*Further praise for the Bobby Girls series*

'Written with warmth and compassion, *The Bobby Girls* gives fascinating insights into the lives of three courageous young women.'
Margaret Kaine, RNA award-winning author of *Ring of Clay*

'This is a story that needed to be told. As a former Special Constable, I love Johanna Bell from the bottom of my heart for giving a voice to the women who first made a way for me and countless others like me – to work as real police officers in the service of our communities. Let us not forget the fight that these women had just to be allowed to put on the uniform and do what was right; in their own small way, the first Bobby Girls changed the world for women everywhere.'
Penny Thorpe, bestselling author of *The Quality Street Girls*

'A well-researched and interesting story giving a great insight into early women's policing.'
Anna Jacobs, bestselling author of the Ellindale series

'A lovely story! The author has researched the era and the theme very well. The characters stood out on the page and through their eyes you are transported back to a different age.'
AnneMarie Brear, author of *Beneath a Stormy Sky*

'I really did enjoy *The Bobby Girls*. It has a lovely warm feeling about it and is excellently written.'
Maureen Lee, RNA award-winning author of
*Dancing in the Dark*

Johanna Bell cut her teeth on local newspapers in Essex, eventually branching into magazine journalism with stints as a features writer and then commissioning editor at *Full House* magazine. She now has more than sixteen years' experience in print media. Her freelance life has seen her working on juicy real-life stories for the women's weekly magazine market, as well as hard-hitting news stories for national newspapers and prepping her case studies for TV interviews. When she's not writing, Johanna can be found walking her dog with her husband or playing peek-a-boo with her daughter.

To hear more from Johanna, follow her on Twitter, @JoBellAuthor and on Facebook, /johannabellauthor.

# The Bobby Girls' Secrets

*Book Two in the Bobby Girls Series*

## JOHANNA BELL

**HODDER**

First published in Great Britain in 2020 by Hodder & Stoughton
An Hachette UK company

5

Copyright © Johanna Bell 2020

The right of Johanna Bell to be identified as the
Author of the Work has been asserted by her in accordance
with the Copyright, Designs and Patents Act 1988.

All characters in this publication are fictitious and any resemblance
to real persons, living or dead, is purely coincidental.

A CIP catalogue record for this title is available from the British Library

Paperback ISBN 978 1 529 33086 1
eBook ISBN 978 1 529 33087 8

Typeset in Plantin Light by Palimpsest Book Production Ltd,
Falkirk, Stirlingshire

Printed and bound in Great Britain by Clays Ltd, Elcograf S.ᴅ.A.

Hodder & Stoughton policy is to use papers that are natural, renewable
and recyclable products and made from wood grown in sustainable forests.
The logging and manufacturing processes are expected to conform to
the environmental regulations of the country of origin.

Hodder & Stoughton Ltd
Carmelite House
50 Victoria Embankment
London EC4Y 0DZ

www.hodder.co.uk

To all my parents: Mum, Dad and Sandy.
For making me who I am today and
always giving me support
and encouragement with my writing.

Dear reader,

If you're sitting down to start *The Bobby Girls' Secrets* because you read and enjoyed *The Bobby Girls*, then I'd like to start by saying 'thank you'. I was overwhelmed by the response to my debut and so grateful to you all.

If you're new to the Bobby Girls series, then I'd like to say 'welcome'. I hope you enjoy getting to know the girls as much as I've enjoyed developing and writing about them.

During my research for *The Bobby Girls* I learned about an army camp that was set up at Belton Park in Grantham during the First World War. The town doubled in size overnight with the arrival of twenty thousand troops. Female police were dispatched to help deal with all their antics and to keep an eye on the influx of so-called 'camp followers' who were drawn to the area.

As I read about it all, I knew that I wanted to send one of the girls there for book two. So, I was delighted when my editor agreed to let me pack Irene off for a new adventure in *The Bobby Girls' Secrets*.

I find it easier to write about a location if I've visited it, so I booked a trip to Grantham and reached out to the town's Civic Society for any help they might be able to give me with my research. They did not disappoint; their chairman Courtney Finn got in touch and sent me a wonderful selection of photos and facts about the town's 'pioneer policewoman' Edith Smith, who served there from 1915 to 1918 and who ended up being the inspiration behind Helen's character.

Courtney came and met me at Grantham train station when I arrived and took me on a wonderful whistle-stop tour of all the relevant buildings and areas – many of which feature in the book. I loved being able to walk the same streets the recruits had walked during their patrols and take in the splendour of all the old buildings they frequented. It was a vital part of my research and I'm so grateful to Courtney for giving up his time and knowledge to help me.

Courtney also put me in touch with Edith Smith's granddaughter, Margaret, who was an absolute pleasure to chat to. It was fascinating to learn more about one of the real-life 'Bobby Girls' from one of her relatives.

I very much enjoyed building a story around the wealth of knowledge I gained during my research into Grantham and the WPS, and I hope you enjoy *The Bobby Girls' Secrets*. If when you've finished it you can't wait to get back to the world of the Bobby Girls, the next instalment, *Christmas with the Bobby Girls*, is available to order now.

# The Bobby Girls' Secrets

# I

Bethnal Green, London, April 1915

The soldier swayed violently and reached out his free hand to steady himself. Finding the wall just in the nick of time, he groaned deeply before taking a swig from the bottle clutched firmly in his other hand. He must only have been in his twenties, yet he looked to Irene as though he was weighed down by the worries of a man three times his age. It was still daylight, and she wondered if he was intoxicated from the previous evening or if he'd started drinking as soon as the sun had risen on the day.

'Come on now, I think it's time we got you home,' she said firmly. The man – taller than Irene by at least a foot and possibly twice the width of her slender frame – leaned into the wall and let out a long, loud belch. Wrinkling her nose, Irene looked over her shoulder at her colleagues Maggie and Annie.

After a rocky start, Irene Wilson, Maggie Smyth and Annie Beckett had become firm friends since joining the Women Police Service, or WPS, at the same time a few months previously. It had been an unexpected bond given their vastly different backgrounds – the only thing the three girls had in common when they met was the fact they were all in their twenties while the rest of the recruits were much older. Maggie had actually only been eighteen when she signed up, having lied about her date of birth to get past the fact that, officially, you had to be twenty-one years old to join. But now they operated like clockwork together, instinctively knowing what each other needed without the necessity of words. Irene was particularly grateful for that in this moment when, on catching her eye, Annie and Maggie stepped forward immediately to help her.

Irene took one of the soldier's arms and placed it over her shoulder, and Maggie did the same with the other. As his body twisted round, he lost control of his legs and suddenly all his weight was on the two girls. Annie swooped in to remove the bottle from his grasp, placing it carefully on to the floor in the alley where they had found him shouting to himself about '*the bloody Kaiser*'. Then, she reached into his pocket and pulled out his identity card to find out where he lived as Irene and Maggie dragged him towards the main street.

The scenario was becoming a regular one during the girls' patrols in Bethnal Green. More and more soldiers were coming home on leave and turning to drink to try and block out what they'd witnessed on the battlefields. When the men weren't too drunk, they also liked to turn to the affections of the area's prostitutes to help blow off steam – and the WPS girls' number one priority was looking out for those women. They were also concerned with any ladies or young girls naive enough to get caught up in the excitement of being in the company of a man in uniform who was risking his life for the country. Some women were desperate to give something back to these heroes, but found they only had themselves to give. The WPS were constantly on the lookout for them, keen to swoop in and move them along before they did anything that could get them arrested and caught up in the legal system, which was set up in favour of the men. They were also tasked with protecting children and women in general in these trying times.

Having escorted the soldier home to a very concerned – and angry – wife, the three friends made their way to Bethnal

Green Police Station to get changed out of their uniforms before the end of their shift at 6 p.m. The group had had a hard time settling into their roles at the station at the beginning of the year. They had found the male officers less than willing to accept them, convinced they were no more capable of carrying out their intended roles than a chocolate teapot.

But the men had been forced to take them more seriously after they had cracked the biggest burglary case any of the officers had seen for years. The girls had discovered who the culprit was purely by chance – not that they would ever admit that to anyone else, of course. As a result, the men at the station had reluctantly accepted them, although they still didn't exactly go out of their way to support them.

The dowager whose jewels had been stolen was so grateful that she had given the girls a cash reward as well as donating money to the WPS. They had immediately decided to pool their money and move into a flat together. They had been tempted by a three-bed in an impressive block in Bethnal Green, to save the journey to the station every day. But although the building was far grander than the horrible little room in a tenement block nearby that Irene had been stuck in for so long, she felt like she needed to move out of the area entirely. And all three girls had agreed it would be preferable to live a good distance away from the area they were patrolling. It wouldn't do well to bump into people they had previously reprimanded while out for a pleasant stroll.

After devoting all their free time to looking for the perfect place, they'd begun to despair. Then they had stumbled upon a flat in the Peabody Trust's Camberwell Green Estate and it had been love at first sight for all of them. Within two weeks of their adventure with the dowager's jewels, they were moving their belongings into their new flat.

When Irene had first come across the Boundary Estate – the area in Bethnal Green the friends spent most of their time patrolling – she had been struck by the big brick buildings and beautiful shared open spaces. She had never dreamed that she would one day end up living somewhere similar. Now she was, and every day she was grateful for the way that her luck had turned.

Before the move, Maggie had briefly stayed with Irene in her tiny room in Bethnal Green. Irene had stepped in to help when Maggie's father had thrown her out of their big family home in Kensington. It had been a brave move for Irene, who up until that point had been hiding her poor means from her better-off friends in the name of pride. But Maggie and Annie hadn't judged her as she'd feared. If anything, the revelation had made her feel closer to them both. And, to Irene's surprise, neither she nor Maggie had struggled sharing a bed or such a small living space. In fact, they had both found it quite comforting. Since moving into the new flat, it had taken some time for her to get used to living somewhere with so much space – they even had their own sink and lavatory, a luxury Irene had never been lucky enough to experience before.

Even with the cash from the dowager, she and Maggie were working factory shifts around the WPS work to pay their way, but they both felt it was worth it. Annie's middle-class family were covering her share of the rent. Her father had insisted she invest her money from the dowager so she had something of her own to put towards a new life with her fiancé Richard when he returned from the war. Seeing as she wasn't doing extra work on top of their patrols like the other two, she was in charge of keeping the place clean and tidy and often went on a cleaning spree while her two friends were at the factory. She had confided to Irene that it helped her pass the time while she was in the flat on her own and stopped her worrying too much about Richard. The girls had been in their new home for just over a month now and the set-up felt perfect.

'I'll see you both later tonight,' Irene said as she let her dark brown hair loose from its ponytail and tied up her shoes. It always felt good to swap her clunky WPS boots for her daintier footwear. She found the uniform as a whole cumbersome, but she had to admit that it did a good job in commanding the public's respect.

'That dress looks wonderful on you,' Maggie sighed. 'Frank's parents will love you.'

Irene smiled gratefully and felt a wave of anticipation pass through her. She didn't own any nice clothes. All her dresses were worn and tatty, so Annie had loaned her a pretty navy-blue number. It was a little on the large side for Irene, but she had to admit she felt good in it. She hadn't thought it possible for clothes to change the way she felt until she had slipped on her WPS uniform. That smart, navy-blue tunic-style jacket and ankle-length skirt made her feel important, even if it wasn't the most comfortable. And now this dress was helping boost her confidence ahead of this very important meeting.

Irene thought she'd hit the jackpot when PC Frank Bird kissed her following the arrest of the jewellery thief six weeks previously. She had taken a liking to the constable as soon as she'd laid eyes on him when he was charged with showing the girls around their new patch in Bethnal Green. He had been the only officer to show them any kindness when they'd first arrived, and he had made her laugh. But, convinced he wouldn't be interested in someone with her background, she had refused to act on her feelings despite Maggie's best attempts to make her. Then, Frank had literally swept Irene off her feet with the passionate embrace following the arrest, and they had immediately started courting.

So far, Frank had taken Irene to the picture house, various dances and even out for dinner. She didn't have much spare time between patrolling and her factory shifts, but although she was exhausted, she felt like the luckiest girl alive with someone like him doting on her. Now, he wanted her to meet his parents and she was full of excited angst about it. It was a big step in the right direction – but what if they didn't approve of their policeman son stepping out with someone who was working in a factory on the side to pay her rent?

Frank had had the day off, so rather than meeting at the police station they were due to meet at Covent Garden tube station to walk to the restaurant together. When Irene made it to the meeting point at the station entrance, she was surprised to find Frank wasn't already waiting for her. He was normally so prompt because he hated the idea of her waiting for him anywhere alone. Looking up and down the street, she pulled her thin jacket tighter around her body. It wasn't exactly cold, but there was a light breeze and she wasn't much used to standing in the same spot for too long as patrolling meant almost constantly being on the go. There was a man selling newspapers at a stand next to her, so Irene decided to check the time – maybe she was ahead of schedule. But her heart dropped when he revealed she was right on time.

'Not been stood up have you, love?' the man joked lightly.

'Not likely,' Irene replied confidently, wandering a few steps away from him again to wait. Frank must have been held up, she reasoned.

'Want a newspaper to pass the time?' the man shouted over to her.

'Oh, I won't be waiting long,' she smiled, but she felt unease stir inside her. Then she silently chided herself for doubting Frank. He had never given her any reason to expect so little of him. There was sure to be a reasonable explanation, and he was certain to turn up soon, she told herself.

An hour later, Irene was shivering and she was starting to give in to the doubt again. She was facing away from the newspaper seller now as she couldn't bear the sympathetic looks he kept throwing in her direction. As another couple greeted each other before going happily on their way, Irene decided it was time to give up. But just as she was about to walk back into the station, she saw Frank's head bobbing along in a crowd coming towards her. Relief rushed through her as she raised her hand to wave to him – swiftly followed by disappointment and embarrassment when she realised the man walking towards her was a stranger with the same floppy hair and slim frame as Frank. A group of girls nearby started laughing and Irene was certain they were cruelly mocking her.

*That's it*, she told herself, *enough is enough*. And with that, she turned on her heel and started the long walk home – too close to tears to get back on the tube and risk breaking down in front of strangers.

Fighting back the tears that were threatening to pour down her cheeks, Irene wondered whether Frank had finally realised this thing between them couldn't go any further. Was he too embarrassed to introduce her to his parents, after all? That had always been her fear. Furiously wiping tears from under her eyes, she scolded herself for being so silly as to believe someone like Frank could ever be serious about someone like her. What had she been thinking? She'd been swept up in it all, encouraged along by Maggie and Annie. She tutted to herself as she remembered how they'd worked together to boost her confidence before the first few dates she'd had with Frank – when she had been so nervous she'd almost called everything off.

Her friends had meant well, of course, but in the end they'd just added to her inevitable heartbreak. She couldn't be cross at them, though – they came from different backgrounds and they had no experience of being treated like a second-class citizen. They didn't realise how different it was for someone like her. She was angry with herself, more than anything, for failing to put a stop to the whole thing before her feelings had grown too strong. She had been so naive.

Pushing the front door open, all Irene wanted to do was get into bed and hide under the covers where she could let all her emotions out without anybody bearing witness to her weakness. But, of course, Maggie and Annie rushed to her side, confused as to why she was home so early.

'What happened?' Maggie exclaimed.

'Are you all right?' Annie asked, taking Irene's arm and leading her into the sitting room.

As they guided her to the sofa, Irene broke down. She hated crying in front of anybody – even her closest two friends. But she was just too overcome with emotion when she saw the concern on their faces to hold it in any longer. Maggie rushed off to make Irene a cup of tea while Annie tried to comfort her. Irene managed to explain, through sobs, that Frank had stood her up.

'He won't get away with this,' Maggie raged when she came in with the steaming drink for Irene. Her normally pale complexion had reddened, and her blue eyes were wide with rage.

Irene didn't have the energy to sit and analyse what might have caused Frank to change his mind about her, and she decided to head to bed early. Part of her was hopeful she'd wake up tomorrow and find it had all been a bad dream. Or maybe she'd discover his bus had broken down, or his parents had been taken ill. Anything had to be better than the possibility that he was too ashamed of her to introduce her to his family.

She didn't get much sleep that night, and her friends didn't push her to make conversation on their bus ride into the station the following morning. When they walked into reception, Irene looked around anxiously and didn't know whether to be happy or sad when she didn't see any sign of Frank.

The three of them stopped in shock when they walked into the side-room the girls had been given as a place to rest and change and found Frank sat at the desk with his head in his hands. He didn't seem to realise they had joined him, so Annie let out a cough and his head snapped up to reveal red, puffy eyes. A look of sorrow spread across his face as his gaze fell upon Irene. She suddenly felt sorry for him when she saw how distraught he looked, and she felt Maggie backing down and stepping back. It was clear to all of them that there was more to this than they had previously thought.

'We'll leave you to it,' Annie whispered as she and Maggie shuffled out of the room together.

'Well?' Irene managed as she walked over to stand in front of Frank. She had decided to give him the benefit of the doubt and let him explain after seeing the state he was in, but she still felt hurt.

'It's about . . . a girl I used to know,' he muttered. He got to his feet and ran his hands through his hair as he paced up and down the room anxiously.

'What about this girl?' Irene almost spat.

'We parted ways just before I met you and I honestly thought that was the end of it,' Frank explained. 'I was blown away when I laid my eyes on you and I didn't think of her again – not even once. But, well . . .' he stared at the floor, his eyes wide. Irene couldn't figure out whatever could have happened – but whatever it was, he was clearly still in shock about it.

'Is she all right?' she asked him tentatively. He raised his head then, looking at her for the first time since Maggie and Annie had left the room. He smiled warmly, but there was a sadness behind his eyes.

'Yes, she, erm . . . she's fine,' he replied quietly.

Irene was beginning to get agitated now – first he stood her up and now he was dragging out giving her the reason why. She couldn't stand it any longer. Just as she was about to demand an answer, he blurted it out. 'She's with child,' he spluttered, staring at the floor again and going beetroot red.

Irene placed her hand on the desk to steady herself.

'*My* child,' he continued. 'She turned up at my place last night just as I was leaving to meet you. I didn't have any way of getting word to you. I'm so sorry. I haven't slept a wink,' he added as he sat down and put his head in his hands again.

He didn't need to say anything else. Irene knew exactly what was coming next. Frank was a decent man – it was one of the things she adored about him. He wasn't the kind of person who would dismiss this kind of responsibility or abandon a child. He would make an honest woman out of his former lover and they would live happily ever after with their beautiful baby. The thought of it brought a tear to Irene's eye.

'Don't worry, I understand,' Irene whispered as she turned to leave.

'Please, don't go yet,' Frank blurted, jumping up after her and grabbing hold of her arm just as she reached the door. Irene turned to face him. 'Can't we talk about this?' he pleaded, staring longingly into her eyes. Her knees trembled as she felt the familiar pang of longing that she always got when she was this close to him. Then she pushed him away.

'There's nothing to discuss,' she said firmly before leaving the room and walking straight out of the station. Annie and Maggie caught up with her further down the road. Once she managed to fill them in, they sent her home and promised to cover for her with Chief Constable Sadwell.

'We'll tell him you have "women's problems",' Annie suggested. That one always got them ushered out of his office so quickly that their feet hardly touched the ground. Irene normally enjoyed picturing the chief's face turning crimson and panicking at the mention, but today her thoughts were consumed with sorrow. Things hadn't even really started with

Frank, not properly, yet she had developed strong feelings for him. The fact that she had allowed herself to hope for a happy future together had been a big leap of faith for her – it wasn't something she took lightly. She didn't normally let anybody in. She had only just started to open up to Maggie and Annie, and that had taken a long time. Frank had made her feel safe enough to allow herself to be vulnerable with him, and now her heart was broken.

By the time she got home, she had switched from upset to angry – but not with Frank. She was furious with herself. She had spent all her adult life working hard to keep romantic feelings pushed deep down inside of her. She'd watched so-called love destroy her mother years ago, and she had resolved to never fall under its spell. *Silly girl, thinking someone would come and sweep you off your feet when you know these things always end in heartache,* she scolded herself.

# 2

A week later, Irene had slowly started to feel better about the situation. She hadn't seen Frank since she'd walked out of the station following his revelation. He had immediately taken some last-minute leave to prepare to receive his new wife after the wedding which, according to some of the station's biggest gossips, had been arranged to take place in a few weeks' time. The haste was apparently due to his mother's wish that her new daughter-in-law wasn't 'showing' too much when she walked down the aisle.

Irene had found it easy to convince herself she wasn't upset about losing Frank when she hadn't had to see him every day. But now she was on the bus on her way to the station with Annie and Maggie in the knowledge he was due back on duty, and she was worried all her old feelings would come flooding back as soon as she laid eyes on him.

'How are you feeling?' Maggie asked tentatively. Until now, both her friends had respected Irene's wishes and neither had spoken Frank's name over the past week. They hadn't even mentioned the break-up at all. Irene turned her head to stare out of the window as the bus pulled away from their stop. She knew that if she looked at her friend, the tears she was working her hardest to keep in would explode out of her.

As the bus made its way out of Camberwell Green, Maggie quickly changed the subject by suggesting they pick up some jellied eels for Sal on the Boundary Estate. Sal was the matron's assistant at the estate's central laundry. She knew everyone and always had the freshest take on a scandal. Her lips were even looser if she had been treated to her favourite snack. Irene nodded along, grateful for the distraction. That was one of the things she loved about Maggie – despite her naturally inquisitive nature, she knew she wouldn't push her on it.

When they walked into their room at the station, Irene's heart sunk when she saw Frank standing in the corner, waiting. All the old feelings she had worked hard to push aside over the last week came rushing back and hit her square in the gut.

'We'll get changed in the toilets,' Annie whispered as she hurriedly collected up her uniform and made her way back out of the room, and Irene silently thanked her for her discretion and thoughtfulness. Maggie, on the other hand, hadn't moved an inch. Irene stared at her pointedly, but she still wasn't getting the message. Despite her sadness, Irene suppressed a laugh – Maggie was obviously dying to know what Frank had to say now he was back. Annie rushed back in, scooped up Maggie's uniform and grabbed her arm on the way back out, pulling her out of the room with her this time. Irene closed the door behind them and sat down at the desk, motioning for Frank to take the chair opposite.

'I'm so sorry about all of this,' Frank said sadly.

'You don't need to apologise,' she smiled. 'You and I were never anything anyway,' she shrugged.

'How can you say that?' he replied, looking hurt.

Irene felt a pang in her chest. Was that love? Was that what it felt like when you saw the person you loved in pain? She pushed the thoughts aside.

'I know it hadn't been that long,' Frank continued, 'but we had something special, Irene, and I know you felt it too.'

'What does it matter now?' she said louder than she had anticipated, trying to stay strong.

'You have to know that I really liked – I *like* you,' Frank said, leaning forward on the desk and gently placing his hands on top of her own.

'Don't talk nonsense. Nothing can ever happen. You have a family to think about now,' Irene snapped, pulling her hands away sharply.

Frank flopped back in the chair, looking defeated. 'I know,' he sighed. 'I just wanted you to know that I really saw us going somewhere and I'm sorry we didn't get a chance.'

'Me too,' Irene said quietly. 'But let's just pretend that nothing ever happened – it will be easier that way,' she added, serious now.

Frank looked hurt again and it took Irene everything she had not to take back what she'd said. The last thing she wanted to do was to forget her time with Frank, but she had to shut it all out to protect herself.

'Right, well, I'll leave you to get changed before the others come back,' he said awkwardly, getting up and walking across the room to the door. Irene found herself wishing he had done something nasty to end their relationship. She had a feeling she was going to struggle being around him when he was such a decent chap. If only she had been right, and he had been too embarrassed by her to introduce her to his parents. It would have stung, of course, but it would have made it a lot easier for her to hate him and move on.

When Annie and Maggie joined Irene back in the room, she filled them in on her conversation with Frank. 'And that's the end of it,' she said sternly, looking Maggie in the eyes. Her friend nodded her understanding and Irene breathed a sigh of relief that she understood it wasn't to be spoken about again.

'Right – jellied eels!' Maggie declared in a determinedly cheerful voice, skipping out of the room. Irene had to laugh. If there was anything that was going to take her mind off her heartache at seeing Frank again it was a day with her best friends and watching Sal devour her favourite snack in her disgusting, fascinating way.

The girls ended up having a busy morning, which was good for Irene as it meant she didn't have any time to think about Frank. They managed to get to the Boundary laundry just in time for Sal's tea break, and she got her helper Mary to go back in and fetch them a cup each when she spotted them walking over. Sal had offered to take Mary in a few months back when the girls had asked for her help in getting her away from a life of prostitution. Mary had flourished under Sal's care and seeing how well she was doing always made Irene feel warm inside, even on a tough day like today.

'Awww, this'll go perfect with me cuppa tea,' Sal beamed, rubbing her hands in anticipation as Maggie produced the paper parcel they'd picked up from the fish shop on the way. The girls had got used to watching Sal gobble down the eels they brought along for her, but the sight still left each of them speechless. As she tucked some stray hairs behind her ear and shoved a handful into her mouth, Mary came back with the tea. It was a welcome interruption and Irene gladly moved her gaze away from Sal.

'Thank you,' she smiled gratefully, taking one of the drinks. Sal's cups of tea had kept the girls going through the harsh weather earlier in the year. Although the temperature was warming up now, they were still always thankful for the refreshment.

'How are you getting on?' Annie asked Mary as Sal noisily made her way through a second mouthful of fish.

'Tell 'em about Glenda Barlow,' Sal interrupted, her voice muffled through the half-chewed eels.

'Ah, she wants you to go and have a word with her youngest,' Mary explained as Sal nodded encouragingly. 'She's worried about her falling into bad ways. She keeps staying out late and talking about men in uniform. I had a go, to try and scare her by telling her what happened to me. She seemed worried at the time, but her mother says it's not done the trick – she's still up to no good from what she can tell.' Mary looked disappointed.

'It was good of you to try and I'm sure you helped,' Maggie offered, placing a reassuring hand on the girl's arm.

'Yes, maybe your advice coupled with a chat with us will be just what she needs to get her back on track,' Annie added positively.

'That's what I told 'er!' Sal shouted and bits of spittle spurted out of her mouth and on to the floor just by Irene's feet. Irene smiled as Sal wiped her face with her sleeve. Sal didn't give a hoot what anybody thought of her and never changed her behaviour for anyone – she would have spoken with her mouth full in front of the Queen. Irene wished she could be like that. She knew she wasted too much time worrying about what other people thought about her, but she just couldn't seem to stop herself.

After bidding farewell to Mary and Sal, the girls had another walk around Boundary before heading to the Taplock block on the estate, which was where the Barlows lived. Home visits were getting to be quite regular for them now that the families in the area knew a bit more about them and were used to them patrolling.

Increasingly, mothers were calling on them to guide their younger children in the right direction. With so many men off training or fighting, many children had a new sense of freedom and no men to answer to, and the women were struggling to keep them in check. Often a friendly word of warning from the three of them when they were in uniform was enough to deter the little ones from getting into any more trouble. Although there were a few families they had ended up visiting on more than one occasion. Irene much preferred those visits to the ones like the one they were just about to make. She found discussing young women's morals and inappropriate behaviour with their mothers extremely uncomfortable.

Mrs Barlow opened the door looking tense, but when she saw who it was she visibly relaxed. The girls had become used to an array of reactions when people spotted their uniforms. Mostly they were accepted and respected now, especially by the women. Occasionally they faced problems, but that was normally when the person in question was up to no good and upset at being asked to stop. Men were often outraged at being confronted in delicate situations and were prone to taking a swing, but that was where the girls' ju-jitsu training came into play. Some of the prostitutes they ran into could also get quite lively. Irene thought that was understandable really when their livelihood was being threatened. But they found the women were mostly grateful for being moved on without punishment.

They hadn't yet run into anyone as violent as the man who had thrown Maggie in front of a moving car just two months ago. That run-in had certainly hardened them all. It meant they were always on their guard, even if the situation at first seemed safe. The brute who attacked Maggie had never been found and Irene was still angry about it, but she was jolted back to the present by Mrs Barlow's voice.

'I'm so glad you're here,' the older woman was saying, drying her hands on her apron. Her black hair was scraped back into a bun and her eyes looked drained and tired. Irene could hear children playing in the room behind her.

'You lot! Out!' Mrs Barlow bellowed, making Irene jump. Immediately, four boys raced through the door at speed and pushed past the girls, shouting at each other and laughing before jumping their way down the stairs. When the block's main door slammed shut below them, Mrs Barlow closed her eyes and took a deep breath. 'We'll be able to hear ourselves think now,' she said. She gestured for the girls to follow her into the flat, adding, 'I love my boys, but they don't half cause a din.' She stopped just outside the living room.

'It's my Rosie I want you to talk to,' she whispered. 'I think she's getting her head turned by soldiers in their uniform.' She peered into the living room before pulling the door to, leaving them all standing in the dark hallway. 'I'm ever so worried she'll ruin her reputation,' she added, looking concerned. 'I don't think she's done anything wrong, though – oh darn, I don't want to get her into trouble, maybe this was a bad idea . . .' She wrung her hands, clearly panicking.

'Don't worry,' Annie said kindly. 'We're not here to hand out any punishments. Even if your Rosie has done something she shouldn't have done already, it doesn't matter to us. We're only interested in making sure it doesn't go any further. We don't want her to get herself into a muddle she can't get out of any more than you do.'

Looking relieved, Mrs Barlow smiled and opened the door to lead the group in to meet her daughter. The morning sun was lighting up the whole room, but the teenager sitting on the sofa had a face like thunder. She scowled as Irene, Maggie and Annie sat down next to her on her mother's instructions.

'Rosie, these ladies are from the WPS,' Mrs Barlow said gently. Rosie's face did not soften on hearing the introduction.

'I'll leave you to it,' Mrs Barlow said quietly, backing out of the room nervously.

'You gonna try and scare me like that other girl did?' Rosie asked, looking bored. 'Ain't nuffin' to do with you what I get up to, long as I'm not breaking any laws.' She stared at them defiantly.

'We just want to make sure you *don't* break any laws,' Irene said, trying to keep the conversation friendly despite Rosie's obvious hostility. 'We know it's easy to get swept up when you think about what soldiers are sacrificing for us and the country.'

Rosie's face softened, and she smiled for the first time.

'I'm in awe of 'em,' she said, looking suddenly emotional. 'Mam's daft if she thinks I'm gonna start letting 'em have their wicked way with me. She really has got it wrong.' Rosie laughed softly to herself, and Irene felt herself relaxing. Maybe this wouldn't be the challenge she had first expected. 'I meet 'em and I just wanna give 'em a bit of comfort before they go off to fight,' Rosie added.

'And by comfort you mean . . .?' Maggie asked cautiously.

'A cuddle and a chat,' Rosie replied, laughing again. 'Besides the fact I know you get arrested for going on the game, I've never even kissed a boy, let alone charged one for that or more!' She stopped and started picking at her cuticles nervously. 'I think it's probably my fault Mam called you here, though, and I do think I should say sorry for wasting your time.' The girls waited patiently until Rosie looked up sheepishly and explained, 'I quite enjoy teasin' her, and I might've got a bit carried away with it all. I was that offended when she first told me what she thought I might be up to – it was as if she didn't know me at all!'

Irene felt sorry for her. It was bad enough to be accused of such a thing, but for your own family to suggest it must have hurt.

'I was upset she could think that of me,' Rosie continued. 'I could see how much the not knowing was getting to her, so I played along a little and had some japes doin' and sayin' things that would get her worried. It was just a bit of fun and I thought that girl from the laundry would be the last of it – I didn't think she'd actually get the pollies round to give me a talking to!'

'Don't worry,' Annie said through giggles – they were all laughing now, and Rosie looked relieved. 'We're just happy you know what's what and we don't have to worry about you getting yourself into any trouble.'

'But go easy on your mother,' Irene added gently. 'The poor woman has enough on her plate with those brothers of yours without you giving her more to stress about.'

Rosie nodded. She agreed to tell her mother the truth to put her mind at ease, and then got up to show the girls out of the living room. Mrs Barlow was waiting at the front door.

'You've nothing to fret over with that one,' Irene said as she looked back to give Rosie a knowing glance. 'But you could give her a few more chores to keep her busy,' she suggested, meeting the teenager's outraged scowl with a playful wink and waving goodbye.

Walking back through Boundary, Irene felt positive and happy again. But her heart started fluttering as they made their way back to the station for lunch. Looking around uneasily as they approached the reception desk, she found that she was desperate to catch a glimpse of Frank, but at the same time determined not to see him to save herself the pain of it. Getting over this man was turning out to be a lot harder than she had anticipated – maybe she wasn't as tough as she thought.

It turned out that Frank was out making an arrest, so Irene was able to eat her sandwich and get back out on patrol in relative calm. She felt bright for the rest of the afternoon, but the feeling of dread crept up on her again as they made their way back to the station to clock off and get changed. When she spotted Frank standing at reception, her nerves made her feel physically sick. Every time she saw him, she was reminded of what she had lost.

'Busy day?' he asked as she hurried past. Before everything had fallen apart, they would have all stopped to talk to him. Irene would have revelled in telling him about their visit to Rosie and the girl's cheeky ways getting her mother into a spin. But now she couldn't bring herself to even look at him. How could she laugh and joke with him when she felt so sad about losing him? Maggie and Annie stuck with her, and they changed out of their uniforms in their room in silence. They were due to meet their friend Sarah and as they rushed back out of the station, Irene was grateful for the distraction from the awkward encounter with Frank.

# 3

When the girls made it to the tea room to meet Sarah Brown, she was already waiting with a steaming pot and four cups. Sarah grinned as the three of them made their way to the table and said their hellos. They had all met during training. The foursome had just started growing close when Sarah's secret eyesight problems had been discovered and, subsequently, she had been thrown out of the organisation. She had been angry at first, but as a writer at *The Vote* magazine, she had thrived back at her main job and had even been promoted.

'So, come on, what have you been up to since I last saw you?' Sarah asked eagerly as she poured the tea.

As Maggie and Annie filled Sarah in on their latest news, Irene excused herself to freshen up. She knew her friends would seize the opportunity to share what had happened with Frank while she was out of earshot and she was glad to give them that chance if it meant Sarah didn't ask her directly about him. As she walked back to the table a few minutes later, the conversation died down and Irene was greeted with carefully blank faces. Her plan had obviously worked.

'Have you heard the latest about Grantham?' Sarah asked in a falsely cheerful voice. Happy to have a fresh topic to discuss, Irene smiled and shook her head.

'Well, they've dropped the curfew at last,' Sarah revealed.

'Thank goodness for that,' Maggie exclaimed. The recruits sent to patrol in Grantham, where a massive army camp had been set up, had caused a stir by helping police officers enforce a curfew against 'women of loose character' between 6 p.m. and 7 a.m. early in 1915. Nina, one of the founders of the Women Police Volunteers, as it was originally called, had strongly disagreed with this, arguing that the point of the organisation was to help women, not constrain and control them – and Irene, Maggie and Annie agreed with her. The other founder Margaret, however, had supported and defended the Grantham recruits' work. Nina had demanded that Margaret resign from her position, but this just ruffled Margaret's feathers and in response she had called a meeting of the whole corps, where she put the case to a vote.

Irene and the girls had assumed everyone would agree with Nina, but were dismayed to discover that they were the only three to vote with her. As commandant of the WPV, Margaret had had a lot more contact than Nina with the recruits and Irene wondered if that had gone in her favour when it came down to the vote. She hoped that was the case instead of the alternative explanation, which was that all their fellow recruits were on a moral crusade rather than trying to help women. Nina was ousted and Margaret took over the reins, reforming the group as the Women Police Service.

Following the burglary, Irene, Maggie and Annie had come up with the idea of asking Sarah to write a regular column for the paper about what they got up to on patrol, to get the word out about how valuable the recruits were. It had never got off the ground, though, because Nina was *The Vote*'s editor, and understandably wasn't keen on the idea of supporting the WPS in her paper. But Sarah loved hearing about their patrol work so much that they met regularly to catch up anyway.

The girls had felt uncomfortable being a part of the WPS while the curfew was still in place, so this news from Sarah was most welcome.

'Of course, the recruits in Grantham are still insisting they only went along with it in the first place to prove it wouldn't work,' Sarah continued. 'It's laughable, really. It actually made the problems there worse – women were entertaining more soldiers and drinking more alcohol in their own homes than they did on the streets. The curfew just forced the problem underground. I think they only lifted it because Nina kept protesting after she left, and she had a lot of backing from other suffragettes outside of the organisation. It's a shame they only backed down once she was gone.'

'Hopefully they'll get back to patrolling how they're meant to now,' Annie said hopefully. 'They should be looking out for the welfare of the women and girls in the town, not conducting witch-hunts and locking them up in their homes.'

'I don't know,' Sarah sighed. 'From what I've heard it's still been very much a case of "them and us" between the prostitutes and the recruits there. An awful lot of them are ending up straight in court instead of being warned and moved on or given any advice on other ways to get by.'

Irene felt herself growing frustrated as she thought about how the prostitutes were being treated in Grantham. They were people too and they deserved to be treated fairly. There were all sorts of reasons women ended up selling themselves, and she was pretty certain none of them did it because they *wanted* to. Some had even been forced into it. She had seen first-hand when she was younger how that happened. *Don't think about it*, she chided herself before turning her attention back to her friends.

'Anyway, the biggest news is that the original recruits who helped impose the curfew have been moved on to Hull. They've got some new women there now, and they're still looking for more.' Sarah said. 'Hopefully, their new volunteers have a different way of thinking. Preferably women who won't be inclined to support the heavy-handed police like the old lot did.'

Irene wasn't so sure, though. All the other recruits had voted for Margaret who was in favour of the curfew, after all – even if she did claim that was only to prove it didn't work.

'Well, good luck to whoever has the misfortune of landing that role,' Maggie scoffed, before taking a large glug of tea. Her long blond hair fell across her face and she flicked it back before adding, 'I can't think of anything worse than trying to win over prostitutes in a town where they've been let down so badly.'

'True,' Sarah sighed. 'But a big draw of the job is that it's a paid one.'

'Really?' Irene exclaimed, blushing when the others turned to stare at her. 'I mean, I didn't realise anyone in the WPS got paid,' she added quietly, shrinking back in her chair.

Sarah flashed her an understanding smile. 'They're not paid by the police,' she explained. 'The money comes from a voluntary committee called the Association for the Help and Care of Girls. They're also given lodgings in the town. So, it may be a tough job but there are definitely some perks to it.'

Sarah's comments stayed with Irene as she made her way home with Maggie and Annie later that evening. She couldn't stop thinking about the women up in Grantham and the short shrift they were getting from the WPS. Surely it was only going to continue, even though the original recruits had been replaced. But what if someone who was sympathetic to them was posted there? Would one friendly face be enough to make a difference? Could that person change the attitudes of the other recruits? Could that person be *her*?

'Come on, slowcoach, or we'll miss the bus!' Maggie called back to her, shaking Irene back to reality, and she hurried to catch up.

Lying in bed that evening, Irene found her mind wandering back to the idea she'd had earlier that day. It was madness, of course. The last thing she wanted to do was to leave her new life with her best friends. They had only just settled into their new flat, and she finally had somewhere she felt happy calling 'home', as well as solid friendships she could truly rely on.

But at the same time, she knew she would never forgive herself if she didn't take the opportunity to try and make things better for the prostitutes in Grantham. What if someone had done that when her family had needed help all those years ago? Would she have been spared from going through everything she had been through since? Would her family still be together now?

Then there was the question of money. Despite Dowager Parsons' generous reward after the burglary, Irene was still having to work factory shifts around her WPS patrols to cover her share of the rent. If she was posted there, she would be free of the financial worries currently weighing on her and able to focus purely on helping the women. She might even be able to finally afford to send money to her aunt Ruth in Sheffield – something she had been desperate to do ever since she had got her first job.

She wouldn't have her best friends by her side, of course. Annie and Maggie were horrified by the goings-on in Grantham so she was certain they would never go with her. Not only that, but Annie had her family in London and her fiancé Richard would be returning here when on leave from the army. And Maggie had just managed to organise visits to her mother without her father's knowledge. With her brother Eddie due to finish his training soon and head off to the front line, Maggie would never move away and leave her mother completely alone with her father. But Irene knew she couldn't stay just for them. Her friends would be fine without her, whereas there were a lot of women she could help in Grantham.

One other person she would be leaving behind was Frank. But maybe that was just what she needed? During the past week, she thought she had come to terms with the fact that whatever they'd had was over. But seeing him again today had hit her hard. She knew that with time it would get easier to be around him – but did she really want to continue working at Bethnal Green while he was filling everyone in on his wedding plans and gushing over his newborn?

Everyone at the station had known about their courtship, and his baby news had spread quickly – along with all the gossip over his mother pushing for a speedy wedding. She knew they would all be talking about her heartbreak, too. She felt like everyone was watching her, waiting for a reaction and feeling sorry for her, which she just couldn't bear. Surely it would get harder and harder for her in the coming weeks and months. The distance was probably just what she needed to expel the last remaining feelings she had for Frank.

With her mind racing, Irene was struggling to get to sleep. As she thought about the possibility of waking up somewhere else, hundreds of miles away from her friends, a single tear ran down her cheek. They hadn't been living together for all that long, but having them close made her so happy. Living with Annie and Maggie, she found that she finally felt she belonged after so long feeling like an outsider and alone. These girls were like family to her.

But one of the main reasons Irene had joined was to help women who needed to escape a life on the streets. She felt an almost physical urge to get involved whenever she thought about what was going on in Grantham. She couldn't ignore it. Even if she couldn't get the more militant WPS members to ease off on prostitutes, she could at least take the place of someone who might have those harsh views – and that was better than doing nothing. Maybe it would go some way towards making her feel better about what happened in her own family all those years ago. If she could save just one family from a similar fate, then it would be worth it.

Finally, after hours of fretting, Irene resolved that it was worth the sacrifice and she would put herself forward for the post in Grantham. She felt a shiver run down her spine as she tried to predict how her friends would react to her decision. They didn't know her background so they wouldn't understand her need to do this. And despite the closeness she felt to them, she wasn't ready to tell them her deepest secrets – things she had never told anybody.

But there was no need to rock the boat just yet. She was only putting herself forward. She might not even get picked to go. She didn't want to upset them unnecessarily. Deciding that there was no need to tell them unless it was definitely going to happen, Irene drifted off to sleep, hoping she was doing the right thing.

The girls were working a night shift the following day, so they all enjoyed sleeping in late in the morning. When Irene opened her eyes, Maggie was already sitting at the end of the bed, ready to start the day.

'Come on,' she giggled as Irene stretched out her arms and then rubbed her eyes. They were always awake before Annie and took great joy in bursting into her room and jumping on her bed to wake her. Annie joked it was like living with two small children. Irene slipped out of bed and ran after Maggie, who was already at Annie's door.

'One,' Maggie giggled quietly.

'Two,' whispered Irene.

'Three!' they shouted together before pushing the door open and both taking a running leap on to Annie's bed. Annie opened her eyes and looked up at them, startled, as they landed together in a heap, then she groaned and pulled the cover over her head.

'Could you not let me wake up naturally just once?' her muffled voice pleaded as they giggled in delight.

'You'd only miss it if we stopped,' Maggie teased, pulling the covers away and sticking her tongue out at their dishevelled friend, whose mousey curls were hanging across her plump face in a mess. Irene stopped laughing then. She was reminded of her plan. The fact that she was all set to put a stop to their morning ritual, and neither of her friends was aware of it, made her feel guilty.

'What's up with you?' Annie asked groggily. 'You look like you've seen a ghost.'

'Oh, nothing. I . . . I just remembered something I forgot to tell Sarah yesterday,' Irene said, trying to sound carefree and forcing a smile. As they ate breakfast together, Irene found herself hoping the WPS bosses wouldn't take long to give her an answer once she had put herself forward. She was dreading her friends' reaction, but keeping it from them was already proving to be harder than she had ever anticipated. 'I've an errand to run before our shift,' she declared as soon as she'd finished eating. She got to her feet, grabbed her jacket and walked to the door without looking back. She couldn't bring herself to look at them. 'I'll meet you both at the station!' she called behind her as she opened the door and rushed out before either of them had a chance to ask for more details.

Irene took a deep breath and started her journey to the WPS headquarters with her head held high. She was about to request a transfer to Grantham, and once she had done so, she knew there would no going back.

# 4

Sub-commandant Frost hadn't uttered a word since Irene had revealed her desire to take up the final available post in Grantham. The superior officer – lovingly nicknamed 'Frosty' – sat at her desk looking thoughtful as Irene stood on the other side watching her intently as the hand on the clock on the wall ticked round. She had thought it would be a quick exchange and she was starting to worry she wouldn't make it back to Bethnal Green in time for the afternoon's patrol. Being late would not only get her into trouble, it was sure to raise eyebrows with Annie and Maggie. She didn't want to have to tell any more lies.

'I can't work out why you want to leave the other two,' Frosty finally commented, staring across at Irene. Her imposing presence, made harsher by her extreme haircut, used to make Irene nervous, but after spending time with her over the course of training she had come to learn that the stern demeanour she put across was a bit of a front. Frosty had shown she was caring and considerate when she'd gone out of her way to make sure the girls stayed together when they got their final placements, having noticed their strong bond.

'I feel like I could really make a difference in Grantham,' Irene said confidently. 'I'd love to stay with my friends, but there's only one vacancy and I didn't join the WPS to make friends – I joined to help women who need it.' That seemed to do the trick, as Frosty nodded approvingly.

'Well, I wouldn't normally send someone as young and

fresh as you, but you might be in with more of a chance than usual,' Frosty admitted. 'There are a hell of a lot of soldiers to keep in line up there with the new camp, and the curfew fiasco and Margaret and Nina's subsequent to-do has made people a bit nervous about what relations are like in the town,' she added, sighing. Hearing that made Irene even more determined to get involved. She thanked Frosty for her time and made a quick dash to Bethnal Green.

Annie and Maggie didn't push Irene for details on where she had been when she rushed into the station that afternoon. She tried to force all thoughts of a transfer out of her mind as she set out on patrol, but every time she, Annie and Maggie stopped to talk to someone or checked in at a shop or pub, she couldn't help but think how lonely she would feel doing those things without them both by her side.

Irene had also started to worry about her pals patrolling in Bethnal Green without her. She wasn't one for thinking too much of herself, but she had to admit that she was by far the strongest of the three of them. Annie had come out of her shell since they had started training, that was for sure, but she could still be a tad timid in certain situations. And moving out of her family home to live with the girls had been a big step for her. She had admitted recently that, even with her parents paying her way, she was struggling fending for herself after spending so long with her mum on hand to tend to her every need.

Then there was Maggie to think about. She would swear blind that Peter attacking her and all the fallout from it hadn't affected her, but Irene knew for certain that it had – after all, you don't just get over being raped overnight, and she had lost a baby, for goodness' sake. She was still fun and cheeky, but she wasn't quite as assertive and quick to stand up for herself as she had been when they had first met. The more Irene thought about it, the more anxious she grew about not being around to look out for them.

'What do you think?' Irene heard Maggie ask as they walked along Bethnal Green Road towards the Lamb pub. Irene looked around, flustered, as she realised her friend was talking to her. She had been lost in her own thoughts *again* and completely missed the conversation. Looking up with a blank expression on her face, she caught Maggie rolling her eyes.

'Are you there, Irene?' she mocked slowly. 'Whatever is the matter with you today?'

'Sorry,' Irene muttered, flushing pink in a panic. 'I, just, I had a bit of trouble getting to sleep last night and I'm rather tired.'

'Well it's going to be a long night, then,' Maggie sighed. 'Let's head to Boundary soon,' she suggested, giving Irene a knowing nod. The bandstand on the Boundary Estate stood so high that they often sneaked off for a rest up there. The men at the station thought themselves far too important to be wandering around the estate or taking on any jobs there – they all got handed down to the girls. So, they were doubly confident they wouldn't get spotted and get into trouble for slacking off on duty. But as much as Irene would have loved a sit-down, she wasn't keen on the idea of being stuck up there with Annie and Maggie. She was feeling so guilty about keeping something so big from them that she could already feel herself being awkward around them. And sitting up there with no distractions would just draw even more attention to her strange behaviour.

'I'll do better if I keep moving,' she said with a fake cheerfulness. 'Let's pop in and see Bob at the Lamb now we're nearly there.' They were just about to walk into the pub when they heard a sudden burst of raised voices. Stopping in their tracks, they all looked around them to try and figure out where the noise was coming from.

'In the alley,' Annie said, already heading around the side of the building at speed. Irene was impressed at the way she had bolted off ahead with confidence. Maybe her friend wasn't as shy and retiring as she had convinced herself she was. She started to follow, but realised Maggie was frozen to the spot, and only then did Irene remember that the commotion was coming from the alley where Peter had first accosted Maggie. Irene was stuck. She didn't want to leave Annie to deal with the disturbance by herself, but she also hated to abandon Maggie when she was obviously feeling scared and vulnerable.

'Get off!' a woman's voiced screeched. With that, Maggie came to life and darted straight into the alley, and Irene followed. They got there just in time to see Annie pulling a portly woman with a face as red as a tomato off a younger and slighter woman who was almost spitting with rage.

'That's enough of that,' Annie said firmly, struggling to keep the woman's arms behind her back as she desperately attempted to free herself and get to her victim. As she bobbed from side to side, both her ample chest and her big chin wobbled dangerously. Maggie jumped forward and grabbed the younger-looking lady and pulled her further down the alley, so she was completely out of reach.

'You're lucky they showed up, Joan – I was just about to show you what-for!' Maggie's woman yelled as she made a quick lunge forward to try and get away from Maggie's grasp. But Maggie had a firm grip on her, and it was no use. Irene decided she should step in and act as peacekeeper.

'What's this all about, then?' she asked calmly, walking into the middle of the two pairs of women. It felt like stepping into a boxing ring.

'She's been up to no good with my Billy!' Joan shouted, growing angry again and trying to thrust herself away from Annie.

'Oh, look at ya,' the younger woman laughed. 'Billy'd try his luck with anyfing!' Before the final sentence had even left her mouth, Joan roared and launched herself forward with all her weight. Irene stepped towards her, frightened that poor little Annie would fail to keep her back by herself. But Joan was quickly jolted back again, and Annie looked out from behind her with a proud grin on her face. She had more power and confidence than Irene had realised.

'Come on, now,' Irene said calmly. 'We all need to be pulling together and supporting each other at the moment. Not fighting tooth and nail. We should be leaving the battles to our brave men, protecting the country.' Both women looked at the floor sheepishly, and Irene felt a wave of relief as she realised that her words had managed to shame them into submission, just as she had hoped they would.

'Well . . .tell 'er that – she's the one what 'it me,' the woman Maggie was holding on to said quietly, bringing her hand up to her reddened cheek. She was still staring at the ground.

'Is it really worth falling out over a man, with all that's going on?' Irene asked, looking between them both.

'I just want Ellie to leave my Billy alone. He's not the brightest and it don't take much to turn his 'ead,' Joan moaned. She looked upset now, but she had definitely calmed down.

'I were only teasing,' Ellie said apologetically. 'I've been really worried about my Ted going off to training. I'm right jealous of you 'aving Billy at home with yer.' She turned to Irene. 'I fink I just wanted to take me upset out on yer, but I know it's not right.' There were tears in her eyes now, and Maggie released her grip as Ellie let out a loud, guttural sob.

'Oh come 'ere,' Joan said sympathetically as Annie stepped back to allow the friends to walk towards each other and embrace. 'Billy's only staying 'ome cos he's a good for nuffin' lump, you know that,' Joan laughed, rubbing her hand up and down Ellie's back. 'I'll be wishing his gammy leg better so he can stop giving me the run around by the end of the week – you watch. You should be glad of the peace and quiet you 'ave at home.'

Joan's words hung in the air as the pair continued hugging for a few moments more. Irene was certain everyone else in that alley knew she was only saying what she thought would make her friend feel better. The truth was that no one wanted their loved ones out on the battlefield during this war. It had already been so bloody, and it didn't look like there was going to be any end to it soon. Once the women had parted, they looked round awkwardly at Irene, Annie and Maggie.

'Don't worry. It's a stressful time and tensions are running high,' Maggie said, her voice full of sympathy.

'You'd be surprised how many women end up taking it out on those closest to them,' Irene added. 'I take it you were on your way for a drink before you had your spat?' she asked them, smiling. They nodded. 'Come on, we'll walk you in,' she offered. 'We were headed there ourselves.' As the group wandered back down the alley and into the Lamb, Irene thought about how brave Annie had been rushing into that situation before checking her friends were behind her. And she hadn't panicked when she'd reached the women alone – she had dived right in and managed to pull them apart with no backup.

And what about Maggie? Although she had obviously felt spooked at the prospect of going back down that alley, she had snapped out of it as soon as she heard her friend might be in trouble. The terror she had felt hadn't held her back in the end. Maybe Irene's friends would be all right without her after all.

Was she just trying to think of reasons to talk herself out of going to Grantham because she was scared that she wouldn't be able to make the changes she was so desperate for there? Now she had seen how strong Maggie and Annie were, she realised she couldn't use them as an excuse to hold her back from doing what she knew she needed to do.

Irene spent the next few days feeling distracted. She was desperate to know if her application to transfer to Grantham had been successful. The uncertainty was gnawing away at her like a rat chewing through a pipe.

'What's bothering you?' Maggie asked as they wandered

around Bethnal Green Gardens four days after she had been
to see Frosty. Irene's heart skipped a beat and she flushed red.
She was terrible at lying – why couldn't Frosty just put her
out of her misery? She had made it sound like she was in with
a good chance, so why was she taking so long to decide? She
was sorely tempted to reveal all to her friends – she couldn't
cope with keeping it from them. But she didn't want to risk
the fallout when there was a chance that she might not even
get the posting. She just had to hold out a little longer.

'Nothing at all,' she answered as brightly as she could.
'Honestly, I'm fine,' she added, laughing at a group of kids
who were chasing each other around on the grass. When they
had first started patrolling, the local children were fascinated
by women in police uniform. But now no one batted an eyelid.

'You're in your own little world,' Maggie pressed. 'I'm worried
about you, Irene. You're distancing yourself from us and that's
what I did when everything was happening with Peter.'

Shame flushed through Irene. Her friends were worrying
themselves that something terrible had happened to her when
the issue was that she had gone behind their backs and she
was keeping it a secret from them for as long as she could to
avoid any confrontation. This was just getting worse and worse.

'I'm just tired, that's all,' she said firmly. She had to work
hard to keep her voice from wobbling. She was touched that
her friends knew her so well they could tell something wasn't
right. She had never been close enough to anybody for them
to show her such love or concern. But it was just making her
feel more guilty.

'If there's something upsetting you, please tell us,' Annie
tried now. 'Keeping it to yourself will do you no good. We
promised we wouldn't keep anything from each other – the
Bobby Girls, remember?'

Irene could feel her heart racing as she tried to suppress
all the uncomfortable feelings that were running through her.

'Look, I don't deserve your concern so let's just leave it at that,' she snapped, marching ahead. She knew they meant well but their questions were making her feel rotten. Not only was she keeping her request for the transfer from them, but that morning she had received a letter from her aunt Ruth, which she had lied to them about.

She had told them it was a letter from an old friend. Her aunt had revealed that her youngest son – Irene's cousin – Henry was ill, and she was desperate for any money Irene could send to help get him better. As far as Maggie and Annie knew, Irene didn't have any family, let alone an aunt and six cousins. She wasn't entirely sure why she had kept the truth from them. Maybe on some level she was frightened that if she revealed just a little bit about her past then the rest would come tumbling out. It had certainly crossed her mind that if Maggie caught even a whiff of her having relatives still alive, she would put one of her big plans into place to get them all together so she could meet them and learn more about her. She knew her friend meant well but that was a possibility she just couldn't risk. If Maggie and Annie ever met Ruth and her brood then the truth about Irene's past would be revealed. She couldn't allow the two worlds to collide, and the safest way to avoid that happening was to keep her family hidden from her friends.

Ruth had been there for Irene when she lost her parents as a child. Her aunt had been desperate to take her in, but at that point she already had three young children of her own and it would have been too much for her. But she visited Irene regularly at the children's home where she ended up. Ruth was her only visitor and a ray of light through those dark days. Since then she had had three more children before losing her husband to influenza.

Irene had been desperate to earn enough money to support Ruth and her children ever since leaving the children's home.

Now her aunt was in desperate need and Irene was closer than she had ever been to being able to help. But it had also highlighted another truth she was keeping from her friends.

The rest of the day's patrol was awfully awkward for everyone. Irene's bad reaction to her friends' concerns hung in the air around them like a bad smell, and she could tell they were both tiptoeing around her for fear of upsetting her further. She decided to go to headquarters as soon as their shift was finished and withdraw her application. It was already ruining her closest friendships – and she hadn't even been accepted. She could take on more shifts at the factory to gather money to send to Ruth. At least if she was exhausted, she would lack the energy to be upset over Frank. She certainly wouldn't have any time to think about him.

When they finally made it back to the station to get changed and go home for the afternoon, Witchy – an officer nicknamed so by the girls because of his pointy nose and nasty demeanour – was behind the reception desk and Frank was leaning against it talking to him. The sight of Frank made Irene feel sick. She had managed to avoid him for the past few days and he was the last person she wanted to see right now. *This day just keeps getting worse*, she thought to herself as Witchy waved the three of them over.

'I hear you're off up north,' Witchy said, staring at Irene. Instantly, she could feel Annie and Maggie's eyes on her as she stopped walking and tried to work out what was going on.

'Wha— how – I mean . . . what do you mean?' she stuttered. She could feel her cheeks burning red as everyone looked at her.

'Your request's been approved – they sent the paperwork over this afternoon,' Witchy replied happily. He was obviously enjoying the fact his revelation had stunned everybody in the room and was making Irene uncomfortable. Irene looked around to see who was there to witness her embarrassment, and with a dart of horror she realised Frank was still standing only a few feet away. As her eyes met his, she knew he had heard.

'That's a mistake,' Maggie said confidently. 'None of us have applied to patrol in Grantham – not after hearing about how recruits treat the prostitutes there.'

'Well, it's all here in black and white,' Witchy boasted smugly, waving a piece of paper around.

'She's not going anywhere,' Annie said defensively. 'It's all right,' she added, placing her hand comfortingly on Irene's arm. 'We'll go and see Frosty and get this sorted out. We'll go right now.'

'There's no need,' Irene whispered. She could feel nervous energy pulsing through her body as she prepared to finally tell her friends the truth. This wasn't how she had planned it. She'd hoped to have been able to break it to them gently – and certainly not in front of an audience. But Witchy had put paid to that. 'I want to go,' she added quietly as a group of officers walked past them, showing interest in the awkward exchange.

'Yes – we'll all go and see her together – as I said,' Annie replied, sounding confused.

'No, I mean I want to go to Grantham,' Irene said, folding her arms to stop them trembling. 'I applied for the position.'

Maggie and Annie stared at her open-mouthed for a few long seconds. Then Maggie turned on her heel and stormed off down the corridor towards their room. Irene looked around at Annie and the hurt on her face cut her to the core.

'I'm sorry,' Irene whispered. 'I have to go. But I can explain.'

Annie wiped a tear from her eye before turning wordlessly and going after Maggie.

When Irene looked back to the reception desk, Witchy was smirking.

# 5

Edging the door open, Irene glanced into their room cautiously to see Annie and Maggie already dressed in their everyday clothes and putting their shoes on in silence. Maggie's lips were pursed, while Annie had tears streaming down her face.

'I don't want to leave you both,' Irene said as she walked into the room. The girls jumped up in shock.

'Well, you ruddy well are!' Maggie said loudly. 'How could you do that? After everything that's happened in Grantham. And to apply without telling us. Were you ever going to let us know, or were you going to just slip away one night?'

Irene found herself wishing she'd been honest from the start. They might have struggled to understand why she'd applied, but they would have had time to come around to the idea and to understand her reasons, and it wouldn't have come as such a big shock.

'I honestly didn't think they'd send me, and I didn't think it was worth upsetting you both if it all came to nothing in the end anyway,' Irene explained.

But Maggie wasn't listening. She picked up her things and barged past her to get through the door. Annie stayed where she was.

'Why would you want to go there?' she asked, her brow furrowed in confusion. 'And why would you leave us? We started this journey together – I only know life on patrol with the two of you. Maggie and I can't do it without you.'

'Yes, you can,' Irene said confidently, walking over and wrapping her arms around her sniffling friend. 'You're both a lot stronger than you realise. You didn't need me the other day when those women were scrapping in the alley! And, besides, this won't be forever.' They sat down and Irene explained her desire to try and change the way the women were being treated in the town, as well as her longing to spend some time away from Frank so that she could heal. It wasn't the *full* truth, but it was as much as she felt able to reveal – and it seemed to be enough for Annie.

'I suppose if anyone can change things up there, it's you,' Annie reasoned with a sad smile. 'Don't worry about Maggie,' she added. 'She'll come around. She just needs some time to calm down.'

'You don't have much time,' Frank's voice offered from the doorway. Both girls jumped up in surprise. He was holding the piece of paper Witchy had used to reveal Irene's fate. 'Says you have a train to catch at the end of the week,' he explained, handing it over to her with a resigned look on his face. Irene was taken aback – she hadn't expected to be sent off so soon. She took the form and read it over for herself. He was right: she was off to Grantham in just three days' time.

'You stay here. I'll speak to Maggie,' Annie assured her as she gathered her things and made for the door. Resting her hand on the knob, she looked back and added, 'Once she hears your reasons, she'll support you like I do. I'll see you at home soon.' Smiling sadly, she walked out, leaving Irene and Frank standing awkwardly in the middle of the room. He gestured for her to sit and she obliged as he brought a chair over to sit opposite her.

'I don't want you to go,' he said, fixing his eyes on her and giving her that butterfly feeling again. 'Is it because of me?' he asked cautiously.

'Don't flatter yourself,' she scoffed. Seeing the hurt on his face, she quickly backtracked. 'I mean, not entirely. I have bigger reasons for going, but I must admit that the thought of not having to see you most days was a big pull. It will make it easier for us both to move on.'

He nodded, staring at the floor. 'I have the next few days off,' he whispered. 'So, I suppose this is goodbye. I know you well enough to know I won't be able to change your mind if you're set on going.' He looked up at her once more.

'I suppose it is goodbye, then,' she agreed. She smiled weakly, trying her hardest not to let the pain she was feeling show through. 'You'll be a brilliant father,' she said, just about disguising the wobble in her voice. 'Your fiancé is a lucky woman.' They both stood then, and Frank placed both his hands upon Irene's shoulders before giving her a kiss on the cheek. He stood back, looking embarrassed. The awkward embrace had been a world away from their first passionate kiss, which had taken place in the exact same spot. Irene wondered if he was thinking the same thing as he walked slowly out of the room – and out of her life for good.

After getting changed, Irene decided to walk home rather than take the bus. She wanted to give Annie time to try and talk Maggie round, and she also felt like she needed some space to get used to the idea herself. It had only been four days since she'd visited Frosty and applied for the transfer, but the wait for news had been agonising and it felt like she'd been in limbo for much longer, not knowing if her life was going to be thrust into chaos or continue on as it was. And then suddenly it was all happening at the speed of light.

When she eventually walked in through the front door, she was relieved to find both her friends sitting calmly on the sofa.

'I'm sorry I overreacted,' Maggie said sheepishly, getting up to hug Irene. 'I was shocked and hurt that you hadn't been honest with us. But Annie's filled me in now, and I think you're so brave to be going there alone to help all those women. We're both very proud of you.'

Irene was touched, and also starting to feel more than a little anxious about what lay ahead. It *was* a bold move – had she really thought it through properly? No matter, it was too late now, and besides, she found almost to her own surprise that she was ready to embrace it.

'It's a paid role, remember,' Irene said as she sat down between them both. She couldn't believe she had forgotten to address the money with Annie earlier. 'I won't have to pay rent while I'm there, and I should earn more than what the factory pays, so I can send some back to you to cover what I should be paying here. I don't want to leave you both in the lurch.'

'Don't be silly,' Annie replied lightly. 'My parents are so happy to see me standing on my own two feet, I'm sure they'll be happy to cover some of the extra until Frosty sends a replacement for you. Also, they don't realise I was so keen to move in with you both. They keep harping on about how guilty they feel that I felt pushed out when my aunt and cousins came to stay indefinitely. They'll jump at the chance to make up for it,' she said with a cheeky grin.

'And I can put in a bit more now I have the factory money coming in,' Maggie added. 'If anyone deserves to not have to worry about money for a while, it's you, Irene,' she added, smiling kindly. 'Maybe you could treat yourself to some new clothes.'

Irene couldn't help but feel guilt-ridden yet again. Her friends had no idea that she planned to send the extra money she made to her aunt Ruth. It was another in what felt like a long list of secrets she was keeping from them.

'There's just one condition,' Annie said playfully.

'Yes?' Irene asked, glad to be pulled back to their conversation.

'You have to apply to come back to us as soon as you've managed to make things better for the prostitutes in Grantham – and once you feel ready to be around Frank again,' Maggie said.

'Of course. I couldn't stand to stay away for too long,' Irene replied. And she meant it.

'And you must write to us and keep us up to date,' Annie chipped in. 'If anyone gives you any hassle you must let us know and we'll be on the first train up there to help.'

'After taking down Peter together, I feel like we can deal with anyone!' Maggie said triumphantly, and they all laughed.

'We'll still be the Bobby Girls,' Irene grinned as she wrapped an arm around each of her friends.

'The Bobby Girls forever!' the three of them chanted happily in unison, and Irene pulled them in tighter.

# 6

The following day was army payday, so the girls were extra busy keeping order on the streets of east London as lonely soldiers drank away their sorrows and searched for solace in the form of female company. This meant that Irene found she didn't have time to get anxious or excited about her forthcoming challenge and, before she knew it, it was Friday night and she was setting her alarm to get her up in time for her Saturday morning train to Grantham. The three girls had each flopped into bed as usual after a busy patrol, and Irene knew both her friends were gearing up for a big farewell in the morning. But, she knew she wouldn't be able to bear to say goodbye to them in person, so she got up extra early and sneaked out before they woke. She left a short note:

*Please forgive me – I would have found goodbye too hard.*
*I will write as soon as I'm settled in, and I will be back before you know it!*
*All my love,*
*Irene x*

She knew her friends would understand. They knew her well enough to appreciate she didn't feel comfortable expressing her feelings at the best of times.

When she got on board the train, she hauled the suitcase Maggie had loaned her up into the luggage rack. Maggie had used the suitcase to transport her most treasured possessions when she'd left her family home to start her new life in Bethnal Green with Irene. Irene thought back to how terrifying it must have been for her friend to leave her life of privilege to share a room in a rough part of town with her. It helped her put her feelings about this journey into perspective.

Irene hadn't packed much – she didn't have much to take with her, after all. There was her uniform, of course, and a few of her tatty old dresses as well as a couple of shawls she had thrown in when she'd seen how empty the suitcase looked. Annie had insisted she take the navy-blue dress she'd loaned her for the dinner with Frank's parents that never happened. Irene hadn't been keen – she felt like the outfit was cursed and she wasn't sure when she would get a chance to wear it in Grantham. But Annie had been adamant she should take it on the off-chance she got an opportunity to showcase it. There were a couple of her favourite books in there, too, and her writing kit.

The train journey was long and lonely, but Irene used the time to order her thoughts about what she was doing and, as she stepped off the carriage and on to the platform in Grantham, she felt ready to take on her new challenge.

As men and women swarmed past her and rushed along the platform, Irene stood clutching Maggie's suitcase with such force her knuckles turned white. Just as she was contemplating stepping back on to the train and heading back to London, the crowds around her dispersed and she spotted an official-looking figure with her gaze fixed upon her. Irene wouldn't have thought she was a WPS recruit had it not been for the familiar uniform she was wearing. The woman was stocky, and her face was round and tubby. Even from a distance, she looked more like a schoolteacher or a country-house cook than a policewoman.

'You must be the new recruit from London,' the officer said, offering out her hand formally when Irene reached her.

Her thick circular spectacles reflected the midday sun. Irene obliged and had to stop herself from wincing as they shook hands – her new colleague's grip was impressive. 'My name's Helen Miller,' she continued, not breaking eye contact.

'It's good to meet you,' Irene replied. 'I'm Irene Wilson.'

Helen nodded before continuing. 'There's a few of us here already, we all arrived a couple of weeks ago, so we can show you the ropes and help get you settled in. It's a busy old patch to patrol but I imagine you're used to that.'

Irene relaxed a little. Helen's tone was warm, and she had a friendly, motherly air about her – even if she did come across as quite firm on first impression. She was close in age to the recruits Irene and her friends had trained with. Irene would have put her in her early forties, although she would never say that to Helen – she was notoriously bad at guessing people's ages correctly. Helen's thick hair was greying, and it was cut to a bob – the ends just stuck out from under the rim of her hat. She had a fuller figure, and Irene imagined she had a brood of children at home.

As the duo made their way from the station into town on foot, Irene noticed how run-down the area seemed. Comparing it to London, it felt more like Bethnal Green than somewhere like Kensington. Helen nodded a greeting to almost everyone they walked past.

'Got another young bobby to take under your wing?' an old chap called out as they approached.

'Looks like it,' Helen replied with a small smile.

'Are the others my age, then?' Irene asked eagerly. 'I'm twenty-six.'

'Yes, love,' Helen said. 'Ruby's twenty-four and Mary's just turned twenty-five – although you'd think she was in her sixties, the way she goes on.' Irene was intrigued, but she didn't push for any more information. She didn't want to come across as a gossip on her first day.

'Gosh, everyone seems to know who you are,' Irene commented as a couple of soldiers waved at Helen from the other side of the road.

'Keeping yourselves outta mischief I hope?' Helen called over to the pair. She sounded serious, but she was giving them a small, playful grin.

'Yes, ma'am,' the taller of the two men replied. 'We're just on our way to the rest home for some food!'

'Glad to hear it,' Helen said firmly, still smiling slightly then turning to Irene. 'Sorry, love, I just wanted to make sure those two weren't thinking about getting into any trouble. I've had to escort them back to the camp a few times over the last few weeks when they've been the worse for wear.'

'Oh, we had our fair share of that in London,' Irene laughed. 'I shall feel right at home here.'

'Going back to your question,' the older woman continued. 'The two recruits who started here last year worked hard to gain acceptance. They were dogged by gawkers when they first arrived – I'm sure you had the same in London when you first stepped out in the uniform.' Irene nodded knowingly. 'Well, crowds of people would follow them around when they were patrolling. They were all so fascinated at the sight of them and desperate to see what they were doing here. You've got to remember it was a strange time for Grantham – the town's population was only around twenty thousand before the war and it almost doubled over the course of a few weeks when the troops arrived at Belton Park.'

Irene had to admit she hadn't realised quite how big the army camp in Grantham was. This could end up being even harder than she had envisioned, and she had known it would be a tough task anyway.

'The locals came around quickly,' Helen sighed. 'They soon understood the women police were here to help and not persecute. The soldiers got used to them pretty sharpish, too,' she added as she made a beeline for a young woman who was carrying a baby and trying to coax a screaming toddler along the pavement beside her. The poor woman's face was flushed, and she looked harassed and ready to cry.

'Come on now, Thomas, it can't be that bad,' Helen soothed. She was crouched down next to the child, who had stopped screaming and snapped straight out of his mood as soon as Helen had approached. His mum took a deep breath and mouthed a silent 'thank you' to Helen.

'Now wipe those tears and help Mummy, will you? You need to be a good boy while your daddy's away fighting for us all.' Thomas quickly rubbed all remnants of tears from his face and put his hand up for his mum to hold. The family continued on their way, and Helen and Irene carried on their journey.

'Of course, there was quite a bit of unrest when the curfew was brought in at the start of the year, but that was mainly between the recruits and prostitutes,' Helen said, picking up their previous discussion. 'Any respectable woman going about her business had nothing to worry about.'

Irene wasn't sure she agreed. She wasn't happy at the idea of any women being locked away in their homes at night, but she kept those thoughts to herself.

'When the curfew was lifted and the first WPS recruits moved on to Hull, we were accepted straight away, and we've settled in well. You'll probably find the problems we deal with here are similar to what you had to sort out in London,' Helen explained. 'Although there's a lot of open space up here and a lot of frisky soldiers, so you'll be separating couples in the lanes and fields around the base several times a day.' Irene fell silent as the words sunk in. There hadn't actually been a lot of that in London – it seemed to mostly take place behind closed doors. She and her friends had found themselves stepping in to help and guide women before things got to that stage. They were more used to moving women along when they caught them trying to pick men up – not stepping in once things were underway.

'Don't worry, you'll get used to it,' Helen said. She was being so blasé about it, and Irene could feel her cheeks turning crimson. 'A sharp whack with a rolled-up umbrella usually does the trick,' Helen added. Irene thought she must have been joking at first, but there was no hint of humour in her voice and when she looked around at her, her expression was serious.

'There are a lot of prostitutes who hang around in the town and near the camp – both local and women who travel in especially. They call them "camp followers",' Helen continued. 'I'm sure you've seen the talk of "khaki fever" in the newspapers, referring to the excitement in the town at all these brave men turning up to stay. Well, a lot of the army recruits are young boys, fresh from school or college, so they're very easily led and tend to think with their trousers. There's also not a lot of entertainment in Grantham so the troops often flock to the public houses, and they come across women willing to pass the time with them on their way.' Irene had heard of both the terms 'camp followers' and 'khaki fever' and she hated them equally. They suggested the women were somehow not in control of their own actions and couldn't help but throw themselves at men in uniform. But although Irene knew there was a lot more to it than that, she didn't dare say anything.

'The men you spoke to before said they were off to a rest home?' she asked instead.

'Oh yes, there are quite a number of them in Grantham,' Helen said proudly. 'They're a home from home for the soldiers – sort of like a club. The men largely rely upon them for rest, recreation and refreshment. We try and encourage the troops to spend their spare time in them rather than the town's pubs, but I'm sure you can appreciate how much of a battle that can be. They're mostly run by religious organisations. There are some in the town and some at the camp. Lots of the local women volunteer – they're good for keeping everyone out of trouble.'

Irene felt a rush of relief that there was at least somewhere she would be able to move wayward soldiers on to, rather than back to camp or a pub.

'Like I said,' Helen continued, 'many of the troops prefer to spend their free time in the local pubs – of which there are many, so drunkenness is a big problem. And quite a few of them have a habit of stealing bicycles to get back to the camp on when they've had an ale too many,' she added. Irene had to stifle a laugh at the thought of tipsy soldiers swerving to and fro through the town on stolen bikes as angry locals chased after them.

'Our lodgings are on this road,' Helen explained as they made a left turn. Irene noticed the street sign and noted they were in Rutland Street. They made their way along a row of stone-built terraced houses until they reached the middle. Helen led Irene in through the front door and then through a door on the left, into a cramped living room. There were two small sofas pushed up against two of the walls, and a small table in the middle of the room. Two young women, who Irene assumed must be Ruby and Mary given the WPS uniform they were wearing, sat on one side of the room while an even younger girl sat on her own on the other sofa.

'This one wants to talk to you, won't say nothing to us,' one of the recruits said sharply, rising to her feet and picking up her hat which had been perched on the seat next to her. She had long red hair, scraped back into a low bun. Her skin was pale, and Irene could make out clusters of freckles on both her cheeks. She was surprised to see how short she was. But she was quite stocky, which Irene reasoned would help her in this job. The second recruit rose too. She seemed much more timid than her colleague. She was taller and slimmer than the redhead, but as soon as she stood up, she stooped so that she appeared shorter.

'Is this the new girl, then?' the first one asked Helen. She didn't even look at Irene or acknowledge her directly in any way.

'Yes, Mary,' sighed Helen. 'Her name is Irene Wilson. Play nicely, please.' Helen turned to face Irene. 'This is Mary, as you've probably already guessed. Mary Green. And Ruby is the quiet one,' she added, pointing at the second girl. 'Ruby Gilbert.' Ruby had shoulder-length blond hair and her brown eyes were so big, Irene felt taken aback, even though she was smiling at her. It felt like those eyes could see straight into her soul.

'Take Irene up to her room please, ladies,' Helen continued, 'while I have a talk with Rosie here.'

Irene followed the pair out of the room and through a door to the right. It led straight to a set of stairs. As Irene climbed them, still clutching Maggie's suitcase, she could see a small kitchen below her to the left.

At the top of the stairs was a small hallway, and Irene's heart dropped when she could only see two doors. She would be sharing a room with one of her new colleagues, then. She had been willing – happy, even – to share with Maggie back in Bethnal Green. But she knew her and felt comfortable with her. She had only just met these girls and she wasn't sure if she was ready to live in such close proximity.

'It's all right, we don't bite,' Mary laughed bitterly.

Irene blushed, mortified that her feelings had shown so clearly on her face. 'Sorry, I just, I'm quite a private person,' she stammered in explanation.

'Well, there's no room for being precious here,' Mary said as she opened one of the doors to reveal two tiny single beds and just enough room to stand in between them. 'Literally, no room,' she laughed to herself. 'You'll be out on patrol all hours, so you'll hardly spend any time here,' she added, shrugging her shoulders.

Irene wasn't sure if that was supposed to make her feel better. It didn't. She was just about to ask who she was sharing the room with when Mary turned around and stomped back down the stairs.

'Don't worry, you'll get used to her,' a voice whispered from behind her. Ruby. Irene had forgotten she was there. She was fairly sure it was the first time she had spoken since she'd arrived.

'You'll be in with Mary,' Ruby added. 'I share with Helen.' They both stood in silence. Irene started to wish she had never left London. 'Our room has a wardrobe. I can clear you some space in it, if you like?' Ruby offered.

'That's lovely, but I really don't have many things,' Irene said as she opened up the suitcase on one of the beds.

'Oh,' Ruby said, failing to hide her shock as she took in the half-empty suitcase. 'Well, you can at least put your uniform in there,' she added hopefully.

'I'd appreciate that,' Irene smiled gratefully.

'I'll leave you to get changed,' Ruby whispered awkwardly as she backed out of the room. 'We're to show you the town this afternoon.'

Ruby was a very sweet girl, Irene decided. And Helen seemed nice enough. They might not be chatty and fun like Maggie and Annie – but then, Irene was here for a purpose. The best thing for her to do would be to get on with it without any distractions. Making more friends wasn't a priority anyway.

She was a little worried about Mary, who had come across as rude and stand-offish. Irene had encountered girls like her growing up in the children's home and she'd always clashed with them, given Irene's lack of ability to hold her tongue when she saw anyone being treated unfairly.

*Maybe she's having a bad day*, she reasoned to herself. Irene thought back to how badly Maggie had come across on their first meeting and smiled. And they were best friends now. As hope filled her heart again, Irene changed into her uniform. Struggling to heave on her bulky boots in the room's tiny space, she decided to give Mary the benefit of the doubt. After all, she knew better than anyone that everyone deserved a chance.

# 7

Irene slowly made her way back down the stairs. The heavy clunking of her boots on each step made her feel self-conscious, but then Ruby stomped down just as loudly behind her, and she felt a little better. There were voices coming from inside the living room and Irene stopped outside the closed door.

'That'll be Helen and Rosie still,' Ruby explained. 'A lot of the girls round here come to Helen for advice.'

'You'll never get a chance to enjoy that room,' Mary's voice boomed out from the kitchen. Irene hadn't realised she was in there, and it made her jump. 'Always full of the town's bad girls asking Helen to help them after they've done something wicked. It's like her own private counselling room in there.'

'They're not *all* bad girls,' Ruby whispered to Irene under her breath. 'Some of them just need a little guidance after falling into the wrong company and getting into a dishonest way of life.'

'Poppycock!' Mary sneered. Irene waited for Ruby to stick up for herself, but her mouth stayed firmly shut and she stared intently at the floor. Irene felt a little lighter knowing at least one of these recruits was as sympathetic to the women they were there to help as she was, even if she did seem reluctant to voice her opinions in front of Mary. She hadn't figured Helen out yet – but what she had seen on the walk over hadn't caused her any concern. Maybe the harsh treatment and support for the curfew had left Grantham along with the two original recruits.

Suddenly she heard movement coming from the living room, and goodbyes being exchanged. The door opened and Helen beckoned them in. 'That's put us back,' Helen tutted. 'We'll have missed Angela's case at the magistrates' court now.'

'Darn it. I wanted to see her face when they took her down to the cells!' Mary cried in frustration.

Irene looked over, horrified. Ruby was staring at her feet and chewing her lip uncomfortably. Helen didn't seem to have reacted to the outburst. Irene stared at the older woman, willing her to put Mary straight.

'I've told you to try and have more compassion for these women and girls,' Helen said to Mary eventually. Her tone was neutral, so it was difficult to tell whether she was offended by her words like Irene was. Helen turned to Irene. 'Angela's one of the more, shall we say, prolific offenders in Grantham,' she explained. 'She turned up from one of the surrounding towns a few weeks ago, and we've had to pull her off soldiers in the fields five times now.'

'But . . . I thought we were here for prevention, not prosecution?' Irene tried tentatively. She was cautious of getting off on the wrong foot with her new colleagues, and although Helen was the same rank as her and the other two, she was clearly the one they looked up to and answered to due to her age. She didn't want to upset her before they had even set out on patrol together, but she couldn't let the matter go entirely.

'That may be so in London,' Helen smiled patiently. 'But this is a small town with a lot of servicemen and a lot of women keen to take advantage of their heavy pockets and empty hearts.' She paused when Mary guffawed and continued when the room fell silent again. 'So, we might not always stick to the original WPS outlook. Sometimes you have to take extreme measures to keep everyone safe. That includes the women. It's all very well moving someone on, but if they keep coming back and doing the same thing again and again, there comes a time to take some firm action.'

Irene had to admit that she couldn't argue with that. If they'd really had to step in five times with this Angela before taking her to the police station to be dealt with, then it seemed like a fair last resort. But she couldn't help thinking that the right approach initially could have ended up with a more positive result.

'I think it's important to try to help the women see a way out of the kind of life they've fallen into, so they don't feel like they *have* to continue on with it,' Irene said. She'd planned on treading carefully to begin with but now she found she couldn't hold back. She was proud of her stance on prostitution and she wanted her new colleagues to know that she wasn't here on a moral crusade.

'I completely agree,' Helen smiled warmly, much to Irene's relief. 'Now, I must go and wash these cups up, and then we'll set out to show you around the town.'

As soon as Helen left the room, Irene became aware of Mary stepping closer to her.

'Don't you dare start judging us,' Mary hissed under her breath.

'I'm not, I just—' Irene started, but Mary continued over her.

'You fancy London types are all the same – I saw it when I was training down there.' She looked over to the kitchen quickly to make sure Helen was still out of earshot. 'You think you know better, don't you? Well, I give you two days patrolling here before you're getting the dirty so-and-sos thrown in the cells, too. Like flies round a carcass, they are – they just keep coming back and you'll quickly get fed up of your nicey-nice approach. We might not be able to arrest them ourselves but there's always someone down at the station ready to help.'

Irene took a step away from Mary, horrified at her attitude.

She looked over to Ruby, waiting for her to say something, but Ruby just shrugged her shoulders apologetically before switching her gaze to the floor when Mary looked in her direction. There was a moment of awkward silence – Irene was too shocked to respond to Mary's outburst. Then, Helen walked back in and the three of them fell into line behind her as she left the house.

'We'll go to the police station to introduce Irene to the chief and get an update on Angela first,' Helen announced, and the girls followed her in silence. They hadn't ventured far before Helen stopped the group outside a large building. Irene stepped into the road quickly to try and see where they were, and a street sign told her they were on Wharf Road. She made a mental note of its proximity to the house. She was confident she would know the way back on her own; she was already finding her bearings.

'I just want to pop in and show you Central Hall before we go to the police station and the camp,' Helen explained as they made their way into a big room filled with women sitting at wooden tables as they sorted through army uniforms. 'The Grantham Labour Exchange have organised a scheme to take care of the soldiers' garments,' she continued. 'It started with the first lot to train at the camp – the Eleventh Northern Division. They've just left and men from the Manchester and Liverpool "Pals", the Thirtieth Division, are on site now. Local washerwomen are allocated twenty-four sets of soldiers' clothing a week and they're paid seven shillings per week for helping out. It pays more than most of the work around here, so it's great for the local women.'

'We're paid by Grantham War Distress Committee, and they get the money back off the military authorities,' an older voice chipped in from beneath a bundle of clothes on the table they were standing in front of.

'Hello, Joy,' Helen said warmly. 'How's Derek getting along?'

'Oh, I had a lovely letter a few days back,' the woman replied, still sorting through her pile of clothes and not looking up. 'He had a close shave with a grenade a month or so ago. I wish he'd keep things like that to himself. It's the sort of thing a mother doesn't need to know about!' She tutted and shook her head, still staring at the garments in front of her.

'Joy's son is fighting in France,' Mary said. Irene had guessed as much, but she nodded politely anyway. Joy looked up for the first time since they'd entered the room. Her eyes fixed on Irene and she smiled.

'Got yer new lady polly then?' she asked.

'My name's Irene,' Irene said, tipping her hat and giving Joy a friendly smile.

'This place'll keep you busy,' Joy said knowingly. She was back to her sorting already. 'But you're in good hands with this lot,' she added. Helen wandered away from the table and Irene, Mary and Ruby followed.

'You won't get much trouble in here,' Helen explained in a low voice. 'But I wanted you to see it so you can get a feel for the town and learn about everything we're doing to help the troops. The kit gets sent here and also to the Middlemore Mission Room and the Springfield Mission Hall. The women mark and mend them before taking them off to be washed. It generally keeps them too busy to get into bother, but there's the occasional scrap.'

Irene bobbed her head, thinking back to the two factory workers Annie had pulled apart in the alley next to the Lamb. Had that really only been a week ago? Her heart ached as she thought of her two friends – she missed them so much already and she had only just left them.

Thankfully, Irene had a lot to learn about Grantham to keep her mind off Annie and Maggie. As she made her way to the police station on St Peter's Hill with her new colleagues, she learned what an interesting set-up it was. The station was tacked on to the side of the Guildhall, where a small area contained the cells and offices. When they reached it, Irene was impressed by the size of the Guildhall, and marvelled at the huge four-faced clock at the top. A large green lawn lay in front of the building, where there was also a magnificent statue of Isaac Newton. 'The town's very proud of the fact he grew up here,' Ruby whispered when she spotted Irene looking at it.

When they walked around the side of the Guildhall and into the part used by the local police, Irene could see why Helen chose to work from the living room at Rutland Street. There was no space for a private room like Irene, Maggie and Annie had enjoyed at Bethnal Green Police Station.

'Afternoon, ladies,' a sergeant smiled when they got to the reception desk, and they all greeted him back. 'Come to find out what happened to your top tom?' he asked, still grinning. 'They gave her two months in prison,' he said proudly.

'Great news!' Mary cried. Irene looked around and stared as she saw Mary grinning like she had just come into a pile of money. She couldn't understand how she could be so happy to learn that another woman had been so harshly punished. She imagined none of the men that this Angela had been caught with had been punished at all! It took all her willpower not to speak her mind, but she just about managed to keep her mouth shut. She didn't want to make an enemy on her first day.

'Well, that will make our lives a little easier for a couple of months, at least,' Helen said, before introducing Irene to the officer, who was called Sergeant Jones. 'We're taking her up to the camp, let her see what she's got to contend with,' Helen said playfully. 'But first I'll introduce her to the chief,' she added, motioning for Irene to follow her along the short corridor. Mary and Ruby stayed with Sergeant Jones.

'Enter!' a strong voice boomed after Helen knocked on an

office door. Irene followed Helen into the room and was struck by the size of the man behind the desk. He was the height of her while sitting in his chair. He was slight with thinning hair, and his spectacles were pushed down to the bottom of his nose as he pored over papers spread out in front of him.

'This is our new recruit, Irene Wilson,' Helen said.

The man finally glanced up. Pushing his glasses on to the bridge of his nose, he stood and offered out his hand to Irene. He towered over her now. His handshake was firm, and he kept eye contact as he introduced himself.

'Chief Inspector Boldwood,' he said in a formal but friendly tone. He sat straight back down and went back to reading the papers as he added, 'I trust Helen here is taking good care of you. You won't have much need to bother us here. Good day.' With that, Helen thanked him for his time and retreated from the room, with Irene close behind.

'He doesn't see us as part of his team,' Helen explained as they walked back towards Ruby and Mary, her voice a little subdued. 'He's not against us being here, but he's happy to leave us to our work. I don't imagine you'll have any cause to meet him again while you're here – unless something goes drastically wrong, of course.'

'It was the same in London,' Irene explained as the four of them stepped back on to the street together and began to walk through the town. 'But Sergeant Jones seemed to be on good terms with you all, and I noticed another few officers nodded hellos as they walked past. Are they not put out to have you here?'

'Well, of course not, dear,' Helen said. 'Why ever would they be?'

'It took them quite a long time to accept us in Bethnal Green,' Irene explained. 'They were convinced we were good for nothing. It was only when we broke a big burglary case that they seemed to accept we were capable of police work.

Even now, they're not overly friendly with us and a few still tend to look down on us.'

'Stuck up lot in London,' Mary sniffed.

'I think they were overwhelmed when the camp went up here,' Helen said, ignoring Mary's comment. 'As I said before, their town almost doubled in population over the course of a few weeks when the soldiers started arriving, and then all the prostitutes and camp followers rolled in. The Association for the Help and Care of Girls – that's who pays us – felt that trained women would be better at keeping girls and young women from evil influences than policemen. And the officers agreed – they were happy to have women here who could deal with those issues, leaving them to do what they do best.'

'I wish they'd seen it like that in London,' Irene sighed. 'Although, I'm glad we didn't have twenty thousand troops to deal with.'

'Get used to it,' Mary said harshly. 'Just because you had an easy time down in London, it doesn't mean that you can leave all the hard work to us!'

'I didn't mean—' Irene started, but Helen stepped in.

'Irene's been sent here because she's hard-working, Mary, so you've no need to worry yourself about her pulling her weight.'

Mary huffed and fell back to walk on her own in silence. She seemed to have a real bee in her bonnet, and Irene felt sorry for anyone not in uniform who happened to cross her. She could already see she had some kind of power complex. She noticed Ruby had gone quiet again, but Helen started talking before Irene had a chance to try and include her.

'We're removing the sources of the trouble to the troops in a way the normal and military police couldn't even attempt. We look after troublesome homes and do rescue work among the girls. We stop a lot of cases from having to go to the police court, although the odd one like Angela slips through.' She made it all sound very worthy, but Irene was still feeling uncomfortable with the joy Mary had seemed to take in learning their actions had resulted in a woman being locked away.

'You'll get to see that many of the recruits are young boys, fresh from school or college,' Helen continued. 'They're very naive and certain women prey on that. They get no formal supervision or control once they're outside the camp perimeter. We've been stepping in a lot to stop them getting themselves into bother. The police really would struggle without us here, and they know it. They leave us to get on with it and we keep out of their way in return. That's why your meeting with the chief was so brief. It was more of a formality – he's not particularly interested in us so long as we're doing the job we were put here to do so that his men don't need to bother with it at all.'

'That's why they leave it to us to investigate when deserters are being hidden by local women,' Mary said, excitement in her voice. 'We're much better at dealing with them.'

Irene bit her tongue. She might have known Mary would have enjoyed the deserter raids. And she was astounded that they were given free rein to search for deserters in people's homes. She couldn't imagine being given so much trust by the officers in charge in London.

As they got closer to the camp, she was distracted from the conversation by the number of street stalls they were suddenly passing. The stallholders were trying to draw in everyone who walked past, and there were so many the air was filled with loud voices offering all kinds of wonderful trinkets and garments.

'Oi! Stop pinching me customers!' a voice shrieked from behind them. The four of them stopped walking and spun around just in time to see an angry-looking woman rushing from a bakery towards them, waving her fist in the air. Irene hadn't expected any sort of action this quickly. She hadn't even seen the whole town yet! She braced herself, putting one foot forward, ready to launch into some ju-jitsu if it was required. But the woman sped straight past them, her flapping apron brushing Irene's leg as she went.

'Mrs Cauldwell,' the woman panted through heavy breaths – the short dash from the bakery to the food stall had her gasping for air. 'Please, I have some pastries in especially for you, come and have a look.'

'Oh, but they're cheaper here,' Mrs Cauldwell replied, indicating the stall and continuing to reach into her bag for her purse.

'You're gon' put me out of business!' the woman in the apron yelled, pointing her finger at the stallholder now, who was grinning and bagging up some cakes.

'Not my problem if you been overcharging these poor folk,' the stallholder shrugged, handing over the offending package to Mrs Cauldwell. As soon as it had exchanged hands, the shopkeeper lunged forward, knocking bread and pastries flying as she tried to get to the owner.

Irene froze and stared, aghast. Without missing a beat, Helen got the shopkeeper in an impressive hold and held her tight as the woman writhed from side to side, trying to get at her victim. Ruby and Mary stood either side of the pair, looking braced for action and ready to jump on anyone who tried to help free her. But no one did. A small crowd gathered as passers-by stopped to see what all the commotion was about. Nobody seemed fazed, though.

'I've told you before, you need to calm down about this,' Helen said quietly but firmly in the shopkeeper's ear. 'You want me to tell the lads to arrest you?' The woman's body visibly relaxed, and Helen loosened her grip before taking a step back.

'I'm sorry, love,' the shopkeeper whispered, looking ashamed now and wiping sweat from her brow. 'Please don't report me. I'm just struggling to make ends meet, is all.'

'You know we can't do anything about the stalls,' Helen said. Her voice was friendly now – understanding. 'Go back in and get baking. I *will* send the lads down later – but only to buy up all your best pastries. They've got more money than sense, those men at the station. And very greedy appetites.' The two women laughed, and the shopkeeper gave Irene, Mary and Ruby a nod before slowly walking back to her shop, her shoulders slumped.

'We get that a lot,' Ruby said quietly as the group continued on their way. Irene was shocked she had spoken, but happy to get the chance to open up a conversation with her. Before she could respond, Mary butted in.

'Travelling merchants pitched up soon as the camp got busy,' she said, her nasal voice grating on Irene's nerves. 'They set up shop wherever they can find a scrap of pavement. They're after whatever they can get from the troops and the locals.'

As they made their way further through the town, Irene could see what Mary meant – temporary shops and stalls littered every street. Alleys were blocked by them. It seemed anything was available, from souvenir cards to send to loved ones, to socks and caps for warmth on the front. Irene made a mental note to buy one of the cards to send to Maggie and Annie as soon as she got her first pay packet.

'You'll often find stallholders arguing with soldiers,' Helen said as they turned a corner and were met by a man in uniform haggling with someone who appeared to be trying to sell him a pair of thick socks. 'It's not just the women who want to take advantage of the troops with a ready supply of cash and too much time on their hands,' she added in a low voice as they passed the pair.

'I want them for the same price you were selling them at yesterday,' Irene heard the soldier saying, agitation in his voice.

'One side feels extorted and the other hard-done-by, and we're expected to somehow maintain order among it all,' Helen sighed. 'It doesn't help when anyone around here in an army uniform is treated like a hero by the locals. It makes it extremely difficult to keep soldiers in line when the locals want to indulge them no matter what crime they commit.'

'We only step in when it gets nasty, like back there,' Ruby whispered. Irene was beginning to wonder how on earth Ruby had made it through training to become a WPS recruit, let alone survived life patrolling this bustling town with its huge army camp. Although, if she was on duty with Helen and Mary all the time then she could understand how it would be easy for her to stand back and let their big characters take over. She was intrigued to find out more about this timid girl who she could tell had a kind soul. But for now she needed to focus on getting to know her way around Grantham, and she was excited to see the army camp that had transformed the town.

# 8

By the time they made it to Belton Park, Irene was exhausted. They had traipsed through endless fields to get there. They had even had to take a diversion to avoid a firing range where troops were practising their shooting.

'There's so much countryside,' she groaned to herself when they finally spotted rows and rows of wooden huts and a grand-looking house, which Helen explained was Belton House. Irene wondered why the Grantham recruits hadn't been supplied with footwear more suited to the terrain. The cumbersome boots had been uncomfortable when she was patrolling the streets of east London in them, and they were even more so now as she waded through the muddy fields. She kept her thoughts to herself, though. She didn't want to come across as negative on her first day, and she definitely didn't want to give Mary another excuse to take a swipe at her.

'We don't report to anyone here,' Helen explained as they walked around the perimeter of the huge camp, passing soldiers and officers who each nodded or smiled an acknowledgement to them. 'They know who we are from our uniform. We only really come out here if we're returning a soldier to camp or on the lookout for women of bad character who have sneaked in. That, and tracking down naive daughters of local families who have escaped from home to creep in.'

'It's not just locals,' Mary took over now. 'They come from all over to try and get their hands on the troops. Lots are arriving from Nottingham at the moment. It's a good three miles from the train station to the camp, which goes to show how determined they are to have their wicked way.'

'But where do they take the men, to . . . you know?' asked Irene uncomfortably. She couldn't help but feel shy when it came to discussing intimate acts, even though she had been dealing with it as part of her police work for months now.

'*Have sex?*' Mary asked loudly. A group of men in uniform looked up from a postcard they had been huddled around and started laughing. Mary grinned at them, obviously taking great pleasure in Irene's discomfort.

'No use being a prude about it, dear,' Helen said matter-of-factly. 'Going back to your original question,' Helen continued, 'they often do their business in the fields surrounding the camps, and of course in quiet alleys in the town. I'm surprised we didn't come across anybody on our way here.'

'That all calmed down when they brought in the curfew,' Mary said now. 'I still can't believe they lifted that. We weren't here then, but the recruits before us said there was much less hanky-panky in the streets.'

Irene was shocked. How could any woman think enforcing a curfew like that was a good idea? She couldn't keep quiet. She didn't care if she riled Mary – she had to say something.

'But how can you support a curfew like that?' she asked. She tried to keep her tone soft, so that she didn't come across too confrontational, but it was hard work. 'The majority of the poor women around here aren't criminals at all, so they don't deserve to be locked up at home every evening.'

'Sometimes, needs must,' snapped Mary, but she seemed a little flustered. She obviously wasn't used to being challenged on her views. 'Besides, anyone respectable wouldn't be wandering the streets at all hours anyhow.'

'But how do you decide who is bad and who is good?'

Irene ventured. She knew she was effectively poking a bear, but she was fascinated by Mary's views. It seemed as though she saw prostitutes as a different species to herself.

'Oh, you just *know*,' Mary said firmly. She sounded as though she was beginning to get frustrated. 'There's a certain way a lady holds herself – and she talks in a certain way.'

Irene was beginning to understand why Mary was so extreme in her treatment of the prostitutes. She looked down on anybody who was less wealthy or educated than she was. Irene had been correct in her suspicions: Mary couldn't stand anyone who she viewed as being inferior to herself, and that covered a rather large group of people. She wondered if she realised that 'respectable' women often fell into prostitution, too.

'There's no use in us getting into a disagreement about this now,' Helen said firmly. 'The curfew was proven not to work, and it was lifted before any of us arrived. We have to respect that and do our best to keep these women off the streets and away from our troops. After a little while you'll come to know the bad girls of the town as we do, Irene, and you'll be able to distinguish them from the professionals moving in to serve the soldiers.'

Irene was happy to have someone step in before things got heated between herself and Mary again. She was going to have to be careful around her – not least because she herself was exactly the kind of woman Mary would be gunning for if she knew her circumstances. She suspected Mary was just about tolerating her at the moment as the WPS uniforms made her think that they were equals.

'How did the army get hold of all this land?' Irene asked Helen, keen to change the subject.

'The earl who owns the estate donated it to the War Office soon after war was declared,' Helen explained. 'He handed over the whole of the park – the area between Belton House

and the eastern side of the river Witham went from pretty
gardens to one of the biggest military camps for the infantry
in Britain in the space of a few weeks. It's no surprise our
little town struggled to cope with the influx of bodies.'

'Are you all from around here, then?' Irene asked. She had
assumed Mary was local judging from her accent, but she
couldn't be sure about Helen and Ruby.

'Oh, sorry dear,' Helen said, smiling. 'That was a little
misleading. I've not been here long but I tend to think of it as
my town already. No, no, I had my family in Merseyside and
later trained as a midwife in London. Ruby here is from Surrey.'

'I'm the closest to local they've got,' Mary boasted. 'I'm
from Newark – about fifteen miles away. It's near here but
it's a very different place with very different people. You
wouldn't catch frivolous young girls wandering the streets at
night in my hometown, I can tell you. My family own a big
house there. It's almost as impressive as Belton House.'

Irene got the feeling Mary was exaggerating. She seemed
to think that she was better than not just prostitutes but the
people of Grantham as a whole.

Irene decided she definitely needed to keep her background
to herself. She didn't want to give Mary any reason to pick
on her. She reminded herself that she had kept her situation
from Maggie and Annie while patrolling with them and living
in the same area. She had grown close to them and they
hadn't discovered the truth until she had chosen to reveal it
to help Maggie. So, she was sure that pulling the wool over
Mary's eyes shouldn't be an issue. She certainly wasn't planning on growing close to her.

'What about you? Have you always been in London?' Mary
asked. It was the first time she had shown any interest in her,
and Irene took a moment to realise she was talking to her.

'Yes, I grew up in Kensington,' she lied quickly. She thought
back to the lovely street Maggie's family lived on and imagined

what it would have been like to grow up there. There was no chance she was going to reveal the years she had spent in children's homes to someone like Mary. She didn't see the harm in telling a little white lie in the name of self-preservation. And she knew Maggie wouldn't mind her 'borrowing' some of her history if it meant Mean Mary left her alone.

'That's a bit fancy,' Mary sneered, looking Irene up and down with a suspicious tone in her voice.

Irene panicked. This would surely backfire – her clothes and demeanour were enough to give her away before she even spoke. She had brought hardly anything with her to Grantham – was that the action of a well-to-do young lady from Kensington?

'I thought it best to leave my better clothes at home,' Irene said hurriedly, thinking back to the tatty dress she had been wearing when she had stepped off the train earlier that day. 'When I was patrolling in London, I found the women were more receptive to someone they believed was more on their level,' she said, gaining confidence. It was a complete fabrication, of course – anyone her and her friends had met patrolling had responded to the uniform and the authority it gave them. People seemed to fall into line when they saw it, assuming the wearer was better educated and wealthier than themselves and therefore commanded respect. She blended into the background in her everyday clothes.

'I find round here they behave better when you let them know who's boss and put them in their place,' Mary replied. 'Maybe you ought to send for some of your nicer clothes,' she added nastily, pursing her lips.

'When do we ever wear anything but the uniform?' Helen said light-heartedly. Irene was grateful to her for coming to her rescue. 'We work seven days a week most weeks, so no one sees us in anything but this,' she laughed, pulling at the WPS letters stitched on to the shoulder of her jacket.

The interruption halted the interrogation Mary had just been getting started on. Irene was sure she could see through her. She hated that people like Mary judged everyone on their class and background. Just because Irene had grown up without her family and hadn't had as good an education as her, didn't mean to say she was less worthy of this role. She had passed the training just as she had, despite all of that.

They came to a big hut and Helen explained it was one of two YMCA huts on the camp. There was also a military base hospital, churches, a cinema and the base even had its own railway line. The troops slept in wooden huts with corrugated iron roofs and each regimental line had its own separate barracks, latrines, wash houses and mess huts. Electricity and water supplies had been organised, too. Irene thought it was more like a little town than a military camp. She had known the base was big, but she hadn't expected anything on this scale.

'The huts and marquees are there for the social and moral welfare of the men, and to attempt to provide places of counter-attraction to the questionable ones,' Helen said, raising an eyebrow at two young lads who were poking each other and chuckling as they walked past them.

'Fat lot of good it's doing,' Mary scoffed. 'Most of the men would rather get up to no good with bad women and beer. Speaking of which . . .' her voice trailed off as they all watched Ruby suddenly dart across the field towards the row of huts opposite.

'What is she doing?' Irene asked, confused. She also wondered why they were all standing still and not going after her to help her.

'Argh, she's spotted one!' Mary cried, throwing her hands up in exasperation. 'That could have been mine!' Ruby disappeared around the side of the hut on the end of the row momentarily before emerging holding the arm of a dishevelled-looking woman who was staring at the ground in defeat.

'There goes your fun night!' a man's voice cried out from inside the hut. There was a roar of laughter as Ruby and her prisoner walked past the entrance and into view of the soldiers inside.

'And another of you lot saved from a bout of VD, thank you very much!' Mary yelled over at the hut as Ruby and the woman approached. Irene was stunned. Ruby had hardly said a word all afternoon and had been acting so timidly. Where had this sudden bout of confidence and assertiveness come from?

'You – keep quiet,' Helen whispered urgently to Mary. 'Let Ruby deal with this her way.'

'But she'll just let her go,' Mary groaned. If Ruby hadn't been walking towards them with a woman in tow, then Irene could have been forgiven for thinking Mary was talking about a wild animal. Irene bit her tongue.

'She says she got lost trying to get into town,' Ruby explained once she reached the three of them. Mary went to say something but winced and scowled as Helen struck her in the side with her elbow. 'I've explained that the camp and soldiers are out of bounds,' Ruby continued. 'I'll escort her back to the train station so she can get on her way home.'

With that, the woman started struggling. She tried to break free from Ruby's grip, but Ruby held tight and thrust the woman's arm behind her back. As Ruby went to grab her other arm, the woman threw it wildly in the air, almost striking Ruby in the face. Irene made to step forwards, but Helen stopped her.

'She can do this,' she muttered, just as Ruby got hold of the woman's other arm and forced it behind her back.

'We'll be off then,' Ruby said cheerily, already pushing the woman, who was still struggling, across the field in the direction of the train station.

'But – shouldn't we go with her?' Irene asked. 'We never

split up in London, it was too dangerous to be out on your own.'

'She'll be fine,' Helen laughed. 'She can handle herself well, that one. She might not be able to get a word in around Mary, but she's a very competent recruit.'

Mary tutted and rolled her eyes. 'Not my fault she can't string two words together in front of me,' she huffed.

'Anyway, it's far too busy around here for us to be sticking together all the time,' Helen continued. 'Just remember how many troops there are in one small area. We often go and patrol different areas on our own or in pairs. You've done the training and you've worked in London, so you'll be fine.' Irene must have let her panic show on her face as Helen added, 'But I won't send you out on your own just yet. We'll help you get to know the town and the people first.'

Irene smiled with relief, although she still felt anxious at the thought of patrolling alone. She had only ever known life in uniform with Maggie and Annie by her side. They were her backup, and she was theirs if anything ever turned nasty. Could she do this without that support? She had to admit she wasn't sure. She'd been so concerned before she left with whether they would be all right without her, she hadn't stopped to think about whether she would be able to cope without them. They were like her security blanket. But there was no question of her voicing her fears – especially not in front of Mary. As her heart pounded like a marching-drum in her chest, she resolved to focus on getting to know the town as best she could. She would worry about the rest when the time came.

# 9

The journey back to the town centre was quicker than the trek to the camp as it turned out there was a main road, Manthorpe Road, that provided a much easier route between the two locations. Helen said she'd wanted to show Irene the scenic route first as that was the one that they tended to take more often. Apparently, they were more likely to catch couples up to no good in the fields surrounding the camps than along the main road. It made sense to Irene, but she couldn't help but feel they could have gone a little easier on her on her first day. She had so much to take in and put in order in her mind that she could do without feeling physically as well as mentally exhausted.

After Irene, Helen and Mary had had a relatively quiet wander around the town, Ruby caught back up with them all. She revealed the woman she had apprehended at the camp had left on a train without any problems. Helen wanted to check in on an older lady who had been to see her the previous day with concerns about her niece, so she left the three of them at Market Place and they agreed to meet back at Rutland Street that evening.

As soon Helen was out of sight, Mary turned to Ruby and Irene. 'I've got my own business to attend to, and it doesn't involve either of you,' she said curtly before walking off.

'Is she always so pleasant?' Irene laughed in her wake, shocked at the way Mary had spoken to them.

'You'll get used to her,' Ruby shrugged before leading her off towards an alley full of stalls and tradesmen. Walking past a stall selling postcards of Grantham, Irene's eye was caught by a young lad hovering around near a tall man as he made his way along the street. At first, she assumed the pair were together – a father and son out to pick up a few items in town. But the boy kept hanging back and looking around shiftily. And as she kept track of them, she was struck by the contrast in their appearances. Even from behind, she could tell they came from very different worlds. While the man was kitted out in a smart suit and wore a watch that glistened in the sun with every step he took, the boy's shorts were dirty, his hair dishevelled, and there was a hole in his shirt.

Irene was just about to point the pair out to Ruby and ask if she knew either of them, when she spotted the boy slide his hand into the man's trouser pocket and bring it back out holding his wallet. He was so swift and light-fingered that the man didn't notice. It had been such a natural move, Irene had to look again at the wallet in the boy's hand to be sure her eyes hadn't deceived her. Before she had a chance to say or do anything, the little tyke sped off down the street. Before she knew what she was doing, Irene was on the move.

'Sir! He's got your wallet!' she cried as she ran towards him. 'Stop! Thief!' she shouted at the top of her voice, sprinting past the man now and towards the High Street. The wallet's owner stared after her, confused, and patted down his pockets before a look of panic swept over his face. For a moment Irene thought she had lost the boy, but then she caught a glimpse of the back of his head as he darted behind one of the stalls. She picked up her pace and followed him. As she came around the back of the stall, she couldn't believe her eyes when she saw him standing there, staring straight back at her. The cocky so-and-so must have thought he had lost her already.

'Stop!' she yelled as he spotted her, turned and started running again. She had been determined to catch him before, but now that he had shown he thought he had nothing to worry about – presumably because she was a woman – well, there was no way she was going to let him get away. She was soon close behind him again. They were on the busy High Street now, and he kept winding between people, so that every time she went to grab his shirt as it blew out behind him, she just missed it. He switched direction suddenly and ducked down an alleyway. Just as Irene rounded the corner, she saw the lad fly up into the air – he had been going so fast that he had tripped over a pile of rubbish. As he landed on the floor, she made it to his side. She watched in amusement as he scrambled to his feet, his face dropping as he looked up to see her face looming over him.

'Thought you were too quick, didn't you?' she gloated. 'Ah – no you don't!' she cried when he went to dart off again. She grabbed his arm and twisted it behind his back. Now she was up close to him, she could see how skinny he was. There was no need to use any force on him, so she did it a lot more gently than she would normally have done. Taking in his gaunt face, covered in dirt, and feeling his bony arm, she felt a wave of sympathy for him. He must have only been around ten years old, and she realised he must have been desperate to do what he'd done, and just trying to get by and survive. She was glad Mary had sauntered off now, as she was certain that had she spotted his crime the poor lad would be on his way to the police cells right now. Irene wanted to find out why he'd gone to such extreme lengths and help him if possible.

Before she could say anything, a man's voice rung out from the entrance to the alleyway.

'Do you need any assistance?' it boomed. Irene looked up and spotted a police officer. She smiled and shook her head.

'I've got it all under control, thank you,' she replied with confidence. The officer tipped his hat and continued on his way. Irene looked down at the lad again.

'Please,' he begged. 'Me mam's sick and I just wanted to

bring her home some bread.' Irene's heart broke for him. She was tempted to just let him go on his way. But then she remembered Ruby had seen everything, and the owner of the wallet was surely awaiting its return. She couldn't risk either of them thinking she had let the boy get away. She didn't know Ruby well enough yet to be sure she wouldn't report back to Helen, and the man would probably be so angry that she was certain the whole town would soon know how useless she was. He'd had an air of importance about him. At least she had saved the boy from being arrested, she thought as she reluctantly guided the lad back along the alleyway. Thankfully, he didn't put up a fight.

'I'm sorry,' Irene said quietly as they walked slowly back along the High Street. 'I understand why you did it. But you can't just go around stealing from people.' He stayed silent, tears welling in his eyes. 'What's your name?' she asked.

'Billy,' he whispered, staring at the ground.

'Well, Billy,' she said kindly, 'I'm sure we can think of a way to get some money coming in for your mum without you getting into trouble.' He looked up at her now, hope in his eyes. 'When I was in London, a lot of the businesses relied on young boys like yourself to help them out,' she explained. 'It might mean some early mornings, but you'd get some honest money for it. And if we can get you some work with a greengrocer then you might get a bit of fruit and veg to boot. That'll help your mum get back to health.' Billy smiled now, and his pace quickened. 'We'll have to give that man his wallet back,' Irene added, 'but let me do the talking, and when I'm done tell him you're sorry. If he accepts your apology, then I'll be happy to let you go without taking this any further. How does that sound?' Billy was nodding his head eagerly now. Irene prayed the man was understanding.

As they approached the row of stalls where Billy had swiped the man's wallet, they found him standing by some freshly bakcd bread talking to Ruby, a small crowd of onlookers having gathered around them. Her heart sank when she spotted Mary making her way through the crowd.

'Well,' the man exclaimed when he looked around to see them heading over. 'I must say I'm impressed. I was sure the little thief was far too fast for you, even with the way you raced off after him. I've never seen a woman run so fast! What an outstanding policewoman you are.'

Irene couldn't help but feel flattered, despite his patronising tone. Now she was getting a good look at his face, she couldn't deny the fact that he was extremely handsome. He looked to be in his forties, but his broad shoulders and his impressive physique, along with the salt-and-pepper stubble around his smiling mouth, gave him a rugged charm. He was greying slightly at the temples, which Irene thought made him look distinguished. And he was very tall – Irene was tall herself, but he towered over her. As she returned his smile and looked into his eyes, they seemed to glisten with kindness.

Irene and Billy were standing in front of the man in silence. Irene realised she needed to speak and pulled herself together. 'Billy here had a moment of madness born out of pure desperation,' she explained, trying to cover the slight quiver in her voice. Mary was standing with them now, and Irene heard her scoff, but continued talking over the noise. 'His mum's gravely ill, you see, and he just wanted to do something to help her.'

'With my hard-earned money?' the man asked sternly. He looked serious now, but there was still an undeniable twinkle in his eye that Irene found intriguing. What was wrong with her? He looked old enough to be her father, yet she was feeling ever so jumpy all of a sudden. She felt Billy shrinking next to her and she forced herself to speak again.

'Of course, it wasn't the thing to do at all. I've explained that to Billy now and he agrees. We've even come up with a plan to get him get some honest work so he can help his mum without breaking the law. And he has something to say.' She nudged Billy gently and he looked up slowly at the man.

'It's all right, I won't bite.' The man laughed as Billy stared at him open-mouthed. Irene noticed that the creases around his eyes showed up when he laughed like that, making his face look warm and kind.

'I'm . . . I'm sorry, sir,' Billy whispered timidly.

'Well, that's very big of you, Billy,' he replied warmly. Irene breathed a sigh of relief.

'Here's your wallet back, Mr . . .?' She realised she hadn't even introduced herself or asked for his name. He'd really sent her giddy.

'Murphy. Charles Murphy,' he said, reaching out his hand, and before Irene knew it, she was shaking it. An excited shiver ran through her body as their skin made contact and his hand gripped hers firmly for the formal greeting. Did he keep hold of her hand longer than was necessary, or was she imagining it? She scolded herself again, before handing back his wallet. His fingers brushed hers again as he took it from her. Had he done that on purpose?

'I own Murphy and Sons over on the London Road,' he explained, holding eye contact with her. Irene nodded, despite the fact that the name didn't mean anything to her. She was still getting to know the town and she hadn't noticed anywhere named Murphy & Sons.

'We were hoping you'd show some mercy on Billy here, seeing as he's apologised and returned your wallet. Of course, I'll escort him home and make sure his mother is aware of what he's been up to,' Irene explained, crossing her fingers behind her back. 'Does that sound agreeable to you, Mr Murphy?'

'Oh, please, call me Charles,' he said lightly. His eyes were playful now, and Irene felt her stomach flip. He fell silent for a few moments, looking thoughtful. Then he reached his hand into his pocket. Irene could hear the jangling of loose change.

He pulled out some coins and counted them out. 'There's six shillings there,' Charles said, passing the coins over to Billy, who took them from him nervously. He looked up to Irene for reassurance and she smiled to let him know it was all right to keep hold of them. 'Take that to your mother, Billy. I hope it helps makes things a little easier for you both until you can find a way to make some money of your own. Just don't resort to thievery again, my boy.'

If Irene had been sent giddy by this man before, she could almost fall down on the floor now, he had made her knees so weak. What a gentleman! To show such compassion and caring to someone who had stolen from him. He was obviously a man of good standing, and she knew from experience people like that didn't normally give people like Billy – like *her* – the time of day, let alone show such understanding for the desperate situations they often found themselves in. Irene nudged Billy again and he took the hint and stammered his thanks for the money.

'That's so very kind of you, sir,' Irene said gratefully.

'Please, it's Charles,' he laughed again. Irene felt herself blushing lightly as he fixed his gaze on her yet again. She wasn't used to calling somebody like him by his first name. 'And I'm afraid I still don't know what to call you?' he added, still not breaking eye contact. Now she felt really silly – even after realising her mistake in not asking for his name straight away, she had failed to offer up her own.

'I do apologise,' she laughed nervously. 'My name's Irene. Irene Wilson.' She wasn't usually so formal when she met people for the first time, but Charles was making her act out of the ordinary in more ways than one.

'Well, Irene Wilson,' he said. Her heart raced when she heard him saying her name. 'It was wonderful to meet you. Even in such grim circumstances.' She smiled. 'I do hope our paths will cross again – for a better reason next time.'

As she watched him walk away, she realised she hadn't responded to his final words. What had this man done to her? She was always so confident and sure of herself, but he had reduced her to a gibbering wreck. She looked over at Mary, who raised her eyebrows.

'Would you like a moment to compose yourself?' she asked sarcastically.

Embarrassed, Irene took Billy's arm. 'Let's just get this one back to his mother,' she said firmly.

She had completely forgotten Mary had been standing there and she was angry with herself for letting her guard down and acting so foolishly in front of her.

'Did you fancy him, miss?' Billy asked innocently as they started walking in the opposite direction to the one Charles had taken.

'What do *you* think?' Mary said mockingly from behind them. Before Irene had a chance to respond, she felt a tug on her arm. She turned and found Ruby had fallen into step beside her.

'Charles Murphy is one of the most important men in this town,' she whispered excitedly. 'I can't believe he was so friendly to you. He was quite terse with me while we were waiting for you to return.'

'Well, maybe he has a bit of a soft spot for our new girl, hey Irene?' Mary said teasingly.

Flustered, Irene continued on her way with Billy in tow, Ruby following alongside them, her face desperate for the conversation to continue.

'I'll talk to you about it later,' Irene hissed under her breath, feeling herself blushing again. All she really wanted to do now was replay the encounter in her head and think about Charles Murphy's handsome eyes and charming smile.

# IO

Billy's mother hadn't seemed at all fussed that Irene had caught him red-handed stealing from one of the big players in the town.

'Murphy surely wouldn't miss a few bob, what with the way he's living,' she had snapped scornfully before her bird-like frame was racked with a terrible coughing fit. Just as she slammed the door on Irene, Ruby and Mary, Irene spotted blood shining wetly on the tissue she had pressed to her mouth.

'He wasn't lying about her being ill, at least,' Mary shrugged.

Irene felt even worse for Billy now. She resolved to visit the boy again soon and help him find some work. She hoped his mother's attitude wouldn't put him off the idea. She also decided to try and find out more about Charles Murphy. She had assumed his business was just a small local set-up, but the reaction from both Ruby and Billy's mother seemed to suggest it was something bigger.

Back among the hustle and bustle of the traders in town, the girls were all shocked when a dishevelled-looking woman came rushing towards them looking panicked. It was clear Mary wasn't used to being sought out by such characters, preferring instead to hunt them down herself, as she didn't utter a word when the woman explained why she needed help.

'There's a soldier down the next alley,' she told them urgently. 'I don't want to get into any trouble – I just wanted to cheer him up. But I can't touch it.' She closed her eyes and shuddered. 'I think he needs help.' She'd barely finished her sentence before running off in the opposite direction.

As the three of them made their way towards the alley, Irene braced herself. She knew the military was fighting a losing battle against VD. One of the reasons prostitutes received such bad treatment was because they were blamed for the men struck down with it being unable to fight for months while they received treatment. Not that Irene agreed with that viewpoint, of course. But she had never seen any of the symptoms up close and personal, and she had a feeling she was about to.

Turning into the alley, she saw the man on his knees. His trousers were undone, and he was cradling his crotch area.

'Don't come any closer! Don't look!' he cried out as the group approached. He put his hand out to warn them away and then, realising it left part of his private parts on show, quickly swept it back in to protect his dignity – or what little he had left. He winced as his hand made contact with the area. In the split-second it had been left slightly uncovered, Irene had seen what appeared to be angry-looking boils and some unpleasant discharge.

'Oh, you poor thing. Just look at what those terrible women have done to you!' Mary cried, rushing to his side. The soldier squirmed, looking even more embarrassed than he had done previously, if that was even possible.

'What *they've* done *to him?*' Irene exclaimed.

She couldn't believe what she was hearing. Did Mary think men had no say in the activities they got up to with prostitutes? If VD was rife then that wasn't solely down to women – it took two consenting people to spread disease like that. But, noticing that Ruby wasn't passing any judgement, Irene decided to keep her thoughts to herself and deal with the issue at hand instead of getting into an argument with Mary while this man continued to suffer. Thankfully, Mary seemed to have missed Irene's remark as she sat down on the floor next to the soldier and mollycoddled him.

'You need medical attention,' Irene said, approaching the two of them.

'My sergeant can't know about this,' he said looking up at her with panic in his eyes. 'I'll get punished and they won't let me fight!'

'You're in no fit state to fight,' Irene replied. 'In fact, I don't even think you're capable of walking right now.'

'I thought if I did something with it, it might sort it out. But as soon as she touched it, it felt worse,' he admitted, looking away

'Not satisfied with infecting you, they come back to put you through more pain,' Mary tutted, shaking her head.

Irene bit her tongue and took a deep breath. 'We need to get him to the camp hospital,' she declared. 'There's no way he can walk there, even with our assistance. We need some help.'

'I'm not leaving him!' Mary barked.

'I'm not asking you to,' Irene said as calmly as she could. Mary seemed intent on starting an argument even when there wasn't one to be had. Irene asked Ruby to run to the police station and get one of the officers to bring a car to the alley entrance so they could give the man a ride back to camp.

'Mary, you stay with him and I'll guard the alley entrance – we don't want anybody walking down here and getting a fright.'

'Yes, and keep those filthy wretches away,' Mary called after her. 'They've done enough damage as it is!'

Irene rolled her eyes, safe in the knowledge Mary wouldn't see. She was astounded that a woman could see the situation as she did, but it wasn't the time or place to debate it.

When Ruby returned in a police car with a PC, Mary insisted on travelling back to the camp with the soldier to make sure he was admitted to the hospital straight away. Irene was only too happy to wave her off.

Irene was keen to know where Ruby stood on the VD situation – did she think the prostitutes were solely to blame, or could she see the bigger picture? But they stopped to talk to so many people as they made their way around the town that she didn't get a chance to broach the subject, and before she knew it, it was time to head back to Rutland Street to meet Helen.

Helen insisted that Irene get an early night while the rest of them patrolled into the evening. From what Irene could make out, they didn't have any set shifts and just kept an eye on things as Helen saw fit. Which meant they didn't have a lot of time for much of anything else.

Irene felt guilty that she hadn't taken the time to write to Maggie and Annie to let them know she had arrived safely and fill them in on her new colleagues. She was eager to put pen to paper for them, to feel some kind of connection to them again, even if it was only through a letter. But the truth was that she was just too tired and she was desperate to get into her new bed. As soon as she had walked into her room, she hung her uniform over a chair that was wedged behind the door, and she could feel sleep coming for her already. Grateful that she no longer had her factory shifts to worry about fitting in, she started to give in to the sleep that was calling her.

As her eyelids grew heavier and heavier, her mind drifted to Frank. She wondered what he'd been up to that day – had he been at the station, or was he helping to prepare for the arrival of his baby? His wedding day was looming closer, and she felt a huge sense of relief that she wasn't in London to hear all about it. Irene realised it was the first time she had thought of him all day. At least there was one benefit to being so busy, she thought as she yawned and rolled over on to her side. Frank had certainly been just as out of mind as he was out of sight. And meeting Charles Murphy had definitely been a welcome distraction.

Irene was achieving one of the things she'd hoped for with her transfer to Grantham already. The second would definitely take longer. She knew already that Mary was guilty of treating the prostitutes – and women in general – badly, and it would take some doing to convince her to be fair to them. She wasn't sure about Helen and Ruby just yet, although they were definitely kinder to the general public than Mary. As sleep finally took hold, Irene felt ready for the challenge ahead.

The following morning, Irene woke with a start as the bedroom door slammed shut. She hadn't even heard the others returning the previous night, but it appeared Mary was now up and about. Irene took a few moments to wake up properly. She must have been out cold – it wasn't like her to sleep through anything, let alone someone coming into the room and getting into the bed so close to her own. After a big stretch and a quick rub of her eyes, she was getting ready to rise and prepare herself for the day when she heard the outhouse door slamming beneath the bedroom window. Then there were heavy footsteps on the stairs, and the bedroom door flung open again.

'Are you going to join us at some point?' Mary asked curtly, raising her eyebrows at Irene in a way that made her feel like a child who had just been caught in the middle of doing something extremely naughty. 'We're ready to go and Helen's insisting we wait for you,' she added, a hint of frustration in her voice. She was dressed in her uniform and her hair was pulled back into a neat bun.

'Sorry, I – I'll only be a minute,' Irene stuttered, feeling flustered by the look of impatience on Mary's face. 'What time is it?' she asked cautiously.

'Nine,' Mary barked. 'We were out patrolling until gone two in the morning and you're the one still in bed. You best get your skates on!' With that, she turned on her heel and left the room, slamming the door behind her again.

Irene couldn't believe she'd slept in so late. All the travelling and new experiences the day before must have really taken it out of her, as well as the long walk to and from Belton Park. But she would have to get used to that. Thankfully, she had never been one to take long getting ready. She was downstairs in her uniform with the others in a matter of minutes.

'Go and freshen yourself up and I'll have some breakfast waiting for you when you're done,' Helen said when Irene entered the kitchen, flashing her a warm and friendly smile. It was so different from Mary's greeting, and so far from what she had expected given Mary's attitude, that Irene was a little thrown. Helen was standing next to the stove, and Mary and Ruby were both sitting at a small wooden table with empty bowls in front of them.

'She means go and relieve yourself outside,' Mary tutted, sounding bored. She turned to Helen now. 'Do we have to wait until she's had her breakfast?' she moaned. 'There's a train due in from Nottingham.'

Normally Irene would have been happy to sacrifice her breakfast to keep everyone happy – she was used to skipping meals to help make ends meet anyway, and in fact she hardly ever ate in the mornings to save money – but she'd been so busy the day before that she hadn't eaten a thing. She had been too tired to think about food when she'd flopped into bed, and the mention of eating now had brought her stomach roaring to life.

'I won't need much, and I can take it with me,' she offered, still wary of rubbing Mary up the wrong way but more worried about surviving the morning without at least a small amount of food inside her.

'You'll do nothing of the sort,' Helen said firmly. 'You look like you could do with a good meal, if I'm honest. And you certainly need to keep your strength up if you're to spend the day with us.'

Right on cue, Irene's stomach let out a loud rumble. She blushed, hoping nobody apart from herself had heard it. When none of them reacted, she relaxed and started making her way across the room to the back door that led to the lavatory.

'Mary, why don't you go on ahead to the train station?' Helen suggested. 'You can look out for any of the usual bad characters getting off the train from Nottingham.' Mary sprung up out of her chair and raced out of the kitchen without a word or a backwards glance. 'Be nice!' Helen shouted after her, just before the loud crash of the front door closing made them all wince. 'Never closes a door quietly, that one,' Helen muttered as she went back to stirring a pot on the stove.

When Irene had finished in the toilet she walked back into an empty kitchen. There was a steaming bowl of porridge on the table and a spoon, along with a cup of tea. Her mouth watered as she sat down to enjoy it. She didn't normally like porridge, but she was so hungry it tasted as good as one of the sandwiches Maggie's family cook Florence used to make for her. The porridge was gone within minutes and when Ruby walked back into the room, Irene felt shame flushing through her cheeks.

'I can never get enough of that the morning after a full day of patrolling,' Ruby said, smiling kindly. Irene was surprised to hear her speaking so freely, and she wondered if it was because Mary wasn't there. 'I've had two bowls already. You want some more?' Ruby asked, walking over to the stove and scooping more porridge up in a ladle. She must have picked up on Irene's hesitation. 'Honestly, it'll go to waste otherwise,' she added.

Irene didn't need any more persuasion and ate the second bowl just as quickly. Once she was done, she washed up her bowl, spoon and cup. She felt ready to start the day.

'It's just you and me this morning,' Ruby said quietly as she rose from her chair. 'One of the girls has popped in to see Helen so she told me to show you around a bit more instead of waiting – she never knows how long it will take and another one will probably turn up before she's finished.'

'Do they come to her a lot, then?' Irene asked as they left the house together.

'She has at least three visitors a day,' Ruby explained. 'A lot of mothers worried about their girls getting caught up with the wrong crowd or being tempted by the soldiers go to her for advice, and even girls themselves once they've done something they shouldn't have done.' Irene was certain now that Helen felt the same way as she did when it came to the way the prostitutes were treated. Ruby seemed to be on the same page, too. Maybe it was just Mary who was continuing the bad attitude of the previous recruits here. Speaking of Mary, now she was alone with Ruby this seemed like a great opportunity to dig a little deeper.

'So, I hope you don't mind me saying,' Irene started cautiously. 'You hardly spoke yesterday and now—'

'You've seen what Mary's like,' Ruby said, cutting her off before she could finish. 'I learned quickly that it's better to just keep your mouth shut around her. She's the kind of girl to go out of her way to make anything into an argument. Helen does her best to keep her in line but she's not really our superior – there's only so much she can do. Plus, she tends to lash out the worst when Helen's not in earshot, anyway.'

'So, you just shut yourself down when she's around?' Irene asked incredulously. They were walking along the High Street now, and it was busy with stalls and locals as well as soldiers wandering around as it had been the day before.

'It's frustrating, but you'll be doing the same soon, I can assure you,' Ruby sighed. 'We have enough to deal with keeping things in order around here without having to stop every five minutes to have a pointless argument with Mary. Take that soldier yesterday. I think her view that it's all a prostitute's fault that he got sick is ridiculous. But what would have been the point in saying anything? She just would have blown up at me, and the soldier would have had to wait longer for treatment.'

Irene could see her point regarding the incident yesterday. She had backed off herself to prioritise getting the soldier to hospital. But she wasn't convinced that was always going to be the best course of action. She had come across characters like Mary in the children's home and she knew she could handle herself just fine. Girls like her were just bullies, and they needed people to stand up to them or else they would just go around picking on everybody – like Mary currently was.

'I won't stand for it,' Irene said confidently. 'I've already seen the contempt she has for the prostitutes here, and the effect she has on you. I was being cautious at first, but now I've got the measure of her I won't be holding back. I won't let her break me down.'

Ruby nodded quietly but Irene could see that she didn't believe her. There was no point talking about it further – she knew actions would speak louder than her words could anyway. She would just have to prove it to Ruby. She was certain that if she stood up to her, she would eventually win Mary round. People like her fed off cowardice, so she had to show Mary she was strong.

As they turned down one of the side alleys, Irene felt like a weight had been lifted. This was what she had come to Grantham for. She needed to work on Mary and somehow change her way of thinking. It was important to make her realise street women are human too and they deserve to be treated with as much respect as anyone else. She was also now determined to help Ruby to come out of her shell around their nasty colleague. She was obviously a good recruit, so it wasn't fair that she felt forced to suppress herself around Mary for an easy life.

Irene had come here fearing that all the recruits would have the same terrible traits that Mary had, so it was a relief to know her task wasn't going to be as big as she had originally anticipated. She only had one person to work on to help make things better for the women of Grantham. The new sense of purpose was breathing life into Irene. She felt like her old self all of a sudden, instead of the one who had been moping around since everything had gone wrong with Frank. She knew now that this had been the right thing to do. All her doubts had evaporated, and she felt positive for the first time in weeks. Irene couldn't wait to make a difference here.

# II

Irene felt a lot more relaxed patrolling without Mary. Ruby was easy to talk to and friendly when Mean Mary wasn't around, and she showed sympathy and understanding to all the women the pair of them ended up talking to during the course of the morning. After wandering up and down the streets of Grantham a few times to help Irene learn her way around, they decided to head out to the fields surrounding Belton Park.

'There's always someone at it,' Ruby said matter-of-factly. Irene couldn't get used to her speaking so frankly after she had come across as being so reserved the previous day.

As they made their way through the first field, Irene was struck by the beauty of her surroundings. She had never actually been anywhere where there was so much green space – miles and miles of it. It felt liberating to be out walking freely through it, even if she was in a bulky uniform and unwieldy boots.

'So, what's your story, then?' Ruby asked, interrupting her reverie. 'Why would you want to come out and patrol somewhere like this, when you're settled in London?'

'Oh, I didn't have a say in it,' Irene lied. She felt bad for the fib straight away. Ruby was a lovely girl and she didn't want to hide the real Irene from her like she had done with Maggie and Annie for so long. She felt confident Ruby would accept her for who she was, just like her friends in London had done. But she needed to keep her lowly past and precarious financial situation from Mary if she was going to get her on her side and have any hope of changing her behaviour for the better. And it would be a lot easier to do that without tripping herself up if she used the same story for everyone.

'What, they just shipped you up here without checking first?' Ruby asked, round-eyed with worry. Her normally pale face had flushed pink and she looked horrified.

'Yes, but I don't think they make a habit of it,' Irene assured her. 'And anyway, I was grateful for the break from London, if I'm honest.' As she told Ruby about what had happened with Frank, it felt nice to open up with her and be honest about it. She had never been good at sharing personal things with other people and it had taken her a long time to get to the point where she felt comfortable enough to do so with Maggie and Annie. Even with them, she still struggled sometimes. Maybe her friendship with them had helped her in that sense. She was just reaching the end of her tale when Ruby stopped in her tracks and put her arm out to stop her from walking any further.

'What is it?' Irene asked, heart pounding. Ruby put her finger to her lips to signal that Irene should be quiet and used her other hand to point to a huge oak tree just off to their right. Irene stared at the tree for a good ten seconds before finally spotting a pair of hairy legs poking out from behind it, with trousers gathered at the ankles. She nodded an acknowledgement and then they both started walking towards the seemingly bodyless limbs. As they got closer, they heard groaning coming from behind the tree and Irene cursed the blush she could feel making its way up her neck. When they reached the tree, they were confronted with the alarming sight of a man splayed on his back and a woman sitting astride him, facing away from Irene and Ruby, bobbing up and down – her long dress thankfully covering their dignity and billowing around from the constant motion.

'*Ahem*,' Ruby coughed loudly.

Irene cringed, expecting the couple to realise they had been rumbled, come to their senses and straighten themselves out immediately. But they were having so much fun that it appeared they hadn't heard Ruby's not-so-subtle interruption.

'Excuse me!' Ruby shouted.

It did the trick; even Irene jumped. The woman spun her head round in shock as the man crooked his neck to the side to see who was there. They spotted Irene and Ruby at the same time and the woman jumped to her feet while the man desperately tried to cover his manhood with his hands and scrambled clumsily to his feet.

'We'll give you a minute,' Ruby said with an air of superiority as she turned her back on the couple. Irene did the same. She could hear clothes being buttoned up and patted down, as well as whispered cursing.

'You told me no one comes out here,' the man hissed under his breath. Ruby turned back around to face the couple again, and Irene followed suit.

'There's not a patch of Grantham land that we don't keep an eye on,' Ruby informed them proudly.

Irene saw that the woman was blushing furiously. The man's face was also red, but Irene couldn't decide if that was left over from the excitement he had just been experiencing or if he was angry at the disturbance and the dressing down that he probably thought he was about to receive.

'But we're not here to embarrass you or make you feel bad,' Ruby continued, her voice softer now. 'We just don't want to get you into any trouble.'

The man's face relaxed visibly and as his shoulders slumped, Irene realised he had probably been preparing for a confrontation. But Ruby's approach had instantly defused any tension.

'You need to think about diseases,' she was saying now. Irene couldn't believe how straight-talking Ruby was being, but it seemed to be doing the trick. 'And are you aware of how many illegitimate babies are turning up in Grantham already?' Ruby asked the couple. They both shook their heads, eyes averted. 'You need to think about how you would cope on your own with a baby out of wedlock,' she continued, speaking directly to the woman, who had turned very pale. 'It's a very real risk if you carry on like that. This one will be off fighting and if he even makes it home, he won't be coming back to Grantham for you and the bastard child.' She waved a hand dismissively at the soldier, who seemed to be deliberately avoiding eye contact with her.

'You don't want to get a nice young woman into that sort of predicament, do you?' Ruby was staring hard at the soldier now, but he was still looking away from her gaze. 'And think of the baby – growing up without a father. Poor thing.' He shifted his weight on to his other side and nervously scratched his head.

'Well, when you put it like that . . .' he muttered, staring hard at the ground.

'Can I trust you to run along – in different directions?' Ruby asked after a few moments of silence.

'Yes, ma'am,' the soldier replied, finally looking her in the eye. 'I'm sorry to have caused you both any trouble.' Dipping his head, he made off in the direction of Belton Park, clearly desperate to get away from them. Once he was out of earshot, the woman looked to them both.

'Thank you for being so . . .discreet,' she whispered.

'We're looking out for you more than for him,' Ruby said. 'You're lucky it was us who found you. Our colleague would have marched you into town and had you thrown in a police cell before you had even got your undergarments back on. I know times are hard, but there must be other ways you can make ends meet?'

'I wish it was that easy,' the woman said sadly as she started walking away.

'Just take a little more care,' Ruby called out after her, but she didn't respond.

Irene was impressed at how Ruby had handled the situation, especially given the state the couple were in when they'd approached them. She couldn't wait to write to Maggie and Annie to tell them. They would be relieved that not all the WPS recruits in Grantham were treating the prostitutes unfairly.

Irene and Ruby decided to wait until the woman was nearly out of view and then head back into town behind her, to make sure she stayed away from the camp for the time being at least. As they picked their way back across the fields, Irene realised she hadn't had a chance to ask Ruby anything about herself.

'Now you know all about me and Frank, do I get to know about you and your sweetheart?' she asked Ruby, looking to the band on her wedding ring finger.

'Oh, erm . . . it's not what you think,' Ruby said as she nervously fiddled with the piece of jewellery. 'I'm not actually . . . married.' Irene was confused – why on earth would anybody wear a wedding ring unless they were married? 'I was going to be,' Ruby added. Her voice had dropped in volume so that she was almost whispering now. Irene leaned in as close as she could to make sure she could hear the rest of what she had to say. 'My fiancé Paul, well, he was killed in action.'

'Oh goodness, I'm so sorry,' Irene said. She felt terrible for asking now. Why hadn't she kept her curiosity to herself? Ruby would have told her when she was good and ready. But now she'd pushed her into it before she was comfortable.

'There's no need to apologise,' Ruby whispered, even though tears had filled her eyes. She looked away from Irene and took a deep breath. 'I should stop wearing this if I don't want people to ask questions. But I just can't bring myself to do it.' She stopped walking. 'Can we sit for a minute? I'd like to talk about him, but I might get upset so I'd rather we were away from prying eyes.' Irene wasn't sure if she meant the people in Grantham in general or just Mary, but either way she was happy to oblige. They sat on the grass in silence for a few minutes before Irene plucked up the courage to speak.

'You don't have to tell me anything,' she said gently, but Ruby waved her caution away.

'I haven't spoken about him since I got here. I've been feeling guilty about that – it feels as if I'm forgetting about him already. But Helen knew what had happened when I arrived and told me she wouldn't pry unless I came to her. And Mary – well, she would be the last person to show any interest in my personal life. And besides, I would never speak to her about Paul anyway. I feel like I'd be tainting his memory talking about him with someone like her.'

Irene understood completely and smiled knowingly at Ruby.

'We'd only just got engaged when he left to fight. He was from a very rich family, and he hadn't told them about me. I grew up the eldest of ten children in a very poor family – my parents often went without food so my siblings and I could eat. I moved away when a position in domestic service came up. But I'm afraid the lady of the house took an instant dislike to me, and I was dismissed after not even a week.' Ruby paused and sighed deeply.

Irene realised she had a lot more in common with this girl than she'd first realised. She was itching to tell her that she, too, had grown up in poverty – what a thing to bond over! But she stopped herself just in time. She had to keep to her story.

'I was desperate not to let my family down, and I didn't want to go home and take food away from my brothers and sisters,' Ruby continued. 'I was sitting in the park in tears trying to figure out what to do when Paul joined me and asked if I was all right.' Ruby's eyes lit up and her voice moved up slightly in pitch when she mentioned Paul's name. 'It doesn't sound likely, does it?' Ruby asked, looking up at Irene now. 'Someone from such a well-off family stopping to talk to somebody like me?' Irene had to admit that she would never have predicted it. 'Well, that's just testament to what a wonderful man Paul was. He didn't see different classes, he just saw people. And he was so caring. He could never walk on by if he saw somebody struggling.' It turned out Paul's friend was managing a factory nearby, and he got Ruby some work.

'I was so grateful to him, and he was keen to stay in touch,' Ruby explained. 'When he told me that he had romantic feelings for me – well, you could have knocked me down with a feather! We started courting and we both knew it was love very quickly. But I'm not exactly the kind of girl you rush to take home to meet your fancy family.' Ruby laughed to herself.

She paused to sniff and, seeing the sympathy in Irene's eyes, she quickly added, 'Oh, Paul wasn't ashamed of me or anything like that. He just wanted to wait until things were official, get the timing right, you know? When the war started, we decided it would be better to wait until it was over to tell his parents about us. He was sure that if they knew I'd waited for him while he was off fighting, they would understand how much we loved each other, and my lack of money wouldn't matter. And, of course, it was all supposed to be over by last Christmas. So, that was the plan – tell them when he returned from the front and then have a big wedding.'

'But he didn't make it back?' Irene asked cautiously after a few minutes' silence.

'I was just about to finish my police training when I read about him being killed in service in the newspaper. Imagine! My own fiancé and I had to read about his death in the paper, along with people who didn't even know him,' Ruby said bitterly. She was staring at the ring as she turned it round and round on her finger. 'That newspaper was wet-through with my tears by the time I threw it away.' Irene's heart was breaking for her new friend. She thought of Annie and Maggie and prayed they would never have to go through the same thing with Richard and Eddie.

'Paul had been paying my rent in London while I was training,' Ruby explained. 'He knew how desperate I was to make something of myself, so when he heard about the WPS he offered to support me if I gave up my factory job in Surrey to train. We also hoped the role would impress his parents when the time came.' She paused to take another deep breath. 'So, when I lost him, I lost absolutely everything. I was about to quit and try and get my factory job back when I heard there might be spaces coming up in Grantham. Everyone knew the recruits here got paid so I thought I'd be up against too much competition to get it.'

Irene nodded in understanding. 'I think the whole mess with the curfew, and how it sparked the row that broke up the women at the top, put a lot of people off,' she said.

'Well, it was lucky for me,' sighed Ruby. *And me too*, Irene thought to herself. 'You probably understand a little more about why I don't tend to speak around Mary now you know my background,' Ruby added. 'We fell out a lot in the beginning. I couldn't stand the way she spoke down to anyone she thought had less money or education than her. But every time I tried to step in, she would just turn on me. I realised there was no way I could change her.'

Irene's blood was boiling now. She felt angry that Mary could make someone as lovely as Ruby feel so worthless.

'I'm poor too,' Irene blurted out. The words had left her mouth before she'd had a chance to monitor them. But she felt confident Ruby would be on her side.

'You don't have to make fun of me,' Ruby snapped, getting to her feet.

'I'm not!' Irene cried, leaping up and grabbing Ruby's hand to pull her back to face her. 'We're more similar than you realise,' she laughed. 'I lied before – they didn't send me here out of the blue. I asked for a transfer partly because of Frank, that part was true. But the other reason was that I needed the money. I was working at a factory as well as patrolling to make ends meet in London,' she added. Ruby's face softened and she no longer looked offended. But then she tensed up again.

'So, why on earth did you lie to me?' she asked frowning.

'That was silly of me,' Irene sighed. 'It's just that once I realised Mary had this bee in her bonnet about people with less money than her, I thought I'd better hide my true past to avoid any unnecessary conflict with her. I thought it would be easier to tell the same story to everyone.'

Ruby nodded her acceptance of the explanation and they sat back down. Irene went on to confess that she had grown up in children's homes and had struggled to make ends meet since leaving. She didn't go into any details about her family – that was a step too far, even if she did feel like she could trust Ruby.

'We can work on Mary together,' Irene suggested. 'I hate the way she treats the prostitutes around here just as much as you do. And I can't stand that you have to hold back so much around her. You should feel free to be yourself.'

'We'll see,' Ruby said as she got to her feet and offered Irene her hand to help pull her up. 'Right now, we need to head back into town and make sure that woman isn't trying it on with anyone else.'

On the walk back, Irene realised she hadn't got to the bottom of why Ruby wore a wedding ring when Paul hadn't made it back from France. Normally, she would have stopped herself from prying any further. But she felt comfortable with Ruby, and confident she wouldn't mind being asked.

'So, I take it the ring is from Paul?' she ventured carefully.

'Oh! Yes, I never did finish telling you, did I?' Ruby laughed. She seemed a lot happier for having shared her story. Irene knew exactly how she felt. 'A week after I learned of Paul's death, I got a letter from one of his friends. They'd been sent out to France together, and he knew all about me. Paul had given him his grandmother's wedding band and asked him to send it to me if anything happened to him. That was how badly he wanted to marry me. I put it straight on and I haven't taken it off since.'

Irene was on the verge of tears. 'That's beautiful,' she said, wiping her eyes.

'I'm sorry – I didn't mean to upset you!' Ruby cried, stopping to pull her in for a hug.

'I'm not normally like this,' Irene said, pulling away almost immediately. She had always struggled to show her emotions and affection, and she felt awkward.

'Why don't you contact Paul's parents?' Irene suggested as they started walking again, desperate to put the focus back on to Ruby.

'They'd never believe me,' she scoffed.

'But you have the ring – they're sure to recognise it,' Irene pointed out. It was a beautiful piece of jewellery. Irene assumed the three small stones set into the middle of it were diamonds. They sparkled and twinkled every time Ruby moved her hand. 'Wouldn't it be a relief for them to know his heart was full of love when he was taken, and that he had someone doting on him, too?'

'I think they're more likely to believe I'd robbed their home for the ring than accept their son wanted to marry someone like me,' she replied sadly. 'It's too much of a risk. If they took the ring back, then I'd lose the only part of Paul I have left.' Her big brown eyes glistened with tears again, and Irene decided she'd pushed far enough. It was time for a change in subject. As she grappled over what to say to lighten the mood and take Ruby's mind off her broken heart, her new friend suddenly broke into a grin.

'Why don't you tell me what you thought of Mr Murphy?' she said, her voice suddenly full of excitement. Irene blushed and looked away. 'Oh, come on,' Ruby begged. 'It was obvious you were both very happy to be getting acquainted.' Irene was desperately trying to think of a response when they were distracted by a loud screech coming from the next field. Without another word they both broke into a run.

Suddenly, a woman's voice started shouting 'Help!' It sounded like it was coming from inside one of the bushes. Irene wondered what on earth could be happening. Her heart raced as they got closer to the row of hedges.

'We're coming!' Ruby yelled when they were nearly there. When they reached the owner of the voice, Irene was staggered. She stood rooted to the spot as she tried to get her head around what was in front of her.

# 12

Mary was laughing so hard that she was gasping for breath. Ruby and Irene stood over her, lost for words, as she tried to compose herself.

'You should have seen your faces!' she cried, bursting into another fit of giggles. 'Help!' she shouted mockingly.

Irene knew Ruby wouldn't say anything. She was so angry herself that she was happy to speak up for both of them.

'That was a cruel trick,' she spat, placing her hands on her hips.

'Oh, come on, I thought you'd like a bit of fun – you seem to be the type,' Mary sneered, getting to her feet. Her good mood had clearly switched in an instant and she was facing off with Irene now, anger etched across her face. Irene felt Ruby step back, leaving her in a stand-off with Mary on her own. 'You need to loosen up a little,' Mary said, jabbing her finger at Irene's chest.

Irene could feel rage building inside her, but she knew getting into a fight with Mary was the last thing she should be doing. Ruby wouldn't back her up and she'd end up kicked out of the WPS. Where would that leave not only her but her aunt, who was relying on the extra money this was going to bring in? Not to mention the women she had come here to help.

'You're right,' Irene smiled, stepping back and putting both her hands in the air in a show of surrender. 'Good work. You really had us going there,' she laughed lightly, trying not to overdo it. She felt foolish for pledging to stand up to Mary previously. She was already beginning to see that keeping her close was probably a better tactic and she should have listened to Ruby to begin with.

'I know!' Mary cried, breaking into a fit of giggles again. 'Your faces were quite the picture!'

Irene had to force her mouth into a smile. 'How did you get on at the train station?' she asked.

'I collared a few suspicious-looking ladies and told them exactly what would be in store if we caught them getting up to no good in our town,' Mary said. She looked pleased with herself.

'Wouldn't it be better to show them a bit of sympathy and compassion?' Irene asked cautiously. She knew she was skating on thin ice, but she was finding it hard to hold her tongue.

'They don't deserve any!' Mary laughed. 'They run around Grantham with their knickers round their ankles, distracting our men and spreading disease among the troops. They're lucky I don't shove them straight back on to the train, the dirty, disease-ridden good-for-nothings!'

'But most of them don't have a choice,' Irene said, trying to keep her voice neutral so as not to antagonise her.

'There's *always* a choice,' Mary said firmly. 'You can try all you like but you'll never convince me.'

Irene took in the firm set of Mary's brow and the almost fanatical glint in her eye. She thought about what Ruby had said about having tried to change Mary's mind before, and then about the long and difficult road ahead of her if she carried on in the hope of convincing Mary to be a better person. In a moment of clarity, she saw it was no good. A leopard like Mary would never change her spots. She decided in that moment to give up trying. Mary had clearly led a life of privilege and never had to struggle like herself, Ruby, and any of the women she was so keen to pour scorn upon. She hoped she never did.

But giving up on Mary didn't mean she would give up on her ambition to improve the lives of the women of Grantham – she would just need to go about it differently. She would speak her mind to Mary as much as she could, but now, she decided, she would try her hardest to get along with the girl. That way, she would be out of her firing line and could go about her business without worrying that Mary would be out to get her.

'Anyway, what have you two been up to?' Mary asked.

Irene filled her in on the couple behind the tree.

'And you let her go?' Mary asked, aghast.

'Ruby dealt with them both brilliantly,' Irene said proudly. 'I think speaking kindly to them probably had more impact than being nasty and hasty. Now they have respect for us, as well as being more informed about the consequences of their actions.' She braced herself for more backlash, but Mary raised her eyebrows, looking thoughtful, as if she were mulling Irene's words over in her head, and Irene wondered if there might be hope for her yet. Then Mary rolled her eyes, and Irene decided there probably wasn't.

'Helen's got a whole queue of wrong-doers waiting to see her this morning, so she's left patrolling down to us. How do you want to do it?' Mary asked, changing the subject.

When no one responded, Mary sighed. 'Well?' she asked impatiently. Irene focused her attention back to the task in hand. She looked to Ruby for guidance, but she just shrugged her shoulders. After a few more seconds of silence, Mary tutted loudly and said, 'Fine, I'll decide. You two can patrol together, and I'll go off on my own.'

Irene was torn. She was desperate to get away from Mary as quickly as possible, so Mary's suggestion was very tempting – but if Mary went on her own then Irene wouldn't be there to try and subtly step in if she got carried away asserting her authority.

'How about we stick together?' Irene suggested with a deliberate smile. 'I'm sure I can learn about the town faster if I have two guides.'

Mary looked annoyed. 'Suit yourself,' she shrugged, walking on ahead on her own.

'She prefers to patrol alone,' Ruby whispered just loud enough so that Irene could hear but Mary couldn't. 'She can get away with more that way.'

'That's exactly why I suggested we carry on together,' Irene muttered back under her breath. 'I want to keep an eye on her.'

'What are you two whispering about?' Mary snapped, spinning around and marching back towards them.

'I was just saying how much I can learn from you both,' Irene smiled innocently.

'Hmmm, I'm sure you will,' Mary said smugly as she stormed off ahead again.

When they arrived back in town, it was busy with street vendors and locals haggling in raised voices. There also seemed to be groups of soldiers at every turn. Mary stopped to chat to one of the stallholders. While Ruby and Irene waited for her, Irene spotted the woman from the oak tree talking to a soldier a few stalls down. She didn't want Mary to catch wind of the situation as she would surely use the fact that they had only just spoken to her as an excuse to get her arrested for improper behaviour, so she discreetly pointed her out to Ruby.

'You keep Mary distracted, and I'll go and have another word,' Ruby suggested. Irene nodded her agreement as Ruby slipped away. It wasn't long before Mary finished her chat and turned back around to spot Ruby was missing.

'Call of nature,' Irene shrugged by way of explanation. 'I said we'd carry on this way up the High Street so she can easily catch us up,' she added, pointing in the opposite direction to where Ruby was now talking to the woman. The soldier had disappeared. Mary sighed and went on her way, none the wiser. Irene was pleased with herself. With Ruby's help she was making a difference already – they had just saved a woman from being humiliated and possibly prosecuted. She hoped Ruby's words would do enough to stop her trying anything with anyone else today, as she didn't see how they could let her go a third time.

When Ruby joined back up with them, Mary didn't seem to suspect a thing and Irene and Ruby exchanged a knowing smile.

The girls spent the rest of the day wandering around the town, helping Irene get her bearings. By early evening she was confident she could find her way around alone with relative ease, so she was feeling a little more relaxed about the prospect of patrolling solo when the time came. The fact that everyone in the small town seemed so friendly was a big help – everyone she'd met so far had made her feel welcome.

Ruby made a point of taking them down London Road, where she showed Irene Murphy & Sons. Irene couldn't believe her eyes when she took in the enormity of the factory buildings – they almost took up the whole street. It seemed that Charles Murphy really was an important figure in the town. She was desperate to know what kind of business took place behind the closed doors, but she didn't want to show any interest in front of Mary, so she kept quiet.

In the evening, Helen was keen for Irene to accompany her on public-house duty. 'You must have noticed the large number of pubs in the town,' she said as the four of them sat down to a dinner of stew. One of the elderly ladies who lived a few doors away had come in and cooked it for them earlier in the day while Helen was giving out advice to girls in the front room.

'They appreciate us here,' Helen had explained when Irene's face had revealed her shock at the kind gesture. 'They know how hard we work to keep their town safe. It doesn't leave a lot of time for cooking.' The stew was delicious – Irene didn't often get to enjoy a cooked meal, let alone one that was home-cooked. Her body was so grateful for the warmth and nutrition that she could feel it responding by growing lethargic and sleepy. She could have closed her eyes and fallen asleep there and then, and it was only five o' clock! She got herself a glass of water to try and wake herself up.

'You two can take the evening off,' Helen said to Ruby and Mary. 'You've both been working all hours this last week. You need some rest.' Neither girl argued, and Irene could understand why – she felt like she needed some time off herself and she had hardly been here any time at all. She now knew for certain that there was no proper shift structure and Helen just decided who was patrolling and who had time off.

Irene and Helen started their public-house duty at the Red Lion Hotel on the High Street. On the way there, Helen explained that shortly after the army camp had been established, the local landlords had been banned from serving alcohol to soldiers in uniform after seven o'clock.

'It didn't last for long,' she laughed. 'They realised how much money the men could bring into Grantham and soon changed their minds.' They had already passed by four groups of soldiers, and as they walked into the Red Lion, they were faced with a sea of uniforms. Irene was struck by the overwhelming stench of liquor, beer and smoke. She only ever went into pubs while patrolling and she didn't think she would ever get used to the horrible smells associated with them. The locals and the soldiers were chatting and getting along nicely, and there was no sign of any women. Happy that there was nothing much for them to do, Irene and Helen had a quick chat with the man behind the bar before heading back out on to the High Street. Nobody had seemed to notice their presence.

'You'll find everyone is used to us popping in and out,' Helen explained as they started walking again. 'We'll go to the George Inn next,' she added. 'That's where the officers and the richer residents drink, so there won't be any prostitutes in there. We find it's good to go in now and then to show our faces though, just so they know we're around in case they fancy getting rowdy.' When they walked in, Irene noticed a distinct difference in the atmosphere. The smells were the same, but there was something about the way that the men held themselves in here that showed her that the George Inn was a rather classier affair than the Red Lion. There was no slouching or shouting across the room. And everyone was smart, not just the officers in uniform.

'Irene Wilson.' Irene stopped in her tracks when she heard her full name being spoken and felt a gentle hand upon her shoulder. Helen must have heard it too, because she stopped and they turned around at the same time to find Charles Murphy smiling at them. Irene's heart fluttered at the sight of him.

'It's a pleasure to see you again,' he said smoothly, holding out his hand. Irene nervously went to shake it, but he pulled her hand up to his mouth and kissed the back of it. She tried desperately to hide her surprise, but a quiet gasp escaped her, and she felt her cheeks immediately flush red with embarrassment. 'Mrs Miller,' he said, extending his hand out to Helen. He went to kiss the back of Helen's hand, too, but she grasped his palm firmly and forced him into a handshake instead. Unfazed, he smiled playfully and chuckled to himself before continuing.

'I met your newest recruit yesterday,' he said, smiling at Irene. 'She left quite the impression on me, I must say.'

Irene's stomach was doing somersaults. How was this man having such an effect on her? The only other man who had made her feel remotely like this was Frank – but this was on another level compared to that.

'Yes, well, we only take on the best,' Helen said briskly. It was clear that she wasn't affected by Charles's good looks and charming manner like Irene was. 'I heard all about it, Mr Murphy.'

'Good. Well, I hope you'll let me treat this young lady to some tea and cake to thank her for her impressive work?'

Irene tried to hide her shock. Did he mean he wanted to step out with her? Or was he just being friendly because she had helped him retrieve his wallet? Why would somebody like Charles Murphy want to go for tea with her? Her mind was racing as she stared at Helen, willing for her to say yes while at the same time feeling terrified at the prospect.

'You can see we're in uniform, Mr Murphy,' Helen replied warningly.

'Oh, please, I've told you so many times that you can call me Charles,' he replied, smiling.

'And you know I take my role very seriously, Mr Murphy. Would the lads down the station address you by your Christian name?' Helen challenged.

'As you will,' he said, waving away her question with his hand. 'But you still haven't told me whether or not I can take Miss Wilson here for some tea.'

'What Miss Wilson does in her own time is up to her,' Helen said. 'But right now, we're on duty and that would not be appropriate.'

Charles held up his hands in a mock play of surrender. Helen hadn't given even a glimmer of a smile for the whole conversation, and she didn't start now.

'I would love to repay your kindness with some tea and cake one afternoon soon. It would be wonderful to get to know the woman behind the impressive police work,' Charles said, speaking directly to Irene now. She found herself blinking furiously as he fixed his gaze on her. 'Next time you have an afternoon off, please do come and find me at Thompson's on

Finkin Street. It's a lovely little refreshment room that I like to visit every afternoon to wind down after finishing work. You'll find me there between five and six. Your company would be most welcome.'

Irene knew her face was crimson once again, and her mind had gone completely blank. She couldn't find any words to say back to him. He picked up her hand and kissed the back of it again as Helen tutted and sighed loudly next to her.

'Enjoy your evening, Mr Murphy,' Helen said tersely as she turned and continued on her way to the bar.

Charles gave Irene one more lingering look before turning around and making his way back to wherever he'd come from. Irene managed to snap herself out of the trance that Charles had seemed to cast upon her during the entire encounter, and she quickly scurried after Helen. They spoke to the landlord for a good ten minutes, but when they left the pub Irene realised that she had no idea what the conversation had been about. She had been lost in her own thoughts – about Charles Murphy.

Irene was worried about getting carried away with the wrong impression, but he seemed to be giving very clear signals that he was interested in her romantically. It wasn't what she had come to Grantham for, but she couldn't deny the attraction. Up until now, she'd still felt incredibly upset about Frank, but maybe Charles was the distraction she needed.

Normally she would shy away from a man of such great standing. Her worries about her background had stopped her from admitting her feelings for Frank in the beginning and she had convinced herself he wouldn't look twice at someone like her, and yet he was only a middle-class policeman. So, what was different now? Charles was certainly being more forward. Was that giving her the confidence to consider taking him up on his offer?

Perhaps her brief encounter with Frank had boosted her

self-worth, she pondered as she followed Helen into another High Street pub, the Horse & Jockey. As painful as it had been in the end, had her relationship with Frank actually been good for her? Or maybe her friendship with Annie and Maggie had helped prove to her that her background really didn't matter – she could hold her own with people of any class, and even make friends with them.

Of course, there would always be exceptions – people like Mary who would never accept anyone of a lower class than themselves. Irene knew she would likely always feel uncomfortable about her background with people like that. But Maggie, Annie and Frank had all helped her realise she didn't have to feel ashamed around everyone. And besides, now she was being paid to patrol, she didn't feel quite as ashamed – she was supporting herself as well as her family with something more substantial than factory work, and that had to be enough to impress someone as well off as Charles Murphy.

'I can tell you're distracted this evening,' Helen remarked as they left the Horse & Jockey. Irene was snapped back to the present. 'And don't think I don't know what started all your daydreaming,' Helen added stiffly. Irene stared at the ground, mortified. 'Don't worry, you're not in trouble,' Helen said kindly, and Irene breathed a sigh of relief. 'Just be careful,' the older woman warned. Irene looked up now, confused as to what she meant.

Helen stopped walking and turned to face her. 'Look, Charles Murphy is a typical charmer,' she explained. 'I can see you've been taken in by his handsome appearance and smooth-talking. He's very good at making women feel special.' Irene was beginning to feel foolish – was he like this with everyone he met? Maybe he wasn't that interested in her, after all. 'I can't stop you from meeting up with him in your own time, but if you do that then you need to find out the truth about his past.'

'What do you mean?' Irene asked.

'It's not my place to tell you,' Helen said stiffly. 'I don't want to cause any problems or start a rift with that man. Just promise me that you'll make sure you have the full story before you think about starting any kind of relationship with Charles Murphy.'

Irene nodded slowly as she panicked about what could have possibly happened in his past to get Helen so riled up.

'I can already tell that you're an exceptionally fine WPS recruit,' Helen added, sounding a little more relaxed now. 'Men like Charles are very old-fashioned when it comes to women. Remember, he is at least twenty years older than you. He won't want a wife who works. He'll want someone to stay at home where he can keep an eye on what she's up to.'

Irene shuddered at the thought. Maggie had told her all about how miserable her mother was living with a husband who wanted to control every aspect of her life. It was one of the reasons Maggie was so desperate to make a life of her own, avoiding settling down too young as a housewife with no life experience to talk of. Irene wanted the same for herself. As for Charles's age, it hadn't really crossed her mind. She had always been an old head on young shoulders, and so age was of little consequence to her, unlike class. But Irene didn't dwell on all that for long as she was too concerned with what Helen had said about Charles' past.

'I would hate for an infatuation with someone like that man to pull your attention away from this very important role,' Helen said firmly, before continuing her patrol along the High Street. Irene had to rush to keep up.

Irene spent the rest of the evening going over Helen's words of warning while the conversation with Charles flashed into her thoughts every now and then. She didn't want to risk her place in the WPS, and she was starting to feel like helping the women in Grantham was something that she was destined to do. Somehow, sticking up for these vulnerable women and stepping in when Mary tried to treat them unfairly felt like a way to honour her mother's memory. She certainly didn't want to give up her role to become a housewife. But she couldn't stop thinking about the spark she felt when she was in Charles's presence. It was so strong – did he feel it too? Surely, she could keep going with the WPS and explore things with him at the same time? And he had been so understanding about Billy . . . how could a man with that capacity for kindness be bad for her? As for his past, well – surely whatever had happened couldn't be that bad or else he wouldn't be such a big name in the town. He was clearly very well regarded and successful. And, besides, Irene knew better than anyone that somebody's past shouldn't define them.

By the end of the evening she had decided she definitely couldn't ignore the pull she felt towards Charles. Maybe Helen was wrong about him. She had been extremely stand-offish with him in the pub, and Irene wondered if she had ever taken the time to get to know him properly. Irene made her mind up to seek Charles out in the tea room he had mentioned the next time she had a free afternoon. She wasn't even sure when that would be – maybe she would have forgotten all about him by then, anyway. But if not, then what harm could a friendly cup of tea do?

# 13

Before Irene knew it, she had been in Grantham for two whole weeks, and it felt as though her feet hadn't touched the ground. She'd been out on patrol every single day and with all the exercise her already loose-fitting uniform was starting to sag off her even more. Her previous worries about being able to navigate her way around the town were long forgotten – already she knew the place like the back of her hand. She must have covered every inch of the fields between the town and Belton Park, and she knew all the best places to look for frisky couples.

She had also tried to secure some work for Billy. But news of the incident with Charles's wallet had spread like wildfire throughout the town and none of the local shopkeepers were keen to take on the lad who'd been silly enough to try to rob one of Grantham's richest and well-known residents. She'd been round to Billy's house a few times to try and check in on him, but he was never there.

Helen always made sure Irene, Ruby and Mary had a bit of time off each day, but she seemed to keep going around the clock herself, advising people in the living room in the mornings before heading out on patrol until late into the night.

Irene's breaks had hardly ever come in the early evenings, and when she did get an afternoon off, she was shattered, so she hadn't had a chance to slip into Thompson's when she was off-duty and find Charles. Irene wasn't sure if Helen had kept her busy on purpose. It was certainly feasible that she was needed most afternoons as the town tended to get busy early on with soldiers looking to let off steam with the women who hung around, but Irene couldn't help but be suspicious. And she couldn't for the life of her work out what terrible thing he could possibly have done in his past to make Helen so intent on keeping them apart.

If Irene was honest with herself, she'd been relieved to be either too busy or too tired to meet with Charles. She wasn't sure she would have had the nerve to seek him out on her own if she had been given the chance. She had wandered past the refreshment rooms on Finkin Street while on duty between five and six o' clock on quite a few occasions, and each time she'd glanced in anxiously through the window and found it almost empty. There was never any sign of Charles. Given his absence on those occasions, she convinced herself he had just been being friendly when he'd made the offer, and that she was better off without the complications of a man in her life, anyhow.

She lay in bed now as Mary got into her uniform. It was nine in the morning and while Mary had enjoyed an early night the previous evening, Irene had been out on patrol with Helen and Ruby until gone 3 a.m. They had escorted a number of worse-for-wear soldiers back to Belton Park and broken up four couples cavorting in the fields. They had also found a soldier flat on his back in an alleyway with his flies undone and no idea of how he'd made it there. When they checked for his ID, they'd found his wallet was missing. He'd sworn blind he hadn't entered the alley with anyone, but they all knew it was likely he had gone there with a prostitute and ended up paying far more than he'd anticipated for the pleasure. After all that, Helen had told her and Ruby to take the morning off and she fully intended to do so.

Stretching out her arms in bed, Irene knew Helen would be up already, making a pot of tea for the latest waifs and strays who had turned up on the doorstep looking for her advice. She didn't know how Helen kept going like she did – she certainly couldn't keep up with her and she was at least twenty years younger.

As she dozed, she heard Mary leave the bedroom and the now-familiar heavy clonking of boots on the stairs. Rolling over, she heard the noise making its way back up the stairs. Intrigued, she sat up on her elbows to try and better hear who had come upstairs and what they were up to. The bedroom door creaked open again and she saw Mary's grumpy face peer in. Irene had hardly spent any time with Mary over the last week or so. Helen had seemed to pick up on that fact that it wasn't only Ruby who was uncomfortable in Mary's presence, so she tended to go on patrol with her herself or send her out alone.

Irene was grateful she didn't have to put up with Mary but also frustrated that it meant she was free to abuse her position when she was out on her own. But she'd decided she was better off prioritising getting to know her way around the place, so she didn't feel so vulnerable when they were out and about. Also, she was eager to try and start helping the women once they were in the system here – making sure they were dealt with fairly by the police and courts. If she couldn't change Mary's harsh treatment, then she could try and make things better once she'd had women arrested.

Now Irene was so confident in the town's layout, she had been meaning to ask Helen to put her on patrol with Mary more, so she could see what she was up to and maybe try some subtle tactics to change her views. She knew there was no point coming up against her, but maybe she could try and lead by example.

But she kept stalling; she enjoyed patrolling with Ruby and the pair were growing closer. She didn't much fancy swapping long hours with someone so friendly for shifts with Mean

Mary. After glaring at Irene as she lay in bed, Mary threw something in her direction and then backed out again, closing the door loudly behind her.

The items landed softly on the end of her bed and Irene realised with a flush of excitement that they were letters. Two of them. Grabbing them greedily, she recognised the handwriting straight away. One was from her aunt Ruth and the other bore Maggie's neat, loopy writing. Putting the envelope from her aunt to one side, she ripped open the one from Maggie. She loved hearing Ruth's news, but she was desperate to feel close to her friends again. She had only managed to write them one letter since her arrival and she was desperate for news from them. She was also keen to learn their thoughts on Charles, who she had written about in her letter to them.

*May 1915*

*Dearest Irene,*

*We thought it best to write you a letter together as we haven't had much spare time since you left – we're confident that you won't hold it against us!*

*We were so happy to hear from you, and to learn that you're settling in well. It sounds like the women in Grantham are getting better treatment now that fresh recruits are in place. It's a shame Mary seems to be the exception, but we know you're more than capable of helping her understand there are better ways to get the job done.*

*As for your most exciting piece of news – we both think you should meet Charles for tea! He sounds delightful, and like just the tonic to help you forget about Frank. You should know, Frank's wedding is taking place in a week's time. Maybe Charles can be the perfect distraction. It doesn't have to lead to anything, but please get out and enjoy yourself and get to know someone new!*

*We have to go now. They are sending a replacement for*

*you, but she doesn't arrive until tomorrow, so we're being kept rather busy but as you know we'll never complain about a hectic patrol!*

*We look forward to an update on Charles very soon!*

*All our love,*
*Maggie and Annie xxx*

Irene was so happy to hear from her friends that she burst into tears. She had been so busy over the last couple of weeks that she'd hardly had a chance to register how much she was missing them. Now, she couldn't hold back the emotions that were rushing through her. When she had read the part about Frank's wedding, however, her heart had dropped. Her happy tears turned to sad ones as she imagined the man she had fallen for promising his life to another.

Maybe Maggie and Annie were right about Charles. She'd been sure the best thing to do was to forget about her fancy for him. But her friends knew her so well. If they thought she should give him a chance then, surely, she should consider it? If only to take her mind off her heartbreak.

As Irene picked up her second letter, her thoughts wandered off to her mother. She closed her eyes and took a moment to remember happier times with her before everything had gone wrong at home. She took a deep breath and carefully opened the envelope from Ruth. The tone of this letter was in complete contrast to the cheerful one from her friends:

*May 1915*

*Dear Irene,*
*I'm sorry I haven't been in touch recently. I've been reading your letters with interest and I'm so proud of everything you're doing with the women police. And now this grand job*

*in Grantham. I always knew you were destined for a better life than that of a factory girl!*

*The reason I haven't written for so long is that poor Henry has taken a turn for the worse. I don't think I explained just how ill he is in my last letter. He's been struck down with consumption and it seems to be getting the better of him, even though I'm nursing him as much as I can, and his brothers and sisters of course do their bit.*

*The doctor says as long as we live where we do then we'll all be at risk of getting it. This horrible illness seems to favour the poor, so we're not in a good position, my dear. And as for Henry, well, the best we can do is feed him well – but you know how I struggle to feed all the mouths as it is, and fresh meat and vegetables haven't been through our door in goodness knows how long!*

*I hate to beg, dear, but I know you mentioned when you wrote to tell me about your new job that it meant you might be able to send some money our way. If you have anything you can send us, then I would love to give Henry a piece of juicy red meat and some fresh veg – see if it doesn't perk him up.*

*We all send our love and we can't wait for the day when we get to see you in that fancy uniform of yours – we will make it happen, I promise.*

*Love always, from your aunt Ruth*

Irene wiped her eyes, but the tears kept coming. *Not little Henry.* At five years old, he was the youngest of her six cousins. Irene had only met him a couple of times. She'd managed to fund a trip to visit Ruth just after he'd been born, and she had fallen instantly in love with the beautiful little baby. Over the next few years she had got to know him and his character in the same way she had done with his older siblings – through her aunt Ruth's stories in her regular letters. Then, on a brief visit the previous summer, the two of them had got along famously. She loved all her cousins but there was something about Henry that made him her favourite.

She had been planning on sending her first lot of pay to Ruth, but she hadn't got around to taking it to the post office. She hadn't realised just how desperate the situation was when her aunt had first written to tell her that Henry was ill. Now she felt a huge sense of guilt for withholding the cash that could go some way to making him better, or at least more comfortable. Irene jumped out of bed – she could catch up on her sleep another time. Lifting up her mattress, she pulled out the envelope containing her WPS wages and threw on her tatty old dress and scuffed shoes.

'I didn't expect to see you up so early,' Helen remarked as Irene stopped at the bottom of the stairs. 'You've just caught me making another pot of tea – would you like a cup?'

'No, thank you,' Irene said as she dashed to the door. 'I've errands to run!' she shouted back behind her as she left the house. The post office was a busy place, with all the letters coming in and out for the troops at Belton Park, and Irene wanted to get her money sent off before the day's rush started. She was relieved to find hardly any queue at all when she flew into the main serving area, hot and sweaty from her run to get there. She scribbled a note to Ruth while she waited:

> *I'm sorry to take so long to get this to you. The new job is going well. I'll write more soon. Please give Henry all my love.*
>
> *Love,*
> *Irene*

She stepped out of the post office and inhaled deeply. She was so relieved that the funds were on their way now, but still felt terrible for not having sent them sooner. A rumbling noise from her stomach interrupted her thoughts, and she realised she was ravenous after the run across town. She decided to head back to Rutland Street and see if Helen had left any porridge on the stove. Then maybe she would get back into bed for an hour or so – her head was starting to ache with tiredness.

Approaching the gardens at St John's Vicarage, Irene could see a small crowd had gathered. As she drew closer, she rubbed her eyes to check they weren't deceiving her. She thought she could see a small aircraft in the gardens. But, surely, she was mistaken. Above the heads of the people standing in front of the large object in the flower bed, she could see a wing. 'B9607' was written on the side. She pushed her way to the front of the crowd and gasped when she saw the front of the aircraft was crushed – and it had just missed the side of the vicarage.

'What happened?' she whispered to no one in particular.

'A biplane from RAF Spittlegate down the road crash-landed,' a voice replied from next to her. She looked to her right and found a policeman. 'Pilot's all right,' he added. 'By some miracle!'

'I'm Irene Wilson – with the WPS. Do you need any help?' Irene offered.

'DS Finn,' he replied, holding out his hand to shake hers. Irene didn't recognise the officer, she'd hardly spoken to any since arriving in Grantham. Helen had been right when she said they were happy to leave them to it. Since the women didn't tend to work out of the police station, regular police and the WPS were able to keep out of each other's way quite easily. Added to that, the fact that Irene was keen not to have any of the girls arrested meant she hadn't set foot back into the police station since her first day in Grantham. Unlike Mary, who seemed to be popping in daily with some poor soul she wanted locked up.

'You're all right, love,' DS Finn said warmly. 'The pilot's been taken to Belton for a check-up at the hospital there, and one of your lot is taking care of the mother and baby,' he pointed to the other side of the plane.

'Mother and baby?' Irene asked.

'It just missed them!' he exclaimed, shaking his head like he still couldn't believe it. 'Luckiest little family in the town, I'd say.' Irene hurried off around the aircraft and almost collided with Mary, who was standing next to a young woman with a baby in her arms. The child seemed to be asleep, but the woman was rocking it frantically, a look of shock etched on her face. Instead of comforting her, Mary was just staring at the mother as if *she* was the object that had fallen unexpectedly from the sky.

'What are *you* doing here?' Mary asked bluntly.

'It's nice to see you too,' Irene snapped back. She was fed up with putting up with Mary's attitude. She may not have been on patrol with her lately, but she had let a lot slip during their interactions at the house over the last couple of weeks. The letter from Maggie and Annie had reminded her of her reason for coming to Grantham and motivated her to start pulling Mary up on her rudeness, at the very least. Mary went to say something, then closed her mouth again when Irene stared intently at her.

'How are you doing there? How's the little one?' Irene enquired gently, turning to the mother and placing a comforting arm around her.

'Oh, they're fine, it didn't hit them or anything,' Mary said nonchalantly.

Before Irene could point out that that wasn't the point, the woman turned her body into hers and started sobbing. Irene cradled the mother and baby and rocked them both from side to side while Mary stood looking on awkwardly.

'Carry on with your patrol, I'll take over here,' Irene told

Mary firmly. She couldn't believe her colleague's lack of empathy. It was one thing to speak to women of the night with disdain, but this woman was obviously upset and in desperate need of comfort. Mary went to protest but Irene fixed her with her stern glare again and she huffed and walked away. Irene was grateful the situation hadn't escalated. But she knew Mary had only given in because she felt vulnerable at being caught in circumstances that she was uncomfortable dealing with. Irene knew Mary would lash out at her at the first opportunity to get her own back. But she would be ready for her. Irene couldn't get a word out of the woman, who was clearly too shocked to speak let alone explain what had happened and give any personal details. She let DS Finn know she was taking her away from the scene and would drop her details into the station once she had them. Then she walked the mother and baby back to Rutland Street, where she was confident Helen would know what to do.

Helen didn't let her down – as soon as Irene led the woman into the living room and she saw the blank expression on her face and the baby in her arms, she ushered the lady sitting on the sofa out of the room.

'Thank you for letting me know, Gill,' she told her visitor while guiding her to the door. 'I'll ask the men at the station to have a word with him. He won't be pestering your Anna any longer.' The woman nodded gratefully as Helen closed the door behind her.

'Put the kettle on, dear,' Helen whispered into Irene's ear. 'There's a secret stash of sugar in the cupboard under the sink – right at the back. Drop a few teaspoons in for this one,' she added with a wink as she led the woman to the sofa and gently and expertly prised the baby from her arms as she sat her down.

Irene had had no idea about the sugar, and she was surprised to find a cup full of it just where Helen had promised. It was in short supply at the moment, and she knew Helen would had to have queued for a long time to get hold of it, and must have been squirrelling it away for a long time to have such a quantity. No wonder she kept it to herself. Walking back into the living room, she was thrown to see the mother smiling at Helen and talking quietly. She knew Helen had a warm and motherly charm about her, but she had never seen it work quite so quickly or drastically.

'Frances here was just telling me about what happened by the church,' Helen explained as Irene handed over two cups of tea. 'It sounds like she and Robert here had a very lucky escape,' she added, looking down at the baby who was still in her arms. Irene wanted to tell Helen about her concerns regarding Mary, but she knew this wasn't the time. And, besides, she wasn't sure there was much point – what would Helen be able to do? She wasn't their superior, she'd simply taken on a role of authority in their group because of her age. No, Irene would have to deal with this herself.

'Go and get yourself sorted before you go on patrol,' Helen said now. 'Frances and I will be just fine now we have our tea, won't we, dear?' When Frances looked up at Irene and smiled, it was like she was seeing her for the very first time. She really had been in a daze when Irene had led her back to the house.

Irene bid them all farewell and decided to head back out for a walk around the town to clear her head. It had been an eventful morning and it wasn't yet ten o'clock. She had only made it about ten steps down Rutland Street when a familiar voice called out her name from across the road.

From the way her heart leapt, Irene knew who the voice belonged to before she looked across the street for its owner. She had only spoken to Charles Murphy two times, but his warm tones were ingrained in her memory and the sound of them sent her heart involuntarily racing. She looked over sheepishly, suddenly remembering her tatty clothes, but he didn't seem to notice her attire as he crossed the road and took her hand in his to kiss it.

'What a pleasure to see you again – and off duty, too,' he said, beaming. Irene blanched as he explained he'd been asking around about her and found out through a policeman friend that the WPS recruits were living together at a house in Rutland Street. 'I was about to start knocking on doors when I saw you. It's like it was meant to be,' he said, smiling that big smile that made his eyes glisten and Irene's knees weak. He certainly knew how to make a woman feel special. But there was one thing nagging at her.

'I've been past Thompson's a few times since I last saw you, and I haven't seen you in there,' she said as casually as possible. She didn't want him to think she was being confrontational, but she was confused.

'Ah, see, now that's why I had to seek you out,' Charles said earnestly. 'I got called away on a work emergency the day after I bumped into you, and I've only just returned. I worried the whole time I was away that you would turn up to meet me and find yourself disappointed, so I wanted to explain as soon as I could. I'm not in the habit of letting beautiful women down.'

Irene blushed furiously and decided there and then, after all her to-ing and fro-ing over it, that she would definitely give this man a chance. He was obviously very busy and important, and he'd gone to a lot of effort to find her and reassure her. That had to mean something.

'I appreciate you taking the time to find me and explain,' she said. She stared at the ground as she spoke, very aware of the fact that if she looked into his eyes then she would trip over her words.

'Please, let me take you for that cup of tea. How about this afternoon?' he asked hopefully.

'I have to work,' she said glumly. The four of them were heading out together that evening on a deserter raid and Helen wanted them all home for dinner beforehand to talk over the plan. She knew there was no chance of getting out if it, and she didn't want to miss the raid, anyway. It was to be her first one and she was keen to see how it all worked. She was pretty sure, though, that after two nights on duty in a row, Helen would give her an afternoon and maybe even an evening off. Feeling brave, she decided to make the suggestion. 'How about tomorrow?' She risked a glance up at his face and was met with a beaming grin.

'That will do nicely,' he said. 'Meet me at Thompson's at five? There's no chance of any riff-raff turning up there so we can have a quiet cuppa.'

Irene felt a stirring of disquiet at the comment – would she not be considered riff-raff in her tatty dress? But she quickly pushed it away. He wouldn't have made the offer if he felt like that, she reassured herself. She nodded her agreement to Charles before scurrying back to the house. Opening the door, she looked back along the street and saw that Charles was still standing there, staring after her and looking bemused at her rushed exit.

She took her shoes off in the hallway and ran up the stairs without making the usual clunking noises. At the top she looked up just in time to see Ruby before bumping into her on the landing.

'What's got you flustered?' Ruby asked, jumping back and laughing.

'I, erm . . .' Irene started. She was growing close to Ruby, but she wasn't good at sharing things like this. She already felt vulnerable opening herself up to romance again after Frank, and the more people who knew, the more people would witness her humiliation if it all went wrong. 'I've just agreed to meet Charles Murphy for a cup of tea,' Irene hissed, smiling nervously. It had come out before she'd had a chance to stop it. Maybe she was more excited about it than she realised.

'*The* Charles Murphy?' Ruby gasped. 'The one whose wallet you rescued the other week?' She stood with her mouth wide open as Irene nodded sheepishly. 'Right, you must tell me *everything!*' she demanded, grabbing her arm and pulling her into her bedroom. They sat on the double bed that Ruby shared with Helen. Irene hadn't been inside the room yet, but she'd known it was bigger than the tiny space she shared with Mary. She looked around and spotted the wardrobe Ruby had mentioned on her first day. She was surprised to see they had room for a small dressing table and a chair, too. Not that there was much on the dressing table. None of them wore make-up on patrol and they didn't really get up to too much else apart from resting or a wander around the town's shops.

Ruby listened intently as Irene brought her up to speed on her situation with Charles. As soon as she'd finished with the encounter that had taken place just minutes beforehand, Ruby jumped up and went to the wardrobe.

'Take your pick,' she said gleefully as she opened the door to reveal a rack of fancy-looking dresses. 'You can't wear your old rags for a drink with Mr Murphy!'

Irene was taken aback by the array.

'Unlike you, I had to bring everything with me when I came to Grantham,' Ruby explained. 'I've never had much, but Paul loved to spoil me and he kitted me out well before he went to war. I never get the chance to wear any of them any more. Some of them haven't even been worn at all. I'd love for you to enjoy them. You can borrow any of them whenever you want.'

Irene was too moved to say anything more than a simple thank you. She got up and ran her hands over the beautiful dresses. A pretty floral piece in brown, pink and blue stood out. She liked the darker colours for their subtlety, and the long sleeves and length would help keep her feeling dignified. She had planned on wearing Annie's dress for this drink – Charles's 'riff-raff' comment still fresh in her mind – but she decided to hold that back in the hope that she would be stepping out with him again.

'Oh yes,' Ruby exclaimed as Irene caressed the material of her dress. 'Yes, this one will be just perfect. It's understated, which is good as you don't want to go too over the top for the first outing.'

Irene's stomach flipped. She smiled gratefully as Ruby took the dress out of the wardrobe and held it up against her. They both had similar slim builds, although Irene was a little taller than Ruby.

'It's a tad long on me so it should be just right,' Ruby grinned. 'Make sure you ask Helen for the afternoon off. She likes to make sure we get enough rest so she's not likely to argue the day after a raid.' She pulled out three more dresses and held them up against Irene. 'These will all suit you too. I'm sure you'll be stepping out some more with him. I'll leave them hanging together at the end of the wardrobe – come and help yourself whenever you need them.'

'Thank you,' Irene whispered, handing back the original dress so Ruby could hang it up with the others. Irene made her way back to her room, where she sat down on the bed to write to Maggie and Annie and update them on the exciting news before it was time to get back into uniform and out on to the streets.

# 14

The patrol that afternoon was quiet. Everyone seemed to be subdued after the plane crash. It had of course just been a training accident, and no one was hurt – but it was a stark reminder to the town about what was going on overseas and that, even here, they weren't safe from the effects of the war. There had been some Zeppelin air raids on towns further south, and everyone was worried about them becoming more frequent. Mary had the afternoon off, having been patrolling all morning, so Irene was happy to be on duty with Ruby. When they arrived back at Rutland Street for dinner, they found Mary and Helen already sitting at the kitchen table enjoying some stew.

'Help yourselves, ladies,' Helen said as they both placed their hats on the side and took off their heavy jackets. Irene had longed for a thicker uniform during the cold winter months in London, but now she was desperate to be able to strip off her long coat as she made her way through the fields towards the camp with the sun beating down on her back. She drunk a whole glass of water before serving up a bowl of stew and handing over the ladle to Ruby.

'Looking forward to your first deserter raid?' Mary asked as she chewed on a mouthful of food.

'I'm not sure, to be honest,' Irene confessed as she joined the table.

'Why ever not?' Mary replied, looking confused. Irene knew exactly why Mary enjoyed the raids – it was her way of exerting her power over other people. With the curfew lifted, these raids were the only chance she now had to barge her way into people's homes and throw her weight around. Especially seeing as they carried them out without backup from the male officers, leaving her to truly show she was in charge. But all Irene could think about was the fact that the fate of any deserter could be to face a firing squad. And she didn't want any part of that.

'The raids look good to male authority, and that will help with our fight to keep policewomen in their roles once the war is over,' Helen explained diplomatically. This argument sat better with Irene, but she still felt uneasy.

'Yes, but it's also important to weed out the cowards!' Mary exclaimed. 'A man cannot desert his duty. My John is fighting in France this very minute. What if he was killed because someone from his regiment had run away scared and wasn't there to help him? It's just not right!'

Irene knew from Ruby that Mary was married. How she had managed to find someone willing to put up with her she wasn't sure. And she didn't agree with this argument – she felt it was a lot more complicated than soldiers being cowards. After all, they had willingly signed up to fight, so it must take something awful to lead them to abandon their post when they risked being shot for doing so.

Irene went to express her thoughts, but she stopped herself. Now wasn't the best time to rile Mary up. She didn't want to send her into an already tense situation with a fiery head and something to prove. That wouldn't do anybody any good. Instead, she gritted her teeth and smiled politely. She risked a glance at Ruby who was staring intently into her bowl. When her gaze landed on Helen, the older woman gave her an approving smile, as if she understood she had held back, and it had been the correct thing to do. But Irene knew she couldn't do it for much longer, and she was getting frustrated that not even Helen would stand up to Mary.

★

They set off for the deserter raid at 9 p.m., having carried out a few hours of normal patrolling beforehand. Helen had been advised that Julie Barnes, a woman with a bad reputation, was harbouring a soldier from Belton Park who had disappeared the night before his regiment was due to leave for France. The woman who visited Helen to give her the information claimed Mrs Barnes was hiding the soldier, despite having a husband of her own away at the front and four children in the household.

When they reached the tiny house in Welby Street, they couldn't see any lights on or any movement from inside. Irene wondered if they'd been given false information and looked around cautiously to check for anybody lurking in the shadows waiting to have a good laugh about having wasted their time.

'Joan's a good source, we'll find him here,' Helen said confidently before she knocked loudly on the door. There was no movement from inside, and Helen had her arm raised to knock again when they heard shuffling and hushed voices coming from the other side of the door. Helen smiled, a satisfied look on her face. Irene looked round at Mary and saw she was bouncing from foot to foot, brimming over with anticipation. Irene's feeling of uneasiness increased, and she prayed they would find everything in order.

A portly woman, who Irene thought was probably around the same age as Helen, opened the door wearing a dirty apron and seemed shocked to see the four official uniforms standing in front of her.

'Whatever's this about?' she asked, straining her eyes to make out their faces properly in the dark. 'There's nothing going on in here you'd be interested in!' she cried before anyone had had a chance to answer her original question. Her indignation set alarm bells ringing in Irene's head.

'Well, you won't mind us coming in to have a little look around, then,' Helen said firmly before gently pushing the door further open and walking over the threshold. The woman didn't have much choice but to step aside to let her pass. Irene moved to follow her in, but Mary barged past her, such was her determination to be the next one in the house. Irene took a deep breath and followed Mary in, and Ruby entered last. 'You took your time coming to the door,' Helen commented casually once they were all gathered in the tiny kitchen.

'I was upstairs, wasn't I? Got kids to put to bed,' the woman said defensively. 'And you best not have woken them with your intrusion.'

'More likely you were finishing off with your coward of a fancy man,' Mary sneered.

Helen shot her a warning look and Irene was surprised to see her shrink back and stop talking. Mrs Barnes looked as though she was just about to respond when Helen cut in.

'You've hidden him well, but I'm afraid you forgot to put his coat out of sight when you hurried him into his hiding place,' she declared matter-of-factly, motioning towards a military jacket hanging over one of the chairs at the kitchen table. On the table were two half-full glasses along with two empty dinner plates. Mrs Barnes's face fell, and her complexion turned pale.

After a pause, she declared defiantly, 'It's my husband's,' straightening up her back and brushing down her apron.

'Come on, now,' sighed Helen. 'You know as well as we do they wouldn't let him into the camp without his full uniform, let alone off to the front line, which is where we know he is. Your number's up. Just call your chap out and we'll get him back to Belton.'

The group stood in a silent stand-off. Irene was on edge,

waiting for either Mary to throw her weight around or Mrs Barnes to try and throw them out of her house. She was certain that given the chance she would be able to reason with the woman, but she was still new here and this was the first deserter raid she'd been on. Helen had taken the lead and she didn't want to overstep the mark, especially when even Mary was holding back.

There were a few more awkward moments of silence before they all turned around at the sound of heavy footsteps on the stairs. A soldier, younger than Mrs Barnes by a good ten years, walked slowly towards them with his head hung low. Mrs Barnes rushed over to him.

'What are you doing, Carl? They'll have you shot!' she hissed as she tried to push him back towards the stairs. But he walked on, not even flinching as she grabbed and pulled at his uniform desperately. He stopped when he reached Helen.

'It's over, Julie,' he said quietly. 'I couldn't face the battlefield again and I knew what my fate could be when I ran away.'

'Don't do this!' Mrs Barnes cried, falling to her knees at his feet.

Instinctively, Irene got on to her knees beside her to try and comfort her. As Mrs Barnes reached up to Carl, he bent down and kissed her forehead gently.

'It's already done,' he whispered.

Mrs Barnes broke down sobbing and Irene threw her arms around her while Ruby rubbed her shoulder. Irene looked up as Carl nodded his go-ahead to Helen, who signalled to Irene to stay put and then silently led the soldier from the room. Irene had forgotten that Mary was in the room until her voice rang out from behind her.

'Now to deal with this one,' she declared.

Irene glared up at her confused. 'What are you talking about? Deal with who?' she asked as Mrs Barnes continued sobbing into her shoulder.

'Well, she was obviously making money out of him being here,' she spat, pointing to a small pile of coins on the counter.

'For heaven's sake, Mary!' Irene shouted angrily. She had reached her limit with the girl now and she could no longer bite her tongue. 'The poor woman's bereft, and the man is gone. Do you not think that she's suffering enough?'

'She should have thought of that before she put the rest of his regiment at risk by spreading her legs. And what about her poor husband? Off fighting for his country while she works her way through all the soldiers back here,' Mary sneered, folding her arms and narrowing her eyes at Irene.

Irene gently moved Mrs Barnes's head into Ruby's arms and then got to her feet. She spoke calmly, hoping to reason with Mary. 'They may well have been intimate, but we can't prove that – let alone whether she was charging for the pleasure,' she said quietly. 'You may not agree with her actions, but that part isn't a police matter. What right do we have to interfere in her private life? Yes, the soldier shouldn't have been here – and it's our responsibility to remove him and take him back to the camp – but anything else isn't our business.' She looked behind her at Ruby, hoping for some backup. But her friend just stared blankly at her.

'Who are you to tell me what to do?' Mary spat, stepping towards Irene, who was alarmed at how furious Mary looked. 'You've only been here five minutes and you've never even been on one of these raids. Helen may think you're a golden girl but she's not here now to protect you!' Irene jumped back as Mary lunged towards her, grabbing for her jacket. As she ran to put the kitchen table between herself and Mary, she saw Ruby leading Mrs Barnes out of the room. She thought Ruby was sensible to get Mrs Barnes out of the way before returning to help her and she decided that if she could just keep Mary at bay until her friend came back, they would be able to placate her together.

Each time Mary moved towards her Irene edged further around the table. Mary was starting to seethe with rage. Irene didn't want to fight her, but it seemed as though she might not have much choice – talking had clearly done no good. She looked desperately to the door again. Where was Ruby? Why hadn't she come back to help her yet? The pair of them continued their game of cat and mouse around the table until Irene finally accepted that Ruby wasn't coming to her rescue. Her heart sunk as she recognised she was on her own and they couldn't continue like this for much longer.

'We don't need to fight,' Irene said firmly, putting her hands up in a show of surrender and stopping still.

The next thing she saw was Mary's fist.

# 15

For someone so small, Mary was very strong. By the time Irene had comprehended what had just happened, she was slumped on the floor. There was a ringing in her ears, almost like a scream, and she winced as she tried to open her eyes. Her right eye felt like it was glued shut and that whole side of her face was aching. She put her hand up to check for blood and was relieved to find none, but her eye was tender to touch and felt swollen already.

She heard footsteps and looked up with her good eye just in time to see Mary scurrying out of the room. Of course – she was a bullying coward, so she'd struck out and now she was running away. Irene groaned as she slowly got to her feet. She heard the front door slam as Mary left the house, and then moments later Ruby peered around the kitchen door.

'She hit you?' she exclaimed, rushing towards her.

'I'm fine,' Irene barked angrily, shrugging Ruby away. She steadied herself on the counter. She felt sick and groggy, and she couldn't open her right eye. Ruby looked hurt at the snub.

'Why didn't you come back in to help me?' Irene asked quietly. The throbbing in her head was constant. 'I thought we were friends.'

'We are, I just . . .' Ruby started.

'Look, I know you have your problems with Mary, but you must have seen how riled up she was getting,' Irene cut in. 'Friends are meant to look out for each other.' Her head was still ringing, and she didn't have the energy to discuss it further. If Ruby couldn't appreciate that what she had done was rotten, then maybe they hadn't been that close to begin with. 'Stay and look after Mrs Barnes. I need to get this looked at,' Irene said. She walked out before Ruby had a chance to protest. But once outside, she became conscious of the fact she didn't have anywhere to go for help. Helen would be dealing with the soldier, and she didn't feel ready to explain what had happened to her, not yet anyway. If she went back to the house then she risked bumping into Mary on her own, which wasn't appealing in the slightest.

Making her way back into the centre of the town, Irene hung her head and put her hand up to her face to hide her injury whenever she passed by anyone. She didn't want people to see her like this and think she was weak. She felt so alone. Ruby's actions – or lack of them – had been a real betrayal and she felt naive for ever thinking they had been building a strong friendship. She certainly wasn't the ally against Mary that Irene had hoped for.

Her thoughts naturally switched to Maggie and Annie. She knew without a doubt that had either of them been there tonight, she would not be wandering the streets alone with a sore head right now. Both girls would have jumped straight in to help her without a second thought. Irene pondered again whether coming to Grantham had been the right thing for her. Her quest had failed miserably – if anything, she'd led Mary to act even nastier than she had been before her arrival. Maybe it was time for her to admit defeat and head back to London.

Then her mother's face flashed into Irene's head. But she didn't look the way Irene liked to remember her. In this vision, her face was bloody and bruised – perhaps similar to how Irene's looked now, she thought as she put her hand up to feel around the swollen area again. She couldn't let everything her mother had been through be in vain. She had come here with a purpose and she needed to see it through. If she didn't rein

Mary in, then would she start attacking other women like she'd attacked Irene? She couldn't let that happen. She wouldn't.

After a short walk she found herself outside The George. She hadn't meant to head there, but she looked through the window and saw Charles talking to some officers from Belton. Had she subconsciously sought him out? She hardly knew Charles Murphy, but at this moment, he was the closest thing she had to a friend. She realised sadly that she had no one else to turn to. She was debating whether to enter the pub when he turned around and spotted her at the window. She smiled and gave a meek wave. His face brightened but then twisted in concern when he took in her swollen eye. She turned around quickly. Why had she come here looking so awful? Irene was about to run off when the door swung open and Charles strode out on to the street.

'Whatever happened?' he asked, cupping her face in his hands and surveying the damage. She winced as he gently ran his finger over her cheek – even that was sore. 'Tell me where he is, and I swear—' he started angrily.

'It wasn't a man,' Irene said glumly. Confusion swept over Charles's face. 'I don't want to talk about it on the street,' she whispered, looking around cautiously.

'Of course,' he said as he put his arm around her shoulder and swept her along the path with him. She was surprised to find herself taking his lead and gratefully walking along with him. His actions were rather forward, and Irene wouldn't normally allow herself to be treated in such a way by someone she hardly knew, but she put it down to the circumstances and her desperate need to be cared for when she felt so low and alone, and actually welcomed it.

Charles lived in a grand house on Avenue Road. They had to pass by the police station to get there, but Charles kept Irene close to his side and made sure the officer on the desk didn't see her. Once inside, Irene marvelled at the size of the place. She suddenly felt out of her depth. This was probably the biggest house she had ever set foot in and she felt completely out of place.

'Please, come through to the drawing room,' Charles said, leading her down the hallway. He hadn't seemed to pick up on the fact that she felt so uncomfortable. Charles summoned a young girl and they exchanged words quietly by the door. The girl left and Charles took Irene's hand and guided her to the sofa, where he motioned for her to take a seat. When the girl returned, she was carrying a big bowl with cold water and a cloth.

'I'll do that, thank you, Mildred,' Charles said softly, taking the bowl and excusing her. Charles sat down next to Irene and she waited nervously as he submerged the cloth and then wrung out the excess water.

They sat in silence as Charles softly dabbed the cloth over Irene's eye and cheek. She was surprised at how gentle his big hands were, and how at ease she felt with his touch. As she watched him at work, she noted how hard he was concentrating, and she was struck by how much care he seemed to be taking. She could see every fine line on his face as he worked meticulously to ease her pain.

After a minute or two, Charles instructed her to hold the cold cloth over her right eye to try and soothe it. Then he finally asked her what had happened. Irene told him all about the friction with Mary over the previous couple of weeks before explaining the evening's events.

'This is why women should be looked after and nurtured,' he said, sighing. 'It sounds as if the power of the police role has gone to her head somewhat. I always said women should be kept out of the physical roles, but I suppose we're all doing what we can in these times. All this stress and responsibility has obviously left Mary feeling overwhelmed and she's lashed out at you,' he added sadly.

'I . . . I don't think that's quite it,' Irene said. She was bemused. Charles clearly hadn't understood what she'd been saying about Mary. Irene wondered if the knock to her head had left her making little sense, or maybe she had misheard him. Surely he wasn't like the bullying officers she had had to deal with back in London who believed the police force was only for men? 'It's got nothing to do with her being in a man's role,' she clarified. 'She's just a bad person.'

'Oh, she is very clearly a little devil,' Charles agreed. 'She would have to be to pick on somebody as kind and capable as yourself. Perhaps this is all down to jealousy. Do you think she feels threatened by the new girl doing such a good job? I've only heard great things about you myself,' he added.

Irene felt herself blushing and she was grateful Mary's blow had left a red mark to cover up the evidence. The suave, charming Charles she remembered from their previous encounters was back – she'd obviously misheard him before, or she had said something to confuse him. He had been impressed with her police work when they met, after all – so it wouldn't make sense that he wouldn't approve.

'So, tell me about your factory,' Irene said. She was keen to learn more about this man. Helen's warning about his past was ringing in her ears but she didn't feel comfortable trying to delve too deep just yet. Maybe as they talked, he would reveal whatever it was that was troubling Helen so much, anyway.

'Oh, it's not all mine,' Charles replied. 'I manage it with my brother.'

As they got to know each other better, Irene learned Charles and his brother had taken over managing their father's factories when he died. Murphy & Sons was a major manufacturer of agricultural machinery, but it had been seconded to producing munitions and engines for the admiralty when war had broken out.

'It's getting tough because with all that going on, we don't have a lot of time for the marketing or manufacturing of new products,' he explained. 'We've been looking for another company to amalgamate with. The munitions work is bringing in the money now, but the war won't last forever and when it's over we'll be left with no new products in the pipeline. The machinery we build takes years to develop, and we'll have to start from scratch so there will be a period where we're making no profit. I went off to investigate a possible merger after I invited you for tea,' he added. 'Don't worry, though: the company is still worth a lot, and my wealth won't suffer whatever happens – my father made sure of that,' he said in a hurry after a few moments of silence.

Irene looked at him blankly, not quite understanding. Then comprehension rushed upon her and she blushed furiously. 'Oh,' she stammered at last, 'I – I'm not the kind of woman who's looking to be kept.' Of course, she would love to not have to worry about money after struggling for so long, but she wasn't interested in Charles for his wealth. And she was proud to finally be making enough to support herself and her family.

'Well, you wouldn't have to worry about going out and doing men's work if you were my wife, that's for sure,' Charles said proudly. She felt winded. They didn't even know each other properly yet, and he was already talking about her being his wife! And there was that reference to 'men's work' again . . . but Charles was holding Irene's gaze with those lovely eyes and speaking in a soft and soothing tone that was bringing her comfort, even though she didn't particularly like what he was saying. Irene felt confused. How could he be drawing her in when normally a man with these views would send her running for the hills?

Before she had a chance to set him straight, he turned the subject to books and spoke at length of his favourite authors. For the first couple of minutes Irene couldn't focus on what he was saying, still feeling off-kilter from what he'd said about being his wife. But slowly, she managed to bring herself back to the present and was soon listening hard. She was delighted to learn Charles was an avid reader like herself. She hadn't come away from the children's home with much, but she had her years there to thank for her literacy skills and her passion for reading. The haul of donated books under her bed in the shared dorm had been vital in getting her through those difficult years.

'You'll enjoy the story behind The George,' he said, leaning into her as his eyes lit up. She noticed again the flecks of grey peppering his otherwise black hair – a reminder of the age gap between them. But she found herself drawn to his maturity and experience and flattered that someone as distinguished as him was taking an interest in someone as young and inexperienced as her. Charles's enthusiasm was contagious, and she sat enraptured as he told her about Charles Dickens' stay at the town's inn on his way to Greta Bridge in 1838. 'My namesake liked it so much there that he referred to it as one of the finest inns in England in his novel *Nicholas Nickleby*,' he said excitedly. 'Isn't that just wonderful? Our very own piece of history immortalised in the book of one of our greatest writers?'

Irene nodded her fervent agreement. She thought back to Frank and their shared love of books. She had thought they had something special, but with Charles, this thing that they had – whatever it was – already felt so much stronger. Yes, she decided she had definitely misunderstood him before. Maybe she just needed to relax, and not be so uptight about things. After all, different people had different views, and perhaps she should be more tolerant of that. She thought back to his mention of becoming his wife, then, and found herself staggered that someone like him could get to his forties without finding one. Maybe Helen's concerns about his past had something to do with that?

'So . . . what's a man like you doing without a wife?' she

asked cautiously as Charles checked over her eye again. She would normally feel uncomfortable asking such a personal question, but for some reason she didn't think he would take offence. Charles's face was so close to hers while he worked on her eye that she could feel his breath on her cheek. The question obviously took him aback, as his breath caught in his throat for a moment before he pulled back from her again and answered.

'I was married,' he said sadly, staring down into the cloth as he wrung it between his hands. Her question was meant to be light-hearted, but it was obviously a sensitive subject for him and Irene felt terrible for prying now.

'It's all right, you don't have to tell me what happened,' she said quickly, instinctively placing a hand over his to try to comfort him.

'No, you should know,' Charles sighed, looking up and meeting her eyes. 'I thought we would grow old together in this house.' He ran his fingers roughly through his hair while he surveyed the room, looking uncomfortable. 'But she betrayed me. It broke my heart so much I feared I would never love again.'

Irene was the one taken aback now. The pain was still clear to see on Charles's face and she grasped his hand again, desperate to say what she could to take it away.

'I hope what I'm about to say doesn't scare you away,' he continued, sounding more positive now, 'but when I met you, Irene, it was the first time I'd ever felt an instant connection with anybody. I know we still hardly know each other, but this has been the most enlivening evening I've had since my wife left me, and it's given me hope that I can find love again. I hadn't thought that possible until now.'

Irene let out a nervous laugh. She wasn't used to men being this open with her. Maybe it was an age thing? No matter, Charles's honesty was refreshing, if maybe a little overwhelming. But she found that what he was saying was making her heart sing. She still couldn't fathom why somebody of his status was so interested in her, but she wasn't going to question it.

'I'm flattered,' she muttered. 'I'm enjoying getting to know you, too.'

'That's all I need to know,' Charles smiled. The movement brought out creases around his eyes.

But a worrisome thought suddenly entered Irene's mind. Was Charles free to fall in love with her? His wife may have betrayed him, but she could very well still be in his life. Were they divorced, or were they living together unhappily like so many married couples seemed to do these days – like Maggie's parents . . .

Irene had to know. She couldn't risk spending more time with Charles and falling for him to then discover he was still bound to another. Her mind wandered to one of her favourite books: *Jane Eyre*. Poor Jane had only found out that Mr Rochester was still married on their wedding day. She couldn't risk going through something like that herself.

'Where is your wife now?' she asked gently. Charles sighed, and Irene's heart dropped. She would have to stop this – whatever it was – right now if he was still married.

'The truth is, I don't know,' Charles admitted. 'I was lucky enough that I had the money to be able to divorce her. I say lucky, but there wasn't really a "good" solution to it all, you understand. The shame and humiliation of going through a divorce was almost too much to cope with.'

Irene's heart ached for him. This was clearly what Helen had been referencing with her comments about his past. The poor man was still having to deal with judgement from others, even though he had clearly been left with no choice.

'As soon as the divorce was finalised, she ran off with her fancy man and I haven't heard from her since. It was a relief in a way, as it meant I was able to rebuild my life and my reputation without the shame hanging over me so obviously. But I know that people still think of me of the man who divorced his wife, and I hate that.'

Irene felt terrible for Charles. He'd been through the worst heartbreak and betrayal and now he was having to deal with the consequences of his wife's selfish actions while she was off enjoying a new life.

'I think you were brave to divorce her,' Irene said confidently.

Charles laughed lightly. 'That's very kind, thank you,' he said, his eyes sparkling again. 'But that's enough about her. I want to get to know more about you,' he added as a smile spread across his face.

They continued talking, and before Irene knew it, it was three o' clock in the morning. Panic set in as she realised she had been enjoying Charles's company so much she'd lost track of the time.

'Helen will be wondering where I am,' she spluttered, jumping to her feet.

'Don't worry, I'll get my driver to drop you over immediately,' Charles said, rising and taking both her hands in his. 'I would walk you home myself, but I don't imagine Helen wouldn't be best pleased to see you arrive at the door with me in tow – especially not with your very impressive war wound,' he added, gesturing to her face.

Irene was confused for a moment, and then remembered what had led her to Charles in the first place. Her head was throbbing, but the distraction of their animated conversations had blocked out the pain. Charles led her back to the hallway, where she was shocked to see her reflection in a mirror on the wall. She lightly tapped the inflammation with her fingertips. The area around her eye was still dark red and swollen, and parts had started to blacken already. She was mortified that she'd been talking to Charles, looking like this, for the last few hours.

'She certainly meant business,' Charles remarked quietly. 'But don't worry, it will go down in a day or two.'

Irene hoped he was right because there was no way she could go out on patrol looking like this. Whoever would take her authority seriously knowing she had taken such a beating?

'You should come and take a look around the factory if you get some time off to recuperate,' Charles said with a smile.

It was like he could read her mind. Her belly flipped at the thought of seeing him again. He must really like her if he wanted to be seen in public with her looking like this.

'I might just do that,' she replied, feeling suddenly shy. He took both her hands in his again and leant down towards her. Her whole body tingled in nervous anticipation as he closed his eyes and put his lips to hers. When they kissed, it felt like fireworks were going off in her head as well as in her stomach. She was grateful Charles was holding her hands as otherwise she feared she may lose her balance.

'You're a very special woman, Irene Wilson,' Charles whispered after gently pulling away. 'I've very much enjoyed getting to know you this evening, even if it wasn't in the best circumstances.' He gave her hands a light squeeze before walking her out of the house. Wordlessly, he helped her into the car parked outside, then went around to the driver's side where he spoke to the man behind the steering wheel. 'Take special care on the roads,' he heard him say, and her heart fluttered once more at the fact that he seemed to care so much for her comfort and safety.

Charles stood on the pavement and watched as the car pulled away. Irene held eye contact with him for as long as she could, entranced by him and well and truly under his spell.

# 16

When Irene walked through the door at Rutland Street, Helen rushed out of the living room and into the hallway.

'My poor love,' she cried, placing her hands on to Irene's shoulders and surveying the damage to her face before pulling her in for a hug. 'Ruby told me what happened. I'm so angry with Mary,' she whispered, stroking Irene's hair gently.

Irene's mother used to do the same when Irene was upset – more often than not over something horrible her father had done towards the end of their time together. She closed her eyes and allowed herself to become lost in the moment briefly, pretending for a short while that she was back in her mother's arms. But all too soon she was transported back to the present and the realisation that she was going to have to face up to what had happened with Mary.

'Where have you been all this time?' Helen asked. She led Irene to the living room where they sat down on the sofa together.

'It doesn't matter,' Irene sighed. She could do without another lecture from Helen about Charles, especially now she knew the truth about his past. She was disappointed that Helen could be so negative about him when he was the victim in it all. But now wasn't the time to discuss that. 'All that matters is that I let Mary get the better of me, and we had a fight instead of talking things through,' Irene whispered staring at her hands in her lap.

'From what I've heard, it wasn't exactly a fight,' Helen said sympathetically. 'Ruby told me what she knows, and Mary herself has admitted she hit out at you while you were trying to reason with her.'

Irene was shocked. Did Mary feel bad for what she'd done?

'Of course, she thinks she was completely justified, so I've made it clear that is not the way she should be behaving with anyone, let alone one of her colleagues,' Helen continued.

Irene tutted. She should have known that Mary showing any sign of remorse would have been too good to be true.

'What happens next?' Irene asked cautiously. 'If she's not going to apologise then I don't think we can keep working together.' She was hopeful Mary's actions might see her thrown out of the WPS, or at the very least sent to work in another town.

'I can mention it to the commandant,' Helen said, 'but Mary's pulling in good results. I know you don't agree with her arrest-happy attitude. It hasn't escaped my attention that she drags prostitutes down to the police station so an officer can arrest them before giving them any advice or a chance to correct their ways. I don't agree with that either, if I'm honest. I do try to rein her in, but you know what she's like. The truth of it is, all the arrests and convictions will look good once the war is over and the commandant is trying to convince the commissioner he should take on female officers. And the more women Mary hauls into the police station to be arrested, the more support and acceptance we get from the officers there.'

Irene put her head in her hands. She couldn't give up and leave Grantham, but it didn't seem as though she was going to make any headway in her quest to make sure the women were treated better.

Helen put a reassuring hand on Irene's back. 'I believe she owes you an apology, though,' she said, 'and I'll try to make that happen. For the time being, I'll keep you two apart. Mary prefers patrolling on her own anyway, so it shouldn't be an issue. How does that sound?'

Irene had to agree it would be better if they spent some time apart. It would give her space to figure out a better way to deal with Mary. Maybe she could focus more of her efforts on looking out for the women already known to the police in the meantime. If she couldn't stop Mary being heavy-handed with her arrests, she could at least try to make sure the ladies she picked on were treated fairly in court.

Irene looked up at Helen and smiled weakly. 'Thank you,' she whispered.

'I don't think we can have you out on patrol until your eye has settled down,' Helen added, rising to her feet. 'We'll see what it looks like in the morning, but I've a feeling you'll be in need of some extra rest anyway.'

Irene nodded gratefully and managed another smile, although even that was starting to hurt her cheek.

Once Helen had gone to bed, Irene crept into the room she shared with Mary and bundled up her bedclothes from her bed. Mary was fast asleep in the bed next to hers and she couldn't abide the thought of lying in the same room as the woman who only hours before had hit her so maliciously. Settling herself on the sofa, she instantly started drifting off. She hadn't realised how tired she was until she was lying down.

As sleep threatened to overtake her, Irene's mind wandered back to Charles and their first kiss. What an eventful evening it had been – it had started out so badly and ended with something so beautiful. She was looking forward to getting to know him better. His comment about how women should stay out of physical roles popped into her head again and threatened to ruin her blissful musings, but she pushed it to one side, reassuring herself again that she'd misunderstood him. She needed a friend right now and he had been so caring this evening – he'd made her feel so safe.

Her mind wandered to their kiss again and she drifted off to sleep thinking about the feel of his soft lips on hers.

# 17

It took four days for Irene's eye to settle down. On her first day off, she took Charles up on his offer of a tour of the factory. He treated her so well on the visit she felt like royalty. Whenever anyone stared at her eye, he jumped in to explain proudly that she'd been injured in the line of duty. Irene became certain she'd misheard his previous comments – his attitude now clearly demonstrated he was in favour of her job.

Knowing she had no friends or family in the town, Charles took it upon himself to take Irene out regularly over the following days. He was understanding of her wanting to keep their blossoming romance from both Helen and Mary, so he picked her up and dropped her off at the end of Rutland Street. They went for countless drives in his car, with him at the wheel, and Irene got to see all of Grantham's surrounding villages and towns. She even went for dinner at his house, and they managed to go for their tea and cake at Thompson's, which turned into a whole afternoon of laughter and chatter. She found to her surprise that Frank's looming wedding hardly entered her thoughts. And when the first Zeppelin raid struck London – thankfully missing Bethnal Green – Charles listened intently to Irene's fears about her friends, and comforted her.

When Helen checked in with her to find out how she was getting on during her unscheduled break from patrolling, Irene found herself lying to her about how she had been spending her time. When Helen asked her outright if she had taken

Charles up on his offer of a cup of tea, she muttered something about having not seen him around and then rushed off to her room. She felt bad for lying to her, as she appreciated the fact that she was just looking out for her. But after getting to know Charles better and learning the whole truth about his divorce, Irene realised that Helen didn't know the real Charles Murphy and so she would never understand.

Irene made sure to cover her dresses during the day with the half-decent shawl she'd thrown into her suitcase at the last minute. She was relieved to find it instantly breathed a bit of life into her worn and tired clothes and covered them up enough that Charles didn't seem to notice how tatty they were. She wore Annie's navy-blue dress for dinner at Charles's house, and she'd silently thanked her friend when he had complimented how she looked. She'd felt uncomfortable borrowing any of Ruby's dresses after what had happened between them.

Faced with wearing Annie's dress again or one of her own for their second dinner at Charles's house, she had opted for Annie's. She reasoned to herself that Charles probably wouldn't even notice, and if he did he wouldn't mind. She was confident that he liked her, but she was still feeling too self-conscious about their different backgrounds to wear one of her dresses for an evening get-together, especially as she was working hard to make sure Charles didn't know they came from such different worlds.

When Mildred showed her into the dining room and she saw Charles looking her up and down with disappointment on his face before looking away again, Irene's heart dropped. Her head throbbed with panic as she walked over to the chair by the fire where he was sitting with a face like stone.

When he looked up and met her eyes, though, he suddenly switched and a big smile spread across his face as he got up to greet her. He seemed delighted to see her, and Irene was so relieved. He didn't make any mention of her dress at all. They had a lovely evening and Irene decided she had imagined his initial disappointment. She put it down to her self-consciousness about her background, and chided herself for being so paranoid.

Charles had stepped in just when Irene needed him. His support and companionship had boosted her waning confidence and given her a renewed vigour for her goal of helping the women of Grantham, even if she couldn't manage to get Mary under control. He didn't mention any more about his views on women working, and she started to wonder if she had imagined it all in her daze.

Thankfully, Irene had been so busy with Charles that she'd hardly seen Ruby or Mary. Mary's busy shifts meant she was often out late so Irene was fast asleep when she joined her in their room to go to bed. The few times she had bumped into her at the house, Mary had grunted and walked off in the opposite direction. She obviously wasn't ready to make her apology.

Ruby had gone into herself and hadn't tried to speak to Irene since their confrontation at Mrs Barnes's home. Irene was glad and she hoped Ruby was feeling ashamed for the way she had acted that night.

During her time off, Irene wrote to Annie and Maggie again to update them on all the latest developments. She was in desperate need of one of Maggie's big plans when it came to helping the town's women, and she was hoping her friend would come through for her. She also missed Annie's thoughtfulness and comfort more than ever.

Once Irene's eye was healed enough that she could go back out on patrol, Helen started sending her out on her own more often than not. Although she found it overwhelming at first, she was soon beginning to enjoy having no one else to look out for or worry about. She had been used to only having to look after herself before joining the WPS, so she found it easy to slip back into that mentality.

She went out with Ruby a few times, but she kept it very formal despite Ruby's attempts at making friendly conversation. Although she was happy to be civil to Ruby, Irene wasn't ready to let her back into her confidences. She just couldn't see how she could trust her any more. She had Charles now, the man who had rushed to help her when she had no one else to turn to, and with him by her side she didn't need friends who would let her down at the first opportunity.

When two weeks had passed since the run-in with Mary and Irene still hadn't received an apology, she accepted she wouldn't be getting one. Helen hadn't mentioned it again, so Irene assumed she was happy keeping them apart and forgetting about it. She hadn't heard back from Maggie and Annie yet after her letter asking for guidance, and she wasn't sure how to proceed now the dust had settled. But she was having so much fun with Charles that she was happy patrolling on her own and protecting the women she came across for now.

She knew that Frank's wedding must have taken place by now, but she had been having such a good time with Charles that she had lost track of when it was happening. When she realised he must now be married, she was surprised – and delighted – to find that she just felt happy for him.

Irene's busy shifts had meant she'd only managed to see Charles during the day since she had started back on patrol. But tonight she finally had an evening off, and they were due to meet for dinner at one of the town's restaurants. She was worried about what to wear – she certainly couldn't wear Annie's outfit again, that was for sure. She was tempted for a brief moment to borrow one of Ruby's dresses, but her pride wouldn't let her.

If Charles really liked her, she thought as she made her way around Grantham on her dayshift, then he would accept her for who she was. Maybe it was time to show him the real her, ragged dresses and all. And maybe she had misread him last time. He was a man, after all – he probably hadn't even noticed her dress!

She was so distracted by her musings that when a soldier screeched past her on a bicycle, she didn't even register the fact it was unusual to see a man in uniform on a push-bike.

She had her latest pay packet in her pocket, and she was planning on posting it off to Ruth when her shift finished. Pausing outside one of the town's ladies' clothes stores and taking in the pretty dresses on display, she contemplated holding some of her money back to buy one for that evening instead of braving wearing one of her old dresses. A smile spread across her face as she pictured Charles's eyes lighting up when she walked in the room. She shivered with anticipation despite the morning sun as she imagined the compliments that he would shower her with, just as he had done the first time she'd worn Annie's dress.

'Did a chap on a bike just come past here, miss?' a rough voice catapulted Irene back to the present and she spun around to find a man in overalls, huffing and puffing and looking up and down the street desperately.

'It's me daughter's bike, she needs it to get to work in a factory in the next town over. We can't do without her pay!' He'd caught his breath now and looked ready to run off after the soldier when Irene placed a hand on his shoulder to stop him.

'He was going too fast, you'll never catch him,' she said. His face dropped. 'I know exactly where he's going – I'll get the bike back for you,' she added confidently. 'You go and find another way for your daughter to get to work today, though, because I won't be able to get it back to you for at least another hour.' She was certain the lad, having stayed out overnight without permission, would have nicked the bike in order to get back to Belton in time for the morning's roll-call, but she would have to make her way there to find it on foot.

'All right miss,' he sighed heavily. 'My name's Paul Glover and we're at Fifty Three Oxford Street. The chap was next door with our neighbour all night – caused a right racket. She's getting worse, that one, she keeps bringing them back at all hours.'

'What do you mean?' Irene asked, her interest instantly piqued.

'Well, she's always been a right one, that one next door – got men coming and going all the time. But she's certainly been busy since the army camp was built.'

'Right, thank you Mr Glover,' Irene said seriously. 'You can leave that information with me, there's no need to pass it on to anyone else. I can assure you I'll get the situation sorted. And I'll bring your daughter's bike back as soon as possible.'

'Thanks, love,' he replied gratefully, marching off in the direction he'd come from.

Irene took a deep breath. She knew she should be reporting Mr Glover's neighbour straight to Helen so they could organise a visit to her house. But that was sure to end in the woman being dragged off to the police station by Mary. She knew she wouldn't be able to protect the woman once they were all in the house – she was likely to get a fist to the face again if she tried. But she could sneak in and try to get the woman to stop her antics without the need for anybody else's input. She could also give her some advice on protecting her health, and ideas for other ways to make money.

Giving the beautiful dresses in the shop window one last, regretful glance, Irene set off for Belton Park. When she got to the entrance gates, sure enough, there was a discarded bicycle lying on the ground. Sighing, she picked it up and gave it a quick once-over. It didn't appear to be damaged, so that was one good thing. She thought about heading into the camp and trying to find the culprit, but she knew it would be fruitless. None of the soldiers would snitch on one of their own.

An officer, however, would take her seriously if there was a suggestion that one of the troops had spent the night with a woman away from the camp. They were terrified of their men being struck down with disease and unable to fight. Irene wheeled the bike into the camp and found an officer at Belton House. He looked out of the window at the bike she had left resting against the wall and gave an apologetic smile.

'I know exactly why you're here, and the man in question will be having his privileges limited for the next week,' he said before she could get a word in. 'He'll also be taking on some extra duties for his insubordination. I meant to have someone return the bicycle to the town later this morning, but I see you ladies are on top of things, as always,' he added.

Irene smiled gratefully. She was still getting used to being appreciated in her role with the WPS. 'Thank you, sir,' she replied. 'But, do you know where your man was all night?' she asked cautiously.

'He admitted to having a few too many ales and passing out in an alley,' the man said, his voice dripping with contempt. 'These young lads don't know how to handle their drink.'

'I'm afraid that's not completely true,' Irene said, before explaining her run-in with Mr Glover. She was fed up with the women getting all the blame for these things. Yes, the soldier was being punished – but only for staying out all night. The toe-rag had tried to lie his way out of the punishment he deserved for taking advantage of a vulnerable woman. The police wouldn't do anything to deal with him, but she knew the army would.

The officer frowned as she finished her story. 'That changes things greatly. I will have to reassess his punishment,' he said. 'I'm disappointed, but I can't say I'm surprised. Now, is there anything else I can help you with?'

'No, sir. I'll leave you to your day,' Irene replied with a nod of her head before making her way back outside. She was pleased the soldier would be facing consequences for what he'd got up to the night before. Now she just had to get the bike back to Mr Glover and try and keep his neighbour out of trouble.

Grabbing the handlebars, Irene contemplated hopping on the bike and riding it back to town – it would certainly get her there a lot quicker. But she had never ridden on one before, plus she wasn't sure how her long, heavy skirt would cope, and she wasn't about to find out in front of the hundreds of troops making their way to the food hut for breakfast. She wheeled it back towards the gates.

'They got you lady bobbies on bikes now, eh?' she heard a voice shout out from the throng of men walking across the camp.

'Mitchell!' she heard an official-sounding voice ring out, and she laughed to herself as she looked over and saw the offending heckler duck his head in shame.

Once Irene was out in the fields and safe from prying eyes, she decided to give the bike a try. She did a final check for any company and, seeing she was definitely alone, she hitched her skirt up and bunched it in the middle to get on to the seat. Mr Glover's daughter must be short, she thought gratefully, as she was able to put both feet on the ground comfortably. Keeping her skirt bunched up so it didn't get caught in the wheels, she started to peddle. She was a little wobbly at first, and she took a tumble almost immediately. Thankfully, she had been going so slowly that she managed to stay on her feet, and it was only her pride that was bruised. Looking around cautiously for any audience to her mishap, she breathed a sigh of relief when she saw she was still alone in the field.

Taking a deep breath, she gave it another go, and this time it didn't take her long to get the hang of it. Peddling faster, she managed to keep her balance. As the light summer breeze flew over her face, she found herself closing her eyes to drink it in. Enjoying the speed, she peddled faster, energy rushing through her veins. What a feeling!

Irene couldn't wait to write to Annie and Maggie and tell them all about her first adventure on a bike. Maybe Helen could write to the commandant and request bikes for all of them – it would certainly help speed up their treks to Belton Park and back. She grasped the handlebars tighter and felt her whole body tense as she rode over a bumpier patch of grass. Once the ground was smooth again, she relaxed and closed her eyes once more to enjoy the sense of freedom the ride was giving her.

She opened her eyes again just in time to see the big mound of dirt in front of her. She panicked as she realised that she hadn't taken any time to work out the brakes. She was almost on top of the mound when she instinctively swerved the handlebars to the right to avoid it.

Irene lost control of the bike and she toppled to the ground, still straddling her new toy. She took a moment to scold herself for getting carried away, and then breathed a sigh of relief when she found nothing seemed to be hurting too much – apart from her pride.

She detangled herself from the bike, got to her feet and checked for any damage, to both her and the bike. They were both fine, apart from a scratch on her right leg which was covered by her skirt anyhow. Feeling foolish, she wheeled the bike back into town. As she got nearer, she started to see the funny side of it, and cheered herself up with the fact it would be a fun story to share with Charles over their dinner that evening. They didn't tend to talk about her WPS work much, so it would be good to have something amusing to tell him about.

# 18

The rest of Irene's shift passed by in a blur. Mr Glover was extremely grateful when she dropped his daughter's bike back, and even happier when she assured him the soldier who had pinched it was in for a harsh punishment.

She knocked at his neighbour's house but there was no answer. She imagined the lady was sleeping off the activities of the evening before, and she resolved to pop back later that day.

Only, she didn't have time in the end – before she knew it her shift was over and she was standing in the queue at the post office waiting to send her wages off to Ruth before she had to go and get ready to meet Charles.

As Irene transferred all her pay into an envelope for her aunt, she felt ashamed of herself for having considered holding any of it back to spend on herself. She had never thought of herself as a selfish person, but she felt like one now. Her desire to impress Charles had almost cost poor Henry and she felt a flash of guilt. She had been stepping out with Charles for almost three weeks now and he had never given her any reason to doubt how much he liked her. Yes, she'd panicked a little when she'd worn Annie's dress the second time, but there had been no hiccups since then and she was certain now that she had imagined his disappointment because her anxiety about it was so strong. It was time for her to show Charles the real Irene.

So what if she only had one nice dress for wearing in the

evenings – one that didn't belong to her, to boot? She really liked Charles, but maybe it was best that he understood she didn't have a rich family bankrolling her and paying for fancy outfits. She was tired of putting on a front and, besides, she was proud of the fact she was out here looking after herself and getting by how she could. She didn't have to tell him her whole sad story, but she shouldn't start spending money that was meant for her family to keep him interested. She was going to wear one of her own dresses this evening, and she was confident Charles wouldn't even bat an eyelid.

Charles had kept their dinner reservation under wraps. Irene was to meet him at the George where they would enjoy a drink before heading to his chosen restaurant together on foot. She had been full of confidence when she'd put her dress on at home, but as she approached the meeting place, she felt the bravado melting away, replaced with apprehension. There was a slight chill in the air this evening, so she had worn a thin jacket over the dress, which she pulled tighter around herself now as a kind of shield.

When she walked in, she felt the usual flutter in her stomach when she caught sight of Charles sitting at a table in the corner. A smile took over his face when his eyes met Irene's, and he stood to greet her.

'Good evening,' he said softly into her ear before tenderly kissing her cheek. He started helping her with her jacket, but then paused midway. Gently putting it back over her shoulder, he quickly looked around the bar. Irene's heart sunk and she silently scolded herself for being so silly as to think Charles wouldn't be bothered by her choice of outfit. Maybe this was it and their dalliance was over.

'There's been a change of plans, we'll dine at my house,' Charles murmured as he placed his hand on Irene's back and lightly ushered her out.

Flustered, Irene dutifully followed his lead. He wasn't calling the evening off, at least. Maybe something else had happened to make him want to change their plans. Charles was silent for the short walk to his house, and Irene spent the whole time in a panic about whether he was about to tell her he didn't want to continue their courtship. When they arrived, Mildred came rushing down the hallway looking shocked to see her master.

'Tell Cook we'll be dining in this evening,' Charles said firmly, guiding Irene into the sitting room. He stepped back into the hallway, pulling the door to behind him. Irene sat down on the sofa, and she could hear urgent whispers as Mildred explained the cook didn't have anything suitable in seeing as she hadn't known he would be eating in – and with company too. 'Well, tell her to work something out,' she heard Charles bark, his voice suddenly rising in frustration. Then there was some mumbling before the door swung open again and he walked back in.

Irene tried her best to look relaxed, but inside she was full of nerves and misery. Charles strode past Irene and then stood with his back to her, staring out of the window at the street outside. The longer he remained silent, the more anxious she grew.

'Is . . .there something the matter?' she finally managed to whisper. Charles sighed before turning to face her. 'I can just leave now, and we won't have to see each other ever again,' she said, rising from the sofa, pulling the jacket she'd kept on even tighter around her body.

'Please, it's nothing that can't be fixed,' Charles said stepping towards her, his arms outstretched. Irene shrugged off his advance. She was too embarrassed to listen to anything else.

'*I* can't be fixed, Charles!' Irene snapped, then turned on her heel to leave the room. But he grabbed her arm and pulled her back.

'I'm not the woman you thought I was,' she exclaimed. 'I

don't have a wardrobe full of expensive dresses. This is as good as it gets and if you don't like that, well . . .' But as she looked into Charles's face, her words petered out. He looked so sincere and she could feel his deep, handsome eyes drawing her in once again. She couldn't help but feel a little breathless, despite the horrible situation she was in. She longed for him to reveal some other silly reason for what was happening.

'Please, take a seat with me,' he said quietly.

Irene softened. Perhaps she had misconstrued what was happening. She should at least listen to what he had to say, she reasoned.

'You have to understand,' he started warmly. 'I love the way you dress – it doesn't matter to me how much your clothes are worth. You could turn up to meet me in rags and I wouldn't care a jot.' Irene felt a wave of calm slide over her. 'You pretty much have turned up in rags tonight, haven't you?' he said, and gave a small chuckle.

He was smiling at her, but there was a hard, steely look in his eyes. Irene was struck dumb. He'd said something so kind then followed it up with something so cruel. But before she had a chance to react, he was talking again.

'I have a certain reputation in this town, my dear, and people look to me as a man of wealth and class. What would they think of me if they were to see me with you in that dress of an evening? It's very well for popping into town in, but it's not *evening* wear, is it?'

'So, I'm not good enough for you?' Irene asked, feeling defeated again.

'No, no, it's not that,' he said, taking her hands in his. 'They would say that I don't treat you well enough, and they would ask why a man with my money hasn't lavished his lady with fine dresses and anything her heart desires! They would think badly of me – and not you – for that reason. And it wasn't until you walked in this evening that I saw how badly I had neglected you. I'm so sorry, Irene. Let me make it up to you, please?'

Irene took a few moments to process what she was hearing. So, he wasn't embarrassed of her, she thought hopefully. He just wanted to treat her properly. He looked so upset she found herself feeling bad for him. But at the same time, he was supposed to like her and yet he had made her feel small and ashamed – had even laughed at her. She didn't know what to think.

'But we've only known each other a few weeks. I wouldn't expect you to buy me anything, Charles,' she managed eventually. 'You know I'm not interested in you for your money and I have no desire to be a kept woman.'

'Please, Irene. This is important to me,' he said, suddenly stern. 'I can't have people thinking I'm not treating you the way you should be treated.'

Irene didn't feel comfortable letting Charles buy her new clothes, but she could see how much this meant to him. And she was so relieved he wasn't ending their courtship after realising how hard-up she was.

'I don't know,' she said hesitantly. It felt wrong to accept clothes from him, but if the alternative was losing him then she didn't feel like she had much choice. She already couldn't imagine life in Grantham without him, he was her only ally. 'Maybe one dress would be all right,' she added quietly.

Charles's face lit up and she felt her stomach flutter all over again. Perhaps this would be a good time to tell him the full truth about her background and her means – the reason that despite now being in a well-paid job, she wasn't able to afford to buy herself any decent clothes. She hated that she felt the need to explain herself in this way, but she pushed those feelings away. If she didn't tell him, she might lose him – and it was only now that she realised how much she had come to rely on him, even need him.

'There's something else I should tell you . . .' she started, but Charles was already on his feet and walking to the door.

'We'll get you measured up tonight and you'll have an array of lovely frocks to choose from the next time we meet. And we can have the restaurant dinner that I promised you!' he called back behind him.

When Charles returned with one of his maids, Irene felt like she had lost the moment to share her story with him. Besides, he had started telling her all about some drama between some of the workers at the factory, and she couldn't have got a word in if she'd tried.

Soon after the maid left with Irene's measurements, they were called to the dining room where they were served a veritable feast. Irene couldn't believe Charles's cook had managed to pull something so magnificent together at the last minute. She was used to relatively small servings from Helen and she was famished after a day on patrol, but she tried to hold back from piling her plate too high.

Before she knew it, her plate was empty, but her stomach was still calling out for more. She waited until Charles had finished his serving, and when he happily helped himself to more, she felt comfortable enough to do the same. But as she reached for a serving spoon, she noticed Charles freeze.

She looked up and was met with a stern expression. She faltered for a moment, unsure whether she should assert herself and take more despite his obvious disapproval. He held her gaze and his eyebrows furrowed. Irene couldn't do it. She was in his house, after all, and she supposed it wasn't attractive for a woman to sit in front of a man shovelling so much food down. She realised she was terrified of upsetting him or disappointing him. She slowly put the spoon down, laughing nervously.

'Good girl,' Charles smiled, making Irene feel a strange mix of indignant and gratified. 'We don't want you getting too round now, do we? The maid will have to retake your measurements!'

Irene gaped at him, speechless, as Charles smiled warmly at her as though he hadn't just said something objectionable, and shoved a forkful of meat into his mouth.

Before she could say anything, he reached out and placed his hand on top of hers. 'Your eyes look so lovely in the candlelight,' he said. 'They're the most extraordinary colour.' He was stroking her hand with his thumb now.

Irene found herself flustered and confused. Had he meant the comment about her measurements? He'd followed it up with something so kind – perhaps it had just been a joke? But it had done the trick: she couldn't bring herself to accept any dessert. Charles smiled approvingly when she turned it down, and then she sat dutifully and watched him enjoy his. Between mouthfuls, Charles talked more about his day at the factory.

When there was finally an opportunity, Irene regaled him with her bicycle mishap. But she was confused when he didn't laugh along at her humorous tale.

'Did I say something to upset you?' she asked cautiously. She had enjoyed telling him about her day and felt deflated by his subdued reaction.

'I'm sorry, my love,' Charles sighed. 'I wish I could join in with your excitement about your little adventure. But the truth is, the thought of it terrifies me. All I can think about is how badly things could have gone for you.'

Irene felt a flash of anger. All she'd done was have a ride on a bicycle – it was hardly a matter of life or death. Why was he being such a misery guts? She was just about to say as much when he continued, his voice softer now.

'There's no need for you to look at me like that. I'm just concerned for you. You must remember, Irene, that I have more experience of the world than you. So, when I can see that something is a bad idea, I rather think you'd do well to at least think about what I have to say about it.' He paused to take another mouthful of cake.

Irene was about to tell him that she had experienced a hell of a lot in her twenty-six years when he started talking again.

'You could have hurt yourself badly and you were stuck out in the fields on your own,' Charles said seriously. 'Who would have found you? What if one of those soldiers had stumbled back, worse for drink, and taken advantage of you in your vulnerable state?'

Irene took a sip of water to give herself time to process his comments before responding. She hadn't even thought of what a tricky situation she could have found herself in if she had injured herself badly. And she was touched by how much Charles seemed to care. She felt silly now for feeling angry towards him. He wasn't trying to dampen her spirits – he was simply worried for her safety. Maybe she should stop jumping to conclusions and doubting his intentions. He was a lot older than her, after all, and clearly thought these things through more thoroughly.

'Yes, I suppose you're right,' she said quietly. 'It was a rather mindless thing to have done.'

'I would hate for anything bad to happen to you, Irene,' Charles said warmly, covering her hand with his again. 'It pains me enough that you're traipsing through those fields on your own at all hours as it is.'

'I'm rather good at looking after myself,' she tried to assure him. But she felt a stab of doubt. Maybe he was right, and she did need someone to look out for her. She had to admit, it was a nice change to have someone worry about her. She had Maggie and Annie, of course, but she hadn't heard from them in a while.

'I just worry about you, that's all,' Charles replied softly before changing the subject.

The rest of the evening was lovely, and Irene felt like she had been truly wined and dined even without leaving Charles's home. When he kissed her goodnight and put her in a car home, she was back to feeling like the luckiest woman alive.

On the short drive back to Rutland Street, she cursed her missed opportunity to reveal her true self to Charles. There had been a couple of times when she had gone to refer to something that had happened during her time at the children's home, and she'd had to stop herself. She was desperate to be herself with him and stop having to watch what she was saying. She felt as though their feelings for each other could really develop once he knew the full picture, and she was confident none of it would matter to him.

They were going to the restaurant he had booked for that evening on her next night off, and she resolved to tell him everything then. She was nervous but also excited at the thought of finally opening up to Charles. It was a big risk, but she felt safe with him and she had to be honest with him if she wanted them to last.

# 19

A week later, Irene popped back to Rutland Street for a rest in the afternoon ahead of an evening patrol. When she walked into her bedroom, Mary was just leaving. Mary looked pointedly at a pile of dresses that were laid out on Irene's bed and then back at her before raising her eyebrows and stomping down the stairs. Irene kept her face neutral but silently told Mary to mind her own business. Once she was certain Mary was downstairs, Irene sat down on her bed and took in the beauty of the dresses.

There were four in total, and Irene couldn't help but feel a little taken aback despite how pretty they looked. She was surprised and a little put out that Charles had got them all without consulting her at all. He didn't even know what her favourite colours were, or what styles she preferred. But as she lifted each dress up and studied them one by one, she admonished herself for being so ungrateful. They were all wonderful and he had obviously gone to a lot of effort to pick them out for her. Irene took her time to run her fingers over the delicate material of each of them. These were even better quality than Annie's dress. She couldn't believe Charles had bought her so many. She wondered if he had pictured her in each of them as he went through the pattern book at the shop.

Although she was exhausted from having been on her feet all morning, she couldn't resist trying them on. She beamed as she found each one fitted perfectly. There was a cream one with a blue sash around the waist, a brown one, which she was certain would bring out the chocolate colour of her eyes, a dark green dress that looked enchanting next to her pale skin, and a black one that she felt she looked quite sophisticated in.

She reprimanded herself once more for having been upset that Charles hadn't consulted with her before buying the dresses. These were items she would never have picked out for herself, yet she had to admit that each one suited her perfectly – he had got the styles just right. She couldn't fault anything with any of them. Maybe Charles knew her better than she knew herself? And perhaps it was time to accept that he knew what was best for her.

Irene was so engrossed in playing dress-up that she didn't hear the footsteps coming up the stairs and she was startled when Helen's voice rang out behind her.

'You can't hang those over a chair like you do with your uniform,' she laughed. Irene jumped and turned around.

'I was just about to get changed and head back out on patrol,' she said in a panic.

'Don't worry,' Helen replied, smiling. 'Any girl would do the same if beautiful dresses like that turned up for her. They look wonderful on you.' Irene beamed gratefully. 'Who sent them?' Helen added curiously. Panic flushed through Irene. She had lied to Helen about spending time with Charles, so how was she going to explain this?

'Oh, I've been saving up all my wages and thought I would treat myself,' she lied, hoping Helen wouldn't notice the redness rising up her neck. 'It seemed easier than sending for my nice clothes from London,' she added. Irene waited nervously as Helen looked her up and down suspiciously.

'Well, you can hang them in my wardrobe to keep them looking good,' Helen offered at last before making her way back down the stairs. Irene undressed carefully and got back into her uniform. It felt so cumbersome compared to the delicate materials she had just been wearing.

Irene was relieved that Helen seemed to have believed her story about the dresses, as she was certain she wouldn't approve of her relationship with Charles. Irene found herself smirking at the word. Was that what this was now? She supposed it was. She was spending all her free time with the man, and he'd treated her to these wonderful outfits. When she looked in the mirror to make sure her uniform was presentable, she realised she was grinning like the Cheshire Cat.

Back out on patrol, Irene dropped into the factory to thank Charles.

'They're all so beautiful,' she gushed, 'and they fit perfectly – even the shoes!'

'That's good to hear,' he smiled. 'I'll let Mildred know she picked well.'

The remark knocked the wind right out of Irene's sails. The lovely mental image she'd built of him taking his time to picture her in each of the outfits shattered into a thousand pieces. 'I thought . . . I thought you had picked them out?' she said quietly,

'Don't be silly, dear,' he laughed lightly. Then he looked up and saw the hurt expression on her face. 'Oh, come on now. You didn't really think I had the time to traipse out to a ladies' clothes shop and go through the pattern books, did you? Irene, you know how busy I am. This factory doesn't run itself.'

'I just, I thought . . . I thought you wanted to spoil me,' she whispered.

'And do you not feel spoiled?' he asked, rather firmly now.

Irene suddenly felt very ungrateful again. Charles had clearly spent a lot of money on the dresses. What did it matter if he hadn't picked them himself?

'I'm sorry,' she whispered awkwardly.

'I can't wait to see you in them,' he said, sounding encouraging again now. 'What lovely surprises I have in store for me, hmm?'

Irene smiled and nodded her agreement. But she couldn't help but feel sad that he hadn't gone to any effort, had just thrown money at the situation.

That evening, Irene decided to head back to Oxford Street to see if she could have a word with Mr Glover's neighbour. When she got to the front door there was no doubt in her mind about what was going on inside. She could hear howling – of what she hoped was pleasure – from where she stood on the doorstep. Looking around her, she couldn't believe that none of the other neighbours had reported what was going on. *Maybe they're all a bit shy*, she thought to herself. She found lots of people felt extremely uncomfortable talking about anything intimate, which she could completely understand.

After knocking a few times and getting no reply, she decided to assert her authority. She rapped loudly on the door with her fist and shouted 'Police! Open up!' at the top of her voice. The noises stopped abruptly, and there was the usual back and forth of hushed voices followed by shuffling and doors opening and closing. Eventually, a bedraggled-looking woman flung open the door wrapped in a tatty dressing gown.

'What can I do for you, officer?' she asked breezily. Irene had to admire her brazenness.

'Do you mind if I step in?' Irene asked.

'I'd rather you didn't,' the woman laughed. Irene heard the unmistakable sound of a man's cough come from a room behind her.

'Is your husband home?' Irene asked casually.

'Something like that,' the woman smirked.

With all the ups and downs her day had already held, Irene was not in the mood for playing games, and she could see that the woman's attitude was a front. 'I'll give you thirty seconds to leave before I get your sergeant down here to haul you back to camp, soldier!' she yelled into the house. Then she took a step back and smirked to herself as a door behind the woman opened and a soldier walked out sheepishly. 'On your way – I'm not interested in you,' Irene said with a sigh before the man scarpered.

The woman looked fearful now, so Irene acted quickly to reassure her.

'I'm not here to have you arrested,' she said kindly. 'I understand that you probably don't have much choice but to entertain men in this way. I just want to make sure you're safe.' The woman's face flushed with relief and she stepped aside to let Irene in. After shuffling off to put on some clothes, she joined Irene in the sitting room where they sat together on the sofa. She introduced herself properly as Jane, and apologised for being rude. Then she fell silent, clearly at a loss as to how to proceed.

'You don't have to explain to me what led you to living in this way,' Irene assured her. 'But if you really do have no other choice then you need to be more careful about how you conduct yourself.' The woman looked confused. 'I could hear what you were up to from the street, and at least one of your neighbours is on to you. Why the other side hasn't reported you I don't understand.'

The woman had the decency to look embarrassed. 'Paul's just jealous I won't let him have a go,' she said, trying on her bravado again. 'And Mrs White next door is deaf as a doorpost.'

'Nevertheless, I've told Mr Glover I'll see to it he's no longer disturbed. If you carry on and he goes to one of my colleagues, they won't treat you as kindly. And anyone walking past while you're at it could report you, too.'

Jane looked sheepish again. 'I've got to keep this roof over my head,' she muttered. 'There's no jobs left around here. What else am I supposed to do?'

All of Irene's stressing about wearing an old dress to meet Charles suddenly made her feel very foolish. At least she had a home, and money coming in to help her family. She couldn't imagine what it would feel like to be so desperate to survive that she had to sell her body to do so. And she had been worried about appearances! But the thought of clothes gave Irene an idea.

'Are you any good at mending garments?' she asked hopefully.

'My mam brought me up right so of course I am,' Jane said proudly.

'Perfect,' Irene beamed. 'Get yourself down to Middlemore Mission Room in the morning. I'm sure they'll be grateful for an extra pair of hands, and you can help the soldiers in a different way – a way that won't put you on the wrong side of the law.' She wasn't entirely sure they needed any extra help, but it was the best solution she could think of right now. She could pop in there herself before Jane and put in a good word for her.

'What's the pay like?' Jane asked suspiciously. Irene sighed.

'I don't imagine it will be as good as what you're making now, but wouldn't it be great to earn a living without having to degrade yourself and constantly look over your shoulder?' Jane looked thoughtful.

'You might have to make a few sacrifices to make ends meet, but you wouldn't be doing anything that could get you into trouble with the police. And you don't want to pick up anything from the soldiers, do you? It's only a matter of time – and then your income will dry up altogether.' Jane looked horrified at the thought, and Irene felt hopeful she had made a breakthrough. But then Jane grew serious again.

'I might not be careful when it comes to the noise, and I can work on that, but I'm careful when it comes to disease,' she said matter-of-factly. 'I keep myself safe,' she added. Irene wasn't entirely sure how that was possible, but she decided not to ask for details. 'I appreciate you trying to help and all, but the truth is that I enjoy what I do – as hard as that might be for you to understand,' Jane explained.

'But . . . it means having to do such . . . horrible things,' Irene stuttered, shocked at the revelation.

'Oh, it's not so bad,' Jane laughed lightly, waving Irene's reaction away with her hand. 'I'm my own boss,' she declared proudly. 'I don't have to get up to no good with anybody I don't want to. I can go out and take my pick around here and bring anyone I take a fancy to home with me where it's warm and safe. I actually quite enjoy making the soldiers a little happier at such a tough time. And it just so happens that I enjoy sex.'

Irene was silent, unable to think of anything to say, and Jane continued, 'I can do it whenever it suits me. And most importantly of all, it means I don't have to depend on a man to keep a roof over my head. My money – which I make a lot of, might I add – is my own so if I don't feel up to it then I can take a couple of nights off and get back to it when I'm feeling better.'

Irene asked for a glass of water so she could have some time to get her head around everything Jane had just told her. She had always assumed all prostitutes did what they did because they had no other choice, that it was a last resort to keep money coming in to keep them alive. But Jane had taken everything she thought she knew about street women and flipped it upside down. Far from being forced into this way of life, she seemed to be in full control and empowered by what she was doing. She even enjoyed the sex!

Irene had never thought about it like that, but she could quite clearly see the other side now. Although she knew most women who resorted to sex work wouldn't choose that way of life, it was almost comforting to know that some were happy with it.

Jane returned with a glass of water and Irene took a sip while she decided how to proceed.

'I've never met anyone who enjoys this . . . what you . . .do,' Irene told her finally.

'What I do?' Jane asked, laughing. 'Come on, dear. It's a job like any other, it's just that folk round here don't like to admit that men need a little bit of help every now and then to let off steam and relieve the pressures they're going through. And if a woman is happy helping them with that, then where's the harm?'

It was a risky step for Irene to turn a blind eye, but she really could see where Jane was coming from. Jane seemed to have thought of everything and was carrying out her work responsibly. And she clearly wasn't about to give up her way of life whether Irene reported her to Helen or not.

'Well, as long as you keep it discreet and you stop drawing attention to yourself with all the noise, I'm happy to keep this to myself,' Irene sighed, hoping that she wouldn't end up regretting the decision. 'It's been eye-opening talking to you, Jane,' she added as she got up to leave. 'Please, keep being safe – and start being quiet!' she joked as Jane saw her out with a smile and a wave.

# 20

When Irene finally got another night off a week later, she couldn't wait to let Charles know. She was excited to show him the first of her new dresses. He had been right yet again; the fact he didn't know what they looked like added to the thrill of the reveal. She thought back to her reaction when she'd learned he hadn't picked the dresses himself and felt bad for expecting so much from him.

'I can't wait for our dinner together,' he beamed when she dropped into the factory to tell him the good news. 'I'll make sure we have a table waiting for us at the Cleveland Hotel. You can meet me there at seven o'clock.' He gave her a kiss before striding off with a spring in his step. Irene felt happy for the rest of the day. Despite the occasional insensitive comment – and what man didn't make those from time to time? – she couldn't believe just how good Charles could make her feel.

After much dithering, she decided on the brown dress for dinner. Everyone else was out when she got herself ready, so she took some time to admire her reflection in the full-length mirror in Helen and Ruby's room. She almost didn't recognise the woman in her reflection. She felt like a new person, and she knew that was all down to Charles.

A wave of guilt swept over her, then. She knew so much about Charles and he was doing so much for her, yet she was keeping such a big part of her life from him. He had even told her about his wife! She decided it was high time to tell him about her years in the children's home. Honesty was the least she owed him. And she knew now that things like that didn't bother him. She'd been so worried about wearing her old dress to dinner, but it wasn't the fact she didn't have anything better to wear that had upset him. The more she thought about it, the more confident she was about Charles accepting her – poverty and all.

At the restaurant, Irene's heart skipped a beat when the waitress showed her to a table where Charles was waiting. His face came alive when he looked up and saw her walking towards him.

'You're a complete vision,' he gasped as he stood to greet her with a tender kiss. Wrapping his arm around her waist, he pulled her in close and raised her hand so he could kiss the back of it. It was such an intimate move, it sent shivers down Irene's spine. As Charles pulled out a chair for her, she tried to regain her composure, but he'd completely flustered her. 'You look beautiful, I'm so lucky to be dining with you,' he said.

Irene couldn't have asked for a better evening. The two of them enjoyed some wonderful conversation and she was feeling so comfortable as they finished their meals that she started gearing up to make her confession. When Charles started talking about his walk to the restaurant, she decided to hold fire until he had finished his story.

'On my way here, a little girl came out of nowhere just as I was approaching the hotel and asked me for money.'

'Poor thing,' Irene whispered, placing her hand to her heart as she thought about how destitute the child must have been to be begging on the streets. She wondered if they might be able to find her on the way home and offer her some more help. She thought back to Billy and how kind and under-standing Charles had been after learning what had led him to swipe his wallet and she felt a swell of pride at how she knew he would have helped this youngster, too.

'I know!' Charles cried. 'I felt so uncomfortable that I almost didn't know where to look. I just ignored her and walked on past. It was frightfully awkward.'

Irene was so stupefied by his comments she was rendered speechless. Her 'poor thing' remark had been aimed at the child – not Charles! Was he playing a joke on her? She stared at him for a few moments, waiting for him to break into a laugh and admit that of course he had handed her some loose change.

'I mean, I know she can't help being poor and I sympathise, I really do. But there's a time and a place, and that was neither,' he said dismissively before going back to his food.

Irene stopped eating herself and sat, frozen, as she tried to take in his words.

'I'm having a rather wonderful evening with you, Irene,' Charles said suddenly, putting down his cutlery to place a hand over hers.

She smiled nervously. She was still trying to work out how his cruel comments about the beggar matched up to the man she had met on that first day, who had been so sympathetic and understanding of Billy's plight.

'I'm so lucky to have someone like you dining with me,' Charles added.

Irene smiled at the compliment, but it could not entirely erase the memory of what he had said about the beggar girl. She coughed lightly to try and get rid of the lump in her throat so that she could speak again. There was no question of her telling Charles about her time in the children's home now.

It broke her heart that Charles felt this way about people who didn't have as much money or privilege as himself. As she watched him talk on, nodding and smiling here and there to make him think she was listening, she struggled to understand how she could feel so strongly about someone who had those views. But, she reasoned with herself, he had been brought up to wealth and plenty – how could he be expected to understand? Besides, there was so much good in him. And she wasn't exactly a saint herself – she had been lying to him for all this time, after all.

Before Irene knew it, the evening was over. As Charles kissed her goodbye, his comments about the little beggar girl crept back into her head, but she refused to let them stay there. If she wanted a future with this man, maybe that would just have to mean forgetting her past altogether – which, to be honest, wasn't such a terrible thought. She did her best to block it out most of the time anyway.

The next few days felt like one long patrol. Irene seemed to be granted hardly any time off and she was exhausted by the time she set out on public-house duty one evening. She had grabbed her hat and coat and rushed out of the front door before Helen had even finished telling her the pubs were her responsibility for the night. She wanted to get out and started before Helen had a chance to instruct anyone else to go with her.

Irene decided to start off in Market Place, and as she stepped into the Royal Oak, she found that the narrow bar area was relatively quiet. Looking around, she could only see locals and no soldiers. But through a brief chat with the landlord, she learned that a couple of men in army uniforms had recently left with a woman in tow. Concerned for the lady, Irene decided to head straight out and try and find the group. But as she made her way back through the bar, she noticed a couple of older gentlemen sitting in the corner talking rather animatedly. Irene paused briefly to check if their conversation was friendly. They seemed jovial enough, so she continued on her way. But just as she went to open the door, one of the men stood up so abruptly that the glasses on the table crashed to the floor.

'What are you on about, Bill?' he yelled. The whole pub fell silent and everyone turned to look at the men.

'I've had just about enough of your temper,' the other man – who was still sitting in his seat, hissed through gritted teeth. 'And you can buy me another drink.'

'The Devil I will, Bill!' his companion shouted. At this, Bill got to his feet too. Irene leapt forward and stepped between them just as Bill was making his way around the small table to grab for his drinking partner.

Irene hurried over to them. 'Gentlemen,' she said calmly, holding an arm out towards each man to keep them at a distance. 'There's no need to get physical.'

'Oh, sorry, love. I didn't see you there,' Bill said sheepishly as he took a step back. Irene often found men were more likely to back away from a confrontation once they saw her in her uniform – especially older gentlemen. Both men sat back down. Irene was just about to bid them farewell and get on her way when the second man muttered something under his breath.

'That's it, Ron!' Bill roared, getting to his feet again and lunging across the table at his friend. Irene dived forward, grabbed his hand and pulled him away just before his fist connected with Ron's face. Bill gave Irene no resistance, but she kept a firm grip on his wrist and turned him away from Ron.

'Why don't we take a walk outside and get some fresh air before I have to get the lads from the station involved?' Irene said calmly and quietly into Bill's ear. He gave a tiny nod and she was just about to loosen her grip a little and guide him out when she felt him being ripped from her grasp violently.

Suspecting that Ron had gathered his composure and come after his pal, she turned around and braced herself to launch into some ju-jitsu. But it wasn't Ron who had pulled Bill away from her – it was Charles.

# 21

Irene stared at Charles, bemused, trying to work out where he had come from. And why he had stepped in when she had everything under control? Glancing around the pub, she cringed as she realised how many eyes were on her. It would do her reputation as a policewoman no good at all if all these people thought she needed rescuing from two elderly gentleman having crossed words.

Before she could say anything, Charles had frogmarched the poor old man out of the door. Irene rushed out after them.

'What are you doing?' she hissed outside in the street.

'What do you mean?' Charles said. The proud look he had been wearing was replaced by confusion. 'I just saved you from losing control of that situation in front of the whole pub,' he said, sounding hurt. 'You could at least show me some gratitude.'

'But I didn't *need* any help. Bill was about to leave peacefully with me,' Irene replied, trying to keep her frustration in check.

'On your way,' Charles spat at the old man, shoving him off down the street. Bill gave Irene a slight nod and a little smile and scurried off. She was even more embarrassed now.

'Irene, I don't think you understand what was going on there,' Charles said, his voice dripping with concern. He stepped forward to push a stray piece of hair behind her ear. 'This is one of the reasons I worry so much about you patrolling around this town on your own.'

'But I had that situation under control,' Irene insisted. She was getting annoyed now – it was like he was refusing to listen to her.

Charles smiled sympathetically. 'You turned your back to that other chap. You put yourself in an extremely vulnerable position,' he explained. 'You seem to be forgetting how many years I've been frequenting the pubs in this town, my dear. I know how these situations escalate. Tell me, had you ever set foot in a pub before you joined the WPS?'

'Well no, but—'

'Exactly,' Charles said, cutting her off gently but firmly.

'But I've dealt with enough arguments like that to know what I'm doing. And I know enough ju-jitsu from my training to protect myself,' Irene argued. She went over it in her head again: Ron had been sitting in his seat when Charles dragged Bill away. He'd been no threat at all.

'And where were all these skills when Mary attacked you?' Charles asked.

'That was different,' she protested. But an increasingly familiar feeling of self-doubt was creeping over her already.

'Was it?' he said, raising his eyebrows. Irene felt some of the fight going out of her. She had judged the situation with Mary terribly and left herself vulnerable. She had been so close to getting Bill out of the pub calmly just now, though. Hadn't she? She felt like she was going mad.

'You've never even had a proper drink,' Charles sighed. 'You don't understand how people act when they're under the influence. I've had my bad experiences with alcohol, and it means I can judge these situations a lot better than you can.'

Irene couldn't argue with that. Alcohol had never really interested her. She'd never had enough money to fritter away on it, for a start. And the few times she'd tried it she had baulked at the taste. Charles knew this about her. She had always stuck to water during their dinners even though he insisted she try some wine every time. Maybe he was right: it was possible he had picked up on something in the pub that she'd missed because she didn't understand how people acted when they'd had too much to drink. Also, she had to admit that she was exhausted after the last few days of patrolling. Maybe she wasn't as on the ball as she had thought.

'I suppose you're right,' Irene said hesitantly. She forced herself to look into his face, despite the blush that she could feel creeping up her neck. 'I'm sorry,' she whispered.

Charles pulled her in for a hug and after a few moments something struck her. 'By the way, what were you doing in there?' she asked, pulling her head back to look up at him. She knew he would never drink in a pub like that because he had a membership at an exclusive club.

'Oh, I was passing on my way to the George when I spotted you through the window,' he explained. 'I decided to pop in and say hello and I walked in at just the right time. Didn't I?'

Irene forced herself to smile. 'Yes, you did,' she said, falling into his embrace again. She was so lucky to have someone like Charles looking out for her. She felt so safe in his presence. And if the price of that was dealing with him being a little overprotective sometimes, so what? And now she'd had time to consider it all, she told herself she was glad he'd stepped in and helped her back there. She might have felt embarrassed at being saved by him, but the alternative could have been a lot worse.

A few weeks later, Irene was lying on her bed and thinking about the fact that she had now been in Grantham for exactly two months. She couldn't believe how much had changed in her life in that short time. Life wasn't perfect, of course, but she was being paid to do a job she loved, had met a lovely man, and still had Maggie and Annie if she needed them. She smiled up at the ceiling and took a moment to thank God for her good fortune.

After getting herself up and dressed, she remembered the letter Ruby had brought up for her. Examining the hand-writing, she knew it was from her aunt, and was excited to hear what a difference the money she had sent was making to Henry's illness. She didn't have time to read it before heading downstairs for breakfast, so she took it with her to read at the table.

But as soon as she started reading, she knew it was not good news. Despite the money she had been sending her aunt Ruth for nutritious food, her cousin's condition was deterio-rating. She found herself shaking as she learned the news in front of her colleagues. As usual, the only conversation that morning had been coming from Helen and as she instructed everyone on their duties for the day, Irene burst into tears. She hated to show any weakness, especially in front of Mary, but she wasn't able to keep it in. Helen leapt up and drew her into her arms. Before Irene knew it, they were standing in the privacy of the living room and Helen was reading Ruth's heartbreaking letter.

'Take the morning off and go and tell Charles,' Helen instructed. 'He won't hesitate to help.'

Irene looked up at her in bewilderment.

'I haven't said anything, but I've been aware of what's been going on this last month or so,' Helen said. 'And your police wages wouldn't have stretched to even one of those lovely dresses.' Her tone wasn't quite disapproving, but it wasn't warm either. Irene felt shame flushing through her veins as she realised she had been caught out in her lies. She remem-bered the suspicious look Helen had given when she had spun the tale and felt embarrassed. 'I'm not your mother, so you weren't obliged to heed my warning about the man. And you're a grown woman so you can make your own choices. Now I know more about your family situation, it seems this union with him may well work in your favour.'

Irene felt uncomfortable at the suggestion she might take advantage of Charles's wealth. Asking him for help had never even crossed her mind. They hadn't been together for long and she was so used to fending for herself. He may have been happy to kit her out with pretty dresses, but this was on a whole other level. What would he think of her if she turned up at the factory, cap in hand? Especially after telling him so emphatically that she didn't want to be a kept woman? Then there was the risk that he would reject her altogether once he found out the truth about her background. She had already decided against confessing all to him for fear of him ending their relationship, but as terrible images of Henry suffering swam around her head, Irene realised she would have to take the gamble and tell him the truth. Charles was her only hope of saving her lovely, innocent cousin, so she had to at least try. She thanked Helen and went upstairs to get changed.

She knew Charles would be at the factory all day, so she sought him out in his office, where thankfully he was alone.

'I thought you were on patrol this morning,' he said as he smiled and got to his feet to greet her. She was constantly flattered by his obvious pleasure at seeing her. Irene looked out through the office window at the munitions workers – mostly women – below. There was a comforting rhythm to the way they worked that soothed her. 'Why are you upset?' Charles asked, putting his arm around her shoulder and leading her to the spare chair across from his own at his desk. She realised she had been staring at the workers in a daze, with tears welling in her eyes. Irene wasn't sure how to ask for Charles's help. This wasn't something she was used to doing. Instead, as she had done with Helen, she handed him the letter. He read it quickly and shook his head slowly.

'This is your aunt Ruth?' he asked.

Irene nodded, wiping the tears from her face and sniffing. She had told Charles about Ruth and her cousins, although of course she hadn't gone into details about their living conditions or the fact that she was sending them her pay. Irene could feel her whole body shaking with nerves. She was terrified Charles was going to throw her out of his office – and out of his life.

'Well, I can see from the address why the poor chap's ill,' he tutted. Shame coursed through Irene. The game was up. Now Charles knew how poor she and her whole family were, he would cast her aside – embarrassed at having been taken for a fool by a pauper. She braced herself. But when she looked up again, Charles was on the phone.

'I have a family I need to get out of the slums. Immediately. The youngest has consumption.' He seemed to stare straight through Irene as the person on the other end of the phone spoke. She fiddled nervously with her fingers in her lap. 'Mmm hmm. Right. Yes, I've heard Switzerland is dealing with it well,' he added, writing down some notes. Then he read out Ruth's address before hanging up the phone. 'They'll be out of that place by the end of the day. I can't believe you didn't tell me what was going on,' he said. He looked livid and Irene wasn't sure what to do.

'I . . .I'm sorry,' she whispered. Charles sighed heavily. Irene felt sick to her stomach at the thought that their relationship was over.

'I could have stopped that poor boy's suffering a lot sooner. I thought we were honest with each other,' he said. He was speaking so softly that she struggled to hear him properly.

'But I didn't think you'd want anything to do with me if you knew the truth,' she spluttered through sobs. 'I've been sending Ruth my pay but it's not nearly enough. I was paid again last week but hadn't got around to sending it on and now I feel just terrible.'

After a tense pause, Charles rushed over and pulled her to her feet. 'I'm not angry with you, you silly thing,' he said, tucking a piece of her hair gently behind her ear. 'I'm furious because someone you care about is suffering, and if I'd known the situation sooner, I could have stepped in to help before things got this bad. The thought of you struggling on your own with this devastates me.'

He paused for a moment, closing his eyes and taking a deep breath. Then his gaze was back on her, those beautiful brown eyes fixed on her own and giving her goosebumps yet again. 'Henry will be fine. I'll see to it that he's sent to a sanatorium in Switzerland. That's where they're getting the best results. And as you heard, I've arranged new accommodation for your aunt and the rest of her children. I can't have them staying in a slum any longer and getting struck down, too. You keep hold of your pay.'

Irene was lost for words. Those were things she would never have dreamed of being able to provide for her family. He was going to save Henry's life. She had come to Charles looking for help, but she hadn't been expecting anything on this scale.

'But . . .why would you do that for them?' she asked quietly.

'Irene, I'm doing it for *you*,' he said, taking both her hands in his. 'I know we've not known each other for long, but I feel like you're a part of me already. I can't stand to see you upset. Especially not when I have the means to put your suffering to an end. Your family feels like my own, even though I haven't met them. I can't stand by and let them suffer.'

Irene couldn't quite believe he was being so generous. Moments ago, she had been panicking that he was about to cast her out of his life, and now this.

'But I lied about my background and I have no money and I grew up in a children's home and—' she started.

He cut her off with a laugh that lit up his eyes and made him look more handsome than ever. 'I've enough money for us both! And do you not think I guessed something was off when you kept wearing those awful dresses?'

Irene was startled briefly by the cruel way he had referred to her clothes but then Charles turned serious again and she found herself drowning in the deep pools of his eyes. 'I've loved spending time with you over the last couple of months – you're like no woman I've ever met before. Knowing all of this just makes me love you *more*. We'll just need to keep the real truth of your childhood between us, of course, for my reputation.'

Irene barely heard the last sentence as she was too fixated on the word 'love'. She goggled at him and Charles laughed gently.

'Yes, I know it hasn't been long,' he sighed. 'But I do love you, Irene Wilson.'

'I don't know what to say,' she stuttered.

'You don't have to say anything,' he assured her. 'I know it's soon, but when you get to my age you learn how to spot these things a lot quicker. I've been through enough in my lifetime to know when something is real. And this is very real, I promise you.'

Irene's only other romantic relationship had been with Frank. That had felt like love at the time, but now in the face of her feelings for Charles, she felt it couldn't have been. But what if she was wrong again? How would she know for sure? Irene was overwhelmed with relief and gratitude that Charles had accepted her for who she was. Maybe what she felt for him *was* love. It was definitely the strongest feeling she had ever experienced. She looked into Charles's eyes again and was puzzled to see he looked worried. Then she realised with a start that she had been so engrossed in her thoughts that she'd left his remarks hanging in the air without responding. She was struck by how upset it made her to see him looking anything but his normal, confident self. She knew in that moment that she would do anything to make him happy – just as she knew he would for her. And if *that* wasn't love, she didn't know what was.

'I love you too,' she whispered.

Charles's eyes glistened, and a wave of emotions like she had never experienced washed over her. She wanted to bottle this feeling up and keep it forever.

'You don't know how good it makes me feel to hear that,' Charles said, then he leaned in to kiss her. The moment seemed to stretch on forever, and Irene was in no rush to end it. But eventually Charles pulled away.

'I'll make all the arrangements for your family,' he beamed. 'And maybe we can even take a little trip to Sheffield to see them soon.'

Irene was overcome. 'How can I ever repay you?' she whispered.

'There is one way,' he said. Charles took her hands in his once more and got down on one knee. He looked up at her confidently, holding her eyes with his so that she could not look away. 'I have spent years searching for the right woman to spend my life with,' he said. 'I know it's fast, but now I've found you I don't want to waste any more time. Irene Wilson, will you marry me?' His expression had been serious the whole time he was talking but now he'd finished he smiled up at her and Irene felt the familiar flip of her belly as the grin took over his whole face and lit up his eyes.

Panic surged through Irene's whole body. Surely, he wasn't serious? They had only just said 'I love you' for the first time! He was right – this was fast. It was certainly moving too quickly for her. Annie and Maggie hadn't even met him yet. But he was going to save Henry's life and make things better for the rest of her family. How could she say no?

But then Charles's previous comments about the beggar girl flashed into her mind, and she wondered if he fully understood just how poverty-stricken her family was. Then she remembered the remark he had made about her 'awful' dresses – and all the other little ways he had undermined her over the last few weeks. Irene's heart sunk. How could he really love her if he felt those things?

And yet here he was, professing such strong feelings for her and asking her to be his wife. He had to love her if he was willing to take such a big step with her – what other reason could he have? And she had just said she loved him. She couldn't let the opportunity to spend the rest of her life with this man go. She would have to push her niggles to the side and take him at his word. After all, love was a journey – she couldn't expect it to be perfect straight away.

Charles had been her saviour through these last weeks and he made her feel like no one had done before. And now he was doing so much for not just her but for her family. As she thought of the difference he would make to their lives, her heart swelled.

'Yes,' she said quietly. 'Yes, I will marry you.'

Charles jumped to his feet and wrapped his arms around her. Then he pulled her over to the door and out on to the balcony overlooking all the workers.

'This wonderful woman has just agreed to be my wife!' he yelled victoriously over all the noise of the machinery and chatter. Everyone stopped and looked up at them. 'We're getting married!' he shouted, louder this time.

The room broke into polite applause and Irene felt a stirring of disquiet once more. Had she been right to accept his proposal so quickly? Maybe she should have asked for time to think about it. But it wasn't as though she had anyone to discuss it with: Helen had been against Charles from the start so she wouldn't get a balanced view from her; she wasn't talking to Ruby and Mary; and Maggie and Annie had been too busy to so much as write to her since she had started courting him.

She smiled through her doubts. Charles was the only person she could rely on at the moment. Irene was on her own without him, but with him as her husband she knew that her family would be safe and that she wouldn't feel so alone. That meant the world to her right now. She decided she had definitely made the right decision.

But she couldn't shake the nagging feeling that, at such an important moment in her life, she should be feeling happier.

# 22

News of Charles and Irene's engagement spread like wildfire throughout Grantham. Following his grand declaration, people were congratulating her on the street before she even made it back home. She found herself swept up in the excitement of it all, and she quickly put her reservations to one side.

'I hear congratulations are in order,' Mary said that evening over supper. It was the most she had spoken to Irene since their altercation, and Irene was stunned into silence.

'I'm really happy for you,' Ruby smiled. Her words sounded genuine and Irene couldn't help but smile back her thanks. She also nodded gratefully at Mary.

'I didn't realise you were courting someone so fancy,' Mary remarked. 'I mean, I thought whoever it was must be wealthy when those dresses arrived, but *Charles Murphy*.' She was raising her eyebrows the way she had done when the dresses had turned up on her bed. 'And to think I was there when it all began,' she laughed. Irene realised Mary was only thawing to her now she was marrying up. It made her angry, but she saw an opportunity to get Mary on her side, so she talked her through their whirlwind romance after that first meeting.

'I hope you'll stay on with us for as long as possible,' Helen said once Irene had finished her story.

'Oh, I have no intention of leaving the WPS,' Irene said cheerily.

'Quite right,' Mary remarked. 'A woman can work and still keep her marriage going – look at me and John.'

Helen's expression stayed serious. 'John's off fighting, and you're both young,' she argued. 'Charles is a lot older than Irene – he's looking for a different kind of marriage.'

'I only said yes today,' Irene replied, trying to laugh off her comments despite the growing sense of unease she felt. 'I don't even have a ring! And I'm not sure we'll be setting a wedding date just yet. There's no rush, after all. We can work all of that out. But I don't think Charles will have a problem with me continuing with the WPS. He's been nothing but supportive,' she said, ignoring the niggling little voice in the back of her brain that was trying to remind her what he said the night of her fight with Mary, and again after the fiasco with the bike.

Helen smiled but she didn't look convinced, and Irene changed the subject. She knew this was the best thing for her family – and for her, of course. After all, she was in love with Charles and he had already been more of a support to her than anyone else she knew.

Ruby stayed silent, but she linked arms with her that night as they all headed out on their separate patrols. 'I'm really excited for you,' she said as the two of them made their way along Rutland Street on the way to Market Place.

'Thank you,' Irene smiled, not looking at her. She was still happy to be civil with Ruby, but she knew they could never have a proper friendship. Irene couldn't be friends with someone if she couldn't trust them to look out for her as she would for them. No, they were better off as colleagues, and colleagues only. Even that brought up its own issues, so she was happy Helen had seemed to have decided that she was doing a better job patrolling on her own most of the time. What was the point in having Ruby with her as backup if she would just run away at the first sign of trouble?

'I saw the dresses Charles bought you in our wardrobe,

they're beautiful,' Ruby offered meekly. Irene could see she was really making an effort, and she did appreciate it.

'Thank you. He treats me very well,' Irene blushed. 'Even after I told him about my poor background,' she added.

'It must be a relief not to have to pretend any more,' Ruby smiled. Irene felt sad that they couldn't be friends – this girl knew so much about her already and understood things about her she'd never dream of telling anyone else. But she had to remain firm. She knew from watching her parents' relationship fall apart that if you let someone back in after they betray you then you live to regret it. She had to stay strong.

When she realised Irene wasn't going to yield, Ruby went off to take a look around some of the town's pubs, while Irene focused on the alleys and side streets. Helen and Mary were sticking together and doing a sweep of the fields between the town and Belton Park.

As she made her way through Market Place, Irene noticed a scraggy-looking woman talking to a soldier. She immediately switched on to high-alert, and then scolded herself for being so judgemental. She knew Mary would have jumped straight in and accused the couple of all sorts as soon as she'd seen them. But they could well have just been having a friendly natter and Irene wasn't comfortable running around the town accusing everybody who looked a little destitute of being up to no good.

But as she dipped into a shop doorway to stay out of view, she saw the woman rub the man's groin area and then grab his hand. She led him around the Conduit, a big stone monument that had provided the first water supply to the town when it was built in the fourteenth century, and out of sight. Irene sighed. She had known her instincts would be correct, but she still felt like holding back had been the correct thing to do. If she stopped giving people the benefit of the doubt then she would end up just as bad as Mary. 'Or Charles,' the small voice whispered in her head, but she pushed it away.

Irene waited a couple of minutes before walking across the square and around the other side of the Conduit. When she laid eyes on the couple again, they were oblivious to her presence. The woman already had the soldier's khaki trousers around his ankles and was getting to work on his underwear when Irene coughed dramatically to let them know they had company.

The woman jumped out of her skin and looked around at Irene in horror. As she started muttering apologies, the man casually pulled his trousers back up and started walking away. Irene suspected he thought he could just breeze off into the night and leave the woman to deal with the consequences, seeing as soldiers never got into any trouble with civilian police for these types of liaison. She was getting tired of this attitude from men.

'I'm keeping my eye on you!' she shouted after him. 'And you can tell your mates to keep it clean, too!'

He didn't even react, which made Irene's blood boil further. She turned around to speak to the woman, just in time to spot her running off in the opposite direction.

With a frustrated yelp, Irene charged after her, and it didn't take her long to catch her up. She was extremely fit these days from the hours and hours of walking. Irene grabbed her arm and pulled her round to face her.

'Please, miss. I didn't mean no harm. Please don't arrest me – my husband will kill me!'

Irene's words died in her throat. She was shocked to learn the woman was married. Most of the prostitutes she had come across were estranged from their families because of what they did, or they hadn't had a family to begin with. She'd assumed that was the case with this woman, especially judging from her thin, hollow face, knotty hair and skinny frame. She had been able to feel bone when she'd grabbed her arm.

'He makes me do it – my husband, I mean,' the woman

whispered. 'He'll beat me if I get caught. Please, let me go and I promise I won't do it again. I'll find some money another way.'

Irene felt overcome with sympathy for her. Her story was too close to home. 'But . . . what will he do if you return home with nothing?' she asked her.

The woman started shaking, and Irene knew the answer. She knew exactly how this story went.

'I'm not having that,' Irene said firmly. 'Come with me,' she added as she started pulling the woman along the street.

'No, please don't arrest me!' she cried, clawing at Irene's hand. Irene yanked her round to face her, and the woman winced.

'Sorry,' Irene said quietly. 'I didn't mean to hurt you.' She loosened her grip before explaining. 'I know what kind of man your husband is.' The woman looked away. 'I know he'll hurt you if you return home with no money for him.'

When the woman still refused to meet Irene's eye, she knew she was right. 'I'm not going to arrest you. I'm going to help you. But you need to trust me.'

The woman looked at her again now and nodded slowly. They walked in silence to St Wulfram's Church, where Irene guided the woman to a secluded spot. 'Will you wait here for me?' she asked. When she nodded, looking scared, Irene assured her again that she wasn't in trouble. 'I'm Irene, by the way,' she told her.

'My name's Stella,' the woman replied quietly.

'It's nice to meet you, Stella,' Irene said. 'Now, please, wait here and I promise you'll be grateful you did when I get back. I won't be long.'

Irene ran all the way to Rutland Street and raced up the stairs when she got there. She pulled out the envelope containing the pay that Helen had handed her the previous morning. Charles had told her to keep it for herself, but she couldn't stand back and send Stella off for a beating when she had cash under her bed that could save her from it. She had all the dresses she needed from Charles, and she was working all the time so she would never get around to spending it anyway. She took out a wodge of notes and stuffed them inside her jacket pocket.

Back at the church, she was relieved to see Stella had waited for her.

'Is this enough?' she gasped, handing her the cash and clutching the stitch at her side.

'My goodness,' Stella whispered. 'I can't take this.'

'You can and you will,' Irene said firmly, her breathing returning to normal. 'But you need to promise me you'll keep off the streets for as long as that will allow. Try and find some work?'

Stella took the money, but she laughed to herself. 'You don't think I've tried?' she tutted. The two of them sat down on the grass in the graveyard and Stella told Irene how she had been working as a barmaid when her husband lost his job. They were struggling to make ends meet, and one night she decided that the two of them would have to go without dinner so their son and daughter could eat.

'That didn't go down well with Dave,' Stella sighed. 'He would rather our children went hungry than he did. That's when he started beating me. The very next night a soldier propositioned me while I was working. The money he was talking about – well, it was more than a week's wages! I hated myself for it, but I was so desperate I closed my eyes and got on with it. And the timing was just right – it was like someone had been looking out for me.'

Irene felt sick at the thought of a woman thinking the chance to get paid for sex was a blessing.

'The pub landlord found out and sacked me,' Stella continued. 'I've looked for more work, but word got around about what I'd done to lose my job and now no one around here will touch me. Of course, Dave found out too. I got another black eye for it, but then he decided he liked the money that came with my new line of work. So now he hits me if I *don't* do it. I'm in such a mess,' Stella moaned, her head in her hands.

Irene didn't know what to say. The situation was hopeless. There wasn't anything she could do apart from give Stella some money every now and then to give her a bit of a break. But that wouldn't stop her husband beating her, or making her do unspeakable things with other men. Irene wished she could report Dave for pimping Stella out and beating her black and blue, but she knew he'd get away with it without so much as a fine – she'd seen it happen time and time again. And it would only make things worse for Stella in the end. Irene sighed with frustration.

'My son's picking up work where he can, and my daughter's doing some cleaning at the Angel and Royal,' Stella said with a false cheeriness. 'I only have to do this now when we're really struggling.' That was something, at least, Irene thought to herself. 'I really appreciate your help,' Stella added. Irene smiled in response, trying to hide her sadness. All she could think about when she looked at Stella was her mother. Stella must have been in her thirties, she guessed – around the age Irene's mother had been when she'd lost her.

Irene had a choice: she could get off her high horse and help Stella, or she could do nothing and risk her children losing their own mother and being left to the mercy of their father. She knew what she had to do.

Before they parted, Irene told her about a couple of spots in town where she was confident Stella could get away with her trade when she really had no other choice. During her various patrols with Helen, Ruby and Mary, she had noticed that they never checked the areas she was sharing with her.

'My colleagues won't be as lenient as I've been,' she stressed. 'I know you have no choice and I'm willing to turn a blind eye to keep you safe from your husband, but they won't do the same.' Stella nodded her understanding. 'Please, when you find yourself short and you have to come out and do this again – look for me before you look for a soldier. If I can, I'll give you more money. I don't have a lot but if it saves you having to do this at least once then I'll be happy.'

'Why are you helping me?' Stella asked, suddenly suspicious. 'The other policewomen treat me like I'm dirt. The other day I wasn't even up to anything and one of them – the redhead – she chased me down the street just to shout at me.'

'I'm sorry about them,' Irene said sadly, cursing Mary in her head. 'And it doesn't matter why I'm helping you. Just let me.'

Stella finally smiled and got to her feet. 'I'll look for you first next time,' she promised, before making her way back towards Market Place.

The rest of the evening was relatively quiet. Irene helped a teenage girl, who had obviously had far too much to drink, get home safely. Then she broke up a couple who were kissing passionately down one of the alleys. It was so dark she would have missed them had it not been for the groans of pleasure coming from the man. Irene had been grateful for the lack of light as she'd felt her cheeks flushing crimson when she'd noticed his manhood in the woman's grip.

As it got later, she decided to pop into Charles's for a cup of tea and a chat, as she had often done over the last few weeks. She knew it was naughty, but she loved their late-night talks and when all four of them were out patrolling she didn't see the harm in slipping away for a quick break.

As Irene filled Charles in on her evening, she had to keep stopping to yawn. They were sitting on the sofa in his drawing room and she always felt sleepy once she sunk down into the comfortable cushions. She hadn't exactly been rushed off her feet, but the long hours and excitement of everything happening with Charles over the last few weeks seemed to be catching up to her.

'Don't worry, my love,' Charles soothed as he rubbed her arm affectionately. 'You won't have to worry about working all these long hours soon.'

'Oh, I don't mind it,' Irene said quickly. She sat up abruptly and did her best to look awake and alert. She was keen to squash any feeling he might have that she was after becoming a kept woman. Plus, she loved her WPS work – a fact she thought he ought to be well aware of by now. 'I love patrolling,' she stressed. 'And, up until you stepped in, it had been a relief to be able to help Ruth out properly after all this time. And now I can enjoy spending some of my hard-earned money on myself for once instead of struggling to get by,' she added proudly.

She felt a tinge of guilt at the fact she had just handed most of her latest pay packet over to a stranger and she was grappling over whether she should share that with him when he asked for more information on her background. They had been so swept up in his proposal following her revelation about being poor earlier that day that she hadn't had a chance to go into any more detail.

Irene found herself being honest with Charles about her upbringing, although she left out exactly what had happened with her parents. Being upfront and truthful with him felt refreshing, but she wasn't quite ready to reveal that part of her life to anyone – even if it was the man she had agreed to marry.

Charles seemed shocked when she mentioned the children's home, and she decided he must have missed her mention of it earlier. He looked a little uncomfortable at first, but then he took her hands in his.

'You poor thing,' he said quietly. Irene shrugged uncomfortably. She felt uneasy with people feeling sympathy for her.

'You've been through so much,' Charles added sadly.

'Yes, but I'm all the stronger for it,' Irene replied proudly. She didn't want him feeling sorry for her.

'The sooner we're married, the better,' he declared as he picked up their cups and went to refill them from the teapot on the coffee table.

'Well, there's no rush—' she started before Charles cut in.

'I want you out of that dive on Rutland Street and living the life you should be living here with me. You deserve the best, my love, and that's what I plan to give you once we're married,' he added, pouring steaming tea into their cups.

'But I thought we could wait until the war is over,' Irene offered hopefully. Everything had happened so quickly and she had been counting on some time to get her head around the idea before walking down the aisle. Maybe even a chance to enjoy being engaged.

'And what would be the point in that?' Charles scoffed as he walked back to her with their drinks. 'No. That won't do. Goodness knows how long this bloody business will rage on. I want you safely under this roof as soon as possible.'

Irene had to admit the thought of no longer having to share a bedroom with Mary was rather nice.

'Well, I'm sure they'll allow me to continue with the WPS even though I'm not living with the other recruits,' she mused aloud. Excitement flushed through her as she realised there would be room to have guests when she lived with Charles. Annie and Maggie would be able to visit whenever they wanted. That would certainly help her deal with the sadness of leaving them for good to settle in Grantham. She pushed aside the knowledge that they hadn't written to her in a long time, telling herself they were probably just busy. She looked up and Charles was watching her quizzically.

'Whatever do you mean?' he asked, his voice full of shock. 'Surely, once we're married, you'll be leaving the WPS?'

Irene's heart started pounding. 'I rather hoped to stay on,' she replied.

'But why?' Charles asked, with genuine interest.

'Well, I enjoy patrolling for a start,' Irene said.

'Yes, but you spend all those hours walking the streets and the fields on your own,' Charles replied. 'You've said yourself it's exhausting. I can see you're struggling to keep your eyes open this evening and it's not the first time I've spotted it. It's clearly taking its toll on you. And you know I worry about your safety out there on your own.'

'I'm not always on my own,' Irene argued weakly.

'Oh yes – there's Mary who hates you so much she gave you a black eye, and Ruby who stood back and let her do it. I hardly think they're the kind of colleagues you can rely upon to help you out of a fix. Why on earth would you want to spend any more time with either of them?' Charles sneered. Irene was stuck for a reply – she couldn't deny that he had a point. 'And then there's Helen, who may be nice enough to you, but she clearly doesn't like me,' he said, shaking his head sadly. 'I don't understand why you're so intent on surrounding yourself with these people when you have no need to do so.'

'I've spent all my life struggling for money, barely making enough to live on. I'm finally in a position where I'm earning a decent wage and I can do as I please with it. I don't want to give that up,' Irene tried.

'But you won't need to worry about any of that when you're my wife,' Charles laughed. Irene pulled a face and he quickly changed tack. 'Yes, yes, I know you don't want to be a kept woman. But after all those years of having next to nothing, would it not be nice to have someone to look after you – and your family?'

He had her there: Charles was covering Henry's medical

care and a new home for the rest of her family. In that moment, she realised she was essentially a kept woman already whether she liked it or not.

'I'm trying to make a difference for the women of this town,' Irene said, more strongly now. 'Yes, I agree that my colleagues aren't particularly ideal, but I'm happy to put up with that if it means I can help the women who need me.' She realised she was leaning forward to make her point and she quickly relaxed herself back into the sofa. She didn't want to get carried away and blurt out something that would give away what had happened to her own family.

Charles sighed. 'I admire your drive and passion, I really do,' he said. 'But helping others is no good if it's putting you at risk.'

Irene felt tears of frustration welling in her eyes. She was between a rock and a hard place here. She loved Charles and she wanted to make him happy. She also felt indebted to him after what he'd done for her and she didn't want to let him down. But she really wasn't ready to leave the WPS.

'Please don't get upset, beautiful,' he said, leaning forward to push a stray lock of hair behind her ear. It was the first time he had used the term of endearment and she smiled despite herself. 'As my wife there will be many ways for you to make a difference,' Charles continued.

'How do you mean?' she asked with interest.

'Well, I can get you on the boards of certain charities, and while the army camp is still here, I can get you involved in the running of the rest homes for the soldiers. They're always looking for organised and capable helpers to keep things in order.'

Irene was flattered at the way Charles had described her. He'd never seemed overly interested in her WPS work, but he had clearly listened when she'd told him what she'd been up to and was obviously impressed with her skills. 'Wouldn't all of that be far more suitable than gallivanting around getting into scrapes with soldiers and prostitutes?' he added.

When he put it like that, Irene had to admit that there was logic to his argument. Yes, she could help just as many people that way, and potentially even more. But she loved 'gallivanting', as he called it – loved the anticipation of not knowing what the next patrol would bring. Did he just want her to be a society woman, content to judge the cake-baking competition at Women's Institute charity events? She understood that someone of his background and class might want a more traditional wife, but if he did, then why did he pick her? It felt like all he wanted to do was change her.

While she had been thinking, Charles had been watching her closely. Now, he got up and strode over to the fireplace and leaned against the mantlepiece. 'Perhaps you're right, though,' he said, eyeing her closely. 'Maybe you should stay in the WPS. Maybe we aren't right for one another.'

Irene jumped to her feet. 'Whatever do you mean, Charles?' she exclaimed.

'I love you, Irene,' he said quietly. 'But all this worrying about you out there patrolling the streets on your own is taking its toll on me.' He ran a hand through his hair and the flecks of grey she loved so much caught the light from the fire.

Suddenly, Irene pictured a life where she would never be able to get close enough to him again to drink in the deliciousness of his hair, his skin, his smell. A life without the warmth and safety of his comforting arms. The thought filled her with panic.

'No! I need you!' she cried, jumping up from the sofa and rushing over to him. She wrapped her arms around him and nuzzled her head into his chest. He was still for a few seconds but then relief washed over her as he relaxed into the embrace and rubbed his hand up and down her back comfortingly.

After a few minutes, she realised she was clinging on to him so tightly he could barely breathe. 'Sorry,' she gasped, releasing her grip and taking a step back. They held hands and stood staring into each other's eyes. Irene felt overcome with emotion as she realised how close she had come to losing him, and how hopeless that had made her feel.

As he led her back to the sofa and they sat down together, she felt confused. She had always been so independent, but she realised now that she couldn't face the prospect of a life without him. She had never felt so dependent on anybody in her whole life and it left her feeling as vulnerable as a baby bird thrust out of its nest for the first time without its mother.

'I love you, too,' Irene whispered finally. 'I didn't realise my WPS work worried you so much.'

'It's torture,' Charles muttered, his head in his hands. Irene couldn't stand it any longer. How could she continue on with the WPS when it was causing so much pain and suffering to the man she loved? Love was all about sacrifice, and this would have to be hers.

'I can't lose you,' Irene said firmly. 'You mean more to me than the WPS.'

'Thank you,' Charles whispered, leaning over to kiss her. As their lips touched, her stomach flipped despite the sadness she was feeling at having to walk away from her beloved WPS. There was so much attraction in their kiss, Irene felt like an electric current was running through her body.

'That settles it. We can start planning the wedding without delay, and you can hand your notice in as soon as we're married,' Charles declared after pulling away.

Irene looked at him in shock. It was all moving too fast. But she knew a wedding wouldn't be happening immediately – these things needed a lot of planning. Even Frank's wedding, which had been a rush-job, had taken a few weeks to get sorted. And she knew Charles would want to pull out all the stops, which would take time. Maybe during that period, she could make him see that she wasn't in any danger when she was out patrolling, and he might have a change of heart by the time they were man and wife. She would cling on to that hope, she decided. But if she had to leave, so be it.

She looked at her watch and was astounded at how late it was. She hurried to finish her drink and headed back out on patrol. There was only an hour or so left before she could crawl into the comfort of her bed. She would have more time to think about everything then, she decided.

But, as always happened after a long shift, she fell into a slumber as soon as her head hit the pillow and she didn't stir until the familiar sounds of Helen banging around in the kitchen as she prepared breakfast for everyone made their way up to her.

Stretching her arms above her head and groaning quietly, she was tempted to roll over and go back to sleep. How delicious an extra few hours would feel. But she knew she would never get away with it. Helen would likely leave her to it, but Irene couldn't stand the thought of the look of satisfaction on Mary's face as she made her explain where she had been all morning.

Hearing her roommate rising, she waited until she was up and dressed before crawling out of bed herself. There was only one thing she needed to make sure she achieved today, and that was writing to Maggie and Annie to tell them that she now had a fiancé.

# 23

Irene ended up being so busy that she didn't get a chance to write to her friends that day. In fact, four days passed before she finally got around to sitting down to put pen to paper. Every time she had a spare moment, she either found herself with Charles or she just didn't have the energy to explain everything in writing. Now, sitting at the kitchen table, she found herself struggling for a way to explain just how quickly everything had moved. She hadn't even been in Grantham three months and Maggie and Annie hadn't met Charles, much less knew anything about him. There was so much to cover.

The truth was, Irene felt slightly foolish for getting swept up with everything and agreeing to marry Charles so soon. She loved him, of course she did, but she was beginning to worry that it was too soon to be making such a big commitment. It was all very well her putting on a front to everyone in Grantham, but she knew her real friends would see through it all and question her actions. And she wasn't ready to admit she had backed herself into a corner through a desperate need to get help for her cousin. In the end, she gave up on the letter, resolving to get back to it as soon as she felt clearer in her head about everything.

As she went about her patrol later that morning, Irene found herself looking forward to the coming afternoon. She had been working pretty much solidly for the last few days, with just a few secret breaks to see Charles, and Helen had told her to take the whole afternoon and evening off. As the time stretched out before her, she revelled in the idea of all those hours with no work. Maybe she would be able to gather her thoughts properly and construct her letter to Maggie and Annie. The more time that passed without them knowing, the more anxious she was growing.

'Ah, I hoped I'd find you here,' she heard Charles's familiar voice booming out as she loitered outside Goode's bakery on Sidney Street. Irene had told him before how she liked to watch from outside on the street as John Goode and his two helpers stacked up all the bread ready to be transported over to the troops at Belton Park. Piles and piles of freshly baked loaves took over the room every morning. It was a wonder for Irene to see so much delicious-looking bread, and her mouth always watered at the irresistible smell of it all. John had told her he was doing a roaring trade since the camp had been set up. Most of the tradesmen in the town were bene-fiting in some way or another. As Charles leaned down to kiss Irene on the lips, she gave a nervous laugh and looked around her anxiously.

'Don't worry, I just called for you at Rutland Street and Helen was there trying her best to get the town's wayward girls back on track,' Charles laughed. Irene breathed a sigh of relief that she was away from Helen's prying eyes. 'Helen's fighting a losing battle with the harlots around here if you ask me,' Charles scoffed, rolling his eyes before quickly changing the subject.

There it was again, Irene thought. The disdain for what she and her colleagues were doing, not to mention the attitude to women it betrayed. But before she had a chance to register and react to the comment, he was talking animatedly about a surprise he had for her on her afternoon off.

'Walk with me so it doesn't look like I'm slacking,' Irene whispered as she started off down the street ahead of him. She had lost count of the number of times she'd told him she really shouldn't be seen standing around chatting to him in uniform. It was lovely he was so keen to be around her that he couldn't wait until she was off duty or at least out of sight, but she was beginning to feel like he was undermining her role. Before she had a chance to get annoyed or say anything to him about it, Charles was talking again about his plans for the afternoon.

'We'll meet at the Angel and Royal at four o'clock,' he said. 'I've got the best treat in store for you!'

Irene couldn't help but get swept up in his enthusiasm, and she was touched he had gone to the effort of arranging something special for her. Just as quickly as her niggling doubts about him and his intentions had entered her mind, they were gone again as her thoughts switched to what he might have in store for her. Charles stayed by her side as she made her way round to the Beehive Inn.

Walking along Castlegate, Irene smiled when she heard the buzzing and humming that she always found so soothing. The pub had a beehive hanging in a tree outside. Through her conversations with the landlord, Edward, she had discovered that this 'living sign' had been there since at least 1791. She loved to marvel at its history while watching the bees busy at work.

Edward was in his thirties with thick black hair. His strapping physique meant that there wasn't often any trouble in his pub. Anyone silly enough to try anything was normally hauled straight out by him and barred on the spot. He didn't suffer fools, Edward. Irene loved talking to him as he had a matter-of-factness that she admired.

'One of the lads got stung last night,' Edward's voice pierced through the buzzing and Irene looked round to see him standing in the doorway with a cup of tea in his hand. He waved her over and Irene smiled before making to head in his direction.

'What are you doing?' Charles hissed in her ear, and she stopped in her tracks, giving Edward an apologetic smile before turning back to face Charles.

'What do you mean?' she asked, taking care to keep her smile fixed on her face. 'I'm on duty. It's part of my job to check in with everyone.'

'You're flirting with him,' Charles said.

Irene blinked up at him. She hadn't even said hello to Edward yet! Thinking Charles was joking around, she laughed, waiting for him to join in. But he held eye contact with her as he grasped her arm just a little too tightly. 'I know what men like him are after,' he said. 'You'd do well not to entertain it.'

Irene was speechless. Was Charles jealous of Edward? Surely he knew by now how much he meant to her, and how desperate she was to keep him in her life. She had agreed to marry him, after all! She felt so uncomfortable, she didn't know what to do next. She couldn't ignore Edward, but she didn't want to upset Charles further.

Suddenly, Charles broke into a big grin. 'Off you pop, then,' he said lightly, kissing her on the top of her head. 'It looks like we both have work to do. I can't wait to see you later,' he added before heading off towards the factory.

Irene stared after him for a few moments, her hands trembling as she tried to work out what had just happened. Then she remembered Edward was waiting to speak to her, so she tried to snap herself out of it and made her way over to him.

'Morning, Edward,' Irene said shakily, happy to see his friendly face after the strange exchange with Charles. Edward didn't seem to notice what had just happened and started chatting away.

Irene nodded here and there, but wasn't really listening. Her mind was still on Charles's strange behaviour. She wondered if she had over-reacted, or perhaps misheard him.

'So, that soldier last night,' Edward laughed. 'Silly so-and-so was trying to climb the tree to see into the beehive. I warned him twice then left him to it. He howled when he got stung. We could hear it at the bar. Goodness knows how he'll cope if the enemy gets him if that's his reaction to a bee sting,' he said, shaking his head scornfully.

'Well, let's hope that bee is the biggest enemy he comes across,' Irene said softly. She knew the soldiers were trying the patience of some of the residents, with their late-night drinking and general boisterousness, but most people in the town appreciated they were just letting off steam at a stressful time. The old barracks on Sandon Road had been turned into a military hospital and many of the locals with motorbikes took recovering soldiers out for day trips on their sidecars. Irene loved the name the British Red Cross, which organised the trips, gave them: 'happy thoughts days'.

'Anyway, I was hoping you'd pop by today,' Edward said before taking a sip of his tea. 'There's been a couple of new faces coming in the last few nights and they seem keen to get friendly with the troops, if you know what I mean,' he added, raising his eyebrows. Irene knew exactly what he meant. 'Ruby was in last night, but I didn't want it to be obvious I was pointing them out. I don't need the trouble,' he explained.

'That's fine,' Irene smiled. 'I'm not on duty tonight but I'll let Helen know so she can send someone along to keep an eye out.' He smiled gratefully, but then his expression quickly changed. 'It won't be Mary, will it?' he asked quietly.

'Oh, I don't know actually,' Irene said, trying to remember if Helen had mentioned anything that morning about who was going to be on public-house duty while she had her evening off.

'Only, she can be a little heavy-handed when it comes to the prostitutes,' Edward cut into her thoughts. 'You and the others are discreet about it, which I find is better for business.'

It seemed like it wasn't just Irene who was concerned about Mary's bolshy ways.

'I'll find out who's on duty before I mention it,' Irene assured Edward before bidding him farewell and setting off for the train station. She didn't often make it out to the station as it was one of Mary's favourite spots. Mary loved putting anyone who didn't look respectable enough to her straight back on a train to where they had come from. But Mary had the morning off, so Irene knew she was safe to go there.

On the walk there, she ran over the encounter with Charles in her head, trying to work out exactly what she had done wrong. She was feeling nervous about their afternoon together now. He'd seemed in a good mood again when he'd left her, but what if he snapped at her again when they met up?

The station was busy, but no busier than normal. There was the usual hustle and bustle as people went about their business, which was good as it kept Irene distracted from her anxious thoughts about Charles. A child was screaming at his mother as they made their way along the platform towards Irene. The poor woman was struggling with a large suitcase in one hand and fighting to keep hold of the youngster as he screeched at the top of his voice about his urgent need for chocolate. Irene was about to step in and offer to help the woman with the suitcase when a man in a suit swept up behind them and took it from her wordlessly. The mother smiled gratefully and hauled her child into her arms. There were a few seconds of silence before more crying broke the peace.

This noise was the piercing cry of a newborn – there was no mistaking it. Irene looked around for a mother and baby to assist, but the platform had emptied of passengers. She spun around to face the York-bound train that was waiting to depart. The guard was about to blow her whistle to signal the train's departure when Irene spotted the owner of the wails through the window. A tiny baby was lying in a Moses basket on one of the seats, but there was no parent in sight. In fact, the whole carriage was empty apart from the baby.

'Hold on!' Irene yelled at the guard. She looked perplexed, but she took her whistle away from her mouth and relaxed the arm she had just thrown up into the air. She made her way towards Irene, who was already throwing the carriage door open.

'Poor love,' Irene whispered, reaching down to pick up the screaming child. Her comforting arms soothed the baby almost immediately, and Irene relaxed when the high-pitched screaming ceased, and he nuzzled into her chest. 'There, there,' Irene soothed, stroking the tot's delicate head.

'I'll search the other carriages,' the guard offered. 'I saw a woman bringing him on a couple of stops ago, she must be around somewhere.'

'I wouldn't bother,' Irene sighed as she reached down into the basket and brought out a handwritten note. Irene's heart sank as she read the words.

> *Please look after my baby. His name is Albert and he's three weeks old.*

'Probably illegitimate,' the guard shrugged. 'We've had a few of those lately. The women get knocked up by a soldier while their husbands are away fighting and need to get rid of the evidence before they come back.'

Irene's heart broke at the thought of the beautiful baby in her arms being described as 'evidence'. She couldn't understand how anyone could abandon a helpless baby so callously, let alone his own mother. 'Stanley in the ticket office will call one of the lads at the police station to get him,' the guard added. 'I need to get this train running again.' Irene held Albert tight against her chest with one arm and picked up the Moses basket handles with her free hand. When she got to the ticket office Stanley was a little more sympathetic, but Irene insisted on staying with Albert until the officer from the station arrived. Stanley didn't seem like an affectionate chap and Irene couldn't stand the thought of Albert being left alone in the Moses basket again.

'What will happen to him?' Irene asked when the officer finally appeared. She was reluctant to hand him over, although there was no way she could look after him herself.

'He'll go into a children's home to begin with. But there are lots of couples desperate to adopt. I'm sure they'll find him a good home,' the officer assured her. Feeling better, Irene handed Albert over.

Making her way back into town, she felt sad. She wasn't sure why the situation had upset her so much. Maybe the thought of a child feeling unwanted by their mother or father had struck a chord with her, after what she had been through herself. She hoped desperately that little Albert would be adopted quickly. She hated the thought of him spending a long time in a children's home. Whatever it was, she tried to shake it off. Her shift was almost over, and she didn't want her sadness to put a dampener on her afternoon with Charles. Especially not after what had happened this morning.

She went straight back to Rutland Street and put on one of her new dresses and her new shoes before letting her hair down and giving it a brush. She hardly ever wore it loose anymore and as she checked it in the mirror, she cringed at the split ends and then tied it back into a ponytail again.

When Irene got to the High Street, she stopped and took in the front of the Angel and Royal hotel. She had only ever been inside while on duty, and she felt rather sophisticated approaching as a customer. She took a deep breath and smiled to herself. Despite what had happened earlier, she was really looking forward to spending her precious time off with her fiancé – it still felt strange to say that!

As Irene walked into the building, the receptionist gave her a welcoming nod. She went straight up the stairs to the hotel bar, where she spotted Charles in a second. He was sitting on a comfy-looking seat in one of the window alcoves and had taken the liberty of ordering some tea. As she approached, Irene wondered who else could be joining them, as there were four cups on the table. Sitting down after greeting Charles, she looked out over Market Place and breathed a sigh of relief that he seemed happy to see her. Whatever this morning had been about had clearly been forgotten.

'Who are we expecting?' she asked, baffled.

Charles grinned, and looked out of the window too.

'Ah, this must be them,' he said smugly, pointing at two figures making their way across the square below.

Irene strained her eyes to try and make out who it was. She could see they were women. As they came nearer, her heart leapt into her mouth and she put both her hands up to cover it and stop herself from crying out. Charles was still grinning at her and looked rather pleased with himself.

Suddenly Irene's excitement vanished, and she panicked. She felt warm and clammy as she tried desperately to gather her thoughts. She should have been over the moon to see these two surprise guests – but how was she going to explain to Maggie and Annie that she had been engaged for so long without telling them?

When Charles spotted Irene's flustered expression, he looked confused.

'I thought you'd be excited to see your friends,' he said. 'I went to a lot of effort to organise this – I'm even paying for them to stay here overnight,' he added, sounding irritated at her lack of response.

'I'm sorry,' Irene whispered, not wanting to make a scene. 'It's just . . . I haven't had time to tell them about our engagement yet and I—'

'I hear congratulations are in order,' Maggie's voice cut

over Irene and she looked up to see both her friends standing next to the table, overnight bags in their hands.

So, Charles had told them already. She couldn't understand why he would do that. He was obviously trying to do something nice, but it felt like she was slowly losing control over her own life. She couldn't say anything now – she had to make things right with Maggie and Annie. And, of course, she didn't want to upset Charles. He may have meddled, but she knew his intentions were good, and she needed to show her friends what a wonderful man he was if they were going to support her decision to marry him. She couldn't risk him snapping and slipping into one of his dark moods in front of them.

'It's so good to see you!' Irene cried out, jumping to her feet and wrapping her arms around Maggie. Maggie returned the hug but stepped away quickly, and Irene's heart sank a little. She embraced Annie before gesturing for them both to sit down.

'Ladies, I'll take your bags and get you checked in,' Charles said smoothly as he got to his feet. 'It's lovely to meet you both after hearing so much about you,' he added before taking each of their hands and giving them a soft kiss.

'I wish we could say the same about him,' Maggie hissed as Charles walked off across the bar. 'But we know *nothing* about him, Irene. And we had to hear of your engagement through him – a stranger!'

Irene couldn't help but feel a prickle of annoyance at the comment. Yes, she knew she was in the wrong for having not told them herself yet, but she hadn't exactly been inundated with letters from the two of them! She was just about to say as much when Annie cut in.

'We wish you'd told us yourself, but we're really happy for you – especially after everything you went through with Frank,' she said, glancing at Maggie warningly. Irene looked back to

Maggie, who was making a visible effort to relax now, and
was smiling and nodding her agreement.

'I'm sorry,' Irene said, deciding to let her gripe go as she
reached across the table and took a hand from each of them
in her own. 'I've just been so busy with the WPS work – you
know how it is – and every time I went to write to you and
tell you about the engagement I struggled. There was just so
much to tell you, and I never had the time to get it all down!
I promise I was going to tell you. In fact, it was top of my
list for my afternoon off today. But how wonderful that Charles
has arranged it so that I can tell you all the details in person!'

Irene was relieved her friends were being understanding,
but she was starting to feel angry with Charles for taking
away her chance to tell them her news herself. She knew she
had been dallying over it, but it was still her news to share
with them and she felt awful they'd had to hear it from a
stranger.

'Well, we haven't exactly kept up our side of the promise
to write to you regularly,' Maggie admitted with a softer tone
now. Feeling lighter, Irene smiled.

'It really has been a whirlwind,' Irene gushed. As she filled
her friends in on the events of the last couple of months, she
found herself feeling giddy when she spoke about Charles. All
the anger she'd felt about his meddling melted away. Yes, he'd
stepped out of line – but look at how well it had turned out.

Annie told her Charles had sent a letter to Bethnal Green
Police Station addressed to her and Maggie revealing the
engagement and inviting them to visit. It was a sweet gesture,
really. And she was so pleased to see them. When Charles
returned to the table, he poured them all some tea – they had
been so busy catching up they'd left the pot going cold.

'It's wonderful to see you so happy,' he whispered into
Irene's ear as she got up from the table to freshen up. She felt
lucky to be surrounded by people who cared so much for her.

But when she returned, there seemed to be a frosty atmosphere. Before Irene could enquire, Charles offered to give Maggie and Annie a tour of Grantham.

'I think Irene would be the perfect tour guide, actually,' Maggie declared stiffly. She finished the last of her tea without so much as looking in Charles's direction.

Irene was surprised her friend was turning down Charles's offer so abruptly. She would have thought she'd jump at the chance to spend some more time with him and find out everything she could about him. What had she missed when she'd been away from the table?

'You've come all this way, and I'd love to show my gratitude by giving you a guided tour,' Charles said, trying to get eye contact with Maggie but failing. 'I've lived here all my life, so I know the town rather well,' he joked. He was smiling, but Irene could see that hint of steel in his eyes again.

'Irene has been walking the streets here for months now,' Maggie said, finally turning her head to look at Charles. 'I'm rather keen to be shown around by her, seeing as it is she who we came to see. Or does she not qualify for the job because she's a *woman*?'

Why was she being so rude? Irene was panicking now about what had been said in her absence. She knew Charles had thoughts on working women that she didn't agree with, but it was all stuff that could be worked on. Maggie didn't know him like she did. She didn't understand that he didn't mean any harm. The last thing Irene wanted was for them to fall out – Maggie and Annie's support was so important to her. She looked over at Charles, who seemed lost for words.

'I'd like to spend some time alone with you and Annie,' Maggie said firmly, addressing Irene.

'But . . .' Irene started. She couldn't fathom what was going on. She was stuck between her best friends and her fiancé – how was she supposed to choose between them? 'It sounds like you two have got off on the wrong foot,' she said as lightly as she could manage, trying to defuse the situation. 'You've come a long way and we don't have much time. It's important to me that you get to know Charles, and—'

'I already know him well enough,' Maggie snapped, getting to her feet. 'He may have pulled the wool over your eyes, Irene, but I grew up with a man like this and I will *not* see my best friend go through it too.'

'What are you talking about?' Charles asked quietly, looking around to check there wasn't anyone within earshot. 'Honestly, I don't know what I've done to offend you, but all I wanted from today was for Irene to get some time with you both as I know how much she's missed you. I'm sorry if I've said something to upset you.' He got to his feet. 'I don't want to spoil your time together, so I'll leave you to show your friends around, Irene,' he said stiffly.

'No, Charles, wait. I want you all to get to know each other,' Irene said desperately. She couldn't believe how quickly this had escalated and she didn't know what her fiancé had said to rile Maggie so much.

'Irene, I'd really appreciate some time alone with you,' Maggie pressed.

Irene looked to Charles and saw the hurt in his eyes.

'I don't want to cause any more upset. I'm sorry this didn't go to plan. Enjoy your stay,' he said to Maggie and Annie before kissing Irene on the cheek and striding out of the bar without a backwards glance.

Irene suddenly felt a flash of anger. Charles had been there for her when no one else had, he had saved her family, and Maggie was not only refusing to take the time to try to get to know him properly, but she was also being exceptionally rude to him. Whatever he'd said, she was certain it didn't warrant the treatment he had just received.

'Charles went to a lot of trouble to arrange this,' she said, trying to keep her voice low and steady. 'How dare you treat him like that. You've no idea what he's done for me.'

'Maybe we should all sit down and talk about this,' Annie offered, desperation tinging her voice. Irene and Maggie both looked down at her – the only one still sitting at the table. Irene nodded and sat back down in her seat, and after a beat Maggie did the same.

'Please, Irene,' Maggie said, calmer now. 'I can see straight through men like that. You have to trust me. He was talking about you as if you were his property. You do know he expects you to leave the WPS as soon as you're married, if not before?'

'Oh, he's not serious about that,' Irene said, waving the comment – and her own qualms – away. 'He'd rather I didn't work, but only because he's a proud man and he wants to look after me. And he worries about my safety when I'm out patrolling. It's sweet, really. I'll be able to make him see that me staying on with the WPS won't be such a bad thing,' she added.

Maggie raised her eyebrows.

'He won't be able to force me to give it up!' Irene snapped. Maggie had only known him for twenty minutes, so why was she so convinced she knew him better than Irene did? Maggie always thought she knew better than everyone else.

'Oh Irene, I thought I was the naive one,' Maggie said, shaking her head. 'Look, I'm not doing this to upset you or ruin your relationship,' she added gently. 'I'm doing this because I care about you. But Charles . . . well . . . he reminds me of my father, and I don't want to see you end up like my mother.'

Her words hung in the air between them as Irene tried to steady herself from the shock of them. They all knew Maggie's father was a brute who had raised his hand to everyone in their family, including Maggie herself. How dare she compare her fiancé to such an animal? And all because he wanted to look after her. She looked to Annie, who didn't seem as shocked at Maggie's claim as Irene would have expected.

'How well do you really know him, Irene?' Annie whispered.

Irene couldn't listen to them anymore. She got to her feet.

'He's manipulating you,' Maggie pleaded as Irene went to leave the table. 'He'll make you think we're the bad ones, so that you shut us out. Eventually you'll have nobody left but him.'

Irene had really had enough now.

'Please, Irene!' Maggie called after her as she stalked off through the bar. 'Just get to know him better before you do this. You need to see his true colours before it's too late!' Maggie's final words rang in Irene's ears as the heavy door slammed shut behind her.

In the corridor, she paused, unsure about what to do next. If she left now, then she couldn't see Annie and Maggie staying in Grantham any longer. Did she really want to leave things like this? Who knew when she'd get the chance to see them again? But she didn't feel like she had a choice. Maggie wasn't willing to listen to reason, and she was angry with her for being so rude to Charles. As for Annie, well – she seemed to be siding with Maggie so there didn't seem any point in trying to speak to her either.

The memory of Charles's crestfallen face prompted her to make her way down the stairs. If anyone deserved her time, it was him. She couldn't stand the thought of him being alone and upset. Besides, the three of them were all too angry to resolve anything right now. Once they'd all calmed down, they could have a proper conversation and the girls could start again with Charles. They just needed some time.

Walking to Charles's house, Irene was desperate to hear Maggie and Annie shouting after her and apologising. She didn't want to part with them like this, but as far as she was concerned it was up to them to make amends.

She looked behind her one last time when she got to Charles's and then knocked on the door with a heavy heart. It really would have to wait. When Mildred answered she smiled and showed Irene straight to the drawing room, where Charles was on the sofa reading the newspaper.

'I'm sorry Maggie was rude to you,' she said as he stood and held out his arms to her. As they embraced, he stroked her hair soothingly.

'*I'm* sorry,' he said. 'I've no idea what I said to offend her so much. We were just talking about the engagement and I was saying that I was looking forward to having you all to myself once we're wed and you leave the WPS.' Irene felt a wave of guilt. As far as Charles was concerned, that was the plan. He didn't know she was secretly hoping she could convince him to allow her to stay on. Yet another of her secrets had caused a rift, she realised as a cloud of gloom descended upon her. She stayed quiet, debating whether she should say anything, before thinking better of it. Now wasn't the time

'As soon as the words had left my mouth, she was shouting at me about how I can't control you, and I can't stop you from working,' Charles continued. Irene felt even more terrible. 'I really felt rather attacked – nobody has ever spoken to me like that before. From what you've said about her father, I do wonder if temper runs in the family . . .'

Irene wanted to stick up for Maggie. She had never seen her like that before, and she knew she wasn't anything like her father – on the contrary, she was a kind and caring friend. But she found herself struggling to defend her to Charles. There was no excuse for her outburst or her treatment of him.

'Maybe some time apart from them was what you needed, in order for you to see their true colours,' Charles said softly, pulling her in for another embrace and kissing the top of her head. 'Thank goodness you have me, my darling.'

A tear rolled down Irene's cheek as she realised Charles really was all she had now. She had just chosen him over Maggie and Annie. There was no going back. She wasn't at all religious, but she found herself closing her eyes and silently praying that this wasn't the end for her and her friends, and that some space would help them see sense and come back to her.

# 24

Irene had been right about Maggie and Annie not hanging around. She spent the whole evening at Charles's wondering if she should go and find them.

Her mood was lifted when Charles presented her with an engagement ring. It was the fanciest piece of jewellery she had ever seen.

'It's beautiful,' she gasped, as he slid it on to her finger over a grand dinner for two. The delicate gold band was a perfect fit, and the diamond was so big it weighed her hand down.

'I wanted to do things properly and get down on one knee in front of your friends,' he said, looking wounded again as she stroked the stone with her thumb in awe.

'I'm glad it was just the two of us,' she said, smiling determinedly. 'It feels more special like this.'

Charles didn't want her to wear the ring on duty in case it got damaged. As much as she wanted to show it off, she agreed. She wasn't used to being responsible for something so valuable and she was happy to keep it out of harm's way.

When Irene ventured back to the Angel and Royal the following morning, she discovered that Maggie and Annie had gone to their room to pick up their bags and checked out soon after her departure from the bar. She was upset but, having had time to calm down, she was less angry. She was sure now that it was all just a big misunderstanding and once Maggie had calmed down too, they would sort things out.

Their friendship was too strong to let anything come between them, and she hoped to one day look back on this with them and laugh about how silly it all had been.

Irene threw herself into her WPS work, but she couldn't help but feel a flutter of hope every time the letter box clunked at Rutland Street – swiftly followed by a feeling of bitter disappointment when she found there was no letter addressed to her in Maggie or Annie's handwriting.

At least she had one positive thing going on in her life, she thought as she made her way across the fields towards Belton Park one sunny morning. It was two weeks since she'd seen Maggie and Annie, and her relationship with Charles was getting stronger by the day. It was almost as if the fallout with her friends had brought them closer. And Mary had backed off completely, while Ruby was keeping a friendly distance and respecting the fact that Irene didn't want to get close to her again.

Before Irene knew it, she was at the gates of Belton Park, having not seen a single soul on the long walk through the fields to get there. She said a brief hello to some soldiers hanging around near the gates and then turned around to make her way back into town. That journey was quiet too, and she decided to stop by Goode's Bakery to enjoy the smell of the fresh loaves before they were transported off to the army camp. As she stood enjoying the aroma, John popped his head out of the door.

'Could we have a natter inside?' he asked quietly. 'There's a cup of tea in it for you and I might even stretch to a loaf to take back for Helen to use for your dinner,' he added with a cheeky grin. The cup of tea would have been enough to get Irene through the door – she was parched after all the walking that morning. Her mouth watered at the thought of the extra bread to go with dinner as she followed John through the bakery and into the kitchen in the back. John filled the kettle and placed it on the stove before offering Irene a seat at a big wooden table in the middle of the room.

'Is there something I can help with?' she asked as she sat down.

'It's my mother,' John sighed, rinsing out a teapot and placing fresh tea leaves in a strainer. 'I wondered if you could check in on her, please? I know it's not really in your job description, but—'

'Of course I'll pop in to see her,' Irene exclaimed happily before he could finish. 'We're here to help anyone who needs us. But *does* she need us? Is something wrong?' she asked cautiously.

She hadn't had much interaction with Gladys Goode, but from what she knew of John's mother she was fiercely independent, and she was another one who didn't suffer fools gladly.

'I don't think so. Oh, I don't know,' John said heavily as he sat down next to Irene. He'd made up the pot of tea and brought it with him to the table. 'She's not really been the same since we lost Joe. Her spark has gone.'

Irene gave a sad sigh, remembering what Helen had told her when she'd shown her around Grantham on her first day. John's son Joe had been killed in France early on in the war. His death had come hot on the heels of John's father, who had keeled over from a heart attack soon after his grandson had enlisted. 'Anyway,' John continued, 'now the neighbours think she's losing the plot – talking to herself late at night. Sometimes there's shouting, but mostly it's full-blown conversations, like there's someone there with her. But, of course, I know she's all alone since father died.

'She won't talk to me about any of it,' John said sadly. 'She won't even let me in the house. She insists on coming to see me here, even though she knows we're run off our feet with all the bread for the camp. And she keeps taking extra loaves away with her, although I'm sure she doesn't eat them as she seems to be getting smaller by the day. I'm sorry to rope you in, dear, but I don't know what else to do – she's so damned stubborn! I thought she might talk to someone kind like you. She's always harping on about you girls in your uniforms helping the town and whatnot.'

'It's no trouble at all, John,' Irene said warmly.

Picking up the teapot, he sighed again as he poured the dark brown liquid into two mugs.

'I just hope she's not going doolally, is all,' he said so quietly it was almost as if he was talking to himself. 'I mean, is she stuck in the past – thinking my father is still in the house with her? Is that who she thinks she's talking to at night, who she takes the bread back for?' He passed a mug to Irene and looked her in the eyes as though they might hold the answer he was looking for.

Irene had to admit it was a curious situation, and she was looking forward to getting to the bottom of it. It was just the kind of challenge she needed to take her mind off things with Maggie and Annie. And if she could help, it would be a good anecdote to tell Charles – and might even strengthen her case for staying on with the WPS. He couldn't argue with a low-risk good deed like helping a confused little old lady.

'Don't you worry,' she said confidently. 'I can be very sensitive when it comes to problems like this. I'll tread carefully and I'm sure your mother and I can figure this out together.' She took a sip of her tea and closed her eyes as the warm liquid made its way down her throat and banished the over-whelming dryness she'd been experiencing since spending all morning walking through fields in the July sunshine in her heavy uniform. 'Now, where's that bread you promised me?' she said with a wink and a smile that had John roaring with laughter.

*

Making her way back to Rutland Street with the warm loaf under her arm, Irene was looking forward to helping Mrs Goode and putting John's mind at rest. She was sure the old dear was struggling to come to terms with her losses and probably a little lonely with John being run off his feet at the bakery. She hoped she would be able to forge a friendship with her and be there to keep her company when she needed it.

After handing over the bread to Helen and explaining the situation, Helen was happy enough for Irene to take Mrs Goode on as her own little project. 'I'll make sure the others know you're in charge of helping her, and if anyone else voices any concerns about her then they should direct them to you,' she smiled.

Irene decided there was no time like the present, and she headed straight over to Mrs Goode's terraced house on Castlegate. She knocked loudly on the door, conscious of the fact that Mrs Goode's hearing might not be at its best now she was in her eighties. There was some shuffling and loud whispering, followed by the sound of a door being shut. Then Irene heard footsteps moving towards her, and eventually the front door opened up just a crack. Mrs Goode peered through the small gap suspiciously.

'Can I help you, dear?' she asked impatiently.

'I'm Irene Wilson, from the WPS,' she replied in her friend-liest voice.

'Yes, well I can *see* that,' Mrs Goode snapped. 'What do you want?'

Irene was a little flustered by her abruptness, but she was undeterred. She decided honesty was the best way forward – this lady wasn't going to be taken in by any cover story.

'John sent me,' she explained. 'He's worried about you.'

Mrs Goode sighed and her body visibly relaxed as she stepped back and opened the door a little further. 'That silly so-and-so. I've told him I'm fine. I don't know why he insists that I'm not,' she said.

Irene was surprised to see how well Mrs Goode looked. Her skin looked fresh for someone her age, and she certainly didn't appear to be as frail as John had suggested when he mentioned his worries about her taking bread for an imaginary friend. She stepped to the side and motioned for Irene to come in. 'I suppose you better join me for a cup of tea if it will put his mind at rest,' she said, rolling her eyes.

'I'd love to,' Irene smiled.

'Not in there!' Mrs Goode cried as Irene went to open a door on the left after getting through the front door. She had assumed it led to the living room because the house layout looked similar to Rutland Street. 'It's a tip in there,' Mrs Goode added quickly. 'Much more comfortable in the kitchen, dear,' she explained as she ushered Irene forward. Irene noticed her hands were shaking, but she decided to leave it for the moment.

They chatted as Mrs Goode – who asked to be addressed as Gladys – made a pot of tea. Irene was delighted to be enjoying her second cup of the day, but she wasn't sure how she was going to get to the bottom of John's concerns. His mother seemed absolutely fine to her, and she certainly wasn't going to ask her if she'd recently developed a habit of talking to herself late at night. She was pondering her next step as she took her last mouthful of tea.

'Look, I know people are talking,' Gladys blurted out of nowhere. Irene looked up to see she was wringing her hands nervously. She put down her mug gently and stayed quiet to allow Gladys to say what she needed to say. 'And I know John won't let up until he knows what's going on. I'm quite happy for him to keep on thinking I've lost the plot, but I don't want to waste your time, dear. There are people in this town a lot more in need of your assistance and it's not fair for you to have to keep coming back and checking on me when I'm actually the happiest I might have ever been.'

Gladys's tone didn't reflect that happiness, though, and Irene was desperate to know what on earth she was talking about. 'Whatever it is, you can trust me,' she said sincerely.

Gladys smiled. 'The truth is that my Joe is back,' she whispered, as if the walls might be able to hear her secret.

Irene was lost for words. How was she supposed to react to news of a soldier back from the dead? *Poor Gladys*, she thought, *she really is suffering a mental episode*. She had seemed so normal and rational during their chat, but John had been right all along.

'Gladys, I—' Irene started, but Gladys held up her hand to silence her.

'Come with me,' she said, getting to her feet and walking past Irene and back to the door she had tried to open when she first entered the house. Gladys paused outside the door and waited for Irene to join her.

Irene's heart was thumping in her chest. She had no idea what was waiting for her on the other side of the door, but something told her this wasn't going to be straightforward. Gladys knocked on the wood three times and then shouted, 'I have a visitor but she's on our side!' Placing her hand on the handle, she looked back at Irene and whispered, 'I hope.'

# 25

When Irene entered the living room, she was overwhelmed by the musty stench that immediately hit the back of her throat. It reminded her of the boys' dorms at the children's home – all sweat and hormones and no fresh air. There was a small sofa pushed up against the back wall, and a round coffee table in front of it. As Irene surveyed the scene, she saw a figure standing stiffly by the drawn curtains. It was a young man in a soldier's uniform. But, surely, it couldn't be Gladys's grandson Joe? Everyone knew he'd been killed in action, and if there had been some kind of mistake about that, then why wasn't he shouting from the rooftops about it? And why didn't John know?

The figure stepped forward into the light and on closer inspection Irene could see he was probably about her age – twenty-six. She knew from her conversations with John that Joe had only been eighteen when he died. This didn't make any sense. He was about a foot taller than Irene and he positively towered over little Gladys. He had greasy-looking blond hair and deep-set brows that made his whole face look sad. He was also in need of a good shave.

'Joe, my darling, I've had to tell this young lady that you're here as your father is asking questions,' Gladys said as she stepped forward and took his hand. He stayed silent and stared uncomfortably at Irene. 'He's too scared to go back,' she said to Irene now. 'They tried to kill him once, I can't let him go again. Nobody can know he's here – not even John. He wouldn't understand and the shame would be too much for him.' Tears were streaming down the old lady's face now as she clung to Joe's hand with both of hers and gazed at Irene. 'I just want to keep him safe until the war is over, please.'

'May I speak with your friend alone?' Joe asked. His voice was croaky and shaky. He seemed nervous. Irene wasn't surprised. Whoever he was – Joe or not – he was definitely a deserter. Irene knew that men who fled their posts in France and were tried for desertion and, more often than not, ended up in front of a firing squad. She hadn't heard of that happening back home, but she knew any soldier who ran away when he was due on the front line could expect severe punishment. The chap who had been found at Mrs Barnes's home was now serving a hefty prison sentence. Something like that would change a man's life forever so she couldn't act hastily. Gladys released 'Joe's' hand and nodded solemnly before slowly leaving the room.

Irene didn't know how she had managed to gain Gladys's trust, but she was glad she had. Of all the WPS members in Grantham, she was confident that she was the one with the most flexible attitude towards their duties. She was willing to listen to this man before deciding if she would turn him in – unlike her colleagues, who would already be marching him to Belton if they had been sent here in her place: Mary out of spite, Ruby out of fear and Helen out of a sense of duty.

'My name's not Joe,' the man said quietly once Gladys had closed the door behind her. He slumped heavily on to the sofa and leaned forward with his head in his hands. 'I don't know what to do,' he groaned as he started slowly rocking back and forth. Irene looked to the door and then back at him. Maggie's terrible experience was still fresh in her mind. Her attacker had tricked her into thinking he was upset and then struck when she was comforting him. Irene couldn't help but think back to that as she grappled over the best course of action to take here. As well as being taller than her, he was well built and she couldn't help but think about how easy it would be for him to overpower her.

But the longer she watched this man struggling, the more confident she felt that he was being genuine. This kind of angst wasn't something you could put on – or at least she hoped not. And he'd been living with a confused little old lady for goodness knows how long without harming her. She couldn't get her head around how Gladys thought this man was her grandson. He was so different from the slight young man that John had described to her. And Gladys seemed so switched on in every other way. Irene decided he wasn't dangerous and sat down next to him.

'Tell me your story,' she said gently.

She wanted to reach out and place a comforting hand on his back, but he seemed so lost in his thoughts that she didn't want to take him by surprise. He stopped rocking and turned his head to look at her. His grey eyes were red and bloodshot, and it looked like he hadn't slept for weeks. She realised the musty stench was coming from him and she wondered how long he had been wearing his uniform.

'I'm nothing but a coward,' he whispered. 'And now I've got poor Gladys caught up in it all. You know she thinks I'm her grandson?' he asked, his voice quivering.

'I figured as much,' Irene answered glumly. He turned his head back, so he was staring at the floor again. His elbows were resting on his knees, and his hands were clasped either side of his face so that his voice came out in mumbles. Irene strained to make out what he was saying as he continued.

'I'll have to give myself up eventually. I can't hide here for ever. The poor love can hardly look after herself let alone the two of us, and she's cutting off her family to protect me. She won't even let her son in the house in case he finds me. Once I'm gone, she'll have to lose Joe all over again. I keep thinking about handing myself in but then she comes in and talks to me like I'm him and I can't face it. She's so happy living in this make-believe world where her grandson came back to her. How can I put her through it all again?'

Irene didn't know what to say. It was certainly a mess of a situation.

'Tell me what happened,' she tried. 'How did you meet Gladys?'

He sighed and Irene wasn't sure if he was going to answer her question. But after a brief pause he spoke again.

'I should tell you my real name first,' he said, still staring at the floor. 'I'm Jack, not Joe, and I was injured during the Battle of Aubers Ridge back in May.'

There was another pause and Irene waited patiently. She thought back to what she had read in the papers about the battle. It had been part of the British contribution to the Second Battle of Artois, and it had been a disaster for their army, which had lost thousands of men in one go. There had been criticism since about the lack of high-explosive shells raising the casualty toll. She hated to think what this unfortunate man had seen.

'I was shot in the leg and ended up at the old barracks hospital here in Grantham,' Jack explained. He had relaxed a little now, although his foot was still tapping compulsively. 'They looked after me for a few weeks and once I was able to walk again, I heard a nurse telling one of the officials I'd be ready to go back to the front with the next lot of soldiers heading off.' Jack leaned forward and put his head in his hands once more, avoiding any possibility of eye contact with Irene. 'I'm ashamed to say I panicked,' he whispered. 'That night I left. I had no idea where I was going or what I was going to do – I just knew I couldn't go back. The things I'd seen . . .' He started rocking again, more violently this time.

Irene couldn't stand to watch him suffer any longer and

reached out her hand and placed it on his back. When she made contact with him, Jack flinched, making Irene jump. But she kept her hand firmly where it was, and eventually he relaxed into it.

'Tell me how you met Gladys,' she said soothingly, trying to pull his mind back from whatever terrible memories were causing him to react in such a way.

'I don't know,' he said, giving a small laugh and sitting upright again. He looked at Irene as he explained, 'I just steamed out of there with no plan and no idea where I was going. I've never even been to Grantham. It's all a bit of a blur when I try to remember now. All I can recall clearly is the overriding need to get as far away from the hospital and the possibility of being sent back to the battlefield as possible.'

His eyes glistened and Irene could see a world of pain when she looked into them. She gave him time to compose himself before he continued.

'I ended up in a church down the road. I'm not religious but something must have pulled me there. Anyway, there she was. Before I knew what to do, she had shouted out Joe's name and thrown herself at me. I was so relieved to be in a loving, warm embrace – just to have that human touch was such a beautiful feeling – that I went along with it. I didn't realise who Joe was and the long-term effect playing along with it would have, I honestly didn't. I wasn't thinking straight, otherwise I would have corrected her there and then.'

'I understand,' Irene assured him.

'We ended up back here and by the time I realised she thought I was her dead grandson, well, I didn't have the heart to tell her the truth. She was over the moon and talking about how her world had ended when she'd seen the telegram and now it was worth living again. By that point I knew the hospital staff would have reported me as having done a runner, so handing myself in wasn't really an option anyway.'

'I'm sure they would understand if you explained this all to them,' Irene said sympathetically.

Jack let out a little laugh and looked at her again. 'One of the men in my regiment wandered off just before the battle. When they brought him back, he said he got lost. He hadn't meant to desert his post. He'd just needed some time to compose himself. But they took him off and he was shot at dawn anyway. What do you think they would do to me? I can't even claim to be lost!'

Irene gulped. She had thought they only used the firing squads on the front line, but now she thought about it she realised that was just an assumption. Who knew what went on up at the camp when no one was looking? The army ruled themselves up there so it was possible they could be dishing out whatever punishment they saw fit.

Irene was starting to panic. She felt completely out of her depth here. She knew what she was supposed to do in this situation: hand Jack in. But could that mean a death sentence for him, as well as breaking poor Gladys's heart all over again?

'I'm going to need some time to work this out,' she confessed. 'But at least you're safe here until I know what to do for the best.'

Jack smiled for the first time. It was a weak smile, but it was a smile nonetheless. 'Thank you,' he whispered. 'I've felt so trapped over the last few weeks, it's a relief to finally tell someone the truth. Even if it does mean admitting how weak I've been.'

'You mustn't talk like that,' Irene said firmly. She didn't know this man at all, but she knew enough about what was happening on the continent to be sure that running away from it wasn't something she could judge him for. 'I can't imagine what you've witnessed and what you've had to go through. I promise we'll work this out,' she assured him, getting up from the sofa.

Before leaving, she popped her head into the kitchen, where Gladys was sat at the table looking worried. She looked up expectantly when she saw Irene's head appear in the doorway, and the naked hope on her face made Irene's eyes fill with tears.

'Don't worry, this will stay between the three of us, at least for the time being,' Irene said.

'Please don't send him back,' Gladys begged, getting to her feet.

'I won't,' Irene pledged, although she didn't know how she was going to keep her promise. 'But we need to do something. He can't stay here much longer. John is already suspicious.'

'Oh, goodness,' Gladys fretted, folding her arms and starting to pace up and down the room.

'It's all right, I'll tell him I've checked in on you and everything was fine. That will buy us some time to come up with a plan. But I can't lie to him for too long.'

'Thank you,' Gladys said, stopping her pacing to face Irene. 'And I'm sorry about the smell. Poor thing hasn't been near a bath since he got back, and he refuses to let me wash his uniform.'

'He's not coping very well, that's for sure,' Irene said sadly before bidding Gladys farewell.

Irene left the house feeling a lot less positive than she had felt when she'd arrived. She didn't want to lie to John, but she couldn't tell him the truth, not yet. From what she could tell, Jack wasn't a bad man. He certainly didn't deserve to be blindfolded and shot dead. Now he'd made the suggestion, she couldn't get the image out of her head. But Jack couldn't hide out with Gladys for much longer. Irene couldn't help but feel a pang of longing for Maggie and Annie – if they were here now, they would know what to do. But things between them were in such a sorry state that she couldn't even write to them for advice.

Wandering the streets of Grantham, Irene tried to think of

someone she could turn to. She knew she couldn't trust Ruby, and Mary was most certainly out of the question. She had a feeling Helen might show some understanding towards Jack and his plight, but her loyalty to the WPS would see her turning him in without a second thought, even if she regretted having to do so. It was too risky.

Finding herself outside the Beehive, she let the hum of the insects take over her crowded mind. After the soothing background noise had helped her clear her thoughts, she realised with a start that she hadn't even considered Charles. *Of course!* He was her fiancé, so it went without saying that he would be there to support her and help her decide what to do for the best.

Making her way to the factory, Irene wondered why Charles hadn't been the first person she'd thought of. Doubts started to creep in as she got nearer to London Road. Maybe he hadn't sprung to mind because she now knew for certain that he didn't approve of her WPS work? She was unsure of his stance on deserters. She'd been so upset when she'd learned the fate of Mrs Barnes's deserter, but Charles had been excited about a potential investor in the factory when she'd seen him that day and, as always, she hadn't had a chance to tell him any of her news.

Regardless, they were getting on extremely well at the moment . . . so why didn't she feel sure if she could she trust him? Charles was the only person she had to turn to, so why was she feeling so reluctant to confide in him? He hadn't expressed any strong views either way on deserters the night she had sought him out after the raid – but then, they'd both been focused on Mary and why she had attacked Irene. Then they had switched to getting to know each other. Maybe he had said something, but she'd been in such a daze that it hadn't registered – or she had let it go over her head like she had with so many of the things he said.

Charles had gone behind her back to get Maggie and Annie to visit and look at how that had turned out. Would he take this information and use it without her permission? She knew he had good contacts in the police as well as at Belton Park.

When she reached the factory, she felt hesitant again. Would this all blow up in her face if she told the one person who she was supposed to be able to tell everything to? The truth was that she didn't know – so maybe she would have to test the waters first.

# 26

As it turned out, there was no need for any testing of any waters. When Irene stepped into Charles's office, she found him deep in conversation with Norman, one of the factory managers who she'd met a few times previously. Seeing her through the glass door, Charles stood up and motioned for her to come in and join them.

'My darling!' he cried over the top of Norman's head. 'We were just talking about your lot!'

'Lovely to see you,' Norman said as he got to his feet and offered Irene his chair. Intrigued, Irene gave Charles a quick kiss hello and then sat down.

'I was just about to get going on my rounds,' Norman said. 'I'll leave your good man here to fill you in,' he added, giving Irene's shoulder a quick pat and waving briefly to Charles as he left the room.

'My lot?' Irene asked as Charles sat down at his chair on the other side of the desk. 'WPS?'

'Yes, indeed. One of Norman's friends up in Scotland says the patrols over that way found a deserter a few days ago. Would you believe he's been sent to rot in jail already? And Norman's brother was picked to be on the firing squad when someone in his regiment refused to go over the top last month. Norman got a letter from him this morning telling him all about it. You can say what you like about the British Army lacking resources on the battlefield, but they're certainly efficient when it comes to executing the cowards!'

Irene's pulse started racing. Did Charles somehow know about Mrs Goode and her visitor? Was this just a coincidence or was he in fact testing her for some reason?

'Whereabouts did they discover the man in Scotland?' she asked as lightly as she could manage. She hoped he hadn't picked up on the quiver in her voice.

'Silly sod was hiding out with his mother! I mean, can you believe it? Of course, that was the first place they looked.' Charles shook his head and laughed loudly. Irene couldn't believe what she was hearing – he seemed to be taking joy in this awful news.

'It just goes to show how incompetent the little blighter was. But, of course, if he couldn't handle life on the front line and had to run home to mummy, then he was probably a bit of a lost cause anyway. If you ask me, they should have shot him like they do with the men in France. Best thing for it, in my opinion. I'd bet any other weaklings in his regiment tempted to run away would give it a second thought.'

He shook his head again and looked through some papers on his desk. He seemed to be finished on the topic. It was like the unfortunate soldier's fate was as inconsequential to him as a speck of dirt on his shoe.

'Those poor men,' Irene whispered, before realising she'd said it out loud.

'What do you mean, *poor men*?' Charles asked incredulously. His cheery tone had been replaced with one of irritation. 'They brought shame on this country with their actions!'

'But it sounds just terrible out there, Charles. The things these men must be seeing . . . it doesn't bear thinking about. Men shot down and blown up in front of them. Their own friends. I don't think I could go back to it after witnessing something like that.'

'Yes, well, that's because you're a *woman*,' he said, and his smile was slightly patronising. 'You're not cut out for such things. That's why there are no females out on the battlefields, dear. My goodness! Can you imagine? You'd all be running scared like these chaps at the first sound of gunfire!'

Irene's blood was boiling now. It was bad enough that her fiancé couldn't show any compassion to someone in such a terrible situation – a dead man, no less. But to turn this around and use it as yet another excuse to put her down?

'My sex has nothing to do with it!' she snapped, unable to hold back any longer.

The shock on Charles's face told her she'd gone too far with her outburst and she immediately panicked.

'What did you say to me?' he asked incredulously, looking out of the window and down at the factory floor to make sure nobody was looking up to try and see what the commotion was about.

'Nothing,' Irene whispered, suddenly terrified.

As she watched his face turn puce with anger, Maggie's words about Charles reminding her of her father started ringing in her ears. She was certain her friend was wrong. Maybe standing up to Charles about something they were both passionate about would prove that. Men like Maggie's father didn't tolerate strong women disagreeing with them. Charles wasn't like that – he would calm down and see where she was coming from. She just needed to explain her side of things for him to understand instead of shying away from the confrontation.

'It's not a gender issue,' she said, gently now, clasping her hands together to stop them from shaking. 'It's about being a human being. Think about how you would feel if you were running through no man's land and a shell dropped down next to you and blew Norman up. Would you just get up and carry on fighting, or might you find that a little hard to wipe from your memory? Could you continue on, knowing that could very well happen to you, too? Or might you struggle?'

'I would ruddy well keep going and stick a bullet in the German who killed Norman – and he would do the same for me,' Charles replied firmly. 'That's the difference between men and women – and cowards. Men don't let these things take over. They get on and do the job they're there to do. If I didn't have this factory to run, I'd be out there doing my bit too and I'd rather die for this country than scurry away and leave my comrades a man down because I was weak. The British Army can no more afford to carry cowards than it can traitors. You won't change my mind on this, Irene. Those men shirked their responsibility and let down their whole regiments. You have to stamp out that kind of behaviour otherwise it spreads and before you know it, we've lost the war.'

'But they're running from the German guns just to be shot by the British ones,' Irene tried to reason. 'They know their fate is to be court-martialled and shot for cowardice when they leave. At the very least they'll lose their freedom for goodness knows how long. Can you not see how terrified of the battlefield they must be to do that knowing what surely awaits them when they're inevitably found?'

'What I *cannot* see, Irene Wilson, is why you are trying to argue with me about this,' Charles spat angrily, suddenly rising from his chair. 'How *dare* you speak back to me.'

Irene cowered in her chair. Her hands were shaking even more now. Was Charles about to confirm Maggie's suspicions?

'I knew this WPS nonsense was getting too much,' Charles sighed suddenly, walking around the table towards her. He was speaking kindly again now, all his rage dissipated. His mood swings could be so confusing sometimes. 'Things like this are bound to give women strange ideas.' He took both her hands in his and pulled her to her feet.

Irene's mind was racing as he took a stray hair and tucked it behind her ear – a gesture that used to make her legs wobble but right now made her feel sick to her stomach.

'The sooner you leave and forget about it all, the better. Maybe you should think about letting it go *before* we are married. I think that would be best for both of us.'

Irene pulled her hands out of his grasp. Now Charles was calm again, she could feel her confidence creeping back. She was desperate to prove he wasn't like Maggie's father.

'This has nothing to do with the WPS,' she said cautiously. 'If I'm going to be your wife then you're going to have to accept that some of my views are quite different to yours and I *will* stand up for what I believe in. I disagree entirely with your attitude towards deserters, but I'm willing to accept it as you're my fiancé. You should be showing me the same respect.'

Charles stared at her in silence and she felt proud of herself for sticking up for what she believed in. As soon as she was talking to Maggie and Annie again, she would enjoy telling them about this moment.

Charles looked behind him to the window overlooking the factory floor, and then back at Irene. 'If there weren't so many eyes on me right now, I can assure you I would knock some sense into you,' he growled through gritted teeth, leaning in towards her.

Irene took a step back in shock and fear. She had always known she and Charles had different views on things, but she had never believed he could behave like this. She had become terrified of life without him, but now she had seen the real man the idea of staying with him was beginning to feel even more frightening, even if it meant she would be alone in the world. There was only one thing she could do.

'I think this was all a mistake,' she said shakily. 'Maggie was right – you're just like her father and I want nothing to do with a man like that.' Without another word, she took the gorgeous ring from her pocket where she always kept it when she was on duty and placed it into his palm.

She turned to walk away but Charles grabbed her arm and pulled her back so quickly she yelped.

'Please, that hurts,' she winced. He had pulled her so close to his body that they were almost touching.

He put his mouth right next to her ear, so she could feel his warm breath against her skin. Anyone looking up from the factory floor would think he was whispering sweet nothings to her, but instead he hissed, 'I've saved your family. If you think you can leave me just like that then you have another think coming.' With that, he released her arm and smirked at her. Then he thrust the engagement ring back into her pocket.

'What do you mean?' she asked quietly as Charles walked back around the desk and sat down in his chair.

'I mean,' he said as he shuffled the papers and started sorting through them again, 'that you owe me. You're in my debt.' He paused and peered up to look her in the eye. 'Do I really have to spell it out, Irene? Heavens above, I thought you were a little brighter than this, I really did.'

Irene didn't know what to say as he sighed and waited for an answer. All her previous bravado from sticking up for herself had vanished. When she didn't respond to his question, Charles continued. 'If you leave me, I'll withdraw the funding for Henry's care. And the rest of your no-good family will be out on the streets too as I'll take their lovely new home away. Do you understand now?'

She felt dizzy as the realisation dawned on her. Charles wasn't who she'd thought he was. She'd fallen in love with a monster and now she was trapped.

'Are you going to answer me?' he roared. Irene jumped. She had been completely lost in her panic.

'Yes, I understand,' she stuttered, not wanting to make him any angrier.

'Oh good, I *am* pleased about that,' he said, smiling sweetly now. 'Now, run along, my dear, and have a good day,' he added cheerily as he got back to his paperwork. 'We'll have a talk about your WPS work the next time you have an evening off to come over for dinner.'

Irene was beyond confused. He'd been so ruthless and nasty to her just seconds ago, and now he'd snapped back to being friendly and was acting as if nothing had happened. He didn't look up from his desk again and after a brief pause Irene slowly made her way out of the office on wobbly legs.

As she stepped back out on to the street, her head felt foggy. Maggie had been right about Charles all along. Why hadn't she listened to her? He was controlling Irene already and there was nothing she could do about it. He had her over a barrel. There was no way she could afford to pay for Henry's care in that fancy spa in Switzerland, let alone the rent on the new house he'd arranged for Ruth and the rest of the children. She couldn't break off the engagement. She would have to marry him and abide by his rules, which meant saying goodbye to the WPS for ever. How could the man she thought she'd loved – and who claimed to love her – treat her like this?

Tears stung Irene's cheeks as it dawned on her that she was stuck fast. And there was nobody she could turn to for help. She felt too ashamed to admit the truth to Maggie and Annie, but even if she did come clean to them, what could they do to help? None of Maggie's grand plans would be of any use in this situation. Since her father had cut her off, she was just as hard-up as Irene. She didn't have the kind of money Charles had available to rescue her from this predicament. And Annie would be kind and caring as usual, but what use was that right now? She knew Annie's family were financially sound but not to the extent that they could fund everything Irene needed in order to get away from Charles.

Irene found herself wandering back towards Belton Park. She often found the fields between the town and the camp peaceful and she needed somewhere quiet to clear her head. Sitting down underneath the big oak tree, she pulled out the engagement ring and moved it around between her fingers as she took some time to think. She knew what she needed to do. In order to save her family, she would have to become Mrs Murphy – and accept everything that entailed.

# 27

When Irene's stomach started to grumble, she realised she had been sitting under the oak tree far too long. It was nearly teatime and quite apart from her personal problems, she hadn't worked out what she was going to say to John, let alone been back to see him. She didn't want him turning up at his mother's house looking for answers. So, she stood up and dusted herself down ready to walk back into town. She hoped the pressure of the deadline might help her come up with a solution, and it would also be a good way of taking her mind off her dreadful situation with Charles.

Her plan worked – by the time she reached the bakery, Irene had decided to buy herself some time by confirming to John his mother was struggling to cope with their two painful losses so close together. It wasn't a complete lie.

'I think some female company will do her good,' Irene insisted when she got there. 'So, leave her be for now but be here for her when she comes by to see you. And I'll make sure I pop in for a cuppa and a chat with her regularly until she's feeling better. I'll also make sure she eats more of the bread you give her.'

John was extremely grateful, and Irene felt terrible for keeping the full truth from him. But she desperately needed some more time to figure out what to do for the best, and her head was clouded with her own dilemma regarding Charles at the moment. She couldn't comprehend turning Jack over to the possibility of the firing squad, but she knew he couldn't stay on at Gladys's with the poor woman convinced he was her grandson for too much longer.

Just before she left, an idea popped into Irene's head. She had put helping Billy to one side after news of him stealing from Charles had reached the whole town. Now that some time had passed, she wondered if John might be willing to help. This was the perfect time to ask him, as he was feeling grateful to her for helping his mother.

'I could do with an extra pair of hands for a few mornings a week,' John said. 'But isn't that the boy who stole from your Mr Murphy?' he added cautiously.

'It is,' Irene replied, her heartbeat quickening with fear at the sound of Charles's name. 'But he only did that because he was in such a desperate situation. Nobody talks about the part where he was trying to get food for his mother, who is really very ill. Charles felt so bad for him that he even gave him some money himself after I caught him.'

Irene's breath caught in her throat at the memory. The Charles she had met that day was so different to the Charles she had just been with. She wondered where everything had gone wrong. But she was pulled back to the present when she realised John still looked unsure. Her mind back on helping Billy, Irene persevered. 'Do you really think Charles's fiancée would be trying to find him work if she didn't believe there was some good in him?'

That seemed to change things for John, and he agreed to give Billy some work on a trial basis. Irene was delighted and went straight to his house to try and find him again. This time, she struck lucky and he opened the door.

'Ah, hello miss. I ain't been up to nothing bad,' he said as soon as he saw her.

'I should hope not,' Irene laughed. She didn't believe him for one minute, but she had a soft spot for the boy and admired his cheekiness.

Once she'd explained about the work at the bakery, he seemed excited. 'Me mam's getting worse,' he told her, 'So we've no money coming in now.'

'Well, now you can bring her home money *and* some bread regularly,' Irene said cheerily. 'I hope the money Mr Murphy gave you helped a little?'

'Not one bit!' Billy cried, shaking his head.

'Whatever do you mean?' Irene asked.

'I went straight out to buy some vegetables and medicine after you dropped me home, and I bumped into him at the end of the road. He led me down a side street out of sight and took the money back! I might be young, but I know his type and I knew it were too good to be true the moment he handed it over – that's why I didn't want to take it in the first place. He probably followed us back here to make sure he could get his mitts back on the money as soon as possible. Rich folk like him only do stuff like that to impress others.'

His face had turned red while he was speaking, and Irene could feel the anger and humiliation seeping out of him. She also felt humiliated – Billy had been able to see through Charles straight away, even before he had taken the money back. But she'd been sucked right in. His charm and good looks had pulled her in and seen her overlook all the warning signs. Nothing had *gone wrong* since she'd first met him – he'd always been selfish and cruel. If she hadn't felt like a fool before then she certainly did now.

That evening as Ruby, Mary and Helen enjoyed the bread Irene had delivered earlier in the day with some vegetable stew, she pondered what to do with her evening off. Helen had sprung it on her at the last minute, which she was grateful for as it meant Charles didn't know about it. The last thing she wanted to do was to go and see him to discuss all the ways he was going to control her now they were both clear on the fact that she had no choice but to agree to everything he desired.

She decided on an early night – she certainly needed the rest. But as the others left to patrol and the house fell silent, she found herself unable to relax. Thoughts of Charles and the menacing way he had snarled at her in his office, along with his threat of violence, ran through her head until she felt ready to scream.

When she could bear it no more, she decided to go and visit Mrs Goode and Jack. If she couldn't rest, then she may as well get started on figuring out what to do about their complicated situation. *And the best way to do that is to find out more about Jack*, she thought as she threw on some of the clothes she had brought with her to Grantham.

When she looked at herself in the mirror, she thought she looked like herself for the first time since she had met Charles. Those fine dresses were all very well, but they weren't who she really was. She'd been playing dress-up, pretending to be someone she wasn't. And now, she realised with a pang of regret, the days when she could be her true self were numbered. Charles would never let her dress like this when they were married. She turned away from the glass so that she didn't have to watch the tears making their way down her face.

When she reached Mrs Goode's street, she looked around herself for the first time since leaving the house. She had scurried across town with a shawl covering most of her face, terrified of bumping into Charles or being spotted by one of his acquaintances, but as far as she could tell she had been successful.

Knocking on Mrs Goode's front door for the second time that day, she felt apprehensive. It probably hadn't been one of her best ideas to turn up unexpected so late in the evening given the circumstances, but she was hopeful that her new companion would answer and welcome her in. She heard hushed voices and shuffling, followed by the sound of the living room door being closed, so she assumed Mrs Goode was squirrelling Jack away again. Then the door was tentatively pulled ajar, but Gladys relaxed when she saw Irene and threw it wider to let her in. Giving three knocks on the living-room door as she passed it on her way back to the kitchen, she shouted back at Irene.

'Close the front door behind you, love!' Irene did as she was told, and then stepped aside as the living-room door swung open and Jack joined her in the hallway. Stubble still covered the lower part of his face, and his hair was still dirty. Confessing to her about his situation hadn't made him feel any better, then, Irene thought sadly. Jack nodded and gave her a nervous smile.

'Hello again,' Irene said warmly as they both made their way into the kitchen, where they found Gladys already preparing a pot of tea and some bread and butter.

'We have a special knock,' she explained without turning around to face them. 'When I give three loud bangs, it means the coast is clear for Joe to come out.' She picked up the plate and approached the table. 'Thank goodness for your father, eh?' Gladys smiled at Jack as she placed the offering in the middle of the table and motioned for them both to sit down. 'His bakery is helping get you back to full health!' She bustled back across the room to tend to the teapot, while Irene and Jack sat down at the table.

Jack looked over at Irene uncomfortably, and she smiled weakly back. One thing was certain: he wasn't taking advantage of poor Gladys's confused state. That look on his face told her that he felt terrible for the fact she was still convinced he was her grandson. But at least Gladys seemed in good spirits.

As the three of them got chatting, Irene forgot all about

her original reason for visiting. Gladys was so animated once she got going and although Jack was quiet, he had a warm, calm air about him that made Irene feel comfortable in his presence. As the evening went on, he started chipping in to the conversations more and it seemed as though he was relaxing in her company already. When Irene looked up to check the time, she was startled to see that it was already past ten o'clock. She made her apologies and excused herself, then hurried back across the town, keeping her shawl over her head.

As she lay in bed, the cruel situation with Charles crept back into her mind, and she found herself unable to stop tears from streaming down her face. More than anything, she was angry with herself for allowing Charles to dupe her. She had been so willing to be swept up by his good looks and his charm that she hadn't seen any of the warning signs. Letting out a loud sob, she felt relieved Mary was out late patrolling and she didn't have to hide her sadness. Feeling free to embrace it felt good – after all, all she could do now was accept the awful position she found herself in – and she had nobody to blame but herself.

Over the next week or so Irene found herself drawn back to number 48 Castlegate more and more. She popped in while on duty whenever she was sure none of her colleagues would notice her absence, and she often stopped in on her way home, too. It became her new salvation – the role Charles's home had taken on previously. Irene had given Helen the same explanation she'd given John and she was grateful to have the cover story in place. But she had to be careful as she knew suspicions would be raised if it was noted that she had been visiting too frequently.

When she thought about it, she was never sure if she was going in order to see Gladys or Jack. She enjoyed the company of them both, and the three of them always sat together in the kitchen and talked over a cup of tea. As she got to know them better, she felt so relaxed in their company that her worries and angst over Charles just melted away whenever she was with them.

She felt like her company was helping Jack, too. He had finally agreed to let Gladys wash his uniform and he had started to wear some of Joe's old clothes she'd had stored away. He was so well built that they were all a little short and tight, and he joked to Irene about how silly he looked when Gladys was out of earshot. Irene found it refreshing that someone in such a terrible situation could find the strength to laugh at himself. And Jack had started to wash himself, too – his hair was now clean, and it looked lighter as it fell in a gentle wave across his forehead. His face looked a little fresher, although his eyes were still bloodshot and sunken. He was definitely coming out of his shell slowly but surely and she was enjoying getting to know his personality.

She had found herself smiling over at him on more than one occasion, and she'd had to look away quickly when he had turned his head and caught her. She wasn't sure what kept pulling her in, but she found him so intriguing. Maybe it was the fact that he never gave away anything about his background or his life before the war. Irene felt greedy to learn more about him, but she never pushed him.

One day she popped over fresh from breaking up a brawl between two drunk soldiers in Market Place. She was feeling a bit shaky and thought Gladys and Jack's company and a cup of tea might help calm her down. She hadn't intended to mention anything about the encounter – she was used to keeping things like that to herself as they just got Charles started on his quest to get her to quit the WPS – but Jack asked her if she was all right and she found herself telling him and Gladys all about it.

'I could see something was on your mind,' Jack said quietly, staring into his cup. 'I can't believe you managed to break up two angry men like that,' he laughed softly. Irene smiled – he sounded impressed and not disdainful like Charles would be if she had relayed the anecdote to him. She felt sad as she thought about how Charles would probably have said something to make her feel like she had acted in the wrong. 'I bet they never saw those ju-jitsu moves coming,' Jack added, looking up at Irene now. It was a fleeting glance, but Irene caught his eye and she was certain she saw a flash of happiness behind them before they seemed to glaze over again and he looked away.

After that day, she told Gladys and Jack all about what she'd been up to on patrol whenever she dropped in. It felt refreshing to be able to share that part of her life with people who seemed genuinely interested in hearing about it. It made her realise anew that it *was* interesting. Yet Charles had never wanted to know anything about it, and now he was intent on her quitting she made sure to keep quiet about her duties while in his company so as not to rile him up about it.

One afternoon, Irene panicked when there was no answer to her knock on the door at Gladys's. Thoughts of army officials storming in and dragging poor Jack away while Gladys wept helplessly flashed through Irene's mind. But when she tried knocking again, she thought she heard a small noise inside. If Jack was alone, he wouldn't answer the door, she thought to herself. She bent down and opened the letterbox.

'It's only me,' she half-whispered, conscious of drawing attention to herself if anyone was walking past. She relaxed as she heard footsteps, and the door was opened a notch. She gently pushed her way in. Jack had released the door and then stepped back into the living room so that no one would see him when it was opened. Irene closed the door behind her and stood with Jack in the living room.

'Are you alone?' Irene asked, startled that Gladys had left him to fend for himself.

'Gladys has gone to get some bread, she won't be long,' Jack replied. Of course, Irene thought. She had forgotten that Gladys was making more of an effort nowadays to visit the bakery and keep up appearances with John.

'I'll, erm, I guess I'll leave you to it, then,' she replied awkwardly. She wasn't sure why, but it felt wrong to be here on her own with Jack – she was used to it being the three of them.

'Gladys will be back soon,' Jack replied. 'We could wait in the kitchen together?' He seemed nervous about making the suggestion, and Irene didn't want to upset him by saying no. But she found that she also felt nervous.

'Yes, of course,' she blustered, while trying to make sense of everything she was feeling. Why was she so jumpy at the thought of being alone with Jack?

He walked past her to lead the way to the kitchen. 'What tales do you have to share today?' he asked once they were both sat at their usual spots at the table. She noticed his knee jerk up and down a couple of times before he slammed his hand down onto it and it stopped. He laughed nervously. 'Has a life of its own sometimes,' he whispered.

Irene could sense he felt self-conscious about it, so she quickly started telling him about how she'd run into Stella that morning. She'd never told anyone about how she was helping Stella – she would lose her job if word got out, after all. But she found herself giving Jack the full story. She found it so easy to open up to him, and she realised that she trusted him.

'You're a very decent woman, Irene,' Jack said warmly. She tried to brush the compliment aside – she hadn't heard one for so long that it made her feel uncomfortable. 'I mean it,' Jack stressed. 'You're putting yourself on the line for me, which is admirable enough. But now you tell me how you're risking everything for these women. I think you might be the kindest person I've ever met.'

As Irene felt her face turn tomato-red, the sound of Gladys's key in the door travelled down the hallway and she breathed a sigh of relief at the distraction.

Back out on patrol, she kept thinking back to Jack's words. She knew he was just being friendly. After all, it was in his interests to keep her on his side. But there had been something in the way he'd looked at her when he'd said those things. The glaze had been lost from across his eyes, and it was like she'd had a glimpse of the true Jack, free from all the horrors of the battlefield that normally consumed him. She pushed the thoughts to the back of her mind when she realised, with a dull thud of dread, that it was time to get ready to see Charles.

She had made sure to keep up her regular visits to see Charles since he'd threatened her at the factory. She didn't want to rock the boat. But, so far, she had always stopped in to see him while she was on duty, so she was able to make an excuse to get away after a short while. They hadn't discussed their deserter disagreement, and Irene found that if she agreed with all his opinions and kept her own to herself, they got on brilliantly and he was his old, charming self with her.

It was easy to get drawn in and forget everything that was really going on sometimes – that's how good he was at it. She felt sad every time she reminded herself it was all a facade, but she was willing to play along if it bought her more time.

Irene knew she had avoided dinner with Charles for long enough now. Every time she lied to him about having an evening off and sneaked off to see Gladys and Jack instead, she spent the next day panicking. She was paranoid he would get fed up soon and visit Helen to demand she give her a night off, and Helen in turn would inform him that she had enjoyed many recently.

So, reluctantly, she got dressed up and slipped on her engagement ring to join Charles for dinner. Thankfully, he was in one of his better moods and Irene made sure to act like the perfect fiancée, laughing at all his jokes and not speaking unless spoken to, so that he didn't get riled. She would have had a pleasant evening if it wasn't for the toxic undercurrent that she felt running between the two of them.

Taking off her green dress to get ready for bed after returning home from Charles's, Irene felt a cloud of sadness enveloping her. They'd had a pleasant enough evening, and, to her relief, he hadn't brought up either the wedding or his desire for her to quit the WPS. But she was tired of playing his games.

Getting into bed, she thought back to her chat with Jack earlier in the day, and how good it had felt to be able to be so honest with him. He'd been showing a real interest in her WPS work and it lifted her waning spirits. She realised she felt comfortable around him in a way she only now saw she never really had with Charles – apart from the early days, of course, when he was playing the part of the perfect man. That's what he was, she realised as she drifted off to sleep: an actor. He had sussed her out immediately, knew exactly what she had wanted, and played to her all-too-willing audience.

# 28

The following day, when Irene popped back to the house for some lunch after patrolling all morning, Helen sprung another evening off on her. It was unheard of to get two nights off in a row and she was delighted at the prospect. She knew she should let Charles know and arrange to do something together, but the thought filled her with dread. Charles wouldn't be expecting to see her again so soon, she reasoned with herself as she made her way through the fields to Belton Park that afternoon.

She found herself feeling lighter once she had made the decision to go and see Gladys and Jack again. She felt so good about herself when she was in their company – and for hours afterwards. She wanted to see them as much as she could before it all came crashing down.

And she knew it would end soon, either when Charles forced her to leave the WPS, or when Jack was discovered or handed himself in. She wasn't sure which one it would be, but she knew they were all living on borrowed time.

Irene found an abandoned bicycle leaning up against the gates at the entrance to the camp. Rolling her eyes, she took hold of the handlebars and started wheeling it across the field to get it back to town so she could try and find its owner. As she made her way, she suddenly grinned at the thought of getting on the bike and whizzing across the field, feeling the wind in her hair again. But then Charles's disapproving face flashed into her mind. She couldn't bear the thought of another lecture from him if she took a second tumble. So, she trudged on, pushing the bike, the smile well and truly wiped from her face.

After locating the owner – an elderly gentleman who'd ridden it to one of the pubs the night before and got so drunk he'd walked home without realising it was missing – Irene did a few circuits of the town on foot. Then she knocked on Gladys's door and told her she would be over that night to spend some time with her and Jack. She didn't like to arrive unannounced in the evenings if she could help it.

When it was quiet like this, Irene would normally drop into the factory to say hello to Charles, but she did a round of the pubs instead.

Making her way back to number 48 Castlegate that evening, her face hidden by a shawl again, Irene decided she was going to have to come up with a solution for Jack sooner rather than later. Charles was going to make sure she left the WPS and she couldn't leave Jack and Gladys in the lurch once she'd handed back her uniform.

When Gladys answered the door, she was dressed in a smart two-piece with frills around the collar.

Irene took a step back to take in her splendour. 'Oh Gladys! How lovely you look,' she gasped.

Gladys blushed and waved away her compliment before motioning for her to come in. Closing the door behind Irene, she explained why she wasn't in her usual attire.

'I know you said I needed to reassure John, so I'm going over for dinner,' she said proudly. 'I haven't wanted to leave Joe on his own at night since he came back, but knowing you'd be here with him while I'm out makes me feel more comfortable about it.'

Irene felt her palms getting clammy. She loved spending time with Jack, so why was she getting jittery at the thought of an evening alone with him? She realised her nerves were born out of excitement, and she was surprised to feel so happy at the thought of more time with her new friend.

'You don't mind, do you?' Gladys asked, concern etched across her face as she took in Irene's expression. 'You two get along so well, I thought you'd love some time alone without this old-timer butting in!'

'Oh, of course not,' Irene said in a rush as she stepped in off the street and made her way along the hallway.

Jack was waiting in the kitchen doorway. As Irene took in his height and his broad shoulders, she realised how imposing his presence was. Or was that just because she was feeling so jittery? No matter, she found she couldn't take her eyes off his smile as it spread across his face at the sight of her.

'I thought we could play some cards,' he said warmly, placing his hand on her shoulder. As his hand made contact with her body, Irene felt shivers run through her. What was happening? She had only ever thought of Gladys and Jack as a pair – until yesterday afternoon she hadn't spent any time alone with Jack since their first meeting in the sitting room. Now she had the opportunity to have Jack to herself once more, she realised she was feeling excited about it. *You're in enough of a pickle with Charles as it is without adding another problem to the mix*, she scolded herself, quickly pushing the feelings away.

The pair of them bid farewell to Gladys and took up their usual places at the kitchen table. As Jack poured out the tea their friend had prepared for them, Irene found she enjoyed watching him at work. She was so used to Gladys serving up that the teapot seemed tiny in Jack's huge hands. She studied him closely as he concentrated on pouring their drinks without spilling a drop. He looked pleased with himself but then he was caught out by a quiver in his wrist as he went to place the teapot down, and Irene looked away quickly to save him any embarrassment.

She decided now would be a great time to start devising a plan to save his future.

'I don't think I'll be with the WPS much longer,' she admitted sadly. 'We need to sort out what you're going to do, Jack. I want to make sure you're safe and Gladys is all right before I leave.'

He looked up at her. She wasn't sure, but she thought she could see fear in his eyes.

'I was glad when Gladys said she was going out this evening,' he said, suddenly dropping his gaze down into his cup.

Irene's stomach flipped and she waited with bated breath for him to continue.

'I've been desperate to talk to you alone about all this,' he added glumly. 'I was going to try earlier but I got scared.'

Irene's heart dropped. Of course he wanted to discuss how he was going to get out of this situation safely. She silently admonished herself for thinking he'd want to spend time alone with her for a different reason. This man's future was on the line – how self-absorbed of her to believe he could be thinking of her instead of what fate lay in store for him at the end of this. And anyway, she was getting married to someone else.

'You're right,' Jack continued. 'This can't continue for much longer. I'm terrified of being found out and things will be a lot worse for me if I'm captured instead of handing myself in.'

Irene's heart raced listening to his words. She'd always known Jack would have to surrender himself eventually – it was the only way. She had just refused to think about it as all the possible consequences were too devastating.

'There's more chance they'll let me live if I take myself back,' Jack continued stoically. 'Although to be honest, a bullet to my head would be a relief right now. At least it would be an end to all the pain.'

'Please don't talk like that,' Irene cried. Before she knew it, she had reached across the table and grabbed both Jack's hands in her own. The contact between them gave her goose-bumps. They sat in silence for a long time, both taking comfort in the sensation of the other's hands in their own.

'What do you mean?' Irene asked finally.

Jack looked up to meet her eyes questioningly.

'What pain are you in? How can death be a better alternative?'

Jack took a deep breath and then stared down at their hands, which were now tightly entwined.

'I haven't slept properly for weeks, Irene,' he whispered. His eyes filled and he pulled his hands away to place his head in them, as he had done the day they first met. Irene longed to comfort him, but she forced herself to hold back. It felt as though his body was in the room with her, but his mind was somewhere else – somewhere terrible.

'Every time I close my eyes it all flashes back into my head like a newsreel,' he groaned. 'I can't escape it. I ran away but it followed me. When I do eventually manage to get to sleep, I wake up shouting. It's getting worse. The neighbours must be able to hear me – someone will work it all out soon, and I'll be done for.'

Irene remembered John mentioning the neighbours commenting on hearing shouting through the walls as well as what they thought was Gladys talking to herself, and she knew he was right. They were lucky to have made it this far.

'Even when I stay awake, I can't hide from it,' he continued. 'The dreams can occur right in the middle of a conversation. I'll be talking to Gladys about where she's been for the after-noon and then, suddenly, a row of soldiers – my friends – are being struck down by machine-gun fire right in front of me. I thought I'd feel better once I knew I didn't have to go back to the battlefield, but I would've been better off back there. At least if I'd died in action, I'd have died a hero.' Jack looked up at Irene, his bloodshot eyes streaming with tears. 'Now I'll die a coward and my family will be too ashamed to even talk about me. I won't even get a proper grave.'

'Why don't you tell me what happened,' Irene tried tentatively, brushing her own tears from her cheeks. 'Maybe talking about what you saw will help you.'

She wasn't sure if it would work, but she knew when she'd finally come clean to Maggie and Annie about her circumstances, she had felt a lot lighter for it. And Maggie had certainly benefitted from revealing everything about her attack to her friends. The experiences were worlds apart from what Jack had been through, but she reasoned that the principle might just be the same. Either way, she'd be in a better position to help him if she understood more about why he had deserted the army.

As the pause lengthened, Irene started to worry she'd pushed him too hard. Then he took a deep, steadying breath and started to talk.

'Everyone was so positive when we started out on the southern pincer.' He was still leaning forward on to the table, but his elbows were resting on the edge of it, and his hands were covering his mouth, so his words came out muffled. He stared straight through her as he spoke. Irene wondered with a shiver if he could see what he was explaining playing out on the wall behind her.

'We opened our bombardment with field guns firing shrapnel at Fritz's wire and howitzers firing high-explosive shells on to the front line. They told us to ramp it up after half an hour, then they started sending men over the top.' He paused, taking his hands away from his mouth and placing them into his lap, his back hunched over. Irene saw his eyes glaze over, so that he wasn't there in the room with her any more.

She got up and moved her chair next to his. He didn't

move an inch as she sat down beside him and put an arm as far as she could around his shoulder. Then he edged himself slowly to the side until he found her shoulder, and he nestled his head into the space between it and her neck. Irene was pleased he felt calm enough in her presence to allow her to soothe him like this. She tried to push aside how good it felt to have him in her arms as she stroked his hair comfortingly while he continued, as she would a frightened dog.

'They started heavy machine-gun fire from the other side. It was cutting the men down before they even got over the top – they were being struck on their ladders and falling back down into the trench. I had to wipe the brains of one of my closest friends off my face while I waited for my turn.' Jack's knee started jittering up and down as he struck his heel continuously against the floor. Irene took her hand away from his hair and placed it firmly but gently on his leg. He jumped and pulled his head away from her shoulder. As he stared at her face, it looked as if he was waking, confused, from a deep dream.

'It's all right, you're in Gladys's kitchen with me,' Irene said, taking care to keep her voice soft, and realisation and familiarity swept over his face.

'Sorry. I went back there,' he croaked. 'That's one of the scenes that comes to me when I close my eyes. It always feels so incredibly real. I can even smell the gunfire.'

Irene blinked back more tears, unable to imagine what it must feel like to experience something so horrific. 'Take your time,' she soothed. He edged back towards her again.

'Can I?' he asked cautiously, nodding his head towards her shoulder.

'Come here,' she whispered, pulling his head gently in place again and running her fingers through his hair once more. She was amazed at how right it felt.

'Even as men were being gunned down and their bodies

falling back into the trench, we were getting orders to keep going over. So, we pressed forward. I didn't want to go over, I really didn't. But all around me the trench was filling with dead and wounded men, and the shouts to attack kept coming.' Jack paused again and Irene continued stroking him, confident he would continue when he was ready.

'Somehow, I made it up and over without getting hit,' he said eventually. 'Men were falling all around me, but I wasn't able to stop and help them – I had to keep advancing, according to the orders of the officers. As we set out across no man's land, the Germans set their machine guns on us.' His voice was shaking worse than ever, and Irene knew he was experiencing all the horror of it again.

'I watched as whole rows of men in front of me were hit. I had to keep going forward as one by one their bodies jolted when bullets struck and they either fell to the ground or staggered around screaming for their mothers, before giving up or being hit again and collapsing at last.' There was another pause before Jack started speaking again.

'Then it was my turn,' he almost whispered, and Irene stopped stroking his hair and instead focused on making out what he was saying. 'I think I cried out when the bullet hit my leg. It sent me straight down. I've never felt anything like it. I lay in a mix of mud and blood, clutching my knee up to my chest, willing all the shots coming past me to find me and put me out of my misery. I'd had enough.'

Irene hoped this would be where Jack's trauma ended – that this was the point where someone came and hauled him back to the relative safety of the trenches. But she could tell from his quick, ragged breathing that there was more to come.

'I wasn't granted the luxury of a quick exit,' Jack continued, his voice bitter now. Irene's heart sunk. 'Either back to the trenches or out of this world. Some poor bugger was hit as he tried to step over me. He fell on top of me like a sack of spuds, taking all the air out of me. As I struggled to catch my breath, he groaned and tried to roll onto the floor, but he stayed where he was. I knew then that he was done for. His head was resting on my chest, and the blood was pouring from his neck and pooling next to us on the ground.'

Irene felt sick at the image it conjured up in her mind.

'I focused on the blood as it seeped into the dirt to try and take my mind off the fact that a man was slowly dying on top of me. I thought about my parents as his breathing grew shallower. Then my thoughts turned to his parents. I wondered where they were at that moment, as their son was taking his final breaths. Had they told him everything they'd wanted to before he left for France? Did he know how much he was loved before he ended up there, waiting for it all to end? What had been left unsaid between them? Surely nobody can truly leave this world having heard everything that they should hear? There are always things left unspoken, regrets . . .'

The dampness of Irene's shoulder told her Jack was crying. She'd never seen a man cry before, and her heart broke for him. She was startled to realise how much his pain affected her.

'I didn't even know his name,' he muttered, sobbing now so that Irene could barely make out what he was saying. 'We lay there for hours as smoke filled the air and the bullets and explosions kept coming. Once he'd stopped breathing, I felt relieved, but also jealous, and guilty at the same time. He was free of it all, but I was stuck there. I thought about rolling him on to the floor, but it seemed so callous. And part of me was enjoying the human contact after so long stuck in the trenches.

'At some point they started bringing the stretchers out to pick up the wounded, and that's when I rolled him to the floor and made myself known. I had no idea they would try and send me back to France.'

Jack pulled himself away from Irene now so he could look

her in the face. 'Why would they send any of us back to face that again?' he asked her, his voice cracking with terror and misery and his eyes searching her for answers she didn't have. 'I wish that bullet had taken my leg away so I could escape all this. I would rather spend the rest of my life as a cripple than go back there.'

She realised with a start that he was shaking like a leaf.

'Oh Jack, you've been through hell and back,' she said gently as she pulled him back in and held him tight.

It was clear everything he'd seen and suffered through had affected him psychologically. She had heard a little bit about war neurosis – hundreds of men were returning from the front struggling to deal with their experiences, and some were being treated for it instead of being sent back out to fight. Maybe if she could make Jack's officers understand why he'd fled, then they might find a doctor to diagnose him.

She still didn't know if the firing squad was a certainty for deserters captured in Britain – how could she ask anyone without raising suspicions? No matter what lay in store, she was sure that Jack deserved help for what he had been through, rather than punishment, whether that be death or a lengthy prison sentence. It was a long shot, but it was his best chance of making it out of this with the help he so desperately needed, so she had to try.

They stayed in the embrace for so long that their tea was cold when they finally broke apart. As Irene rose to make a fresh pot, it was clear that Jack wanted to change the subject, but as she cast around for a safe topic, he started to talk.

'Anyway, enough about me. You said you wouldn't be with the WPS much longer,' he said, sounding concerned. 'Why on earth would you leave when it sounds like you're doing so well?'

Irene felt a swell of pride. She hadn't felt good about her WPS work for a long time – Charles never showed any interest and she hardly spoke to Mary or Ruby. Then she felt a wave of guilt. Jack had been so honest with her about something so personal, and yet she had never opened up to him about her private life. Jack had become a firm friend, but he didn't really know anything about her – he didn't even know that she was engaged. Since learning the truth about Charles, she only wore the ring when she was in his company. This was the perfect opportunity to set everything straight, but she didn't know how to explain her situation with Charles without coming across as weak and naive – things she found she was desperate not to be in front of Jack. And she felt like she and Jack had enough on their plate to get sorted as it was.

'I think they'll probably send me back to London soon,' she lied. She felt an overwhelming heaviness in her heart at the betrayal, but she pushed it away. She didn't want to burden Jack with her problems, not with everything he was already having to deal with.

'That's a shame,' Jack sighed. 'I look forward to your visits.'

'Well, we both know this has to end soon anyway,' she said, feeling a dart of sadness at the thought.

'I don't want to run. I can't spend the rest of my life hiding. It's no way to live. I'm not a coward, you know,' Jack said, rare pride sparking in his eyes. 'I need to face the consequences of my actions.

'I think that's best too,' agreed Irene. 'We have to get you back to your regiment before you're discovered. Like you said, it will be better for you if you hand yourself in rather than them getting a tip-off from one of Gladys's neighbours.' Her mind flashed to Mary. She had been keeping her distance recently, but she certainly didn't trust her to not run straight to an officer up at Belton Park if she caught even a whiff of what was going on here.

'Will you keep in touch?' Jack asked hopefully.

'I'd love to,' Irene smiled. But deep down she felt a stab of pain. She knew it would never work. Once she was living with Charles, she would never be able to get post from Jack past him. She knew Charles would never allow their friendship to continue in any form. Besides, she was sure that Jack wouldn't be interested in someone like her once he was back on his feet. He was only leaning on her now as she was his only option.

They heard the key in the lock, and a few seconds later Gladys joined them in the kitchen. 'That was a lovely evening,' she smiled. 'Irene will you join us for a cuppa, and I'll tell you all about what John's been up to?'

'I must get on,' she replied apologetically, getting to her feet. She had to be up early for patrol, and she could already feel her eyelids becoming heavy. The emotions of the evening seemed to have drained all her energy.

'Don't worry, Jack, we'll figure it out,' she whispered as Gladys clattered about by the stove. She thought she had said it quietly enough so Gladys wouldn't hear over the din she was making, but she must have had hawk-like hearing.

'Jack?' she squawked, turning around to face them. 'Why did you call my Joe "Jack"?' she asked, baffled. Irene panicked and Jack, who was still sat in his chair, just stared at her helplessly.

'Oh, it's, erm, it's just a joke that has stuck, that's all,' she lied, pleased with herself for thinking on her feet but feeling flustered at the silly mistake. She waited for a reaction, praying that Gladys wouldn't ask for more of an explanation. She shrugged and got back to the stove.

Irene pretended to wipe sweat from her brow and Jack laughed silently at her. As their eyes met, Irene felt a shiver run through her body. Before she knew what she was doing, she had placed her hand on Jack's shoulder. They held eye contact as he put his hand on top of hers and gave it a squeeze.

Irene jumped and pulled her hand away when Gladys clattered a pan so loudly the sound seemed to vibrate through the kitchen. Flustered for a different reason this time, she rushed out of the room.

'I'll see you both soon,' Irene called as she headed down the hallway and let herself out.

Had that been what she thought it had been? It had felt as if that contact had meant something. Was Jack just grateful to her for her help, or did he feel something deeper? Did she feel something deeper for him? She was slowly coming to the realisation that what she'd had with Charles wasn't love. She had simply been infatuated with him, and then drawn in further when he rescued her family. She knew someone who loved her would never treat her the way Charles was treating her – he was, after all, essentially blackmailing her. And yet, she still felt drawn to him. She wasn't sure if that was because she felt so indebted to him, or if she was still clinging to the idea of the man she'd thought he was in the beginning.

When it came to Jack, Irene knew everything about him was genuine. He had been so honest and open and raw with her. She'd seen deep into his soul and she understood everything he'd been through. Their relationship was pure, and she couldn't help but compare it to the tainted one, built on lies, that she had with Charles.

Walking back to Rutland Street, Irene's thoughts darkened as they were taken over by what poor Jack had been through. She was so consumed by it that she forgot to put her shawl up to cover her face. When she realised, she ducked into an alley to cover herself up and found herself staring at Stella. She hadn't seen her for weeks. She had been happily assuming she was back on her feet, but the look on Stella's face as their eyes met told her she was desperate for cash again.

'I told you to come and find me before doing anything like this again,' Irene hissed.

'I've been looking for you, honest,' Stella said. 'I've only just given up.'

Irene felt awful. There was no way Stella would have found her while she was holed up at Gladys's. With everything she'd heard that evening, she didn't think her heart could cope with anything else.

'Come with me,' she ordered Stella.

'Irene, love, I really need some business tonight,' Stella hissed under her breath. 'I don't have time for another heart to heart with you. Dave found the money I've been stashing from the kids' earnings and drunk it all away at the pub so I need to make some back so we can pay the rent. I know you mean well, but please just leave me to it.'

'Trust me, you need to come with me,' Irene said through gritted teeth. Why wasn't Stella getting the hint that she wanted to get her some money so that she wouldn't have to do any of this tonight? She couldn't stand the thought of anyone having to do it at the best of times, but tonight it was just too much.

Stella grumbled but followed Irene obediently in the end, and when they got to the top of Rutland Street, Irene ordered her to wait until she came back. She crept into the house as quietly as she could. As far as she knew, Ruby and Mary were both out on patrol and Helen was taking a rare evening off and had gone out for the evening, but Irene knew she still had to be careful.

Once in the safety of her bedroom, she lifted the mattress and pulled out the envelope containing her most recent pay packet. As long as she was in Charles's clutches, the one positive was that she didn't want for anything. So, the notes that kept stacking up under her bed were of no use to her. There would never be enough to fund Henry's care, even if she convinced Charles to let her stay on with the WPS to allow her to continue saving. So what use was money to her?

She stuffed the envelope inside her shawl and hurried back outside to Stella.

'Come on, love,' Stella whispered. 'I'm losing valuable time here. The lads have just been paid so I'll have fresh pickings tonight.'

Irene thrust the envelope into her hand. 'Go home, Stella,' she ordered.

Confused, Stella opened the envelope and gasped when she saw the contents.

'Not here!' Irene panicked, looking around them to make sure nobody was watching before snatching the envelope back and shoving it into Stella's bag.

'I didn't expect anything else from you so soon,' Stella whispered. 'Especially not this much.'

'It's a bit more than last time, so it should tide you over until you've saved up again from the kids' wages,' Irene explained. 'Make sure you hide it from Dave until you can get it to your landlord.'

'Irene, I can't . . .' Stella started, but Irene had to get away – she'd taken too much of a risk as it was, talking to Stella in plain sight in such an open area, let alone handing over a package to her.

'Just promise me you'll go straight home now,' Irene urged. When Stella nodded, Irene turned on her heel and rushed back to the house.

Confident they hadn't been spotted, she got ready for bed and settled in for the most peaceful night's sleep she'd had in months. Her good deed had overpowered the terrible feelings of guilt and powerlessness that had been consuming her since leaving Jack, and she was happy that she'd been able to help Stella – even if the cash would only tide her over for a little while.

# 29

Ruby had the following morning off, so Irene went down for breakfast with Helen and Mary. The two of them were already sitting at the table when she walked in, and they fell silent when she joined them. Irene was so busy thinking about the moment she'd had with Jack the night before that she didn't even register the frosty atmosphere.

'Mary was just telling me she caught a couple in the act just off Belton Lane last night,' Helen explained.

Irene nodded and took a big gulp of water. She didn't much fancy listening to Mary's boasting about the punishment she'd doled out. She was just relieved she had managed to ensure Stella didn't need to 'work' last night. The last thing she wanted was for her to run into Mary while she was doing her business. She made a mental note to warn her again next time she saw her about where she took the soldiers. She obviously hadn't heeded the last one. Maybe she could find somewhere truly safe for them.

Irene was brought back to the present by Helen's voice. 'I need you to stay back for a little while this morning,' she was saying. Irene assumed she was talking to Mary, but when she looked up Helen was staring at her, and she looked over at Mary to see her smirking into her porridge. *This doesn't sound good*, she thought suspiciously.

Irene was eager to know what Helen wanted to discuss with her, but Mary was taking an uncharacteristically long time to finish her breakfast. Each mouthful she took filled Irene with more angst, and she could tell she was enjoying it. She normally wolfed down her food, so keen was she to get out and start terrorising the women of Grantham. When she finally finished, she got up slowly and gave Irene a lingering look as she left the room. Something was up, and Irene's first thought was of Jack, and her heart pounded.

'I'll get straight to it,' Helen said as Irene pushed her half-finished bowl of porridge into the middle of the table. 'Mary's been following you, and she's told me what you've been up to.'

Irene's heart sunk down into the pit of her stomach. She'd felt so good just moments before – was it all about to end? Her heart stayed in her stomach while it thumped at what felt like a million miles an hour.

She knew she had been dropping into Gladys's far too often. Why had she been so foolish? She'd been so desperate for friendly company and something to take her mind off the fact she'd lost Maggie and Annie and been lumped with Charles in their place – and now her selfishness had led to Jack's discovery. How would she ever forgive herself? If Mary or Helen reported him, he would surely get dragged back to face the firing squad. Tears filled Irene's eyes as she tried to think of an explanation good enough to buy her some time to get Jack to safety.

'Now, now,' Helen soothed. 'This is nothing we can't get sorted between us, I'm sure.'

Irene looked up. She wasn't sure she understood what Helen meant.

'I know Mary's treatment of the prostitutes can be a little harsh at times,' she continued, 'and I don't want you to take quite as hard a line as she does. But you do need to deal with them appropriately. You can't be handing them care packages in the middle of the street for everyone to see. This is a punishable offence, Irene.'

Irene tried hard not to let the relief that was washing over her show on her face. Mary had seen her with Stella – she hadn't managed to find out about Jack! She tried to think of an explanation quickly: she was still in trouble, after all, even if she felt like she was walking on air.

'What were you giving the woman?' Helen asked firmly. Irene's mind went blank as she stared back at Helen. All she could think about was how devastated she had felt at the thought of losing Jack. With no time to think up any more cover stories, she decided to go with the truth. *I'll be leaving the WPS soon anyway*, she thought sadly, *so what's the worst that could happen?* She didn't feel like she had anything to lose anymore. The only thing she wanted to do was to protect Jack.

'I was giving her my wages again,' Irene confessed matter-of-factly. 'I just couldn't stand the thought of her having to put herself through another night of degradation. I wanted to buy her at least a few nights off this time.'

Helen stared at her. 'I thought last night was the first time you had slipped up, but now you tell me you've been turning a blind eye to her immoral behaviour before that?' she asked. Her tone had changed from firm and friendly to outraged. 'I was willing to work this out with you – you're such a good recruit. I was certain there would be some simple explanation. But this . . . Irene you do know you could be thrown out for this?'

Irene remained silent and stared down at the table.

'Why would you risk everything for some prostitute you don't even know?' Helen asked, incredulous now.

'Because she reminds me of my mother,' Irene blurted out before she could stop herself. Her face flushed red as she realised what she had just done. In the stunned silence that followed, Irene realised it felt like a weight had been lifted to have finally said that out loud. She looked up at Helen, whose expression had softened. Maybe there was hope after all.

She'd never told anybody the full truth about what had happened at home. Her aunt Ruth knew, but even they had never spoken about it. Over the last few months, she had started to think Maggie and Annie would be the first people she would open up to about it. She'd even been building up to it before the Grantham posting came up. She laughed to herself about how quickly friendships and relationships could change.

Maybe it was time now – time she revealed her true reasons for joining the WPS.

'Whatever do you mean?' Helen prompted Irene.

'I mean, my mother was one of them,' Irene said, staring into her hands in her lap.

Helen stayed silent, and eventually Irene looked up to see concern etched across her face. She took a few more seconds to gather her thoughts, and then she continued. 'When I speak to these women, I see more than the dirty, seedy, immoral things they do. I see the other side. The women who've been left with no choice. Like my mother, and like Stella – that's the woman from last night,' Irene explained. 'They *have* to do these things. Why would anybody choose to live like that? They deserve some kindness. My mother was left with no choice and I lost her because of it.'

'Oh Irene, I had no idea,' Helen said gently. 'What happened to your mother?'

'I haven't spoken about her for so long,' Irene sniffed, wiping a tear from her cheek. 'Sometimes I think I've forgotten how to.'

'Take your time,' Helen said, and Irene took a moment to compose herself. She decided the best place to start would be the beginning, so she told Helen all about how happy she had been growing up – as an only child her mother and her father were her whole world. They didn't have much as a family, but their unwavering love for each other held them together like glue and made even the toughest of times bearable. But when Irene turned ten, everything suddenly changed.

'It was gradual at first,' she said. 'My father stopped going out every day and instead he stayed at home. At first it was fun. I loved spending time with him so to have him to myself all day felt like the best thing in the world. I didn't realise it was because he'd lost his job. Soon, our meals started getting smaller, and it seemed that the smaller they became, the angrier my father grew. Before long, it seemed like he was angry about everything.' Irene sighed as the memories she normally kept locked away came flooding back.

'I started spending most of the day in my room to avoid him because he seemed to snap about everything. He was rude to my mother and started to act like I was some kind of inconvenience to him. Every day I went to sleep praying he would wake up back to his old self, but he just seemed to get worse. I think I probably lost my faith around that time.' Irene had never admitted that before – even to herself.

'Then, one morning when my mother was out, I noticed his eyes looked red, like he'd been crying. It broke my heart to see him upset so I went over to give him a hug and he exploded. He pushed me away and shouted that he didn't need my pity. I was terrified of him after that. He'd turned from a loving and happy man into a bitter and angry one in the space of a few months and I felt like I didn't know him anymore. I was devastated.'

Irene took a deep, steadying breath. 'My mother got into bed with me that night and ran her fingers through my hair until I fell asleep,' she continued. 'The next morning my father burst into the room and dragged my mum out of the bed. We were both crying and screaming as he raged at her about finally bringing in some money herself and paying her way. The bedroom door closed behind them and I ran up to it to listen in as he told her he'd made an arrangement with the landlord to cover the rent. I didn't understand what he meant or what was going on. My mum was begging him not to make her do it. Then I heard a loud thump followed by her crying out in pain. I wept as I heard her sobbing.'

Irene paused again as Helen's hand shot out to grip hers. No wonder she had never spoken about this before – recounting it was bringing it all back to life and she felt like she was living it all over again. Now she knew a little of what Jack must feel when speaking about his own traumatic experiences, and how hard it must have been for Maggie to talk about her attack.

When she felt ready, Irene picked up the story where she'd left it.

'I ran to the other side of my bedroom and crouched in the corner with my hands over my ears to block out the sounds of a man puffing and panting that were coming from my parents' room,' she whispered, bile rising in her throat at the memory. 'I was only young, but I knew what the noises meant, and I understood what my mother had been forced to do with our landlord to make up for the fact they couldn't pay their rent,' she said, looking into Helen's eyes now.

'That's not the worst of it,' Irene said when she saw the look of horror on Helen's face. 'My mother was never the same after that night. She had always been so happy and carefree, but she became withdrawn and timid – she hardly ever spoke around my father. And she had only covered the rent that night. We still had to eat, and my father had developed a drinking habit that needed funding. He kept sending her out at night after I'd gone to bed. I overheard them one evening when she asked for a night off from it all. He told her he would take me out and find someone interested in a younger lover if she refused to go. He said he could make more money off me anyway. I heard the door slam close behind her immediately. That was the night she got arrested for soliciting.'

'I'm assuming your mother didn't receive very fair treatment,' sighed Helen. 'I know things are starting to change but it's been a very long time coming. It's why what we're doing with the WPS is so very important.'

'Yes, and it's the reason why I'm so upset recruits like Mary are getting away with treating the women around here so badly,' Irene snapped.

'You know there's not much I can do about that,' Helen said firmly. Then her tone softened, and she gave a conciliatory smile. 'But let's not get distracted – I'd like to know what happened to your mother, if I may.'

'She was allowed home while they waited for the court date,' Irene explained. 'I came home from school and found my father kicking her in the stomach as she lay helpless on the floor. There was blood pouring from her head.' She paused as the memory flashed back into her mind. She had worked so long on blocking it out that the horror of it hit her as if she was seeing it for the first time again. 'He stopped kicking her to look round when he heard the door closing. He saw it was me and he carried on – he didn't even care.'

Irene broke down then. As Helen put a comforting arm around her shoulder, she couldn't help but think back to the evening before, when she had been the strong one comforting Jack. Thinking of him set something off inside her. Mary was clearly gunning for her again, and from what Helen had said it sounded as if she had been following her for a while now. For all Irene knew, she was close to finding out what she was hiding at Gladys's house, which meant Jack's life could be at risk. Even through the pain of telling her story, she was astonished at how much the thought of that hurt.

'I ran to a neighbour for help,' Irene explained, keen to finish her story now and get her punishment over with so she could get to Gladys's and warn her. 'By the time we got back, he'd beaten my mother to within an inch of death and then done a runner. I didn't want to go home anyway, so while she was treated in hospital, they sent me to stay with her sister, my aunt Ruth. When my mother was well enough, they sent her to court, and she was sentenced to nine months' hard labour. She could barely walk, let alone do all the things they expected – she was still in so much pain from the attack. She never fully recovered from what my father did to her, and she died before completing her sentence. The official cause of death was pneumonia, but I knew the truth: my father was responsible for ending her life. Then, to make matters worse, when he was finally caught, he received a two-month suspended sentence for beating her.' Irene scoffed and shook her head. Helen shook her head and wiped a tear from her eye.

'My aunt did her best for me, but she had children of her own and hardly any money, so I ended up in a children's home.' She spotted Helen's quizzical expression. 'There was no way I would have gone back to live with my father, not after everything he'd done. He was no longer the man I spent those first ten years with. He'd have ended up pimping me out, just as he had with my mother. I was happier to grow up in the children's home than with him.' She shuddered at the thought. 'I assume he's still out there somewhere, but I tell everyone he's dead. As far as I'm concerned, my father died the day he lost that job.

'I always wanted to do something to better myself and make sure I didn't end up like my poor mother, and I've been looking for a way to help others like her for as long as I can remember. So, when the WPS opportunity came up, there was more to it than female empowerment for me. I had to get involved to honour my mother's memory.' She went on to explain how closely Stella's situation mirrored her mother's. 'That's why I haven't been able to take a hard-line with her,' she shrugged, feeling defiant now.

'Now I know all of this, I can understand your actions,'

Helen said. 'But this can't go on, Irene. I'll have a hard time convincing Mary I've disciplined you if you carry on giving this woman help. It absolutely has to stop or else I'll be forced to take the matter higher. It's fine to warn women and move them on once, but you know that if they defy you and carry on regardless you have to take firmer action.'

'You mean, you're not going to tell the commandant?' Irene asked, hardly daring to hope.

'Not this time,' Helen said. 'I can handle Mary this time around, but you know what she's like – she'll be keeping an eye on you and if she reports anything else back to me then I'll be forced to take action.'

'I understand, thank you,' Irene said gratefully. But already, she knew she wasn't going to stop helping Stella. She would just have to be more careful from now on. She had been reckless last night because she was shaken up by everything Jack had told her. She wouldn't slip up again. She'd help her as long as she was with the WPS, however long that was going to be, and afterwards too if she could get away with it.

But she had to focus on Jack right now. If Mary mentioned Irene's visits to Gladys to Helen, she knew she would be all right as Helen had given her permission to help the old woman. But Mary was sneaky. What was to stop her from turning up at the house in uniform and convincing Gladys that Irene had sent her? She knew Mary would be desperate to get in and find out what had been going on. Irene had to go straight there and warn Gladys. As for Jack, well, he was going to have to hand himself in at the earliest opportunity – as much as Irene hated the idea.

Irene headed straight to Gladys's house as soon as Helen dismissed her. There was a train due in from London and she knew Mary wouldn't miss an opportunity to give 'dirty-looking women', as she liked to call them, a dressing down as they stepped off it. By Irene's reckoning, she would have just enough time to get in and talk to Jack before Mary made it back into town to keep an eye on her.

As luck would have it, Gladys was just about to head over to the bakery to pick up some bread from John when Irene arrived at number 48 Castlegate. She was relieved to find she would be able to talk to Jack without upsetting her. She would have to worry about how all this was going to affect the poor woman later – right now, Jack's safety was more important.

'I managed to get some sleep last night,' Jack said as they took up their usual places at the kitchen table once they were alone. Irene smiled, despite the panic that was coursing through her. She was happy he'd had the chance to talk about his experience and that it had helped him. 'I don't think I was asleep for long, and I did get woken by my usual nightmare – but it was a definite improvement.'

'A little sleep is better than none,' Irene reassured him. 'But I'm afraid I have some bad news.' She wasted no time in telling him what Mary had been up to and the trouble she had found herself in with Helen that morning. 'Mary's out for me, Jack,' she stressed. 'And if we don't get you out of here soon then she'll be the one to discover you, I just know it. You need to hand yourself in to make sure they go a little easier on you.'

He stared at her in mute horror for a moment, then sagged in his seat. 'I knew I was on borrowed time as soon as I came back here with Gladys. I'm ready to face whatever consequences are coming my way,' he said solemnly. 'And now I know you'll be here to pick up the pieces with Gladys, it makes it easier to go.'

'We'll go back to the barracks hospital together,' Irene said firmly. 'Tonight.'

It seemed so final, but she knew time was of the essence. 'We'll wait until Gladys is asleep and sneak out under the cover of darkness. I'll explain you were unwell when you ran, and then that you were caring for a poorly relative. It's not too far from the truth and hopefully it will sound more plausible coming from someone in a police uniform.'

'But what about poor Gladys when she wakes up and I'm gone?' Jack asked, tears swimming in his eyes.

'She'll be all right,' Irene said with more confidence than she felt. 'I'll tell her I found a sympathetic officer to give Joe another chance. I'll have to explain everything to John, and we can both look after her. Hopefully, when the war is over, he'll agree to let you come and see her again before you go home and we can tell her Joe has been promoted and is moving abroad. I'm sure John will understand and play along if it keeps his mother content.' She couldn't bring herself to think about the alternative – that Jack would be locked away for good, or worse.

She told Jack to warn Gladys not to let any other WPS recruits into the house that day, just in case. Then she left him to get out on patrol before Mary made it back into town to look for her. She spent the rest of her morning looking over her shoulder and doubling back on herself to try and catch her colleague out. She knew she was watching her – she could *feel* it – but she never once spotted her. No wonder Mary had caught her out with Stella as soon as she had let her guard down.

Irene tried not to let her mind wander to Jack – she couldn't seem to help but feel distracted when she thought about him. But she was so confused about her feelings for him. Was he just a friend or was there something more there? She felt overcome with emotion when she thought about what lay ahead for him. It seemed so unfair that she had finally found someone who truly cared for her – whether that be romantically or not – only for him to be ripped away from her. She also couldn't get over the fact that he had put himself forward to help this country, and now he was being punished for the trauma he had experienced as a result.

Before she had a chance to get too upset, she came across two soldiers loitering outside the Beehive. One of them was tall and lanky with jet-black hair and the other was short and stocky and almost entirely bald.

'It's a bit early for the pub isn't it, lads?' Irene asked lightly.

'Day off, love, and what else is there to do around here?' the tall one replied.

'I hear there's fun to be had at the rest homes,' Irene suggested.

'Ah, come on, one drink won't hurt, miss,' the shorter one pleaded.

'You know I can't stop you,' Irene countered. 'But I can let your superiors know you're seeking out alcohol at this hour. And I'm sure it wouldn't go down too well if they found you at the bar in the middle of the day.'

She gave them a meaningful look and hoped it would do the trick. Both men looked at each other and rolled their eyes playfully.

'Come on, have you tried the rest homes?' Irene asked. 'They really can be quite fun!'

The soldiers laughed lightly.

'All right, we'll give it a go,' the almost bald one sighed. 'But only because you've promised we'll have fun.' He gave her a wink as they wandered off and Irene felt her face flush red with embarrassment. She thought back to Charles's suggestion that she help out at the rest homes. Maybe she could make a difference – she certainly had a few ideas of ways to make them more exciting and enticing for the men. They certainly didn't seem to be drawing them in at all at the moment.

Getting on her way again, Irene tried to clear her mind of Jack and Charles. She found that looking out for Mary kept her mind distracted from what lay ahead that evening, but as soon as she went back to Rutland Street for a short rest in the afternoon, she found herself breaking down. She ran up to her bedroom and threw herself on the bed, where she allowed the tears that had been building up all morning to flow. She was so distraught that she didn't even stop to check if Mary had been on her tail when she'd sprinted upstairs, so she jumped when the bedroom door swung open.

# 30

Looking up, Irene was relieved to see Ruby stood at the foot of her bed. She peered around her to check Ruby was alone. When she was sure Mary wasn't hot on her heels, she let her head fall back down on to her pillow once more.

'I did knock . . .' Ruby said cautiously as she softly closed the door behind her and crept into the room to sit down on Mary's bed.

Irene would normally have been horrified to be showing such weakness in front of anybody, but she found she wasn't able to pull herself together as she so desperately wanted to. All the pain and anger of the fallout with Maggie and Annie, the fear and frustration of realising what sort of man she was going to have to marry, and now the heartbreak at having to hand Jack over – it had all exploded like a grenade of emotions going off inside her and she couldn't stop the stream of tears. Ruby sat patiently as Irene tried to speak through sobs.

'Take your time,' Ruby said quietly, and with that, Irene turned her head back into the pillow and let out a big, guttural cry. She felt better for it, and a minute or two later she sat up and took some deep breaths. Once she was able to talk, she found herself telling Ruby everything about Jack. She was the one who had lectured Jack about how important it was to talk about things, yet she was suddenly aware of the fact she herself had been keeping everything bottled up for far too long, refusing to trust those around her. The two of them had been getting on so well before the night of the deserter raid and Ruby had been desperate to try and gain Irene's trust back after the run-in with Mary, but she had dismissed her without a second thought. As she sat here with no one else to turn to, she decided once more that she had nothing to lose. Maybe Ruby would surprise her and come up with a way to save Jack.

'I might be able to help,' Ruby said eagerly once Irene had finished. Her eyes had lit up and she looked excited, which was strange given how upset Irene clearly was about the situation. Irene realised how determined Ruby was to be friends again and felt a sudden rush of affection for her. 'I know one of the officers at Belton Park really well,' Ruby explained. 'Give me some time to go up and have a chat with him this afternoon, but I think it'll be better if we can arrange for him to pick Jack up from where he's staying and take him in, rather than have Jack walk back into the hospital unannounced and risk causing a scene.'

'That sounds good,' Irene sniffed. 'Sorry for burdening you with all this. I just . . . I've had a lot going on that you don't know about and—'

'You don't have to explain it to me,' Ruby cut in gently. 'I wish I could have been here for you through whatever's been happening, but I know I ruined things when I didn't stand up for you with Mary. I really am sorry about that, you know,' she added.

'I know,' Irene sighed. 'I'm sorry for shutting you out like I did. I can be really stubborn. Loyalty is the most important thing to me, so I admit I might have over-reacted,' she said, not meeting Ruby's eye. 'I know more than anyone how nasty Mary can be so I should have given you the benefit of the doubt. And I've been caught up in everything so much since that I haven't taken the time to make amends with you when I really should have done.'

'Well, we can save Jack together and use that to start afresh,'

Ruby said, full of positivity. Irene admired her optimism, and even felt a spark of hope herself.

'I do hope so,' Irene replied. 'What's this officer of yours like?' she asked nervously. 'Do you think he'll be sympathetic? I'm so very frightened they'll kill Jack for what he's done, and he really doesn't deserve that. He's not a coward, he needs medical help.'

'I've spoken to him about issues he's had with some of the men at the camp, and he's always come across as supportive and kind-hearted,' Ruby replied. 'Plus, I've only heard of deserters facing the firing squad in France. I can't say for sure, of course, but I think it would have to be an extreme case for Jack to be shot here.'

Irene hoped with all her heart that Ruby was right. She also wished she had spoken to her sooner to put her mind at rest about it all. But then she felt a rush of panic. Ruby was so desperate to get Irene on her side again – was she just saying what she thought she wanted to hear to make her happy?

'You're doing the right thing,' Ruby said, cutting into Irene's thoughts. She placed a comforting hand on her arm. 'It's certainly going to go a lot better for your friend if he hands himself in, rather than being captured.'

Irene ended up walking to Belton Park with Ruby that afternoon. She was anxious to know the outcome of her talk with the officer and she knew she wouldn't be able to concentrate on anything else in the meantime. She wandered around the perimeter looking out for women, and Mary, while she waited for Ruby, fraught with worry.

To try and take her mind off Jack's fate, she pondered Ruby's use of the word 'friend' when she had referred to her relationship with Jack. Were the two of them just friends, or was there more to it? He had certainly never expressed any feelings for Irene, but she definitely felt strongly towards him and she felt as though that was reciprocated – or was that just her being hopeful? As she struggled with the question, she spotted Ruby making her way back through the camp towards her.

When Ruby emerged through the gates and revealed the meeting had gone well, Irene gave her a relieved hug. Officer Sergeant Simmons was going to be at Gladys's house at eight o'clock that evening with a colleague, and they would take Jack back to Belton with them. Irene went straight over to John's to ask him to invite his mother over for dinner again that night. Thankfully, he was only too happy to spend another evening with her.

'Please tell her I'll be over to see her just before she leaves,' Irene said as she left the bakery. She was hopeful Gladys would understand that meant she would be there to keep Jack company while she was out, stopping her from turning the invitation down as she didn't want to leave him alone for the evening. She could have popped in to see Gladys herself and tell her, but she didn't want to risk leading Mary to the house when they were so close to getting Jack out safely. Plus, she wasn't sure she could look at Jack without breaking down now she had made the arrangement final.

At quarter past seven, Irene walked past the Beehive and spotted Mary inside giving a lone woman at the bar a hard time. The soldiers were still busy spending all their wages, including the two she had chatted to earlier that day, so she knew Mary would be too busy with public-house duty to follow her for a few hours at least. She made her way to Castlegate, knowing that Gladys would be waiting for her so she could head over to John's.

'You won't be staying long if you're on duty, dear,' the old woman said, looking concerned when she opened the door and took in Irene's uniform.

'Don't worry, things are quiet tonight so I can stay for a little while,' she lied. She felt bad for the fib, but she knew it was better for Gladys to be kept in the dark. A drawn-out goodbye would be painful for her, even if she thought Jack was going for treatment rather than uncertain punishment. That was if she would even allow him to leave. No, this way forward would be much better for everyone involved, she told herself. She said goodbye to Gladys and made her way into the kitchen to find Jack.

'Hello, Irene.'

She heard his voice before she saw him. She refused to follow the sound for a moment, knowing this would be the last time she would get to greet him like this, in this room. She wanted to savour the moment one last time.

Finally, she looked up. Jack was sitting at the table staring up at her, his eyes wide with anticipation. She wished she had better news for him. She edged closer to Jack, giving him a slight nod. When she stopped, she found that even though she was now almost standing over him, he still had the same over-powering presence she'd noticed previously. She took in his kind features one more time. She found them to be in stark contrast to his strapping physique, which he had managed to keep despite the weeks hidden away eating a diet that consisted of, from what she could make out, mostly bread and tea.

'I've found an officer to come and pick you up,' Irene said quietly. 'He'll be here soon.'

Panic swept over Jack's face.

'It's all right – Ruby knows him,' Irene said as she reached out and grabbed hold of his hand, which had started shaking. 'She's explained everything to him, and they want to come and get you. It's better to do that than take them by surprise, I think,' she added.

'Yes, yes I suppose so,' Jack whispered, as Irene took a seat and moved it opposite him before sitting down. She reached out and took both his hands in hers now. The two of them stared down at their entwined fingers. 'When Gladys said John had invited her over for dinner again I, well, I was rather looking forward to another night alone with you,' Jack confessed. 'Who knows what will happen to me, Irene. I had so much more to say to you.'

'And you *will* get to say it to me,' she said confidently. 'They're going to listen when you tell them you're suffering from trauma, and they're going to get a doctor to tell the court martial that you need treatment.'

He was still staring at their hands, his expression vacant, and Irene could tell he hadn't heard a word she'd just said.

'Jack, we don't have much time – you need to listen to me!' she cried. She so wanted to hear what he wanted to tell her, but this was far more important. Her voice wobbled with emotion and she tried to stop herself from breaking down completely. She needed to make sure he understood what he had to say once they took him away. It was all very well her and Ruby telling the officers Jack needed help instead of punishment, but they wouldn't be there with him at the hearing to plead his case.

When Jack looked up into her eyes and nodded his under-standing, she was struck by the fact that she didn't know what she would do if she lost him. She knew in that moment she had fallen for him. She grappled with herself as they stared into each other's eyes. What was it he longed to say to her this evening? Did he feel the same way as her? She was bursting to tell him how she felt, but she knew he needed to stay focused if he was going to get the treatment he so desperately needed. And the truth was, they could never be together anyway as she was stuck with Charles. So, it would be cruel of her to confess her feelings to Jack. Irene looked up at the clock and panic almost overwhelmed her.

'We don't have long,' she whispered. 'Do you want me to let your family know?' she asked.

Jack had never really spoken about them. She had told him about her years in the children's home, albeit leaving out the exact circumstances that had led to her being there. But she didn't know much about his background at all. In fact, she didn't even know where in the country his family lived.

'I'd rather they didn't know their son was a coward,' he said bitterly, not meeting her eyes.

'Jack, I don't know how many times I have to tell you—'

'I know, I know – I'm not a coward,' he said, impatiently waving her comfort aside. 'It's great you believe in me, and I really hope this officer who's coming to get me does too. But you don't know my family. They're very proud people, and the shame of this would devastate them. I can't do it to them – not while I'm alive to bear witness to their disappointment.' He paused for a moment. 'If I face the firing squad then at least I won't have to face them.'

Irene's heart ached for him. She thought fleetingly about trying to find and tell them anyway, but she had to respect his wishes. 'If I'm shot then it's best that they learn about it from the army when I'm gone,' he added sadly. Jack went upstairs to get changed into his uniform, and Irene waited nervously alone in the kitchen.

As she heard Jack's footsteps coming back down the stairs, there was a loud knock on the front door, making Irene jump in fright. Jack made his way into the kitchen where Irene was frozen to her chair. She looked up at him, misery etched on her face. He looked so handsome in his uniform, she wanted to reach up and take him into her arms, and never let him go. She desperately wanted to ignore the knock at the door. She wasn't ready to say goodbye yet. But she had no choice.

Reluctantly, she got up and opened the front door. The two officers removed their caps and she showed them in quickly. She didn't want Gladys's neighbours getting wind of any of this.

'Please, can we have a few moments?' she asked them.

'Yes, but make it quick,' the taller of the two said as he

stared straight down the hallway and into the kitchen at Jack. He was standing at the table now, his head hung low and his cap in his hand.

Irene rushed back to him and threw herself into his arms. She didn't care how it looked to the officers. To her delight, Jack clung to her just as tightly. She took the opportunity to run her hands up and down his back, feeling as much of him as she could. She wasn't sure she would ever get the chance again. She breathed in the smell of him – so different to how it had been when they had first met. That stark difference reminded her how far Jack had come in the space of a few short weeks and, despite everything, she was glad for him.

'Thank you for helping me,' Jack whispered into her ear. 'I'll never forget you.'

She pulled away and looked up at him before answering. 'You won't have to,' she said, her voice full of furious determination. 'I'll see you soon.' She had to believe she would see Jack again, or else she would never be able to let him go. She also needed to give him something to hope for.

Irene put on her bravest smile and then she went up on her tiptoes to plant a kiss on Jack's cheek.

'This isn't goodbye,' she said firmly.

He looked into her eyes for a long moment then leant down to kiss her cheek. 'Look after Gladys for me,' he whispered before turning and walking down the hallway to the officers.

Irene had to place her hand over her mouth to stop herself from sobbing. She needed to hold herself together until he was gone. Jack looked back at her one final time as he reached the front door, and Irene took her hand away from her mouth to give him a wave. She tried to keep her head clear, but a little voice kept asking her if she had just led him to the treatment he needed – or to his death. She silently pleaded for Ruby's claims about the firing squads not being used over here to be true – but how could she be sure?

# 31

As soon as the door closed behind them, Irene dropped to her knees with her head in her hands. Now the reality of it was hitting her, she was certain she had just lost Jack for ever. What had she done? She wished she could have kept him safe and hidden away with Gladys for a little longer. She felt lost without him already. She sat on the cold, hard kitchen floor crying as the minutes ticked by.

She didn't care about the fact she should be out on patrol and Mary would soon be reporting back to Helen that she was almost certainly bunking off somewhere. She was ready to end her WPS days there and then herself – she didn't need any help. Her WPS work had led her to lose Jack, so what was the point in clinging to it anymore? Staying on was only upsetting Charles and if she let that go on for too long he could very well stop paying for her cousin's care, without which Henry would surely die. Maybe it was time to just give in to Charles and live the life he wanted for her. She might not have been able to save Jack, but she could save Henry.

When she heard a key in the door, Irene realised with a start that she still had to deal with Gladys. She pulled herself together enough to tell her the story she had previously come up with. She knew she should be telling her the truth but she wasn't ready to do that yet. She would need to be strong to help Gladys through losing 'Joe', so she needed to buy some time to deal with it herself first.

'But he didn't say goodbye,' Gladys said tearfully once Irene had explained.

'We thought it would be easier that way,' Irene explained. 'He's going to get the care he needs now, and he doesn't have to hide away anymore. It's for the best.'

Bile rose in her throat as she spoke, and she longed for what she was saying to be true instead of what she was certain was the alternative. Thankfully, Gladys finally accepted the explanation and took herself off to bed with only a few more tears and remonstrances.

Irene headed straight back to Rutland Street. All she wanted to do was climb into bed and wait for word of what had happened to Jack. She didn't care if it got her into trouble with Helen.

When she got home, Ruby was waiting for her.

'Thank goodness I caught you,' Ruby gasped as soon as Irene walked through the front door.

'I need to be alone,' Irene said, brushing past her to get to the stairs.

'You need to hear this,' Ruby said firmly, grabbing hold of Irene's arm and pulling her back around to face her. Irene pulled her arm away sharply. Whatever Ruby had to say, she didn't care. She was at rock bottom and nothing could make her feel any worse.

'Charles knows about Jack,' Ruby announced before Irene could walk away again. Irene stood, glued to the spot, as a rush of nervous energy flew down the whole length of her body.

'What do you mean?' she panicked. 'How did he find out?'

Then it hit her. Mary. Of course.

'She was outside the bedroom listening in when you told me earlier,' Ruby explained. Irene thought back to how she had purposefully checked Mary wasn't there before talking to Ruby. She had to admit, Mary was good at this skulking-around business.

'I bumped into her this evening and she was boasting about how she told Charles all about it when she saw him in the pub,' Ruby continued fretfully.

Irene hung her head and sighed. She knew how Charles felt about deserters – he was going to be so angry she had helped one. And a young, attractive one at that. But at least Jack was back at Belton now – that was the most important thing.

'There's more,' Ruby said quietly. Irene wasn't sure how this could get any worse, but she waited anxiously for her to elaborate. 'I've been looking for you since I saw Mary, to try and warn you. She seems to think you and Jack had a romantic relationship. It sounds as if Charles believes that, too.'

Irene slumped on to the bottom step of the stairs and put her head in her hands. But she didn't have time to come up with a plan because as soon as she closed her eyes to try and focus, there was a loud bang on the front door. 'The final thing I had to tell you,' Ruby said as her voice quivered, 'is that Charles is on the warpath and he's been storming around town looking for you.'

'Irene!' Charles's voice boomed from the other side of the door. 'There's someone in there, I can hear you!' Irene got to her feet, but Ruby blocked her path.

'I'm not leaving you to deal with a bully alone again,' she whispered fiercely. Irene looked up at her, confused. 'Oh, he seems like a dream man, but just because we've not been talking properly doesn't mean I can't see the effect he's had on you,' she hissed.

There was another round of banging on the door. Irene was growing anxious – aware that the longer they left Charles standing on the doorstep, the more agitated he would become. 'You've been quiet and withdrawn for weeks now,' Ruby added.

'It's all right,' Irene said softly. 'I need to face him sooner or later so I may as well get it over with.' She took a deep breath and walked slowly to the door.

Charles flew through the door as soon as Irene turned the latch. She had to catch her balance as the force knocked her flying.

'I can't believe you thought you would get away with this,' he spat. 'Who on earth do you think you are to embarrass me like this?' His face was bright red as he stepped towards Irene. She froze.

'Good evening, Mr Murphy,' Ruby said with a loud confidence. He caught himself and swung around to face her.

'I didn't see you there,' he said smoothly, stepping back again and flattening down his jacket. His voice was a lot quieter now although he still sounded furious. Irene was grateful to Ruby for not running away like she had when Mary had attacked her. She felt certain Charles would have struck her if they had been alone. She willed Ruby to stay put and protect her with her presence.

Charles looked over at Ruby uncomfortably, obviously waiting for her to leave, but she stood her ground and didn't budge an inch. Irene breathed a sigh of relief. Charles leaned down so his face was almost touching hers. 'You won't get away with this. I've seen to it that your lover will never see the light of day again.' Irene's whole body went numb as she waited to hear just what Charles meant. 'Your pathetic little coward will be gone by the time the sun rises in the morning,' he said, his voice full of triumphant venom. 'I have my connections, Irene. Everyone in this town does what I wish, and you would do well to remember that.'

Irene felt her legs give way and she reached out to grab hold of the wall and steady herself. Were Charles's connections really strong enough that he could order a soldier to be shot at dawn the very next day? She looked up at him and was taken aback by the hatred spilling from his face.

'Please, he doesn't have to die,' she whispered through tears.

'If only you could have felt this level of emotion for me,' he spat bitterly before storming out of the house.

As the door slammed shut behind him, Irene rushed past Ruby and made it to the kitchen sink just in time to vomit. When she was finished, she walked back past Ruby to the front door. She didn't know where she was going, she just knew she had to get away. She couldn't be in the house when Mary came back, couldn't stand to see her smirking face as she rubbed in what she'd done. She didn't trust herself not to lash out at her in anger – and she didn't want to lower herself to that level.

'Maybe he didn't mean—' Ruby started.

'You heard him, Ruby. He said "by the time the sun rises". Everyone knows those sentenced to death are shot at dawn.' Without another word, Irene stepped out on to the street, closing the door firmly behind her.

Irene walked for hours. She made her way past two soldiers squaring up to each other in Market Place without doing anything to intervene. She didn't even notice the amorous couple fumbling in the dark corner of an alley as she wandered along it in a daze.

It was still dark when Irene sat down on the grass under the oak tree between the town and Belton Park. Her thoughts were consumed with Jack and everything she wished she had said to him before he was taken away. When she closed her eyes, she could see his face staring back at her. She shivered as she remembered the pain behind those deep, grey eyes – his deep-set brows always making him look sadder until the moment he smiled, bringing his whole face back to life. Poor Jack had been relying on her to help him and she had let him down. He didn't deserve to die this way. It wasn't supposed to end like this. If only Mary hadn't stepped in to bring it all crashing down, maybe Irene could have saved him. She should have been stronger and done something to help Mary become a kinder person. If she'd done what she had intended to do in Grantham, Mary wouldn't have been so determined to ruin lives and hurt people, and she probably would have left Jack alone. Would she have been able to find a doctor willing to diagnose Jack properly, and stand up for him in court if she'd had more time to try and save him?

It didn't matter now. Any hope there might have been of rescuing him had vanished. Charles had said it himself: he would be gone by the time the sun rises. Irene was well aware of how influential Charles was in this town. There was no question in her mind that he had been able to ensure Jack's execution. He would want any evidence of Irene's 'lover' eliminated before there was any risk of anybody else finding out. She shed bitter tears as she realised Charles didn't care that she had feelings for another man. All he cared about was what everybody else thought, and that had cost Jack his life.

As dawn started creeping in, Irene began to shake. She wasn't sure if it was because she was cold or because she was in some sort of state of shock. Either way, she did nothing to try and ease the tremors running through her body. Instead, she stared defiantly at the horizon, waiting for the sun to appear. When she finally started to see a hint of yellow emerging slowly above the fields, Irene knew it would soon be time for Jack to face the firing squad.

The mist that was sitting just above the grass made her think of the smoke that would rise from the rifles after the soldiers had taken their shots at Jack. She knew one of them would fire a blank round so that none of them would ever be sure who had been responsible for the fatal shot. She took solace in the fact none of them would know Jack personally – they wouldn't be from his regiment, as would have been the case if this were happening in the field. It would be hard enough to have to shoot a man like that, she thought, let alone if it was someone you knew, someone you'd trained with, laughed and joked with, shared meals and stories with. Tears stung her eyes at the realisation that Jack would never get to do any of those things again.

She closed her eyes. She'd heard of soldiers refusing to wear a blindfold when they were tied to the stake. Would Jack look his killers in the eyes, or would he choose to block them out with the thin, white material? She hoped with all her might that it would be over quickly for him. The officer in charge would have to finish him off with a revolver if the firing squad didn't kill him straight away. She didn't want him to suffer, even if it was only for a few moments while the medical officer examined him to check for life. When Irene opened her eyes again, the sun was almost up.

'I'm sorry, Jack,' she whispered into the air. She knew now for sure that what she had felt for Frank wasn't real love. And as for what she felt for Charles, she was now certain beyond a doubt that had been nothing more than a fleeting infatuation. What she felt for Jack was pure and real and all-consuming. She knew she would never feel that again in her lifetime. Even if it were possible, she wouldn't get the chance – after this, Charles was sure to keep her hidden away unless she was in his company being presented on his arm.

The future she had to look forward to would be very much like the life she knew Maggie's mother was currently living – stepping on eggshells for fear of provoking her husband and never speaking out of turn or without his permission. *It is all I deserve*, she thought to herself. *Maybe it's the best thing for me. At least this way I won't be able to get caught up in any more drama or cause any more harm.* She would live out her days obeying her husband and keeping out of trouble. But Jack would always have her heart.

# 32

Helen was in the kitchen preparing breakfast when Irene walked back in.

'I thought you were all still in bed,' she spluttered. 'You haven't been out on patrol all night?' she asked, full of concern.

Irene couldn't think straight. She felt as if she was walking through a dream. Every time she closed her eyes, she saw Jack tied to a stake, a blindfold covering his eyes, his legs trembling.

When no words left her mouth, Helen rushed over to her side. 'You must be exhausted – goodness knows you look it,' she said, taking hold of her arm and guiding her into the room. 'Have a cup of tea and then you must go to bed and stay there as long as you need. I know you're trying to prove yourself to me after what Mary discovered, but you mustn't make yourself ill.'

For a moment, Irene thought Helen was talking about Jack.

'All you need to do is put your past to the side and stop being so soft with some of these women,' Helen added, and Irene realised with an echo of relief she didn't know anything about Jack.

'No tea,' she whispered, waving Helen away and slowly making her way up the stairs. When she got to the top, she found Mary standing outside their room. Their eyes met and she saw something flash across Mary's face – was it relief? She didn't have time to work it out because it was gone as quickly as it had appeared and replaced with a look of bored superiority. Then Mary brushed past her to go downstairs. Irene was glad she hadn't tried to speak to her. She wasn't ready to deal with her.

After undressing, she collapsed onto her bed. Seconds later, there was a light knock on her door. 'Yes,' she croaked. She was desperate to fall asleep so the image of Jack would leave her mind.

'Did Mary say anything to you?' Ruby asked after coming in and closing the door behind her.

Irene shook her head but didn't raise it from the pillow.

'She came into my room as soon as Helen went downstairs earlier. She was really worried about you last night. She was awake for hours waiting for you to return. So was I. Where were you?'

'Hang on, why was *Mary* worried about me?' Irene said, sitting up.

'I think she realises she overstepped the mark by telling Charles,' Ruby explained. 'I mean, she would never admit as much, but that's what I gathered from the way she was talking. It was one thing to follow you to try and get you into trouble with Helen, but going to Charles about Jack was a step too far. Especially when she didn't know the full story. She sounded quite taken aback by his reaction. She said she hardly slept last night because she was worried that he'd hurt you and it would be her fault.'

'She does have a conscience, then,' Irene scoffed.

'Where were you? Are you all right? I'm so sorry about your friend,' Ruby said.

'I was just walking,' Irene admitted.

'All night?' Ruby asked.

'Pretty much,' Irene shrugged. 'I couldn't be around Mary, and I wanted to say a proper goodbye to Jack.' Tears stung her eyes once more as she said his name aloud.

'It will have been over quickly,' Ruby said, pulling her in

for a hug. They held the embrace and Irene felt herself dropping off to sleep on her friend's shoulder. 'Go to sleep now,' Ruby whispered, as she pulled away and gently guided Irene to lie down. 'Mary and I have agreed to keep this to ourselves. She won't tell Helen if it means Charles goes easier on you,' she added, creeping out of the room. Irene felt a small sense of relief before sleep took over.

When Irene woke, she could hear voices downstairs. Knowing it would be Helen advising one of the women who came to her daily for help, Irene realised she couldn't have been asleep for long. Helen normally had visitors up until lunchtime, when most people knew she headed out to check everything was in order in the town. The sleep she'd had must have been deep, as she found herself fidgety and unable to drift off again when she tried. Admitting defeat, she got dressed and made her way to the factory.

After what Charles had done, he was the last person she wanted to see. In normal circumstances, she would have been done with him for good. But she had to think about her family, and if she wanted to keep them safe then she would have to beg for his forgiveness and take whatever punishment made him feel better and able to go ahead with his plans to marry her. Besides, after what he'd done to Jack, she felt even more trapped. If he was capable of doing something so terrible to a stranger, what would he do to her if she tried to leave him? She was ready to accept her life with Charles if it meant keeping Henry alive, and she would rather face him again for the first time in public where she knew he couldn't lose his temper and lash out at her.

As she walked into Charles's office, Irene braced herself for his fury. So, she was surprised when his face lit up as he looked up from his desk to see her.

'Hello,' she said nervously as he stood and skirted around

the desk to greet her. She tried to look him in the eyes but found that she couldn't. She could never forgive him for what he had done, but she would try to block it out. When he reached her, he grabbed her hand and kissed it. Her instinct was to flinch at the gesture, but she tried to hold firm.

'My darling, I'm so glad you came,' he gushed.

Irene had no idea what was happening. Where was the angry and raging Charles from the night before – the man who had sent Jack straight to his death? He was acting as if none of it had happened, just like he had done after their previous disagreement. It was baffling. There must be something wrong with him to act in this way.

'I knew you'd see sense and come back to me,' he smiled.

'Jack wasn't my . . . we never—' she started, but he gently put a finger to her lips to silence her.

'We don't have to talk about it ever again,' he said. His voice sounded calm and kind, but his eyes were boring into hers with an uncomfortable intensity. It wasn't a suggestion, she realised, it was an order. She felt sick as she thought about what Jack had suffered because of him, and her hands trembled in his.

'Now that little *obstacle* is out of the way,' he continued, 'I have a surprise for you.' Her stomach started doing somersaults as she panicked about what he meant. Was he going to take her somewhere away from prying eyes and teach her a lesson? 'I've booked the wedding,' he stated proudly. 'This time next week, you will be my wife!'

Irene felt like she wanted to vomit again, but she forced herself to swallow back down the bile that was rising up her throat and she put on her best fake smile. 'That's good news,' she managed to croak.

'I see you're not in uniform for once,' Charles noted as he made his way back around the desk to sit down again. 'I take it you're done with all that WPS nonsense?' he asked lightly.

As he stared hard at her waiting for an answer, it was clear what she was supposed to say. And she found herself saying it without having to lie. 'Yes, I don't think it's for me anymore,' she said quietly as he sat grinning at her. She'd already lost Jack – she didn't want to lose Henry too. She *had* to leave. It's why she hadn't been able to face putting the uniform on again that morning.

'I knew you'd come around to my way of thinking,' Charles said happily. 'I expect you'll need to give Helen some notice, though. We don't want to leave her high and dry now, do we? I don't want to give her any reason to bad-mouth me, so why don't you take until the end of the week? You can take your time telling everyone the good news about the wedding, and then the town can get used to you being Irene Murphy instead of police officer Irene.'

He looked so smug, and Irene wanted to wipe the smirk right off his face, but she stayed calm. 'That sounds like a good idea,' she replied evenly.

'You can move into my place as soon you've handed back your uniform,' Charles declared. 'Of course, we'll be in separate bedrooms until the wedding night,' he added with a glint in his eye that made her feel nauseous.

Irene didn't feel strong enough to get back out on the beat with the WPS, but if it meant staving off moving in with this monster then she would do it. She also felt like she could do with some time to build up to telling Helen she was leaving. She knew she would try to convince her to stay and right now she felt too fragile for that – she would break down as soon as the discussion started.

On top of that, she needed to tie up the loose ends with Gladys and John before quitting. Yes, she would still be in Grantham, but she had no idea how much control Charles was going to have over her once they were married and living under the same roof. Was she going to be able to leave his house without him or his staff keeping tabs on her? She didn't know if she'd get the chance to see either of them alone once she was Mrs Murphy, and their conversations were going to be so delicate that she was going to have to tread carefully without rushing.

Over the next few days, Irene found herself walking around like a ghost. Whenever anything interesting happened, she looked forward to telling Jack about it and then felt empty when she remembered that she couldn't. She avoided Helen as much as possible – deliberately missing mealtimes and eating her food cold on her own once everyone else had gone back out on patrol or to bed. When Helen questioned her, she claimed she was just run off her feet with people to check in on and things to do, but the truth was that more often than not, she found herself sitting under the oak tree mourning Jack. She was angry at herself for not pushing him for information about his family. She hated the idea of them thinking he was a coward and never finding out the whole story.

As for Mary, she didn't utter a word to Irene. Ruby had told her it was best to keep her distance, given everything that had happened, and she'd promised to leave Irene completely alone. It was a relief not to have to look over her shoulder all the time, but it was too little too late.

Irene dropped in to see Charles every day, keeping up the pretence so that he wouldn't tighten the leash even more. She tried her best to act as excited as he was about the wedding. Whenever she struggled, she thought about Henry getting better and about the rest of her family thriving away from the slums, reminding herself why she was marrying a monster.

As the week drew to a close, Irene pulled her suitcase out from under her bed and started placing the few items of clothing she'd brought with her back into it. When she was finished, she collected the dresses Charles had given her from the wardrobe in the other bedroom and rammed them in angrily, not caring if they were damaged in the process. She still hadn't decided what to tell Helen, but she felt maybe it was best she told her she had been right about Charles all along, and hope she believed that a life as his housewife was what she wanted.

Just as she was folding up her uniform, there was a knock on the door and Ruby walked in. 'What are you doing?' she asked, looking from the suitcase to Irene and back again.

'What does it look like?' Irene sighed. 'Charles wants me to leave the WPS. I'll be a guest at his house until the wedding.'

'And you're going along with it?' Ruby exclaimed. 'After everything he did? Irene, I thought you were more sensible than that! He's nothing but a bully – and a dangerous one at that! He killed your friend out of petty jealousy!'

Irene didn't have the energy to explain herself to Ruby. There was so much to it she didn't know. And while they might have been getting back on track as friends since moving on from Ruby's betrayal, there didn't seem much point in going over everything with her right now. There was nothing she would be able to do to help the situation.

'It's complicated, but believe me, I wouldn't be doing this if I had a choice,' Irene said firmly, hoping she'd made it clear she didn't want to discuss it any further. Ruby hung her head sadly.

'If you see Helen on your travels, will you ask her to pop back please?' Irene asked, keen for Ruby to leave her to it. 'I'm almost ready to go, but I don't want to do so without talking to her first.' Ruby took the hint and left the room without another word.

Irene felt bad for dismissing her so rudely – but she was better off keeping her at a distance now, anyway. She was certain Charles wouldn't be allowing her to build any close friendships any time soon, especially not with someone in the WPS. Irene took her suitcase in her hand and draped her uniform over her arm, then made her way down the stairs to wait for Helen to return. She was still sitting at the kitchen table with a cold cup of tea an hour or so later when she heard the front door. Getting to her feet, she prepared herself to greet Helen, but she was faced with Ruby again.

'Have you seen her?' Irene asked her. 'I really just want to get this over with now,' she added, slumping back down into her chair.

'What I've got to say might change things,' Ruby said eagerly. 'At least, I hope it will.' Irene rolled her eyes. She knew Ruby was only trying to help, but it was impossible to do so. 'Hear me out,' Ruby pleaded, sounding frustrated.

'You've got until Helen gets back,' Irene said, offering her the chair opposite hers at the table.

'Right,' Ruby said, sitting down and placing both hands palm-down on the table in front of her. 'This might take a while, so bear with me.' Irene rolled her eyes again but waited to hear what Ruby had to say. 'The idea of Jack getting shot so quickly didn't sit right with me. I mean, I know Charles has connections up at the camp, and he's certainly influential around here. And I know the army is swift to deal with deserters, but I've never heard of the firing squad being used so soon after someone was taken in – especially as there was no real urgency given that we're on home soil, not the front line.'

'Me neither, but you were here when Charles told me he'd seen to it that Jack would be shot,' Irene sighed, frustrated that she didn't know what Ruby was getting at.

'Let me finish,' Ruby tutted. 'For a start, Charles didn't actually say that, did he? He just said Jack would be gone by the time the sun had risen, and that he wouldn't see the light of day again.' She stared at Irene pointedly while she took in what she had said.

'But I pleaded with him. I told him Jack didn't need to die. If he'd meant he was being sent away to prison, then surely he would have corrected me?' Irene argued. She didn't want to get her hopes up, but as she spoke the words, she realised Charles was callous enough to let her believe what she had feared.

'I asked around at Belton Camp, as I wanted to be sure,' Ruby continued. 'No one would tell me anything and Sergeant Simmons has been on leave for a few days. But it's odd that no one has been talking about an execution. You'd think it would be the talk of the town, wouldn't you?'

'I suppose so,' Irene said. She hadn't really been thinking straight for the last few days – the locals could have been talking about a two-headed lion running loose and she wouldn't have batted an eyelid.

'Then this morning I got a letter from one of the girls I trained with,' Ruby said. Irene looked up at the clock anxiously. She wished Ruby would get to the point. 'I was going to read it over breakfast, but Mary was prying, and I wanted to keep it private. So, I took it out on patrol with me and I've only just read it. My friend knew Paul – they met when he got some leave and visited me in London during my police training. Well, Paul brought his friend Jonathan from back home in Surrey, and we all went to a dance together,' Ruby said. 'Anyway, in her letter, my friend told me she got word recently that Jonathan had been court-martialled for desertion, but he was picked up in Britain and his family paid for an expensive doctor to argue his case, and he's been sent away for treatment. No word of a firing squad or years stuck in prison!'

Irene said nothing. She was happy Paul's friend had made it out alive, but she didn't see what that had to do with Jack.

'What was Jack's surname?' Ruby asked now.

'I don't know,' Irene replied, confused. 'If I knew that then I would have spent the last few days trying to track down his family and tell them the truth about what happened to their son,' she said. 'I don't understand why that matters?'

'Paul's friend Jonathan – everyone called him Jack,' Ruby said excitedly. 'He was called Jonathan after his father, so to make it easier to differentiate between them, everyone called him Jack from birth. But Paul found it funny and used to call him by both names all the time to confuse people. That's how I knew, and it meant I made the connection when I read my friend's letter. Don't you see?' She asked eagerly as Irene's face stayed blank. 'This is too much of a coincidence, Irene – it *has* to be your Jack! If only I'd met him myself while he was holed up with Mrs Goode, or we had his surname to confirm it . . .but I can't see there being any other explanation. I don't think Jack's dead at all!'

Irene's body tingled as it all sank in. Could Jack really be alive? 'I need to know,' Irene said, her voice shaking. 'When is Sergeant Simmons back?'

'He was due back today,' Ruby said. 'I was going to go straight to see him, but I wanted to catch you first before you spoke to Helen. Promise me you won't quit until I've spoken to him?'

'I promise,' Irene whispered. She was trying not to get her hopes up, but she had to admit that Ruby's argument made sense.

As Ruby dashed out of the door, Irene thought about what Jack being alive would mean. It certainly wouldn't mean a happy ending for her – she was still indebted to Charles and destined to be his sad, lonely wife. She wasn't going to be running off into the sunset with the man she truly loved. But after the last few days of grieving for Jack, she realised that knowing that Jack was safe and getting the treatment he needed was all that mattered. Jack being alive, even if he wasn't by her side, would be her happy ending.

# 33

Irene took her suitcase and uniform back up to her bedroom while she waited nervously for Ruby to return. Now she thought about it, she had to admit she'd been so caught up in grief she hadn't stopped to think about how unlikely it would have been for Jack to have been court-martialled and sent to face the firing squad in just a matter of hours. Charles had been so terrifying and convincing she had just taken his word for it that he'd had the power to hurry it along.

She knew how powerful he was, but now she thought about it, it would be unlikely that his influence would extend to the military, where there were rules and regulations that needed to be adhered to. It made far more sense that Charles had simply ensured Jack was out of Grantham by the following morning. He would have been desperate to ensure she didn't get to see him again before he was shipped out. She hoped beyond all hope that Ruby's theory was correct.

Even so, it would have been incredibly sinister and cruel of him to lie to her and let her believe Jack was dead. And it still seemed too good to be true that Jack could have avoided the most brutal of punishments for his crime. It also left open the possibility that he had been sent to rot in jail.

As they hadn't really shared much about their respective backgrounds, Irene didn't know what kind of family Jack came from. He'd come across so humble that she'd never suspected his parents would be rich. He had never seemed particularly posh. Irene was sensitive to that kind of thing as she was always so worried about people judging her for her poor circumstances. And he hadn't given any kind of reaction when she had mentioned her children's home upbringing, which usually meant someone was from a poor background themselves. He had also never made her feel uncomfortable in her own clothes, like Charles did. But if his parents had managed to send in a doctor to argue his case – and win – they must have a lot of money.

All the ifs and whats were driving her to distraction, so she was relieved when Ruby burst back through her bedroom door.

'I saw Sergeant Simmons,' she said loudly. She was clearly excited, so Irene knew it had to be good news. 'Jack's surname is Walker – the same as Jonathan. It *has* to be the same man!'

Irene tried her best to remain calm. 'What happened to him? Does he know?' she asked.

'He was moved quickly out of Grantham,' Ruby said. 'Apparently Charles made such a fuss they felt they had no choice. Sergeant Simmons said Charles was like a wild animal, trying to get in and see Jack for himself. They wouldn't allow it despite his connections, but they agreed to send Jack elsewhere for the court-martial to calm him down. I guess he didn't want you being able to see him before he was dealt with. Sergeant Simmons doesn't know what happened to Jack after he was shipped out, but I just know he's fine. It can't all be coincidence.'

'I need to know,' Irene stressed. 'I have to be sure. Please, there must be a way.'

'Well, I never met his parents, of course, having only met him the once.'

Irene threw her head back on to her pillow. This was so frustrating.

'But they lived in the same village as Paul's parents,' Ruby added. Irene sat bolt upright again.

'Do you know the address?' she asked hopefully.

'No,' Ruby admitted, crestfallen. Irene rolled her eyes and was just about to throw herself back on the bed again in exasperation. 'But the village is only small and I'm confident I could find their house if we travel there,' Ruby said.

Sitting on the train, Irene wished she could click her fingers and be transported straight to Surrey. The journey seemed to be taking so long already and they'd only just set off. They had left straight away, writing Helen a note to say Ruby had had a family emergency and Irene was accompanying her home as moral support, but they would be back the following evening. She wouldn't have dreamed of taking such a liberty normally, but her need to find out what had happened to Jack was greater than her fear of getting into trouble with the WPS.

And she was about to pack it all in, anyway, so what did it matter? Even if Jack was alive, she was still going to have to leave the police and marry Charles. And if it did turn out that Jonathan was indeed Jack, then it didn't sound like his family were the type to welcome somebody like Irene into their brood with open arms. Everything was against them. She would just have to be happy with knowing Jack was alive. If he was alive.

She was touched Ruby was taking such a big risk for her – it meant a lot after what had happened previously. She had certainly proved herself worthy of Irene's loyalty, so it was a real shame their friendship was about to be snuffed out as Charles would never let her be friends with Ruby once they were married.

They got off the train when it pulled into a station called Walton-on-Thames. Irene hadn't heard of the place until Ruby had filled her in on their travel plans. From here, they were to walk about a mile to a village called Hersham, which was where Paul and Jonathan's family homes were.

As they set off on the walk, Irene marvelled at the huge houses running along the tree-lined roads. She had thought Maggie's house was grand, but it was nothing compared to these with their huge windows and well-kept front gardens.

When they arrived in Hersham, they stopped on the village green to discuss the next step.

'There's a post office nearby,' Ruby said. 'It's probably best to ask in there.'

The postmaster didn't let them down. He knew who Ruby was talking about straight away and directed them to a house just on the other side of the green. Irene grew even more nervous as she realised how well known Jack's parents were in the village.

'Do you want me to do the talking?' Ruby asked when they reached the door. Irene nodded nervously. This was it. She was about to find out if Jack really was still alive. Maybe he was even on the other side of the thick wooden door.

A butler answered, and as Ruby explained why they were there, Irene felt grateful for the shield of their uniform. They might have been dismissed before even having a chance to speak without it, but the man took Ruby seriously as soon as he took in their attire. Ruby had wanted to go in their normal clothes, but Irene had insisted. They weren't supposed to wear the uniform in public unless they were on duty, but Irene argued they were taking such a big risk anyway that it was worth doing it properly and making sure they got past the front door after going all that way.

The butler left them on the doorstep for a few minutes and then returned to let them in. As they followed him along a corridor towards the drawing room, Irene scoured the photos hanging on the walls. Her heart skipped a beat and she almost lost her footing when she got to the third one in – it had obviously been taken a few years previously as his face was a lot fresher and fuller and his hair was longer – but Jack's beautiful face was beaming back at her. There was no hint of the pain she had seen so often when she'd been sat across from him in Gladys's kitchen. His eyes looked fresh and sparkly. This was the Jack she had managed to catch glimpses of on just a few occasions.

Ruby had been right, and it meant that Jack was alive after all. Irene wanted to jump forward and shout it to her, but she somehow managed to keep herself composed. They had agreed Ruby wouldn't reveal her links to the family. There was no point in complicating things and upsetting Paul's parents when word got back to them, as she knew they wouldn't have approved of the relationship. Irene thought it was a shame, but she didn't try and change her mind; she knew she would do the same in that situation.

'I understand we have you ladies to thank for our son's return,' an elegant woman declared when they entered the drawing room. She was tall with long, blond hair that was fastened in an elegant knot at the nape of her neck. Her purple dress showed off her slim frame, and she seemed to glide across the floor towards them. Irene noticed straight away that she had the same deep grey eyes as Jack and her heart fluttered at yet more confirmation that he was safe. 'Please, take a seat,' the woman offered, pointing towards a table where a man was sitting. He looked up at them with a smile – but somehow, he already looked bored. They both had brandy glasses in their hands.

The woman had spoken kindly, but she looked them both up and down as she did so. Irene felt as though she was being judged despite the WPS uniform. How could people like this *tell*? 'I'm not entirely sure what we can do for you. I'm afraid I'm not quite sure why you've come at all,' the woman said before letting out a deep sigh. Irene suddenly felt very unwelcome.

'Oh, we won't take up much of your time,' Ruby stuttered.

She was clearly as uncomfortable as Irene around people with this much wealth.

Irene realised she loved Jack even more knowing he'd made her feel so comfortable in his presence regardless of the differences in their backgrounds. He had never made her feel inferior, like people with money tended to. Like this woman, who hadn't even deemed them important enough for introductions, had made her feel. She was acting as though they were just an inconvenience.

Ruby and Irene sat down, but Jack's mother didn't join them. Instead, she leaned against the drinks cabinet and poured herself another measure.

'We've spoken to Jack and we know what happened. He's not here. So, I'm afraid you've had rather a wasted journey,' she said, her voice oozing with disinterest.

'We just wanted to make sure he was safe,' Irene said. 'We've been worried sick since he was taken away, what with the threat of the firing squad,' she added as she played with her fingernails.

'Oh goodness!' the woman cried. 'Don't tell me you developed a little crush on our silly boy? He really does know how to charm the ladies, doesn't he, Jonathan! Even when he's running scared from the Germans!' She was gesticulating so wildly that the brown liquid almost sloshed out of her glass, but Jack's father's expression stayed neutral.

Irene wanted to give her a piece of her mind, but she was also desperate to know what had happened to Jack. Just because he was alive, it didn't mean he was out of danger. 'Please, we just want to know he's getting the treatment he needs,' Irene said, her voice firm now. She was certain the bad reception they were receiving was because Jack's mother knew just from looking at her and Ruby that she was a lot wealthier than them, and Irene didn't appreciate that one little bit.

'He's fine, dear,' she sighed. 'Thankfully, his father has

connections in the military, so we were told about his court-martial before it was too late. Whichever one of you thought to get him out of Grantham was really earning her money that day. If they'd court-martialled him there, he may well have been sent to rot in prison by the time we even heard about the whole sorry mess. He might have even ended up in front of the firing squad if they'd have wanted to make an example of him. As it was, we were able to hire one of the best doctors to assess him and put forward a case for a condition called "shell shock". Apparently, it's happening to lots of soldiers, makes their brains go funny, or something. The army don't usually listen to those arguments, but it helps when you know people in the right places.'

Irene couldn't believe what she was hearing. By trying to force his way into Belton Park to get to Jack and then making sure he was sent away as soon as possible so there was no chance of Irene getting a chance to see him before he was dealt with, Charles had inadvertently bought his family time to save him.

'He's being treated at a military hospital and they expect he'll be well enough to return to the army within a couple of months. He'll be taking up a desk job, of course,' Jack's mother added.

'That's brilliant news,' Irene gushed. She knew she should hold back in front of his parents, but she couldn't help but let the emotion she was feeling out. She wiped her watery eyes with her sleeve. 'Where is he? I'd like to write to him,' she declared.

'Ah, I don't think that will be a very good idea,' Jack's father said now. He got to his feet and walked around the table to join his wife at the drinks cabinet. As he poured them both another measure, Irene waited for him to continue.

'I'd like to let him know how happy I am to know he's safe

and getting the treatment he needs,' Irene offered when no explanation was forthcoming. 'I'm confident he'd be happy to hear from me,' she added when she was met with two blank expressions.

'I'm sure he would,' Jack's mother said unconvincingly. 'It's just that the doctor has advised against anything like that. The emotional upheaval of hearing from you might . . . *upset* his recovery.'

As Irene looked back and forth between them both, she decided she didn't believe a word of it. The woman had clearly made it up on the spot – but what could she do? This was his mother. She was making it clear she didn't approve of Irene having any contact with her son. Without her help, she had no way of reaching him, so she would have to make do with knowing he was safe and well.

'Would you at least let him know we came here to make sure he was safe?' Ruby asked politely. Irene wasn't sure why she was bothering. The message would clearly never reach Jack. But it was nice of her to try.

'Yes, dear, now we must get on – if you wouldn't mind?' Jack's mother said, motioning towards the butler who opened the door and held out his arm to direct them out of the room.

It had taken them so long to get to Hersham that there was no possibility of making it back to Grantham that evening. The girls decided to huddle up on benches at the train station and get what sleep they could before starting on their journey back when the trains started running again the following morning. Irene pretended to fall asleep as soon as she curled up on a bench. They had walked to the station in silence and she didn't want to give Ruby a chance to ask how she was feeling or try and discuss the encounter. She used her jacket as a blanket, and she was grateful for the mild evening air.

To her surprise, Irene slept relatively well considering the circumstances. And she woke up feeling positive. Jack was safe and well. She had always known a future with him was impossible, so this was probably the best outcome she could have hoped for. It would have been silly to think his parents would welcome her with open arms and they would all live happily ever after.

To her relief, Ruby didn't push her on what had happened, and they spent the train journey back to Grantham in a comfortable silence, chatting every now and then about their surroundings or the next stop.

It was early evening when they arrived back at Rutland Street, and neither of them much fancied going out to find Helen and face the music.

'I'm sure she'll wake me when she comes to bed,' Ruby sighed. 'I'll stick to the story, don't worry.'

'I'm sorry for dragging you out there, especially when we were treated so rudely,' Irene said.

'It's not your fault,' Ruby smiled. 'You're my friend and I wanted to help you. I'm just glad Jack is alive. Has that at least brought you some comfort?'

'Oh, of course,' Irene assured her. 'I'm sorry for being so quiet on the way back. I was just going over everything in my head.'

'You're going to stay on with us, aren't you?' Ruby asked. 'Surely you can't still be planning on marrying Charles? He made you think your friend was dead – and that he was responsible!'

'Please, Ruby. I've told you there's more to it,' Irene replied. 'Believe me, I don't *want* to marry that man. Not anymore.'

She knew she'd probably feel better if she filled Ruby in on everything. Keeping secrets hadn't done her any good in the past. But she was tired and emotional, and she had already decided there was no point in sharing her predicament with Ruby. She needed a lot of money to get out of this situation, and that was one thing Ruby didn't have.

They said goodnight and Irene was surprised to find Mary already tucked up in bed in their room. She'd assumed she would be out on patrol with Helen.

'Is everything all right?' Mary whispered as Irene undressed.

Irene froze. Why was Mary of all people showing any concern?

'I'm fine,' she replied quietly but firmly. 'No thanks to you.'

Irene climbed into her bed and turned to face the wall, hoping that was the end of it. She didn't have the energy for a quarrel.

'I make out like I have the perfect family, but the truth is that my mother turned to drink when she discovered my father had been visiting prostitutes,' Mary whispered into the space between them a few minutes later. 'It ruined my family,' she added.

Irene froze again. Was that why Mary hated prostitutes so much? She blamed them for her unhappy family life? Irene didn't know what to say. She wished she had known this about Mary before – she would have been able to make her see that what had happened was her father's fault. After all, he was the one who had ruined his marriage with her mother and devastated life for all of them, not the women who were forced into sleeping with him for money through desperation.

Instead of feeling sympathy for Mary and her plight, Irene felt angry. Too angry to respond. Everything she had been through with Jack could have been avoided if Mary hadn't been taking her personal vendetta out on the women of Grantham. They could have even avoided their run-in at the deserter raid, which led Irene running to Charles, injured and vulnerable! Would she have been so quick to fall under his spell if their relationship had started on a different footing? Had her confidence not already been knocked by Mary's attack, would it have been so easy for Charles to chip away at her himself?

Of course, Irene felt bad for Mary in light of this revelation, but at the same time she felt sad for herself. She couldn't bring herself to respond, so she stayed silent, hoping Mary would assume she had already fallen asleep.

'I'm sorry,' Mary whispered into the night.

Irene was lost for words. The last thing she ever would have expected from Mary was an apology. Maybe she had finally learned her actions had consequences. Irene was glad about that, but furious it had taken all of this for her to come to her senses and learn some compassion. Her apology was too little, too late, as far as she was concerned.

# 34

When Irene came to, Mary's bed was empty. She normally woke when Mary got up and dressed. She wondered whether the relief she'd felt after learning of Jack's safety, coupled with a night on an uncomfortable bench, had led to her finally getting a decent night's sleep.

Thinking of Jack made her smile. But then she remembered his parents seemed intent on her never seeing him again, and she felt sad once more. The ache in the pit of her stomach grew further when it dawned on her she would have to finally hand over her uniform to Helen that morning. That was if Helen hadn't already decided to boot her out.

Once that was sorted, her plan was to visit John and Gladys and straighten everything out with them. Thank goodness she had some positive news for Gladys. Then she would hand herself over to Charles. Everything was a day late now, but Charles had been busy getting ready for a meeting with a potential investor this week and she was sure he would be so happy she had finally quit the WPS for him that it wouldn't matter. She slipped the engagement ring into her pocket with a heavy heart, sad in the knowledge that the next time she put it on her finger that would be it – it would be staying there forever.

The kitchen was quiet when she got downstairs, but Helen must have heard her on the stairs as she listened in through the door while she told the woman she was with in the living room to give her five minutes. Then the door opened, and she emerged looking serious.

'I wish you'd just told me yourself,' Helen sighed. Irene was surprised. What was she talking about? 'You didn't have to go to such great lengths to try and force me into dismissing you – and to drag Ruby into it with you!' She sounded angrier the more she spoke. Then she took a deep breath. 'I'm just disappointed, Irene,' she said quietly. 'I thought you could be honest with me.'

'What do you mean?' Irene asked, baffled. 'Yesterday wasn't about trying to get myself thrown out of the WPS.'

'It doesn't really matter, does it? We both know you're ready to leave and become a housewife. I just wish I'd heard it from you instead of Charles Murphy. I think it's such a waste for you. He's already betrayed one wife, I don't see what's to stop him philandering again after he's married you. But if it's what you want—'

'What do you mean you heard it from Charles?' Irene cut in.

Helen looked shocked. 'Well, he came knocking for you last night. He said he was here to put an end to all your *WPS nonsense*, and he told me all about your wedding plans.'

Rage coursed through Irene as she tried to process what had happened. Not content with forcing her out of the life she loved and into one where she had to answer to him, Charles had made sure he had control over the way the transfer was conducted, too. He hadn't even given her the chance to resign the way she wanted to. She was ready to find Charles and give him a piece of her mind. But then she remembered what else Helen had mentioned.

'Hang on,' said, trying to keep her voice even through the storm that was raging through her mind and heart. 'What did you mean about him being a philanderer? Charles and his wife divorced after *she* betrayed *him*.'

'Oh, that's the tale he spun you, is it?' Helen sighed, shaking her head. 'Charles Murphy is nothing but a cad, Irene. I wanted to warn you when you first got involved with him, but I didn't want to push you away by interfering. I hoped my obvious disapproval of him would be enough to make you think twice, if I'm honest. At first, I thought it had – but then those dresses turned up and it was obvious he was digging his claws into you. I dithered over whether I should say anything to you at that point, but then the next thing I knew you were engaged to the man! By then it was too late, so I made myself feel better by convincing myself that you would have been sensible enough to find out the truth for yourself and that you were happy to trust him despite his terrible history. I'm sorry, I should have anticipated his manipulative ways. I feel like I've let you down.'

'But, they're divorced,' Irene said quietly as she tried to make sense of what Helen was telling her. 'Isn't it near-on impossible for a woman to get a divorce if her husband has been the adulterer? How were they able to get everything finalised if he was the one in the wrong?'

'It was an open secret that Charles was a philanderer during their marriage,' Helen sighed. 'From what I've heard – and remember, a lot of the women around here confide in me, including her old friends – his wife would have agreed to anything in order to get away from him in the end, even if it meant telling the court she had been unfaithful. She was so miserable with him that she would rather have been an outcast in society than remain in his clutches.'

Irene's mind was racing. Helen's attitude back then made sense now. If only she had said something! Would she have listened, though?

'I tried to keep a close eye on things, and when he stepped in to help your family I was hopeful he had changed his ways,' Helen continued. 'But if he's been lying to you the whole time then, well, I'm afraid to say it, Irene, but I would think twice before trusting that man. Please, think about whether this is what you really want.'

Irene's head spun as she tried to take in this news. Their relationship really had been a farce – and right from the very start.

'Well, is it?' Helen asked again.

With a start, Irene realised they'd been standing in silence for the last minute or so.

'Is it what you want?' Helen pressed.

'No,' Irene said firmly. Then she swiftly spun around and stormed out of the house.

Marching towards the factory, Irene was consumed with indignation. She was maddened by Charles's move to take away her control over the one final thing she had to do before signing away her life to him. Not to mention the lies he had spun in order to manipulate her. She couldn't think about anything else through the fog of fury enveloping her. When she got to London Road, she burst through the factory door with such force that it swung back and made a huge cracking noise as it struck the wall. Everyone looked up at her, but she carried on walking. All she could think about was getting to Charles.

'Miss Wilson! He's with the investor!' a voice cried out from the factory floor. 'You'll have to wait!'

Irene ignored the cries and stomped up the iron steps before throwing open the office door. Charles and his potential investor were standing by the window looking out over the factory floor. They wouldn't have seen Irene enter the building from their lookout, so they both jumped at the noise as the door burst open. Charles immediately looked livid and his companion bemused. Irene didn't let their reactions fluster her.

'You couldn't just let me leave on my own terms, could you?' she shouted. 'You had to take that away from me too!'

Charles looked at his potential investor apologetically and stepped towards Irene with his hands up in surrender.

'I think there must have been a misunderstanding, my love,'

he said smoothly. 'Please, say hello to Mr Gill. This is the businessman I've told you about. Why don't you sit down and tell him all about how we met? It's a lovely story,' he added, placing his arm on the small of her back and trying to guide her towards the desk. He sounded so smooth and confident it made Irene's blood boil even more.

'Get off me,' she hissed, taking his hand and pushing it away from her back. 'I've had just about as much as I can take of you controlling my life – and we're not even married yet!' She paused. She knew she was making a big mistake. Charles would never marry her after she'd embarrassed him like this. But she couldn't stop herself. All the hurt and anger from the last few days was pouring out of her. She had to finally be true to herself, and she would just have to deal with the consequences later.

'Come on, dear, I know you've had a busy few days but there's no need to get hysterical,' Charles said, laughing off her remarks. He looked over at Mr Gill and rolled his eyes playfully. 'Why don't you get yourself home and get some rest and we can talk about this properly this evening.'

Irene could see he was trying to act like the reasonable party in front of this businessman, but she could see the steely glint behind his eyes that told her she would pay for her behaviour later, and it made her even angrier. She couldn't contain her feelings any longer. All the pain she'd felt over Jack, all the hurt she was suffering from the fallout with Maggie and Annie, had started to boil over. And it was mixing with the frustration she felt at the fact Charles and Jack's parents all felt like they had power over her because they had more money than she did.

'You let me think Jack was dead!' she said, her voice full of icy rage.

Saying the words out loud made her realise how ridiculous she had been to stay with Charles. She should have called everything off as soon as he'd let her believe he'd sent Jack to his death. She'd felt trapped by the money he was sending her family, but she would be able to find a way to help them herself – she'd always managed to get by before. He'd broken her down and made her think she couldn't do it without him, but he was wrong. She didn't need a man, and especially not one like Charles Murphy. What had she been thinking? Before she could stop herself, she spat, 'I'd rather sell my body on the streets to help my family than marry you!'

Charles's hand flew out so quickly Irene didn't even see it before it struck her face. She was on the floor by the time she realised he'd hit her. As she scrambled to her knees, she looked up at him and noticed a moment's panic flash across his face. Then he turned to Mr Gill and shot him a wry look.

'These women – you've got to keep them in line. I'm sure you have the same problem,' he said with a small laugh.

Charles stepped towards Irene and held out his hand to help her up, but she sprang to her feet on her own, pushed him away and ran to the door. She was just about to fly through it when she remembered the engagement ring in her pocket. She paused and took it out. The sight of it made her feel sick. She never wanted to lay her eyes on it again. She turned around to face Charles, who was still standing in the same spot, sneering at her. Irene flung the ring in his direction with such force that he flinched, then she turned back around and fled the room.

Once she was outside on the street, she slumped to the ground. Pulling her knees up to her chest, she rested her elbows on them and then laid her head on top of her hands. She needed to get money together – and quickly – if she was going to save Henry.

She thought back to what she had just said to Charles. She'd spoken in anger, but she'd shocked herself. Could she really turn to prostitution to save her family? She knew so many women who'd found themselves in such a desperate place that they'd felt like they didn't have a choice. She understood what led them to it, how enticing the cash was when you had no other option. But she'd never dreamed she would find herself in such a place. She wasn't sure how much money Charles had been sending to the rehabilitation centre to care for Henry, but she knew that even if she managed to get her factory job back and worked day and night that she wouldn't even come close to covering it. And then there was the rent on her aunt Ruth's new accommodation.

Irene wept as she accepted her life might be about to take the same path as her mother's had all those years ago. Maybe this was where it had always been leading. Was it all she was good for? Had this been her destiny all along? No matter the reasons – she couldn't see any other option.

When the factory door opened, Irene didn't bother trying to compose herself or dry her tears. She was at rock bottom and she didn't have the energy to try and cover that up. She was contemplating turning to prostitution, so what did it matter if a stranger saw her like this?

'Please, let me help you up. Are you hurt?' a man's voice said.

She looked up to see the businessman from Charles's office reaching out a hand to her, concern etched over his face. Irene shook her head at him and moved her gaze back to the ground. The last thing she needed was another pompous man-of-wealth trying to help her. Look where she had ended up last time.

The man sat down beside her, right there on the ground, even though he was wearing what was clearly a very expensive suit. She looked at him in bemusement.

'Sorry, I just—' the man broke off, looking uncomfortable. 'You see, I always knew there was something off about Charles Murphy, but I didn't think he'd end up proving I was right quite so dramatically!' He ran his hand through his soft white hair and stretched his legs out in front of him. 'I'm not quite as nimble as I used to be,' he joked, looking pointedly at her bent legs. His eyes were kind, and his gentle smile radiated out to soften his whole face. His whole demeanour made her feel comfortable. Irene chuckled through her tears and stretched her legs out, too.

'I'm Roy Gill, by the way,' he said. 'Please call me Roy, though.' Irene held out her arm and they shook hands.

'Irene Wilson,' she said. 'Charles Murphy's *ex*-fiancée.' They exchanged a wry smile and then sat in silence staring out across the road for a few minutes.

'I was reluctant to invest in Mr Murphy's factory,' Roy finally announced. 'But my business partners were adamant it was the best fit. I came here today to see if I could get to the bottom of my misgivings.' He paused and shook his head. 'I still didn't like the chap but just before you stormed in there, well, I was about to admit defeat and sign on the dotted line.'

'And I've stopped the deal going through?' Irene asked.

'I would say hitting a woman in front of me – and in full view of all his workers – will be reason enough to convince my partners to invest their cash elsewhere,' Roy said seriously. 'If that makes you feel any better?' he added.

'It really does,' Irene smiled. He may have hurt her physically, but she'd hit him where it was sure to hurt the worst: his wallet. And she knew how quickly word got around about things like this. She was certain he would struggle to find anybody else willing to put money into his factory after this.

'I hope you don't mind my prying,' Roy said cautiously. 'But what you mentioned, about saving your family—'

'Oh, don't worry about that,' Irene said, feeling flustered. 'I was just being dramatic,' she lied. 'I can sort my money troubles out.'

They sat in silence as Irene found herself wishing her words had been true. She had never felt more alone and vulnerable as she did at this moment, despite the kindness this stranger was showing her. Irene felt a desperate need to be alone and she was getting ready to get to her feet and bid Roy farewell when he spoke again.

'You've done me a big favour today,' he said. Irene turned to look at him. 'It would mean a lot to me if I could pay you back in some way.' He cleared his throat before continuing. 'I know we're strangers, but I have a daughter who's probably a similar age to you, and it would break my heart if anything happened to her and there was nobody to help.' Irene looked into his kind eyes again and realised what it was about him that made her feel so comfortable – it was his fatherly compassion.

'It would be more a long-term investment than a one-off donation, if you wanted to help me,' Irene smiled ruefully. 'But thank you anyway, it's very kind of you.'

Roy wouldn't leave it there though. He pushed her for details and Irene surprised herself by telling him all about Henry and the rest of her family. 'I'm sure I'll find a way to help them,' Irene sighed as she finished the sad story. She looked up at Roy and saw he had tears in his eyes.

'I wasn't completely truthful when I told you I had a daughter who was around your age,' he admitted. 'I mean, I do have a daughter – *had* a daughter. But we lost her to diphtheria ten years ago. I would have done anything to save her, but it was before I made all my money and we just didn't have the means to try any of the remedies they were saying could help. Not that it turned out any of them would have saved her, but I've never felt so helpless in my life. I had to sit back and watch her die a slow and painful death – I couldn't even afford to make her feel more comfortable.' He took a moment to blow his nose on his hanky, and Irene wished there was something she could say to make him feel better.

'My business took off after that,' he said, sounding more positive now. 'And I swore that I would never stand by and watch another family go through that suffering. I made a pledge to myself – and to my daughter – that if I ever came across a similar situation that I would step in and help however I could. I made my fortune too late for it to help my daughter. Please, let me use it to help you and your family. In her memory.'

Irene was lost for words. She was amazed by Roy's kindness and generosity. But after everything she had just been through, she couldn't help but feel a little cautious. On the one hand, he seemed like a genuine, honest man. On the other, she had thought that about Charles, and look where that had got her.

'I'm not anything like Charles Murphy,' Roy said warmly, as though he could read Irene's mind. 'I can promise that I won't expect anything from you in return. Well, except maybe the occasional letter to update me on your cousin's health. If you let me give your family this money, you'll be helping me enough. And, I don't want to embarrass you, but I do hope you *were* just being dramatic about the prostitution, but I wouldn't be able to live with myself if I walked away from here today knowing you might have to resort to that at some point, when I could have stopped it so easily. Really, this kind of money . . . it's pennies to me but it would mean the world to you. Please let me help.'

Irene was struggling to speak, she was so overwhelmed by this stranger's kindness.

'We can make it official if you like,' Roy suggested. 'If that would make you feel more comfortable about it? Why don't we go and see your boss, and we can draw up some kind of contract?' He paused for a moment and scratched his head. 'But there is one problem,' he added slowly.

'What's that?' Irene asked, sighing inwardly: she knew there must be a catch.

'You'll have to help me up – I won't be able to manage myself, with these knees!'

Irene looked at him for a silent moment, stunned, then burst out laughing. In that moment, she decided to trust him. She got to her feet and hauled him up, both of them chuckling all the while.

As they made their way to Rutland Street together, Irene struggled to get her head around the turn the day had taken for her. She'd started out in such a hopeless position, about to give up everything for a life of misery with Charles. And now she was going to be able to keep her family healthy while continuing to do the work she loved with the WPS. That was if Helen would take her back.

She needn't have worried. As soon as Helen was done with the morning's waifs and strays, she invited Roy and Irene into the living room. She listened intently while Irene explained the truth behind her relationship with Charles, and how she had felt like she had no choice but to marry him. When she was finished, Roy took over and filled Helen in on what had happened at the factory that morning and their subsequent agreement. Helen was only too happy to take Irene back into the house and let her continue her police work.

Once they'd sorted out the details of how the financial arrangement would work, Roy got himself ready to head back home.

'What are you going to do about your friends in London?' he asked Irene. 'They must be worried sick about you.'

'I'd better write to them to update them and let them know they were right,' Irene said. 'I feel terrible for not listening to them. They only had my best interests at heart. But it was like Charles had cast a spell over me. He knew how alone I felt in the world, and he exploited that. And I couldn't see any other way of saving Henry. I felt like a cornered animal.'

'You should go in person,' Helen said. 'This is too big of an issue to address in a letter. You need to properly build bridges with them. I think you deserve some time off, and your latest pay has arrived so you can afford the train fare.'

'No need,' Roy piped in. They both looked at him quizzically. 'Did I mention I live in London myself?' he said happily. 'I'll give you a lift there if you can be ready in the next hour. And I won't hear of you getting a train back here. I'll arrange for one of my staff to drive you home.'

'Thank you so much,' Irene gushed. Before she knew it, she was pulling them both in for an out-of-character hug. She truly couldn't believe how lucky she was to know so many caring people.

# 35

It was late when Roy pulled up outside the familiar block of flats in London with Irene in the passenger seat.

'Don't worry, I still have my key,' she said. 'Thank you again for everything, I'll keep in touch,' she added, waving the piece of paper with his address scribbled on it.

'Make sure you do,' Roy grinned.

As she waved him away, Irene realised she fully intended to keep her promise. Roy had already shown her more kindness than all the men in her life ever had. Neither of them had any close family left; perhaps they could each fill that gap in the other's life.

Irene was relieved there was no answer when she knocked on the door. She assumed the girls were out on a night patrol. After letting herself in, she experienced an overwhelming feeling of home. But it wasn't just down to the fact she had previously lived here; the warm and happy feeling running through her was also due to the familiar items lying around the place that belonged to her friends. Annie's hairbrush lay on the sofa – Irene had always moaned at her to put it back in her bedroom when she was finished with it and she laughed to herself at the memory. Then there was one of Maggie's half-finished books on the side. She took forever to get through novels, but Irene loved to talk to her about them when she was finished.

She went and checked her old room and found unfamiliar clothes strewn on the bed and a few trinkets on the side. So, the girls had been sent a replacement for her. She felt sad that they hadn't had the opportunity to tell her about their new recruit. While she had been living her life away from them, they had been busy building a new life without her. Well, that was about to end. She was determined to make amends with Maggie and Annie and get their friendships back on track. And she was looking forward to meeting their new friend, as she was certain they would have welcomed her with open arms. Irene laughed to herself as she thought that from the look of this girl's messy bedroom, she had probably fit right in with Maggie and Annie.

Irene made her way back to the sitting room and sat down on the sofa to try and figure out what to say to her friends when they returned. They had left things so badly. She started to worry that they might react negatively to finding her in their home. After all, they may have promised to welcome her back whenever she was ready, but she didn't live here anymore and a lot had been said and done since that promise had been made.

As Irene grappled with what to say to her friends, she found her eyelids growing heavy. It had been a long and emotional couple of days, and she wasn't sure she was going to be able to stay awake long enough to greet Maggie and Annie upon their return. She was soon sound asleep, but she stirred about an hour later as the sound of a key in the door rattled along the short hallway.

'Well, look what the cat's dragged in,' boomed out a voice so familiar to Irene it made her feel warm inside, despite what it had said. Irene looked at her friend blearily, trying to work out if Maggie was happy or annoyed to find her on the sofa.

Maggie walked over and stood over Irene as she sat herself up. Her expression was neutral, and Irene started feeling anxious. Then Maggie's face broke into a wide grin. 'Come here, you silly sod!' Maggie sighed before pulling her to her feet and giving her the warmest embrace. 'Hmm, you're getting better at affection,' she muffled into her ear as Irene wrapped her arms firmly around her. She had never been one for cuddles, but she'd surprised herself lately. A stream of emotions hit her as she breathed in Maggie's scent and enjoyed the feeling of closeness she had missed so much.

'Do I get a turn?' Annie's voice sung out from beside them, and before Irene knew it, she had forced her way into the embrace, so it was now a three-way hug. They stayed like that for a little while, before collapsing onto the sofa together.

When Irene looked up, she was surprised to see a woman in WPS uniform standing just inside the doorway. She was older than the three of them; Irene guessed she might have been in her thirties and she suddenly panicked that the commandant had sent someone to fetch her back to Grantham or discipline her for the help she'd given Jack.

'Oh, gosh, I'm so sorry – this is Poppy!' Maggie exclaimed, getting up and taking hold of the woman's hand before leading her over to the sofa. 'Sorry Poppy, we got carried away in the moment there,' she giggled. 'This is Irene – as I'm sure you've guessed by now. Irene, Poppy has heard a lot about you.' Poppy gave Irene the warmest smile.

'It's so good to finally meet you,' Poppy said. Despite her age, she was shorter than the rest of them and her thick, black hair fell neatly on to her shoulders. Irene smiled back. She could tell straight away that she was kind and genuine, and she felt comfortable in her presence. It made sense to Irene that her replacement was older than all of them; they had been the youngest to go through the training when they'd joined up, after all.

'I hope they've been kind,' Irene said cautiously. She wouldn't have blamed Maggie and Annie for talking negatively about her after the way she had treated them.

'Oh, you have the best of friends in these two,' Poppy said kindly. 'And I appreciate you have a lot to catch up on so I'll leave you to it and head to bed if that's all right,' she added.

'Of course, and thank you,' Irene replied. 'It was lovely to meet you.'

'You too,' Poppy grinned. 'Night, girls!' she called, heading off to Irene's old bedroom.

'She seems nice,' Irene said.

'You'll love her,' Maggie replied, sitting back down.

As Maggie and Annie kicked off their cumbersome boots and stripped off their jackets, it felt like no time had passed since they had all lived here together. Irene was so grateful to have such a strong bond with them that they could welcome her back into the fold without question. But she had to address the elephant in the room.

'You were right about Charles,' she whispered, her eyes downcast.

'Did he hurt you?' Annie asked. Her tone had turned fierce, and Irene was taken aback.

'Not particularly, no,' she answered, gently patting her cheek, which still felt a little tender since Charles had struck out at her that afternoon. It seemed that, luckily for her, he wasn't as strong as Mary. 'It appears I came to my senses just in time.' The two of them listened intently as she filled them in on everything she had been through. 'I'm so sorry I didn't listen to you,' she added once she'd finished.

'We knew you were blinded by love – or infatuation, I should say,' Maggie said warmly. 'We hoped that given time you would see for yourself, and we knew you were strong enough to get yourself out of the situation – and too stubborn to listen to us!' They all laughed. 'But we had no idea he had your family situation to use as a hold over you. If only you'd told us, we could have found a way to help.'

'It just felt hopeless,' Irene admitted. 'And he had caught me when I was feeling vulnerable. He was so good at making me feel like I couldn't live without him that I truly believed I couldn't.'

'It doesn't matter how hopeless any situation feels, you should always share it with us,' Annie said firmly.

'We can't help you unless we know the full story,' Maggie added.

'No more secrets,' Irene promised. 'And I mean it this time.' Then she felt compelled to finally share her childhood with them. All three girls had tears in their eyes by the time Irene was finished.

'I remember you sounding elusive when we first met and talked about our reasons for signing up,' Maggie said. 'I knew there was more to it and I got a right bee in my bonnet about finding out the truth. I had no idea it would turn out to be something so dreadful. I'm sorry you went through that.' She reached over and gave Irene's arm a comforting rub.

'No wonder you've always been so protective of the women – and I can understand now why you were so keen to help out in Grantham,' Annie said.

'Yes, well, I've rather failed there, haven't I?' Irene said light-heartedly, although she felt deeply disappointed in herself. 'I think it might be time to give up and come back.'

'No, you mustn't,' Maggie cried. Irene was shocked. She thought her friends would have jumped at the chance to have her back with them.

'It's not that we don't want you here again,' Annie rushed in quickly to add, seeing Irene's deflated expression. 'I just feel strongly that you can't let the last few months go to waste. It sounds like you're very nearly there with Mary – you can't give up now!'

'Yes, you said you got an apology from her?' Maggie chipped in. Irene nodded. 'You need to keep going with her while she's feeling remorseful. This could be the opportunity you've been waiting for. You've got a real chance to turn her attitude around now you know what's behind it all. And look at everything you've done for Stella and Billy – I wouldn't call that failure, would you?' Irene had to agree.

'Well, I guess we'll be apart a little longer, then,' she sighed. She was grateful to have had their input. She'd been so caught up in everything else that she hadn't even spotted the potential for a breakthrough with Mary.

'And what about Jack?' Maggie asked hopefully.

'What about him?' Irene asked sadly.

'Well, you were robbed of a big reunion and the chance to reveal your true feelings when you found out he was alive because you were still set to marry Charles. Now you're free of that bastard, so surely it's time to track him down?'

'It would never work,' Irene whispered sadly. 'You heard what his mother was like. Even if I *could* track him down myself, she would never allow him to court someone like me. I'm fed up of being made to feel ashamed for who I am.'

'It sounds to me as if his family's wealth isn't something that defines him.' Annie offered. 'You said yourself you never got even an inkling that he came from a rich background.'

'So?' Irene asked.

'So,' Maggie pitched in, 'if he's not bothered about his family's money, then maybe he'd pick you over them!'

Irene raised her eyebrows and snorted.

'It's got to be worth a try!' Annie cried.

'No,' Irene said firmly. 'I'm so grateful Jack made it out of Grantham alive. He very nearly didn't and that would have been down to me. I've caused him enough problems, and I've suffered enough heartache over him. I think it's best we both move on with our lives now.'

'But you still love him?' Maggie asked.

'With all my heart,' Irene replied, feeling a pang in her chest as the words left her mouth. 'And I think about him all the time. But I can't risk it, girls. There are so many ways it could go wrong and I don't think my heart could cope with any more pain. Please, let's just leave it now.'

They both nodded sincerely – they still knew when it was time to let something go with Irene, no matter how stubborn they felt she was being.

'Well, you always have the two of us to love, and you have so much love from us in return,' Annie said.

'I think the last few months have proven our bond is as strong as can be,' Irene declared. 'Even though we've had a rough patch, being back with you both feels as though no time has passed at all.'

'We don't need to be writing to each other all the time,' Maggie said as they all got to their feet for another group hug. 'Our Bobby Girl bond is strong enough to see us through our time apart.'

'No matter what, I'll always love you both,' Maggie said.

'The Bobby Girls forever!' The three of them chorused in unison, then collapsed back onto the sofa, laughing. In that moment, Irene felt the happiest she had ever felt. She was still sad about losing Jack – but she was thankful he was alive, even if it wasn't by her side. And she had broken free of Charles's grasp while managing to keep her family safe. With the love and support of her two amazing friends she felt like she could achieve anything. She couldn't wait to get back to Grantham to continue her work helping women in her mother's memory.

# *Epilogue*

Approaching Rutland Street on foot, Irene felt the usual cloak of sadness coming down to cover her as she prepared for yet another evening off alone. Although she had tried her best, she'd found life hard since returning to Grantham and getting back into her WPS work a few months before. It wasn't so bad when she was on patrol as she was normally so busy she found herself distracted from how much she was yearning for Jack. But when she returned home, the fact that she had nothing to look forward to would hit her right in the gut. Then, when she climbed into bed and tried to sleep, her thoughts were filled with their time together.

Jack was all she could think about in her moments alone, and she had come to realise just how important he was to her. Knowing he was out there somewhere but that she couldn't be with him somehow felt worse than when she'd thought he was dead. At least then she would have been able to mourn him and would have eventually moved on. As it was, she felt stuck in a cruel nightmare without him.

Gladys missed him too, and Irene had found herself lying on her visits to the poor woman, claiming to have had letters from 'Joe' telling her how well he was doing. Gladys's health was quickly deteriorating, and her memory was starting to get even sketchier. It was little wonder she had mistaken a complete stranger for her grandson, now Irene could see the full extent of her illness. But when Irene told Gladys about the letters, she came to life again. Irene didn't see any harm in the little white lies if they were giving Gladys something to live for. But it made her pain harder to bear as every time she spoke about hearing from him, the fact that she hadn't, and probably never would, stung her even more.

Irene had ended up coming clean to John about Jack and how Gladys had been convinced he was his son. Much to her surprise, he hadn't been angry.

'Even now when I talk to her about those few weeks he stayed and you spent time with them, she brightens up and it's like I get my old mother back,' he'd told her. 'I knew there must have been more to it.' He even wanted to meet Jack if he ever came back to visit Gladys, but Irene warned him it was unlikely.

One ray of light in Irene's life was the regular updates from her aunt Ruth and Henry, who were both writing her frequent letters after settling into their new accommodation. Ruth still wasn't quite sure how her hard-up niece had managed to convince millionaire Mr Gill to help them, but Irene had promised to fill her in as soon as she was able to visit them. There was just too much to say in a letter and she didn't want her family to worry about her.

As for Charles, the first time Irene had walked past him in the street he had let out a scornful laugh in her direction before marching past her with his head held high. It hadn't been what she was expecting at all. She had been braced for a confrontation. She found out later that Roy had convinced more potential investors to pull out of deals with his factory, and promised him he would continue to spread the word among anyone else he explored future deals with if he gave Irene any trouble.

Then, when Helen had become the first WPS member to be given the powers of arrest a few weeks ago, she had popped in to see Charles to warn him that one step out of line would result in him being led out of his factory in handcuffs. He seemed to have kept out of Irene's way since then, and she was relieved. She was also delighted that he seemed to have pressure bearing down on him from all angles and no choice but to stay in line. She hoped he felt a little bit of how she had felt through the previous months.

The funds for her family from Roy meant Irene had her pay packet to use as she wanted to again, and she was giving a lot of it to Stella as well as some of the other more regular faces in the town. She knew it was by no means a solution and she wished there was something more she could do to help, but it was a start. She'd also started buying vegetables for Billy and his mother. She didn't have enough money to completely change anyone's life, like Roy had done for her, but just knowing she was doing something to make a small difference made her feel better – and she knew her mother would be proud of her if she were still alive.

Irene had grown ever closer with Ruby, and Helen had been happy to let them patrol together a lot of the time after commenting on what a great team they made. Irene did find it easier to forget about Jack for a few hours when she was out with Ruby, but she also liked to patrol on her own every now and again.

Mary had been pleasant enough to Irene since her return, but they still hadn't had a proper conversation about everything that had happened. Irene had attempted to bring up what Mary had told her about her father, hoping to be able to help her see that he was the one at fault and not the prostitutes he had slept with behind her mother's back. But Mary had shot her down immediately, pretending to have no idea what she was talking about. She even acted offended at the suggestion her father had been immoral. Of course, Irene realised straight away that Mary's remorse had only been fleeting and she had missed her chance to discuss any of it with her.

But Irene was keeping a closer eye on her colleague and

had even stepped in a few times when she felt she was being too heavy-handed with a suspect. Instead of lashing out at her, Mary had backed off every time and seemed to listen to Irene's point of view. She wasn't sure how long it would last, and if any of her reasoning was sinking in, but she felt positive about it for now and that was good enough.

Turning into Rutland Street, Irene was surprised to spot a figure outside the house. It was normal for people to wait outside in the mornings while Helen let them in one by one and worked through their issues with them in the living room. But it was mostly women who sought her advice, and even though she was still some distance away she could tell this figure was that of a man. Also, it was late afternoon now, and everyone knew Helen headed out on patrol after lunch.

As she got closer, Irene could make out the familiar style and colour of the British Army uniform. She wondered why on earth a solider would be hanging around outside their house. Maybe he was there to complain about being hassled by one of the local women. She steeled herself to deal with him, squaring her shoulders and putting on her most professional expression.

Then, the man looked up and smiled, and her breath caught in her throat. She stopped dead in the middle of the street as she tried to figure out if her mind was playing tricks on her. She had longed to see Jack for so long – could he really be standing outside her door right now? He took his cap off and laughed nervously, and Irene knew he was real.

She let out a yelp and ran straight into his open arms. A warmth rushed through her as their bodies came together. She ran her fingers through his hair to double check he was real, and then they pulled away at the same time and stared at each other's faces, both grinning from ear to ear.

Irene took a moment to take him in. His hair had been cut shorter, his face looked fuller and his eyes were brighter. She could see joy radiating out from them. This man looked more like the Jack in the photo at his family home than the haunted Jack she had grown to love. She was struck by how handsome he looked, and she was overwhelmed with feelings for him.

'I don't understand,' Irene managed at last. 'What are you doing here?'

'It's nice to see you, too,' Jack laughed.

'Sorry, I mean . . . I didn't think I'd ever see you again!' she cried. 'I can't believe it's you!'

Jack gently wiped the single tear that had escaped from her eye and was running down her cheek. Then his thumb moved to her lip and rested there as he looked into her eyes. Her lip was tingling where he was touching it and when he leaned forward and kissed her, the tingles became an explosion.

'That's better,' he whispered as he held her face so close to his that their noses were touching. Irene felt like she was in a dream. 'I've wanted to do that for so long,' he added softly.

'Let's get in off the street,' Irene said, all a fluster when she saw a curtain twitch out of the corner of her eye. 'We'll be the talk of the town by the morning,' she giggled as they sat at the kitchen table together.

'It's so good to see you, Irene,' Jack said as he placed both his hands on top of hers on the table. 'I would have come sooner, only I wasn't allowed any outside contact while I was in hospital.'

'Did they help you deal with . . .everything?' Irene asked cautiously.

'To some degree,' Jack replied gravely. 'I don't think I'll ever get over it all, but I had help from a brilliant doctor who gave me psychotherapy sessions every day. We talked about what I'd seen and how it made me feel – like you and I did. He also encouraged me to write about how I was feeling. You helped me more than you'll ever know, Irene. I'm not sure I would have been able to hand myself in if we hadn't had that discussion beforehand. And the fact I'd talked through it with you already made it easier for me to explain it all to a stranger. I fear they might have given up on me if I'd refused to take him through it all.'

Irene was so happy to hear she had helped him in some way after all, and she beamed at him across their clasped hands.

'All the time I was at Gladys's, I knew I felt something for you, but I was so confused about everything I was going through,' he added shyly. 'I was consumed by the battlefield, so I didn't know if what I felt for you was real and I had too much to deal with to think about it properly. But when I was led away and realised I might not ever get to see you again, all I could think about was you. Nothing else mattered. I was angry at myself for not telling you how I felt and terrified I would live out the rest of my years in prison without ever getting the chance to do so.'

Irene squeezed Jack's hand as she remembered the night she'd sat under the tree to watch the dawn and say goodbye to him. 'I felt exactly the same about you,' she whispered.

'It's funny how the threat of having your freedom ripped away from you can make you realise what – and who – is important to you,' Jack laughed, squeezing her hand back. Irene was relieved he hadn't gone through the fear he was about to face the firing squad.

'They released me a week ago and I went back home,' he continued. 'I was desperate to come and see you, but I started to worry my feelings for you were one-sided. I convinced myself you'd just been doing your job, and that was all it was to you. You help soldiers like me all the time and you don't fall for them,' he shrugged. 'I told myself that if you wanted anything more to do with me, then you would find me and tell me – even though I hadn't given you any information that would help you do that! I ended up telling our family butler, Gerald, about you. I'd learned how important talking about my feelings was and I was bursting to make you more real by telling someone about you, as silly as it sounds.'

Irene thought it sounded lovely!

'My parents and I have never been close. They'd never admit it, but they love their money more than me. Over the years I've grown close to Gerald. When I told him about you, he confessed that you and a colleague had been to the house to try and find out what happened to me. My parents had told him not to tell me. Irene, the relief I felt when I heard that you cared!' he cried.

Irene was speechless. She had thought that had been such a wasted trip, but it had been vital in leading Jack back to her. From what Jack had said about his parents, she also now understood why they'd been so stand-offish with her and Ruby – and why she had never cottoned on to how wealthy Jack was.

'I asked my mother why she tried to keep it from me, and I'm afraid to say she was rather disparaging about you.' He hung his head, looking ashamed. 'My parents want me to marry into money, you see. Like I said, it's all that matters to them.'

Irene's shoulders drooped. She knew this had been too good to be true. Had Jack come here to make sure she knew there could never be anything between them? Did he simply want to make sure she didn't try and track him down again?

'It's all right, I understand,' she whispered through the tears that were now brimming in her eyes. She felt foolish for ever thinking somebody like Jack would want to be with her. For once, Maggie and Annie had been wrong.

'I don't think you do,' Jack said, wiping the tears from her face once more. Irene looked up at him, confused to see him beaming down at her. 'I told my parents they couldn't keep me from you, and that I meant to marry you. They weren't at all impressed, as I'm sure you can imagine – but I told them if they didn't like it, well, then they could jolly well lump it!' He was laughing and Irene was still trying to wrap her head around it all. Had she heard him correctly? He intended to marry her?

'I'm sure they'll come around soon,' Jack added. 'I'm their only child and despite their questionable priorities, I'm usually able to get them to come around to my way of thinking in the end.'

Irene was searching his face for an answer to the most important question she thought she might ever ask. She couldn't quite find it, so she took a deep breath and asked it out loud.

'Did you mean it?' she said, her voice quivering.

'Did I mean what?' Jack asked. It was his turn to look confused.

'That . . . you mean to marry me?' Irene asked, barely able to form the words through the nerves.

Jack got to his feet and took hold of Irene's hands to pull her up too. He kept hold of her hands in his. 'Of course,' he replied, grinning from ear to ear. Then, a little cautiously, he added, 'That is, if you'll have me?'

Blood rushed to Irene's head and she gripped hold of his hands even tighter to steady herself as his words sunk in. 'Yes!' she gasped. 'Yes, yes, yes! I love you, Jack!'

'I love you, Irene,' he grinned and they kissed again. It was truly the best kiss she had ever had in her life. When they finally broke apart, they stood holding each other close, each so happy to be in each other's arms at last.

When Irene settled into bed later that evening, she was exhausted from all the excitement and emotion. Jack had managed to get himself some work in the offices at Belton

Park, so they were going to be seeing a lot of each other while they sorted their wedding plans. As much as she longed to switch off the light and drift off into a delirious state of sleep, there was one thing she just had to do first. She was too tired to go into all the details, but she had to share this news with two of the most important people in her life – there was no question of her keeping *this* a secret from them. She got out her writing paper and her pen and wrote a quick note:

> *To my dearest Bobby Girls,*
> *No secrets, this time. You were right – again!*
> *So . . . How do you fancy being my bridesmaids?*
>   *All my love,*
>   *Irene xxx*

**The next book in the irresistible Bobby Girls series, *Christmas with the Bobby Girls*, is available now.**

# Acknowledgements

The first person I must thank is my editor Thorne Ryan: the brainchild behind The Bobby Girls series. Without you there would be no Bobby Girls and I'm so grateful to you for trusting me with your idea, being a constant support and continually waving your magic wand over my work!

Thanks must also go to copyeditor Justine Taylor: I feel very lucky to have benefited from your keen eye and knowledge. Thank you for sprinkling some wonderful finishing touches over this book.

To my agent, Kate Burke at Blake Friedmann; I feel like I can always rely on you!

A heartfelt thanks must go to Courtney Finn, for transporting me back to 1915 Grantham and helping me picture what the town was like for the recruits patrolling the streets back then. You have taken out so much of your valuable time to help me and this book wouldn't be what it is without your endless knowledge. Also, Elizabeth Finn – who is so kind she prepared a packed lunch for a complete stranger – thank you!

I must also thank Courtney for putting me in touch with Margaret Smith, who is the granddaughter of a real-life Bobby Girl. Margaret, you have been a delight to chat to, and you are every bit as kind and loving as your grandmother was. I hope you enjoyed Helen's character, who was inspired by Edith.

Thank you to John Pinchbeck, ex editor of *The Grantham Journal*, Ruth Crook, Grantham Civic Society Treasurer,

Living History Enthusiast Ian Houghton and Ann Burroughs, retail manager at the National Trust's Belton House Gift Shop, who all supplied valuable help and information.

My warmest thanks must also go to the staff at The Imperial War Museum, and its research rooms, where I have spent many fascinating hours.

To Beverley Ann Hopper, Janice Rosser, Deborah Smith and Louise Cannon – thank you so much for your continued online support, for which I am forever grateful.

Moving on to family; huge, loving thanks to Hewy for all your support and encouragement, and to my brother-in-law Steve: thank you for guiding me through the intricacies of a black eye!

Thank you, Aunty Lee, for stopping people in the supermarket to tell them about my debut novel! And also, my Great Aunt Dot, who has been buying copies of *The Bobby Girls* in their droves and posting them off to everyone she knows; it warms my heart to know that you are both so proud of me.

Big thanks to my Mum for not only being my soundboard and helping me work out various plot lines, but for being Nana Daycare so I could finish this book so quickly. And special thanks must also go to my Dad, for always having the best advice, my Stepmum Sandy and my in-laws Gary and Ella for all their constant love and support.

Thank you – as always, to my wonderful grandad George, and to my cousin Adam – who sparked my interest in the great wars and will both always be inspirations to me.

Finally, thank you to the real Roy Gill – for always being just as charming and kind-hearted as the fictional Roy Gill.

I love this photo of Pioneer Policewoman Edith Smith, who served
with the WPS in Grantham during WW1 and who was the inspiration for
Helen's character. Her granddaughter, Margaret Smith, kindly supplied the
photo and gave me permission to use it at the end of the book. It is her
favourite photo of her grandmother, and shows her in her nursing uniform –
a career she trained for before joining the WPS and which she
carried out after leaving at the end of the war.

I wrote a scene around this photo after coming across it in
*Bygone Grantham Volume 5*. I couldn't believe how close the plane had
come to hitting the church – and then through further digging I
discovered it had also narrowly missed a mother and her baby!

This photo of a bakery in Grantham, from *Bygone Grantham Volume 5*, made
it clear to me just how much of an impact the army camp had on the town
during WW1. All those loaves of bread were ready to be transported off to
Belton Park for the soldiers!

# Bookends

## When one book ends, another begins...

Bookends is a vibrant new reading community to help you ensure you're never without a good book.

You'll find exclusive previews of the brilliant new books from your favourite authors as well as exciting debuts and past classics. Read our blog, check out our recommendations for your reading group, enter great competitions and much more!

Visit our website to see which great books we're recommending this month.

Join the Bookends community:
# www.welcometobookends.co.uk

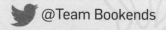 @Team Bookends   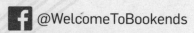 @WelcomeToBookends